Billy rode [illegible] they moved along under a fresh new sky, his heavy feelings began to lift. They were again on their way to a cave that was filled with more gold than fifty men could spend in a lifetime. The gold carried with it the promise of more excitement from every direction. Maybe, thought Billy to himself, there was still a place in life where he could carve his name. When they got to Fort Smith, he would use some of his share of the money to buy him a saddlebag full of dime novels. Only this time, he would read them as a man of experience.

"HOW THE WEST WAS AND HOW IT OUGHT TO BE REMEMBERED... A PLEASURE TO READ AND HARD TO FORGET... QUARLES'S CHARACTERS SEEM TO STEP RIGHT OUT OF THEIR ERA, COMPLETE WITH THEIR HARDSHIPS AND THEIR STRONG SENSE OF PERSONAL INTEGRITY. I CAN'T REMEMBER READING A WESTERN I'VE ENJOYED SO MUCH IN A LONG, LONG TIME."

Clay Reynolds, author of *Franklin's Crossing*

FOOL'S GOLD

JOHNNY
QUARLES

AVON BOOKS NEW YORK

FOOL'S GOLD is an original publication of Avon Books. This work has never before appeared in book form. This work is a novel. Any similarity to actual persons or events is purely coincidental.

AVON BOOKS
A division of
The Hearst Corporation
1350 Avenue of the Americas
New York, New York 10019

Published by arrangement with the author
Library of Congress Catalog Card Number: 92-90439
ISBN: 0-380-76813-5

First Avon Books Printing: February 1993

Printed in the U.S.A.

RA 10 9 8 7 6 5 4 3 2 1

Dedication

I want to thank God for any abilities I might have. A special thank-you to my wife, Wendy, for all the help and encouragement she gives me. Thanks also to my agent, Ethan Ellenberg, a vegetarian; and to a man who has humbled me with his belief in what I do: my editor, Tom Colgan.

Writing is a rewarding career. It's a lonely business, but that small discomfort is more than made up for when I receive letters and comments from you, the readers. One aspect of being a writer that I particularly enjoy is doing my book dedications. In a small way, it enables me to recognize some of the fine people who have been helpful and kind to me along life's pathways.

Al and Judy Fields; Denny and Ann Price; Frank "Watermelon" and Wanda Campbell; Jim and Doriene Kesner; Vance and Jeannie Sharp; Jimmy and Barbara Faust; David and Jean Proveaux; Wayne and Darlene Shirey; Al Gaites; Bunie, Irene, and "Whip" Harper; John and Mary Usher; Art James; Eddie and Ann Payne; Bobby Cremins; George, Brandy, and Alice Felton; Bob Stefancik; David McGill; William Arthur Jackson; Bill and Kathy Baxter; John and Doris Roth; Joe Pinner; Travis Dyer; Marilyn Gail Layne; Roger Noble; Jacque Floyd Kvashnicka; Mickey Druiett; Mike and Anetta Bartlett; Larry and Peggy Layton; Billy and

Carla Smith; Steve Ayers; Gary Williams; Hayes Wicker; Herb Rhea; Don and Janell Diehl; Bruce Campbell; Doug Faulkner; Jeff Mullin; Mark Rountree; Randy Legg; Richard Billo; Sonny Lawrence; Alex Perry; Art Cox; Beth Lilley; Warren Frey; Gary and Sherry Slater; Billy Quarles; Garland and Wilma Quarles; Karen Payne; Mitchell Goc; Waldo and Ann Quarles; Ron Damon; Jerry Dushane; Jackie Griffey; Jim Randolph; Al Phillips; R. V. Hilderbrand; George and Wanda Floyd; Daryl Davenport; Elmer Winfield; Al Hinton; Keet Eaton; Paul and Helen Spears; Henry and Carolyn King; Tom Larkin; Billy Joe Nance; Kevin Cantwell; Tubby Smith; Keri Layne; J. D. Smith; R. G. Hilderbrand; Gary Don Johnson; J. E. Riley; Jon Donnell; Larry and Jacque Perry; Chet Cockrell; David Shields; Jack Mildren; Norval Rucker; Rev. Finis O'Neal; Roylue and Margie Campbell; Betty Southern Allen; Patty Southern Toney; Karen Southern Atwell; Ray Southern; Kim Tackett; Dusty Eby; John Kocher; Jerry Stevenson; Pat Moirano; Carol Semrad; Jeff Stoss; Laurie Anderson; Kris and Mark McKenzie; Karen Johnson Thomas (for Wendy); and, that female Italian Stallion, Bernadette Peters.

Other writers I admire: Liana DeFeo; Judith Henry Wall; Karen Evans; Elita Sharpe; Marsha LaMunyon; Shelley Stutchman; Linda Phelps; Sela Castleberry; Hugh Hairs; Jory Sherman; Maggie Gurley; Richard C. House; Doug Williams; Shirley Eaton; Larry Buckley; Randall Osborn; Shannon K. Jacobs; Clay Reynolds; Randy Greenwood; Curtiss Ann Matlock; Herman Wouk; Charles Wilson; Sara Orwig; Larry McMurtry; Clive Cussler; Georgina Gentry; Helen Carnell; Georgia Parks; Betty Watson; Anita Bridal; Sharon Sala; Janis Reams Hudson; Elmer Kelton; Elmore Leonard; Nancy Landon; Steven Wedel; Lou Mansfield; Howard Domnick; and the late John Vater.

Once, I had one of those boyish adolescent crushes—the kind that makes your heart flutter. I've never forgotten that girl and the wonderful feelings that ran through my veins over her. To the memory of Joni Harrison, I dedicate *Fool's Gold.*

1

When Holt Flynn stepped off the porch, the sun smacked his face with blinding force. He quickly averted his eyes from the harsh rays and searched the skies. Not a decent cloud could be seen anywhere. The thought of another scorcher brought a frown to his tan, windburned face. It was a face that looked the color of leather, and as tough, to boot, except when you reached the line at his forehead. From there and on up into the hairline, his skin was as white as the rest of his face was tanned. He'd forgotten to grab his hat on the way out, and the blazing sun felt especially hot on that tender part of his skin. Slowly, he turned and walked back across the dried and rotting wood of the porch, causing the boards to pop and groan, to retrieve the hat from a nail just inside the door.

When he'd gotten his hat pulled securely on, Holt went back out to survey the pond west of the house. The summer sun usually did some damage, but this year things seemed to be drying up faster than ever. Little squares of parched earth were turning up at the water's edge, caked and crusty. Just looking at them made his mouth feel like cotton. This fact concerned him greatly, for it wasn't even mid-morning yet. Sighing, he squatted down on the porch steps and undressed, then walked barefoot to the pond. The dried squares of earth crumbled under his weight into sharp fragments that cut into his tender soles. He started to step gingerly toward the water, like some prancing cat. When Holt finally reached the part that was mud, it was too hot to offer any comfort, and the water wasn't any better. He cursed as he stepped into what felt like a warm bath. This wasn't the cool relief he was looking for, but still he walked out into the center of the pond, which by this time was no more than a foot and a half deep, and sat down. His naked backside sunk into the slick bottom.

Holt was distracted from his misery as he watched the fish swimming about, searching for the deepest part of the pond, which he was now occupying. The backs of the bigger catfish were clearly visible, and in some of the shallow places, their bodies swam half in and half out of the water. He watched them awhile, trying to figure out which one he should catch for dinner. The thought nearly made him ill, though. Catfish had been the only meat on the dinner table for the last few weeks.

He was eyeing a nice one, maybe a six-pounder, when he looked up and spotted Walter Krenz riding toward the house. As Walter grew nearer, Holt's spirits picked up. Hanging from Walter's saddle were two long objects that looked like ropes.

"Well, I'll be hanged! Rattlesnakes!" he said.

The snakes would be a welcome delicacy. They hadn't had anything so tasty since Walter had killed a young chicken hawk a month before. Holt smiled happily, forgetting all about how hot and miserable he was, sitting in that slimy, half-dried pond. Walter rode his horse in until its feet were in the mud. He slung down two rattlers that measured almost five feet apiece, and said disgustedly, "What in blazes you doin'? We drink that water, and I don't cotton to drinkin' after your stinkin' butt's been wallerin' in it!"

Holt shrugged stubbornly. "If we don't get some rain, you'll not have to worry about such trite things as me dirtyin' up your drinkin' water. Best be grateful for what we do have," he said, eyeing the snakes. Deep down, he felt more than a mite ashamed of what had become of his life. It was a downright disgrace, he thought, when the epitome of excitement was having a rattler on the table.

Walter, apparently deciding it was too hot to argue, and useless anyway, rode on toward the house, leaving the snakes lying in the mud. Their heads had been smashed flat, but the rest of their bodies seemed for all the world like they were still alive. Holt stared at them for a while, then looked back down at the catfish that swam close by.

It had been six years since the two of them had been released from the Yuma Territory prison. That had been their second time behind bars. They had served twin eight-year sentences, and all for robbing a train that happened to be carrying a load of Arizona Rangers to a meeting with the governor. Holt still felt a shudder when he remembered how those lawmen had come barreling out of that train car, their hands full of pistols.

From prison, they'd come here to the Panhandle of Oklahoma Territory. "No-man's-land," it was called, and for Holt's money it damn well earned its name. In fact, the last six years had been unbearably tame ones, but not from their lack of trying. Trouble was, there just wasn't anything in comfortable riding distance to hold up. Their only attempts had been occasionally robbing the scattered neighbors of a few chickens or, once in a while, a calf if there was one to be found.

It pained the two no end, especially Holt, to know that they were considered harmless by the Panhandle residents. Even if they hadn't made a practice of hawking over their checkered past, it was still a hard pill to swallow that folks looked upon them as a pair of poor dirt farmers.

Just rethinking these thoughts worked hard on Holt's temperament, just like every other day at this time when the sun got to heating things up. He flat hated this place near as bad as being in prison. In the summer, it was miserably hot and dusty. Winters, it was colder than Alaska with the cussed winds blowing almost constantly, and nothing to break them up in the way of trees. Holt and Walter had settled here with the idea of raising a few cattle and living out a respectable life, but the three cows they had originally bought had never lasted out their first winter. Two froze to death, while the last had been butchered for food. Their plans for a thriving ranch died that winter, too.

They had both threatened to leave many times, but all they had left were two horses that weren't much more than a pair of nags. A man best be well-horsed if he did any traveling in this land, Holt had pointed out, and besides, where would they go? Still, it was a dream that Walter sometimes stopped to ponder, and that Holt pined over all the time.

Holt reluctantly pulled himself from the water, and had just retrieved the snakes when he spotted riders coming in. His face brightened. It would be Billy Cordell and Charlie Johnson—better-known to Holt and Walter and everyone else as Charlie One Eye. Charlie's good eye, the left one, was a bit cockeyed, and the blind right eye pointed off to the side, giving him the appearance of a bullfrog that had just experienced a skull-cracking jolt to the head. Charlie One Eye was a dull-thinking man in his forties, and as far as Holt knew, had never been good for much more than a day's work at a time, mainly up on the smaller spreads in Kansas.

Billy Cordell, on the other hand, was young, barely in his twenties, and full of energy. His sole ambition in life was to be a notorious gunfighter. He spent nearly every cent he came across on ten-cent novels about the West and its gunfighter heroes. He studied their descriptions, and had taken to walking like he thought a proper gunhand should walk. He even carried his Colt hung low on his right hip, his hand constantly rubbing the handle. He was sure it had to look impressive, and mistook the hard stares he received as respect.

Billy and Charlie One Eye would drop by and stay a few days here and there, whenever either one of them would quit or get himself fired from work. They often worked together, and when one was let go, the other quit his job on the spot. They always made their way back to Holt and Walter, anxious to hear their stories about the days when they robbed banks and trains for a living.

Holt stood still, letting the muddy water roll down his legs as he watched the two riding closer. He was always happy to see them coming, for it meant something to go along with the catfish on the table. He eyed a big burlap sack hanging from Charlie One Eye's horse.

"By dang! Potatoes!" he mouthed, his spirits picking up considerably. He was just starting to think about what fresh stories he could tell that night, when he suddenly saw something that made him realize how ridiculous he must look, dripping wet and naked. There was someone riding double behind Billy.

Not knowing exactly what else to do, Holt just stood there, holding a rattler limply in each hand, until the riders had come close in.

Billy Cordell pulled up with a pleasant smile, scrutinized the snakes whose smashed heads hung submerged in the water, then said, "Howdy, Holt."

"Howdy yourself, Billy."

Charlie One Eye had a puzzled look on his face. Holt couldn't be too sure exactly what Charlie was looking at. He hated getting caught all the time staring at Charlie to determine which way his good eye was supposed to be pointing. Sometimes it was hard to remember just which eye was the one that could see.

Charlie One Eye finally lifted his hand to point at Holt. "You got a-holdst of two snakes with no clothes on. Why's that?"

"Why, hell, Charlie!" Holt said, "that's the way I catch 'em. The snakes are less nervous that way." He lifted the snakes up high until they were completely out of the water, the smashed heads exposed. "What's that you got in the poke, Charlie? Somethin' to dress up these rattlers with, I hope."

"Taters."

Holt nodded, then took his first good look at the rider behind Billy. It was an old Indian man with white hair and wrinkled skin that had turned to leather in the sun. He sat quietly, staring at nothing in particular; in fact, he was the only one who didn't seem to be interested in the fact that Holt was standing there, totally naked, holding the snakes. "Where'd you boys git the Indian?"

"We found 'im wanderin' around over in Kansas," Billy said.

Holt turned away and started for the house with the snakes. He called over his shoulder, "You found 'im, just like that, you say? Well, what in the world you boys gonna do with 'im?"

Billy grew excited as he and Charlie followed Holt to the house on their horses. "We're gonna take 'im back to Georgia, wherest he come from. You see, he was a medicine man at one time, and I guess he done some bad medicine or something. Anyhows, he got run off or lost or somethin'."

Holt gave Billy an amused look as he flung the snakes down on the porch. He hurriedly pulled on his clothes. Billy and Charlie One Eye jumped down off their mounts, but the old Indian still sat, stone-faced, atop Billy's horse, until Billy spoke up.

"Climb on down here, Chief," he said. The Indian slowly dismounted, his body quivering with the effort.

Holt snorted. "Why, hell, Billy! That old Indian don't look like he's got a whole lot of time left here amongst the livin'! Why, he's got the shakes!" He bent over struggling to pull his boots over his wet feet.

2

BILLY AND CHARLIE ONE EYE SAT ON THE PORCH ALONG with the old Indian. They had hauled themselves up to watch Holt skin the snakes. Billy was as close to the side of the house as he could get, hoping to get far enough under the overhang to best keep out of the scorching rays of the sun. Charlie One Eye and the Indian were perched out near the steps in full view of the harsh rays. Neither seemed to notice how hot it was, and neither seemed to care.

No one said much as Holt went about his skinning. The old Indian sat with his face turned into the bright sunlight, watching a chicken hawk that had appeared in the cloudless sky. The hawk floated about, looking for any movement below. Holt, who had also noticed the circling hawk, commented dryly that he could have told the bird it was wasting its time.

"That there chicken hawk is kinda like a man," he added as he flung a skinless snake onto the dried wood at his feet.

Charlie One Eye blinked absently at the hawk. "How's that? I don't see where a dern chicken hawk is like any man I know of," he said.

Holt wiped his hands on his pants, then shielded his eyes so he could study the hawk better. "Well now, Charlie.

That's because you never look past the surface of anything. Now, you take that hawk. He could fly a few miles from here and find some jackrabbits to catch, easy enough. But instead he chooses to waste his time in this sun-baked dustbin where there ain't been a jack seen in months! You see, Charlie, a man's like that," he observed as he started in on the other snake.

Charlie One Eye frowned as he bit off a piece of chewing tobacco, still studying the hawk. He shook his head. "That don't make no sense," he insisted. "Why, a man wouldn't do such a thing, a-tall."

Holt noticed the tobacco and put down the snake. "Toss me your plug," he said. He caught the tobacco in his bloody hand and bit off a generous chew. After he'd moistened it inside his mouth a spell, he put it in its permanent spot in his jaw. Comfortable with the placement, he spat once and said, "Take Walter and me. We're just like that there hawk, inasmuch as we stay here, day after day, in this forsaken spot. Why, we know there's more fittin' places to live your life in! And what about you, Charlie? Hell, look at you and Billy. Why, I can look at that ole hawk there and see a bit of all of us. Yes, sir."

Charlie One Eye took off his hat and, as he often did, rubbed his hand across his balding head. His hands were big, with long slender fingers. When his thumb touched the top of his right ear, the long fingers would reach all the way to his left ear. He ran his hand down to the fringe at the back of his head, then smelled his sweaty palm. He spat and said, "That's about the craziest thing I ever heard. I ain't nothin' like no blamed chicken hawk."

Holt smiled to himself and quickly finished off the second snake. The others watched him as he cut both into pieces suitable for cooking. All done, Holt settled back to talk. Billy had leaned way back on his elbows, and looked like he could fall asleep if it weren't for the heat. Charlie One Eye had picked up his tobacco and was idly turning it over and over in his hand. The Indian sat, stoop-shouldered, still staring as if there was something interesting to look at.

"So," Holt said, "you boys plan on takin' the Indian to Georgia? Why, I'd say that's a mighty ambitious plan."

Billy had let his eyes close as he leaned back. He often did that while other men were sitting around talking. Many times, he'd been accused of being a catnapper, but the truth was Billy just liked to daydream with his eyes shut. While other men might seem to enjoy expounding on what they had seen and done, Billy had nothing in life so enjoyable as his daydreaming. Most times, he'd dream about gunfights that put him against some faceless adversary. They were all of the same nature, with the opponent pulling leather first, then Billy firing just a twinkling of a second faster. He and Charlie One Eye had witnessed a lot of arguments on the many spreads they'd worked on and the saloons they'd frequented along the way. Billy could replay every one of them over in his mind, putting himself in the shoes of the one he considered the "good guy." It always ended the same way. Billy would find himself in a shoot-out, and each time he would plug his foe in the heart. If it weren't for these little scenarios playing through his mind, life would indeed have been a mundane affair.

Holt's voice jolted him from his dream. "Wake up, Billy Boy! Tell me why you're takin' the Indian to Georgia."

Billy's eyes opened into slits. "I weren't sleeping. Just thinkin'." He peered at the old Indian's back, and a smile crossed his face. "Chief there he wants to go back home and die. Back to north Georgia wheres his people come from." He let his eyes close again, hoping to finish up on his daydream before Holt interrupted him again.

"Why, that ole Indian's likely pullin' you boys' legs!" Holt declared. He stared hard at the Indian.

Charlie One Eye, who was wiping more sweat off his head and smelling his hand, stretched his neck and frowned at Holt. "What makes you think a thing like that?" he asked.

"Hell, Charlie! I been to Georgia, and by dang, I never saw no Indians there! 'Sides, he looks like a Plains Indian to me,'cept for his clothes. They're white man's clothes, at least them britches are," Holt said.

"He's from Georgia, all right," Billy said. He sat up with an irritated look on his face. "Ain't that so, Chief?"

The old Indian's eyes were still fixed on the floating hawk. If he was aware of the conversation that was taking place about him, he showed no outward signs.

Holt watched the Indian a moment, then shook his head. "Hell, Billy! Can't that Indian even speak English?" he asked.

"Better'n some white folks I know," Billy answered, still sounding irritated.

"Well, if that ain't the problem, then I reckon his hearin' must be near gone." Holt scooped up the pieces of snake meat and stood up to go inside. Like Billy, he studied the old Indian for a minute, then said, "You boys try carryin' that ole Indian halfway across the country, and I bet you don't make it out of the Panhandle before he croaks! Why, look at him. He can hardly draw a breath."

The observation brought Billy to his feet, a look of concern on his face. "Chief, you all right?" he asked loudly.

The old Indian sat silently, his face turned skyward.

Billy nudged him with his foot. "Dern it, Chief! Speak to me!"

The old Indian's head turned slowly. His eyes were squinting as he faced Billy.

"You okay?" Billy asked, the concern back in his voice.

The Indian closed his eyes and barely nodded, then turned back toward the circling hawk.

Billy gave a sigh of relief and turned to make some comment to Holt, who had already disappeared inside the dark doorway of the house.

"Gonna get the chief back home, just fine," he muttered to himself and Charlie One Eye.

It was mid-afternoon when they sat down to a meal of fried potatoes and rattlesnake. As always, they ate ravenously and without so much as a word spoken among them. When the food was all gone, Holt and Walter began reminiscing about their early days. One of their favorite stories was about the time they had tried to rob the same train as Jesse James and his gang. Holt and Walter had boarded the train as passengers. The car was filled with wealthy-looking travelers. Just as they jumped out of their seats with guns drawn, there'd been shots fired outside the train. At first, Holt and Walter had thought the James gang were lawmen who had somehow found out their intentions. They had been too surprised to put their guns away as the James gang came on board.

Jesse had taken a liking to them. He'd let them keep what little money they had between them, and had even invited the pair to join up with him and the "boys," as he called them. But, shaken up as he was, Walter would have no part in the idea, and, years later, the memory was only good for storytelling after a meal with Billy and Charlie One Eye.

Today, though, was different. Billy wasn't plying Holt and Walter with his usual endless string of questions. Instead, he just smiled a lot, like a kid about to bust with something to say. Holt noticed, but he didn't let on. He sat back like he wasn't the least bit concerned with the new development. Billy had something on his mind, that was for sure, and Holt knew he wanted them to query him on it. But Holt wasn't going to do that, either. No, he'd just wait Billy out, he decided. It wouldn't take long, because Billy never could hold a thing inside, a fact that Walter had pointed out to Holt many times. Billy, Walter claimed, would get caught in a heartbeat if he was ever to try to live out his fantasy of robbing banks and trains and the like.

Holt's eyes slid across the table to Walter. It was obvious that he was right about Billy's being so full of something he was about to bust. Walter had noticed, too. He raised his eyebrows and tilted his head toward Billy in a questioning gesture. Sometimes, Walter could irritate Holt to no end, with his carrying on about Billy and Charlie One Eye's visits. He'd be hospitable to the pair at first, then turn quiet after the first couple of days. By the time the two of them were riding away, Walter would be muttering, "Good riddance." It wasn't that Billy and Charlie One Eye displayed any special kind of irritating behavior; Walter usually managed to find fault with anyone who stayed within talking distance for any length of time. But, after a spell had passed, Walter would always go back to looking forward to their next visit. He'd never said as much, but Holt could tell.

Holt stared back at Walter's questioning look and shrugged. Walter snorted and shook himself, then turned to Billy and blurted out, "Well, you gonna grin us to death, or tell what the big news is?"

That made Billy's smile stretch even wider. "What makes you think I've got any big news, Walter?" he asked, picking his teeth with a fingernail.

The way Billy answered made Walter's mouth drop open. "Why, your dern face is the color of a overripe tomater! But you don't have to tell us a dern thing if you don't want to, that's for sure!" he said. He yanked his tobacco pouch from his pocket to roll a fixin'. Holt noticed that his fingers shook a little as he tried to hide his irritation.

Billy let them wait awhile longer, then finally turned to Charlie One Eye. "Should we tell 'em, or what?" he asked with a grin.

Charlie One Eye looked at him absently. "I thought we came here for that purpose," he said.

Billy cocked his head and bit his lip, giving Charlie One Eye a disdainful stare. It was plain that no one was giving Billy the special attention he had thought he'd get over what was on his mind. Not even Charlie One Eye. He fiddled with his coffee cup, staring into it like a gypsy gazing into a crystal ball. Walter started to say something, but Holt silenced him with a glance. Walter threw up his eyes and silently lit his smoke, then stared at Billy with thinly disguised impatience.

When Billy had salvaged what little suspense he could, he smiled into the cup and said softly, "We—that is, Charlie and me—we thought maybe you boys would like to go along with us in takin' Chief back to his final buryin' ground."

Walter, who had leaned back in his seat, let his chair fall to the floor with a loud bang. He gave a harsh laugh. "Why, dern, Billy! Are you loco or somethin'? Why, I thought you had somethin' of importance to tell!" He got up and walked to the door, shaking his head as he stared outside.

Holt laughed. "Hell, Billy! Much as I hate to agree with Walter, you gotta be crazy to think we'd wanta ride all the way to Georgia!" He laughed again. "It's not that we don't enjoy your company, you understand," he added.

Walter grunted at the door, and Billy stared at him a minute before he said, "Go on and have a good laugh." He nudged the Indian, who was still chewing on a piece of snake. "Okay, Chief, let's have it."

Walter turned to face the table, still frowning but with a hint of curiosity. Holt's face still held a bit of a smile, but he watched the Indian closely.

The Indian sat, holding a piece of snake meat, and looked slowly around the table. His leathery face was as emotionless as before, but his eyes had picked up a twinkle. They could all see it, even though the only light in the room came from the afternoon sun, which shone through the back door in a long stretch on the floor, to just within a foot of the table.

They all waited as the old Indian carefully finished chewing his meat and swallowed. Then, with shaking hands, he laid the uneaten portion on his plate and reached into the pocket of his britches.

"What in tarnation is this all about?" Walter breathed softly as he moved closer to see.

From his pocket, the Indian pulled out what at first looked like a small rock.

Holt leaned over to study the stone. He studied it for a long time, then all at once he murmured, "Hellfire! That's gold!"

"One hundred percent real thing!" Billy beamed.

3

THE ROOM FELL SILENT AS THE MEN STARED INTENTLY at the gold piece in the Indian's hand. He held it out for them to study for as long as they wanted, the shine still in his eyes.

Gold has a way of affecting different men in different ways, and this group was no exception. Walter gazed at the nugget, and a life full of "ifs" passed through his mind. He remembered his widowed mother. A big cache of gold would have provided the money to help her. After his father had died a young man, she had been left with five daughters and a son to raise on her own. The five girls had helped all they could, but instead of becoming the man of the family, Walter had turned to outlawing. It had damn near put his mother into the grave, with her pleas that he turn to a decent life falling on deaf ears. He had sent her what little money he could spare, until the day the law caught up with him. He was in prison when he heard she had died of heart failure. A broken heart, Walter had told himself. He was ashamed of his life, and though he thought about them often, he had never tried to look up any of his sisters after he'd been set free. He felt pretty sure they would have forgiven him readily enough, but somehow that would have made him feel even worse.

Holt was having his own fantasies as he stared at the nugget. To him, the beautiful, odd-shaped chunk of gold brought pictures of pretty whores and good whiskey. He thought of San Francisco, with its fancy saloons and dance halls. He'd been headed there, years ago, to see what kind of fortune he could find, when he'd run into Walter in New Mexico Territory. They'd met in a dingy little settlement where a leaning shack had been converted into a makeshift saloon, and somehow Holt's plans for San Francisco had never materialized. That had been so many years ago. Holt closed his eyes to take them away from the gold, which seemed to light up the entire room. He could almost taste the whiskey and smell the perfume. He felt resentful when Billy's voice broke the silence.

"There's plenty more wheres that come from!"

The old Indian, satisfied that everyone had taken a good look, slowly pushed the gold nugget back into the pocket of his britches, then picked up the snake meat and returned to his eating.

Walter still seemed skeptical. "By damn, Billy! What in blazes does that gold have to do with us takin' that Indian feller all the way to Georgia?" he asked.

Billy's know-it-all smile returned. " 'Cause that's where it come from, and there's a whole lot more! Ole Chief, here, he knows right where it's at!" he said, patting the Indian on the shoulder like they were old friends.

Holt let out a guttural, somewhat sarcastic laugh. "Why, hell, Billy! You and Charlie One Eye ain't stupid enough to believe that this old Indian is gonna take you to any gold? What would he want to do that for, if'n there even was any gold?"

Billy looked once behind his shoulder and leaned forward in earnest. "Have your laugh. I guess I understand, but I'm tellin' you. Old Chief here, when he was a boy back in Georgia, he done saw a big cave that was just loaded with gold!" He tapped his finger on the table with every word. His eyes were dark and serious.

Holt shifted his gaze away from Billy's unbroken stare and looked at the Indian, who still seemed oblivious to anything other than the snake meat on his plate. Holt had serious doubts about what he was hearing, but he had to admit one thing. He wanted in the worst way to believe it. He reached over and gently nudged the old Indian with his hand.

"Well, what about this story Billy Boy is tellin' us? Is it true that you know where a cave full of gold is at?" he asked.

The Indian paused in his chewing and smiled into Holt's eyes. "Yes, it is true," he said softly.

Walter made an impatient gesture and grabbed a chair, scraping it across the floor before he plopped down in it. "Now, don't you start!" he said to Holt. "These boys ride up with some cock-and-bull story about gold in Georgia, and by danged if I can't see there's interest startin' up in you!"

"Hell, Walter. I ain't said I believe any of this," Holt said.

Walter snorted. "The blazes you say! You think after all these years I don't know that look on your face? Well, if you say you don't believe it, you best just keep it that way!" he exclaimed.

Holt turned away from his partner and eyed Billy and Charlie One Eye. They were both watching him and Walter with great interest. Holt could see their enthusiasm. "Hell, boys. I got to agree with Walter. What makes you think he's tellin' you boys straight?" he asked.

The Indian's voice surprised him. It came out low and gravelly, but filled the room eerily.

"I am old. I want to return to the Great Spirit in the land of my birth and that of my father and his father before him. What I say is the truth." The Indian's head drooped forward, and the snake meat in his hand shook, as if the effort to talk had drained his energy.

Walter dismissed the old Indian's claim with a grunt and drained the rest of the cold coffee from his tin cup.

Billy and Charlie One Eye, even if they were disappointed by Walter's reaction, still seemed to be excited about the prospect of becoming rich in the mountains of Georgia.

Holt, for his part, couldn't take his eyes off the Indian. In his mind, he could see that cave, bulging with nuggets of gold that jutted out from all sides. His stare turned blank, eyes widening, and his head cocked involuntarily to one side. He imagined being inside that cave, holding up a candle. The gold was so thick it seemed to blind him with its sparkle. Somewhere off, a piano started playing, and two San Francisco whores suddenly appeared at his side. The first held a bottle of good whiskey. The second, a short, full-breasted blond, cuddled a bottle of champagne and smiled at him invitingly. Grinning, Holt reached out to touch her.

"What in thunder you think you're a-doin'?" Charlie One Eye's startled voice rang out.

Holt's eyes blinked several times. He drew back his hand, which had caressed Charlie One Eye's arm. Flushing a deep red, he tried to look at Charlie One Eye to say he was sorry, but for the life of him he couldn't make out the good eye from the bad. He glanced from one eye to the other, then stammered, "Nothin', Charlie. Never you mind. 'Tweren't nothin'."

Any other time, the late afternoon heat would have felt unbearable in the airless house. Only the flies seemed to possess any kind of energy as they found their way to the scraps of food on the table and buzzed around the men's heads. Today, though, flies and heat were of little consequence as the subject of gold was tossed around. They stayed there and talked around the table until well after the sun had made itself scarce.

Through bits and pieces of conversation with Billy and Charlie One Eye, and scattered information from the old Indian, Holt was finally able to put together a rough account.

As their story went, the Indian was a member of the Cherokee tribe in the mountains of north Georgia. The tribe had outlasted the large 1809 migration of Cherokee to land west of the Mississippi, and although the Indians had been friendly with the white men since 1794, there was still a large amount of distrust between the two. It was back in '21 that the Indian had been off hunting by himself, when he supposedly discovered a hidden cave that was filled with gold. He had told his people about it, and the Cherokee had used the gold to barter and deal with the white men, careful to guard the secret of the hidden cave. Soon after, the Indians had discovered yet another vein of gold, but the white men found out about it, and before long the Georgia people had clamored to get the Indians moved out so they could claim the riches. The Cherokee had finally been driven away in the winter of early 1823, but the tribal elders had made everyone swear secrecy about the undiscovered cave. Today, all who had known of its existence were dead, except for the old Indian who now traveled with Billy and Charlie One Eye.

They talked through evening—talked until the old Indian's head was nodding and Billy and Charlie One Eye were yawning. The three travelers went off to bed down, but Holt and Walter were wide awake from the story they'd just heard. They took themselves to the front porch to talk, sitting out under a bright starlit night.

By this time, Holt was convinced that the story was true, but Walter was even more doubtful than he'd been at the start. He brushed at a june bug that had blindly flitted against his neck, caught it in his hand, and threw it against the hard dry ground. "Hell, that cussed Indian don't know any more about a cave full of gold than I do," he said.

Holt could barely see the dark shape of the june bug as it crawled slowly away from the spot where it had landed. He watched its struggles a moment, then said, "Where you suppose he got that gold rock, then?"

"I don't know! Why, he coulda got it anyplace! And I'll tell you right now, I don't think he's even been to Georgia!" Walter said.

"Now, why would he lie about a thing like that?" Holt reasoned.

"Hell, I don't know. Just a feelin' I got," Walter said.

Holt picked up the plug of tobacco which he'd slipped from the table after Charlie One Eye had generously left it there. He took a big bite from the shrinking plug, worked it awhile, then said, "I think we oughta go with 'em."

"Why, I'll be hanged! You what?" Walter exclaimed. His irritation was growing as he jumped to his feet and started pacing back and forth. His boot heels pounded on the hollow wood, so loud that Holt wondered if the noise would wake the others up. "By golly, you go then! But don't expect me to go traipsin' off on some harebrained chase! No, sir!"

Holt spit tobacco juice at the june bug, satisfied with his aim. "Aw, come on now, Walter! How can you be so dang sure it ain't true? What have you got to lose, anyway?" he asked.

Walter turned and leaned over close to Holt, his face showing his agitation in the pale light. "What have we got to lose? I'll tell ya what we got to lose!" he said. "A whole bunch of time, for one! And more saddle sores than I care to think about! All for some dang crazy story!"

"Well," Holt commented thoughtfully, "we can sit here till we die and blow away, I guess, just like the rest of this dirt. That may be all right with you, Walter, but dern it, I think I'd like just one more bit of excitement before my Maker comes for me." He knew that arguing with Walter was useless, but he did it anyway. The afternoon talk had put a feeling back inside him that had been missing for a long time. It suddenly felt good to have something to look forward to—something a lot more interesting than worrying about what to eat for the evening meal. He set his resolve and stared back at Walter, the white of his eyes glistening in the moonlight.

Unfazed, Walter stood up straight and said, "You're serious."

"As can be," Holt answered.

Walter held up his hands. "Let's say," he said, "that old Chief is tellin' the truth. Why, we don't even have horses good enough to ride fifty miles out, let alone a thousand!" He shook his head. "I'm goin' to bed."

A voice spoke into the night air. "I know wheres you can git horses. Good ones, too."

Holt and Walter both reeled around and were surprised to see Billy standing in the doorway. He was in his underwear, with his Colt strapped to his leg.

Holt smiled at the sight. "How long you been spyin' on us?" he asked.

"Weren't doin' no spyin'. I do know where some good horseflesh is, though," Billy repeated.

"Shit fire!" Walter said in a surly tone. "Findin' good horses ain't no problem. It's the money to buy 'em with." He was clearly disturbed that Billy had interrupted with more silly talk about what, in his opinion, was wild speculation.

Holt agreed with him. "That's right, Billy. You don't think we're keepin' those nags of ours around here 'cause we're softhearted, do ya? No—"

Billy cut him off. "Don't need no money. The Trapp sisters said they'd sell you a pair on credit."

Red exploded across Walter's face, and anger laced his words. "Did they, now?" he said. "Them dern Trapp sisters! We don't want none of their credit! Nor nobody else's, neither!"

The Trapp sisters were a well-known topic of many conversations in the Panhandle area. Katy Trapp Wilson and Nikki Trapp Daniels had been on their way from Missouri to Denver with their husbands, planning to settle there and begin their families. The foursome had been overtaken in Kansas, however, by a small party of Cheyenne, who had happened upon them. The Cheyenne had killed both of the men and were just about to do the same to the sisters when a detachment of the cavalry had shown up, just in the nick of time. The soldiers had been tracking the Indians, who had been on a savage killing spree all across the Territory. The sisters, being of hearty stock, had never left Kansas. After they buried their husbands, they had settled right there, pooled their savings, and opened up a saloon. It was right in the middle of nowhere, but enough traveling herds passed by that the cowboys kept the place flourishing. Over the years, they had added groceries and horses to their fare, along with anything else a cowpoke might need on the trail. Now every cowboy within riding distance would make it a point to stop and do business with the Trapp sisters.

For reasons no one could understand, the sisters had taken a big liking to Holt and Walter. That was a pleasurable turn of events for Holt. In fact, any time he had any money, he would ride the forty or so miles to drink with them. Especially Katy. The two of them had burned many a candle into the night, nursing a bottle of rye and talking about places like Paris, London, and, of course, San Francisco. Holt loved to talk about nearly any subject, whether he was familiar with it or not. Conversation was a scarce commodity around these parts. On occasion, he would manage to get a conversation, going with Walter—or at least he could get Walter to listen while he talked. Billy had read enough dime novels that he could carry on a decent enough conversation, even if it was limited to the subject of gunfights and such. Charlie One Eye, on the other hand, was strictly a listener.

Katy Trapp, though, was the best thing to come by in a long time, for Holt's money. He could converse with her for hours on just about any subject he'd choose. It didn't matter a bit to her, as she could hold up her side of the topic no matter what it was. To say that Holt admired her verbose ways was an understatement.

Walter, however, held an entirely different viewpoint about the sisters, in that he regarded them with disdain. Nothing but trouble, he would claim. Walter's idea of a good woman companion did not include the gift of talk. It was a cheap, silent whore that could best suit a man's needs, he often said. This observation had been made right after they had first met the Trapp sisters. Walter had frolicked with Nikki once, but when the frolicking was over, Nikki had stayed right there in that feather bed and talked about how a man like Walter should be married. She had dern near proposed marriage to him, right there in that bed. Walter had been so badly shaken that he'd waited until the early morning hours when Nikki had finally given up and gone to sleep. Then he had slipped off of that feather mattress and nearly pushed his horse to death in getting back home. To this day, Walter didn't go back unless he had to. Nikki Trapp, in Walter's thinking, was a viper that just wanted to get her fangs into him.

"Aw, hell, Walter!" Holt's spirits had picked up at the thought of seeing Katy again. "For a cave full of gold, I reckon we could do with a little credit with the Trapp sisters," he said.

Walter raised an angry fist. "I'd rather steal 'em as do credit with those women!" he said gruffly.

It had always amused Holt that Walter could get so mad over such trifles in life. He'd known Walter to get red as fire over things that the normal man would not have blinked twice at. "Shoot! They hang ya for stealin' horses," he said, enjoying the effect his words were having on the irritated Walter. He looked at Billy, who was still standing in the doorway, watching Walter as if he wasn't sure he'd be welcome if he stepped out on the porch. "Billy Boy, don't you ever worry about shootin' yourself, sleepin' with that dern gun?" he asked.

Billy blinked several times. He always blinked whenever he didn't know how to respond to something Holt said. He pulled absently at a long string that hung from his underwear and blinked some more.

"Walter," Holt asked his partner, "do you remember that Limpy Davis from Lincoln County?" He turned back to Billy. "He woke up from a bad dream one night and mistook his big toe for a tarantula! Shot it clean off!" He stared down at Billy's white feet until Billy started shuffling his feet nervously.

Walter stretched. "Well, you two can sit out here and jaw all night if you want to. I'm goin' to bed."

Holt stood up slowly and flexed his legs. "He's right, Billy. We best carry this conversation on in the mornin'."

Billy held his post in the doorway, so that Walter had to stop from entering. "What about the Trapp sisters?" he asked.

Walter stared at Billy as if he thought he might be daft, but Holt said, "We'll talk about them in the mornin'. Let's sleep on it first." He pushed past Billy, but paused to glance down at Billy's feet. "Dern if them naked toes don't look a little like tarantulas in the dark," he commented in a low voice.

That set Billy to hopping back and forth even more. "Hey, stop that!" he protested. "I don't reckon I'd be so dumb as to shoot my dang toe off!"

Holt said, "That's what they used to say about Limpy Davis from Lincoln County."

4

HOLT AWOKE BEFORE MORNING HAD OFFICIALLY ARrived. It was still more dark than light outside. He pulled on his britches and grabbed his fixin's. The snoring that filled the room was enough to give a body a good headache, he thought.

Walter, Billy, Charlie One Eye, and the Indian were still sprawled out, and most of the snoring was coming from Charlie One Eye, who was flat on his back with both arms spread. The old Indian lay curled up in a corner on a thick blanket that Billy had laid out for him in his efforts to keep the man alive.

Outside, the air had lost most of the heat of the day before, to where it felt right comfortable. Holt liked to get up early, before any man or animal had a chance to muddle up the silence. He walked past the pond to the corral. There he rolled a smoke and waited for the sun to come up. He carried his Winchester along, for he never knew when a deer might appear. Every month or so, he would spot one that had smelled the pond water and moved in for a drink. Venison on the table was a rare and welcome delight.

He was just crushing the stub of his second smoke with the toe of his boot when something caught his eye. At first, he thought it was the silhouette of a wild turkey, moving slowly toward the shallow pond. That didn't make any sense, though, since there hadn't been a turkey seen in these parts for years.

He squinted through the dimly lit sky, and after studying the form briefly, he saw that it was a young doe. It had always amazed Holt how an animal as big as a deer could sneak up on a scene so quickly and without a man knowing it was coming. Why, he could be staring one way, glance briefly away and back, and there it would appear, right before his eyes, just as if it had entered the world in that exact spot.

But no matter how it got there, it was food. Holt raised his Winchester, leveled it, and squeezed off a round at the dark silhouette. The young doe jerked, and bolted. It ran about twenty yards, then fell. When Holt got close enough to see, its sides were still moving, and the heavy gasping filled the air.

"Sorry about that, lady. I'd much preferred it if you didn't have to suffer any." Holt quickly took out his Bowie knife and plunged the blade into the doe's windpipe. The doe shuddered and was still. Satisfied that it was dead, Holt pulled the animal by its hind legs away from the pond to a spot behind the corral.

Desiring to make quick work of dressing the animal, Holt made a cut from between the doe's legs to the breastbone, careful not to puncture the stomach lining. He then reached up inside the rib cage to where the windpipe had been severed and pulled it out, along with the entrails. The liver was separated and laid on a corral post. The thought of fried liver on the breakfast table made his mouth water.

The morning sun was up to where it sent a splash of fresh color over the land by the time Holt finished skinning the doe. He was hanging the carcass on the corral gate when he heard a door slam. Billy and Charlie One Eye had spied him and walked over to see what he was doing.

Billy wiped his eyes and said, "Mornin'."

"Mornin' yourself, Billy," Holt answered, without looking their way.

"I'll be damned! Look, Charlie! Holt's killed himself a deer," Billy said with surprise in his voice. "I didn't hear nothin'," he added. "Did you hear anything, Charlie?"

Charlie One Eye shook his head.

Holt draped the deer hide over a nail and stood back, amused. "Hell, you boys sure wouldn't make no Indian fighters," he commented. "I 'spect that shot must've woke up my neighbors, the Martins. And they live five miles from here!"

Billy blinked hard a time or two and stared down with embarrassment. It pained him like nothing else to be considered incompetent when it came to anything dealing with a gun. He shuffled his foot in the dirt and grew quiet.

Charlie One Eye didn't even seem to hear Holt's remark, or apply it to himself, anyway. He went over to examine the carcass, peering at it so closely that Holt thought his nose would touch it. "No more'n eighty, eighty-five pounds, tops," he said and sniffed.

"Why, that's right, Charlie," Holt said. "That's why I chose this lady! 'Cause she's just the right size. Ought to feed us all real good for a few days. You got any more of them taters?"

"A few."

"Good."

"Damn the taters!" Billy said, still smarting over Holt's earlier remark. He threw back his head and shoved his hands on his hips. "You and Walter goin' with us, or not?"

Holt answered the challenge with a casual smile. "Aw, let's have a little breakfast first. Then you 'n Charlie 'n me will ride over 'n have a nice talk with the Trapp sisters."

Billy grinned and slapped his leg. Even his desire at that moment to be considered as dark and mean as a snake could not mask the relief he felt. He let out a whoop that startled Holt and Charlie One Eye both, and kicked up his heels.

"That's great! Just great!" Then, as a new thought hit him, his face turned serious. "What about Walter?"

Holt shrugged. "We'll leave him and the Indian here whilst we go see the Trapps. It'll give me some time to think on it," he said. He was wishing by now that Billy and Charlie One Eye hadn't found him quite so early in the morning and come over to talk his ear off. He'd pretty much made his own decision on the question of going to search for gold, but having to convey that decision and deal with Walter was another matter. Mornings were the best thinking time for early risers, when the heat hadn't yet crawled back over everything. Billy, though, didn't seem to know or care anything about Holt's wishes.

"You think it's a good idea, leaving Chief here with Walter? I mean, Walter ain't exactly keen on any of this," Billy said, concerned.

"Hell, boys! That old Indian needs all the rest he can git, if'ns we're gonna keep 'im alive all the way to Georgia, which, I might add, I'm not so sure we can do in the first place! Far as Walter's concerned, he ain't gonna bother 'im none." Holt grabbed up the doe and headed for the house with Billy and Charlie One Eye on his heels.

"You really think there's a chance that ole Chief won't make it to Georgia?" Charlie One Eye asked with a worried tone.

"Hell, Charlie, Georgia's a long ways. There's a chance that none of us will make it," Holt said. He was noticing how neither Billy nor Charlie One Eye was helping him tote the deer, which wasn't that heavy, but it wasn't that light, either.

Charlie One Eye's good eye stared hard at Billy, who shook his head. "Pay no attention to that. We'll make it all right," he said.

Holt was glad when the two decided to wait for their breakfast on the porch. Walter hadn't stirred yet, and the house was quiet enough to do some pondering.

He hated to force Walter's hand in the matter, but Holt

knew he was going to Georgia, whether Walter did or not. The excitement that had filled him since the night before was a grand feeling, and he couldn't pass up what just might be his last chance at making something of his life. He looked at Walter. Holt knew the man well, and as much as Walter hated the idea of going to Georgia, he would still balk at the prospect of being left here alone. No, Walter would be mad as hell all the way, and his companionship miserable, but this time Holt didn't care.

He sliced the liver thin, and soon the aroma of fried liver and potatoes filled the house. Hoping the breakfast might lift Walter's spirits some, Holt waited until they were eating before he told his plans to ride with Billy and Charlie One Eye to visit the Trapp sisters. He was waiting for a high-pitched protest. It surprised him, then, when Walter didn't say a word, but just threw him a look that said plenty. Charlie One Eye kept his good eye on his plate, for the fresh liver was the most important thing at the moment, but Billy fidgeted, his eyes darting back and forth between Holt and Walter.

When Holt went on to say that they planned to leave the Indian behind, he was sure Walter would fly into a fit. Instead, he was again taken aback when Walter pursed his lips and nodded his head.

"I don't see as how I could stop a grown man from doin' what he wants," he said. "As for the Indian, I reckon he's welcome to stay as any, but you're a bunch o' fools if'n you think I'm gonna watch over 'im."

That was as big an encouragement as Holt could hope for, coming from Walter. Right after breakfast, he, Billy, and Charlie One Eye saddled up and headed for the Trapps'. Walter didn't bother to answer when Holt said good-bye, but he stuck a chair out on the porch to sit while the day was still pleasant. The Indian walked slowly to a spot by the front door and sat, cross-legged.

Billy kept glancing back as they rode out, concern showing on his face. He held a constant worry over the Indian's health, and Walter's remark hadn't reassured him any that the Indian would still be alive when they got back. Once they'd moved out of sight of the house, he voiced his concern to Holt.

Holt was philosophical. "Hell, Billy," he said, "that ole Indian has seen a whole lot more sunups than any of us. I reckon he'll survive livin' with Walter for a few days. 'Sides that, I reckon when his Maker, or the Great Spirit as he calls it, comes to take 'im, it ain't gonna matter one bit where he's at or who he's with." He gave Billy a stare and added matter-of-factly, "and there ain't one dern thing you can do about it."

Billy bit his lip and fell silent, but he seemed to feel a little better, as if it really wasn't on his shoulders anymore to keep the old man alive.

They rode at a slow pace so as not to kill the old mare under Holt. Charlie One Eye took up the rear. Billy seemed lost in his thoughts. With only the sounds of horses' hooves and the wind, it was a good time to think.

Holt had turned melancholy. He'd started thinking about Katy Trapp, and the more he thought about her, the more wistful he felt. The woman had often hinted that it would be a nice idea for them to get married. Not a bad idea, he told himself. It would, indeed, be a decent life. He could move right in and live over the prairie tavern with her. There would be plenty to eat and lots of good whiskey. Best of all, he could have many intellectual chats with Katy.

His spirits picked up some when he switched his thoughts to a gold-filled cave in Georgia. Why, he thought suddenly, after they struck gold, he could take Katy to San Francisco with him! They could live out their years in a fine house filled with stimulating conversation. They'd eat in the best restaurants and do the things they'd always wanted to do. Holt had a curiosity about the theater. Of course, he'd never gotten a chance to go. He'd only seen posters of a stage show once, but the lure of it had never left him. He had been foolish enough once to voice his desire to Walter, even though he knew better, and Walter's response didn't surprise him any.

"Why would anyone want to pay good money to watch a bunch of overgrown kids playact?" he'd said with a puzzled look. Holt had since held his tongue on the subject.

It was late when the three rode up to the Trapp Tavern and Mercantile. As they tied their horses, Holt was tired from the long ride, but he could feel a stirring inside himself at the thought of seeing Katy Trapp.

5

"YOU KILT MY BROTHER, AND NO SON OF A BITCH IS gonna get away with that!"

The man stood, rooted in the path of the horse that approached. His hand was clenched around his gun.

Joe Harbin started at the sound of the voice. It disturbed him that he'd been riding along, not paying attention to anything around him. Now, this cur of a man had gotten the drop on him. As cool as November wind, he said, "Listen, mister. I don't know who your brother was, but you're blockin' my way." His face bore no expression. He chewed at the inside of his jaw.

The angry cur shook and took a step forward. "Don't try and deny it!" he shouted. "I know you. You're Joe Harbin!"

Harbin silently responded by letting his steel-blue eyes pierce into the man's own. The cur started to blink.

"You son of a bitch!" The cur thumb-cocked his Colt and raised his arm to take aim, but before he could squeeze the trigger, his eyes suddenly went blank and his mouth flew open. The cur hadn't heard a sound. His face turned puzzled as he stared down at his chest. A small red hole was growing larger in his sweat-stained shirt. The Colt fell harmlessly from his grasp and struck the ground, the round in its chamber exploded. Very slowly, the eyes moved in bewilderment from the little red hole to the Colt that lay smoking. Then the cur, still with a score left to settle, fell dead.

Harbin climbed down from the big red gelding and, after he'd replaced the spent cartridge in his gun, moved to get a closer look at the man who'd tried to kill him. He rolled the cur over and stared down. He still had no idea who the man was, but he didn't linger over the fact. Shoot-outs like this were not uncommon, for when you hunted men for the bounty on their heads, you never knew what enemies you might be making. Harbin's list was long, and he'd grown to expect such behavior from any stranger he might run across. The only thing that bothered him was the fact that he'd let this one get the drop on him.

He made a brief search of the dead man's pockets, but found no information as to who he might be. Not that it made all that much difference. Harbin gathered up the body and propped it against a tree that stood alongside the trail, then retrieved the man's hat and covered his face. A tan mare was tied among some trees a short distance away. Harbin brought the horse close to the body and tied it to the tree. He then took out a small pad of paper from his shirt pocket, wet the end of a stubby pencil with his tongue, and wrote:

"I, J. Harbin, was jump by this unknon man. Shot him for he shot me."

He attached the note to the dead man's shirt, then climbed back atop the gelding. Soon, the shooting of the cur was completely out of his mind.

Harbin rode to the south, letting the gelding keep its own pace. The horse needed no guiding; they had been traveling south ever since they'd left Montana, crossing through Wyoming and then entering Colorado. Harbin was glad that Texas was near. It would be good to get back to familiar territory. He'd been Tennessee born and Texas bred, but his bountying took him to many different places.

In fact, he was just now returning from a wild chase that had begun in Arizona, then taken him through New Mexico and on up north. He'd finally caught up with the man on the muddy main street of Castle, Montana, a town that had gone loco with silver-mining fever. There had been a shoot-out between the two, but Harbin had walked away with the bounty of one Asa Mead. Mead had robbed and murdered a Texas banker, then fled to Arizona, where he'd done the same to a saloon-keeper. He'd managed to escape the law quite nicely, until the unlucky day when his wanted poster fell into the hands of Joe Harbin. The chase had taken months, but the reward was a decent one.

He rode until the sun was just an orange glow in the west, then made camp next to a mountain stream that ran cool, clear water. The gelding seemed grateful to stop for the night, although travel through Colorado was pleasant enough. Harbin caught a couple of trout for supper, and soon had a crackling fire going with the pleasant smell of fried fish filling the air. He ate contentedly and drank deeply from the stream, then opened his bedroll. It was best to get bedded down early, for after the sun had left to make its nighttime orbit, the mountain air could turn mighty cold.

Harbin fell asleep under his wool blankets, keeping close to the flickering flames that danced and cast shadows across his face. He would appear to be as content as a man could be, but then the nightmare would start again, contorting his features as he slept.

In his dreams, Harbin would find himself in the darkness of a nameless town, walking down a street that had no end. He would hear his name called out, and a faceless man would appear, gun drawn at his waist. Harbin would turn and meet fire with fire, only to have the faceless man walk slowly, closer and closer, flame bursting from his gun. As bullets ripped through his body, Harbin felt no pain, only frustration as he held out his gun and fired again and again, each bullet missing its target.

The faceless man would disappear as instantly as he'd come, and as Harbin lay dying in the street, he would call out to the curious faces that appeared to look down at him with their dark, twisted smiles. No one heeded his pleas. The nightmare would then break, jerking Harbin awake in a cold sweat with his heart slamming against his chest.

It had been a year since the dreams had started, only occasionally at first. Then they had occurred so often that Harbin had reached the point where he often fought off sleep. The life he had chosen was molded by guns, and there was no room for fear of any man. The nightmares, though, had done what no human could do. Harbin found himself waking up at three or four in the morning, trembling like a child. The fear would sometimes get so great, he'd spend the night cradling his Colt in his arms, his eyes wide open. Rocks and trees would suddenly turn into the figures of faceless foes.

He awoke just before four o'clock. The night was teeth-chattering cold, but Harbin was drenched in sweat. His breathing came in short, ragged gasps, and his chest ached. He thought he might be sick if the shivering didn't stop. That had happened too many times before. Close by, his horse must have sensed his restlessness. It nickered softly and stamped its feet.

He couldn't go back to sleep, so he lay there until the sun, though still hidden, had lit things up a little. The rocks and trees had become black silhouettes against the deep azure sky. He was wide awake, but he stayed in his bedroll, waiting for the ache in his chest and stomach to ease up, and pondered his life.

It seemed so long ago when he had first started hiring his gun during the big range wars. Bountying had come next, and it was a livelihood that he had settled into, almost too easily. Now it was something he would just as soon have shed years before. Sighing, he pulled a folded paper out of his pocket and opened it. In the semi-darkness, he could see the faint picture and the name underneath. He let his fingers rub across the worn page, then put it to his face and breathed against it while he thought about the words it bore. It was a wanted poster for Jesse James. He'd carried it with him for nearly two years now, keeping close to mind the fact that a bounty as high as James's would be a big payoff, indeed. Enough money to buy a nice little spread to settle down on, maybe someplace in the hill country around San Antonio. He seldom dared to dream about such a possibility, but he had to admit that it was sounding better and better.

Even when the sun had finally established itself over the east horizon, Harbin still lay there in his thinking. The big gelding was becoming nervous at the unusual delay. It snorted and pawed at the earth, wondering why they hadn't followed their usual routine and headed out at daybreak. This morning, though, Harbin just didn't feel like climbing out of his bedroll, or doing anything at all. He couldn't remember ever feeling this weak and tired.

The Jesse James poster was back in his pocket, but it kept burning its way into Harbin's thoughts. Why, he wondered, hadn't he just dropped everything and gone after James way back then? It was a puzzlement that worried him these days. Two years ago, when he'd first pulled the poster down off a jailhouse wall in Kansas City, he'd just figured on someday getting around to hunting the elusive James. Besides, he'd reasoned, it was most likely that every bounty man west of the Mississippi would be out looking for James. All this time had passed, and not one man had been lucky enough to catch the outlaw. If any man could get the job done, Harbin knew that he could. Now, though, as he lay in that bedroll and thought about it, retirement seemed to be the overwhelmingly pleasing thing to do.

He didn't emerge from his bedroll until nearly noon. When he dragged himself atop the big gelding, the horse instinctively turned south, but Harbin pulled on the reins to face east, toward Kansas.

The gelding protested a time or two by nudging its nose southward, reckoning its rider must have forgotten where they were supposed to be headed. Harbin didn't mind, for how was the horse to know about Jesse James, rewards, and retirement?

6

KATY WOKE UP SLOWLY, REALIZING FROM THE ACHE IN her head that she did, indeed, have a hangover. It wasn't only from the bottle of rye that she and Holt had nursed between them, but also from the fact that the two had stayed up most of the night talking.

Katy had been tending to a sore-legged mare that was heavy with colt when the trio had ridden up the night before. She had cursed herself for not being better dressed than she was, but it had been so late. Besides, Holt didn't seem to care one way or the other how she looked. Instead, he'd helped her with the mare and then escorted her inside for food, followed by a long discussion over the rye. It seemed like they could always pick right up on their conversations, as if not a day had passed since they'd left off.

Nikki had just put up their latest customer for the night in the stable. It was a cowboy who was headed to Texas for a job he'd heard about. The man was down to his last dime, and, as she had countless times, Nikki picked up his tab and stocked him with a healthy supply of food for the rest of his trip. At first, she had peered eagerly out the window, hoping that one of the trio riding in would be Walter. When she saw that he was absent, she hid her disappointment by busying herself with cleaning the bar. By now, she had gotten used to the fact that Walter was not going to come. She left Holt and Katy to their private conversation and wordlessly tended to Billy's and Charlie One Eye's drinks.

Through their efforts, the Trapp sisters had ended up with quite a nice establishment. Downstairs, a long bar ran down the left side of the building. There were several tables and chairs in the middle, with homemade tablecloths and chair covers. To the right was the mercantile store, and in back was the kitchen. The upstairs consisted of four bedrooms. Katy and Nikki lived in two of them and rented out the others. Those cowboys who didn't have the dollar rent were allowed to sleep out back in the stable for free. The stable and corral had been well-tended by the two women, and were stocked with several fine horses.

Katy pulled herself from bed and reached for her britches while trying to rub the soreness from her head. She was a seasoned drinker and a tomboy by nature, but she would be hard-pressed to admit it to anyone. She had half a leg inside the britches when she stopped and thought about Holt. Suddenly, she tossed the britches in a corner, found a blue cotton dress in her closet, and pulled it over her naked body. At five-four, Katy was small in stature, but her frame had become muscular from years of working like a man. She ran her fingers through her long brown hair. Her skin was naturally dark, but unlined by the hands of harsh sun and wind. Though her brown eyes were as wide as a fresh-born fawn's, they held a high sparkle when she talked. Katy Trapp was a woman who could keep a man captive and confused all at once. She was strikingly pretty, in an earthy way, no matter what she wore or how she fixed her hair.

Before she left the room, she took a quick look at herself in the mirror, a gesture rarely made for any man on any occasion. For Holt Flynn, though, the matter was different. Katy had known from their very first meeting that she was forevermore in love with the man. She ran her tongue over her teeth, smiling so that the slight overbite shined back at her. Satisfied, she ran happily downstairs to the smell of coffee and bacon and the sound of muffled voices.

When she reached the bottom of the stairs, she stopped. The four men sitting around the table—Holt, Billy, Charlie One Eye, and the moneyless cowboy—all turned to look. Their eyes fastened upon her. She ran her hand through her hair and blushed at their long stares. Nikki was at the stove, stirring a large skillet of gravy. When Katy left the bottom step to walk to the kitchen, the four men's eyes followed her. At first, she thought there must be something wrong, but from the pleased looks on their faces, she knew different. Except for Charlie One Eye. Katy couldn't really tell whether he was staring at her or at something on the other side of the room. From the looks of the others, she figured he must be pointing his good eye at her, too.

"What in the world's wrong with you varmints?" she said finally. "Ain't you ever seen a lady enter a room before?" She hurried over to stand next to Nikki and sniffed. "Ummm! Sure smells good, hon."

Nikki paid no mind to the remark. She blew at a strand of hair that had fallen across her forehead, then grabbed the handle of the skillet with the skirt of her apron.

"All right, boys. You can eat now," she announced.

The men pulled their eyes off Katy and turned toward their plates. Besides the gravy, there was a platter of fried ham, a dozen fried eggs, and a heaping pile of biscuits. Within seconds, the men had their plates filled to overflowing and were shoveling the food in like they hadn't eaten in days.

Nikki watched them for a moment with mild amusement on her face, then turned a stern face to Katy. "Out back," she said simply.

Katy waved her hand. "In a minute. I wanta watch this! It never ceases to amaze me how men remind me of a pen full of hogs when they eat!" She laughed.

Nikki frowned and pulled at Katy's sleeve. Nodding her head toward the door, she said in a low voice, "Now!"

Katy sighed and gave her sister a hard stare. It pained her that Nikki felt she could have the run of things. Even though Nikki was two years older and three inches taller, it still didn't mean she was always right. Nikki seemed to think she was, though. It had been that way since they were children. Nevertheless, Katy followed her older sister out the back door, where Nikki turned with a scolding on her tongue.

"Mercy sakes, anyway!" Katy broke in first. "What in the world do you want? I was just beginning to enjoy myself, watchin' that eatin' exhibition!"

Nikki threw her hands on her hips and glared. "The only exhibition around here is that blamed dress you have on! Now, get back upstairs and take it off!" she ordered.

"Are you crazy?" Katy exclaimed. "I guess I'll wear what I please! I don't tell you how to dress!" She looked down at her outfit, then back up at Nikki. "If I remember correctly, you made this dress," she added defensively.

Nikki groaned. "I declare, Katy Marie! What am I gonna do with you, child? I'm sure you must have noticed them men were all gawkin' at you. Didn't you wonder why? Land sakes, girl! The reason they were all starin' is 'cause you can see right through that dress, and you ain't got any underwear on!"

Katy's face went red. She grabbed up her skirt and peered down at it, then held her hand on the other side and looked hard. "I can't hardly make out my hand," she said. "You sure?"

Nikki shook her head. "When you got to that bottom step and the sun hit you, why I declare! You were next to naked! Now, get on upstairs and either put on a shirt and britches, or at least put on some underwear!"

"I ain't gonna put on no underwear! You know I hate underwear!" Katy said. She stood there and thought a moment. At first, the idea of all those men seeing through her clothes had embarrassed her, but now it seemed mildly amusing. She wondered what had gone through Holt's mind, and the thought excited her more.

Nikki was watching her sister suspiciously. "Well." She sighed. "I guess I can't make you change clothes, but I'm telling you, it ain't decent."

Katy smiled and gently pushed back the errant strand of hair on Nikki's forehead. "Why, sister, I reckon if they did get their eyes full, it wouldn't hurt 'em none! Why, I doubt if Billy and that Texas boy have ever seen a naked woman. I'd say it's right educational. And Charlie One Eye! Who knows what that good eye's even looking at, anyway!" She paused a moment. "And Holt—" She stopped without completing her thought, and took Nikki by the arm. "Come on. They're likely to be eatin' the silverware by now!"

Inside, the men were just wiping their plates clean. Katy had been right—the platters were empty except for one egg, a piece of ham, and a biscuit, all of which she quickly salvaged for her own breakfast. When they had finished eating, Nikki cleared the table, signaling for Katy to sit right where she was, and they all sat back with their coffee. Holt unbuttoned his britches and smoked, while Billy and the young cowboy swapped stories about some of the more rowdy places they'd come across. They were trying to one-up each other, and the stories got more and more adventuresome. Charlie One eye quietly nursed his cup of coffee and stared out the back window at the horses in the corral.

Katy and Holt hadn't spoken. She had seated herself next to him, and every so often they would smile at each other in a companionable way. There would be a lot more conversation later, when they both felt the need to talk.

Finally, the young cowboy stretched and said that it was time to leave. Nikki busied herself with seeing him off, clucking over him like a mother hen. When he had gone, she fetched the coffeepot and began filling the cups. That done, she set the pot down and pulled up a chair. Nonchalantly as you please, she announced, "We've talked it over, and Katy and I have decided to go along with you boys."

Holt, who had just leaned his chair back and taken a pull on his smoke, nearly choked, falling forward with a thud. He coughed. "What?" he managed to say before he coughed again. "Goin' where? With who?"

Nikki smiled. "Why, Holt Flynn! You heard me. We're goin' with you after that cave o' gold!"

Holt's eyes widened. He stared first at Charlie One Eye, then at Billy. "Why, hell, boys! Why didn't you two just put an advertisement in the Dodge City newspaper?" he said in a loud voice.

"Oh, it ain't like that, a-tall," Billy said. "We had to tell the sisters."

Holt slapped the table. "Like hell you did! Why, who else did you boys feel compelled to share your little secret with?"

"Nobody! I swear it," Billy held up his hand. "Ain't that right, Charlie?"

Charlie One Eye nodded, his good eye whirling nervously around. "He's right, Holt. We ain't told another soul, no siree!" he said.

Holt sat up straight in his chair. "Pardon me, ladies." He glanced their way, then leaned toward Billy. "But suppose these girls feel compelled to tell somebody else? Why, there'll be a run on that cave like you ain't never seen!"

Billy was shaking his head. "We had to tell 'em," he repeated. "Shoot, you and Walter ain't got horses enough. You said that yourself!" He smiled at Katy and Nikki. " 'Sides, they're gonna be our grubstake for an equal share."

Holt gave a harsh laugh. "Well, you can wipe that smile right off'n your face, Billy Boy. I can tell you right now that Walter ain't about to go nowhere with any females!" He stopped and thought about what he'd just said. He couldn't help but see the amusement in how violently Walter would react. He managed to cover up his smile as Billy spoke, almost pleadingly.

"I swear, Holt! It was the only way. And 'sides, it won't be so bad having the sisters ride along with us. Why, I 'spect they can ride dang near as well as some of the cowpokes that Charlie and I have rode with." He sat back, straightened his shoulders, and tried to gain back some of the cocksure attitude he usually carried.

Nikki moved closer to Holt and poured more coffee. "Surely you ain't afeared of having a couple of females along, are you?" she asked, challenging him with her smile.

Holt stopped her at a half cup. "Aw, shoot, Nikki. It ain't fear. Why, I 'spect Billy's right about you ladies' ridin' abilities. Speakin' for myself, I reckon I could get real used to ridin' with you 'n Katy. It's just that—well—Walter. He don't see things the way I do."

Katy broke in. "Dang Walter!" she exclaimed. "Look, we've gone and cut out our best horses. There's one," she added, "that we never gelded yet. He's a bit spirited, but I'd bet he's the best horseflesh in all of Kansas. You could ride him, Holt," she said with her eyes twinkling at him.

Holt sat there and gazed at her thoughtfully. A man could do a lot worse than riding along with such a handsome woman. It was during the times spent with Katy that he most longed for a different life than the one he and Walter had. She had a way of making him see another side to life. A softer one, respectable even. Unawares, his eyes fell shut and he could once again see that shining cave full of gold. He even thought he knew what that cave must smell like.

Katy knew that her words had hit their mark. She slipped her hand into Holt's, and was pleased when he accepted it. Katy didn't believe for one minute that there was a real cave with gold in it, undiscovered after all this time. When Billy and Charlie One Eye had first told her and Nikki about their plans to take Holt and Walter along to Georgia, Nikki's face had lit up like Katy had never seen. Whether it was gold fever or not, Nikki wanted to go, and Katy felt grateful for that. She wondered how far it was to Georgia. She wasn't sure, but it would most definitely be a good long spell to spend with Holt.

7

THE NEXT TWO DAYS BECAME BUSY ONES, WITH THE Trapp sisters closing and boarding up their establishment. Holt was amused at this sudden change of events. Walter hadn't even been talked into going yet, and here were the sisters getting packed up and ready. He'd casually asked them if they weren't somewhat worried about leaving all that merchandise behind in their store. After all, it would surely be raided sooner or later. Nikki tossed her head and said why worry about a few dollars' worth of cloth and nails, when they were going to be rich? Katy merely shrugged. In her estimation, it was a small price to pay to get to be with Holt.

They picked out the Trapps' seven best horses, which happened to be the finest stock within several days' ride in any direction, and turned the rest of the horses out to pasture. Holt watched them load up two horses with extra bedding, the sisters' clothing, cooking pots and skillets, coffeepot, forks, and plates. They packed flour, jerky, salt pork, coffee, a hundred pounds of potatoes, and numerous other items. By the time they were all packed up and ready to head south, Holt had his doubts whether the packhorses would make it to his and Walter's place, let alone all the way to Georgia. He'd never in his life seen two animals with so much attached to their backs. He figured half of the stuff would have to be dumped along the way, but he said nothing.

The morning sun was already getting nasty, even though it wasn't even nine o'clock yet when the group set out. Katy looked back and said she wished they had left a sign up that said "Gone South," or something like it, but Nikki laughed and called her foolish.

Billy, Charlie One Eye, and Nikki took the lead, while Katy and Holt dropped back. Holt wanted to keep up a slow pace for the two overloaded packhorses, which were tethered behind his mount, along with two other horses for Walter and the old Indian. He hoped the situation didn't get touchy with the big stallion under him. The horse was more frisky than Katy had let on, and Holt was already riding rigid in his saddle, ready for a sudden buck.

Up ahead, Nikki and Billy chattered about the cave of gold as if they'd already found it and laid claim. It was all speculation, of course, since neither of them had ever been east of the Mississippi. Billy had read stories about the big war, and he assured Nikki that he pretty much knew the layout of the land in north Georgia. "It's mostly hilly country, I s'pose," he said, to which Nikki nodded her approval. Beside them, Charlie One Eye rode along amiably enough, offering very little to the conversation but an occasional nod.

Katy pulled her horse close to Holt's. "What about it?" she asked with a smile in her voice. "Do you think they know what they're talking about?"

Holt said dryly, "To tell the truth, I doubt if Billy and ole Charlie One Eye could carry on much of a conversation with any substance about anything, less'n it's about some character out of one of Billy's books."

"Yes, I think you're right." Katy nodded. "But do you think there's any truth to this story about a cave full of gold?"

Holt pushed back his hat and looked at her slyly. "You

don't think I'd ride a thousand miles if I didn't, do you?"

"Well, I'm a-fixin' to, and I don't," Katy answered.

Holt was surprised. "You don't?" he asked. "But you and Nikki seem all worked up over it."

"Nope." Katy shook her head. "Least, I'm not. Shucks, that Nikki! She'll believe about anything, I reckon."

Holt started to say something back, but shut his mouth. It totally amazed him that Katy didn't believe there was gold to be found. Why, he wondered, would a woman want to leave behind a good home and a thriving business to set out on a long, dirty trail, after something she didn't even think existed? Women had a way of being confusing at times, but Holt was sure that they were supposed to prefer a soft, comfortable life with pretty clothes. They should want respectable company, instead of this raggedy bunch. He stole a glance at Katy. Whatever the reason, he couldn't help but feel glad that she was there. Besides, he thought, maybe to her thinking, her life was at a standstill.

But what about himself? He hadn't believed there was any cave of gold either, at first. The excitement of knowing there was the slightest chance, though, had caught him along with the others. Maybe, Holt reasoned, he was just hoping, instead of believing. Wanting something to be true could be just as convincing as knowing it. He let himself imagine they were already in Georgia, and soon he was back to daydreaming.

They rode all morning, stopped to eat at high noon, then hit the trail again until almost sundown. They were just talking about whether they should make camp or ride on after dark, when Holt saw the Indians.

It was a party of ten. He recognized them as Cheyenne. It was unusual to see them this far north, he thought, but then the Cheyenne had always been a defiant lot, and had often been seen far away from the land in Oklahoma Territory that had been assigned to them by the government.

Holt didn't say anything, hoping the Indians would ride off in another direction. The others quickly spotted them, however, and while it normally wouldn't have caused any concern, they all noticed that the Indians were up to something peculiar. For one thing, they had changed their westerly direction and were moving along at the same pace as Holt's party.

Nikki jerked on the reins of her horse and pulled back to ride next to Holt and Katy. Her eyes were dark with concern. "That's that blamed Spotted Pony!" she said in an angry tone. "His father, Tall Tree, killed our menfolk. He's as worthless as his father."

Holt had never met Spotted Pony, but he'd heard plenty about him. The army had never been able to prove it, but Spotted Pony was suspected to be the culprit who had stolen cows and murdered a family not far from Holt and Walter's place.

He said grimly, "Ladies, it's obvious these Injuns ain't switched direction for a change in scenery. I'd say it's the horses and supplies they're after." He motioned his head toward the horses tethered behind him.

Nikki's eyes flashed. "Just let him try it! I'd love to put a bullet in him," she said.

Holt looked past her and nodded. "Well, you just might git your wish,'cause he's ridin' this way." He unhooked the trailing horses and handed the string to Katy. "If anything starts, you let go of the horses and ride as fast as you can toward that creek bed over yonder."

Katy nodded solemnly. She and Nikki held their mounts close together, while Billy and Charlie One Eye joined Holt. They faced the Indians. Spotted Pony was riding in, along with two other braves. The rest had stopped about seventy-five yards back.

Holt turned to Charlie One Eye. "You stay with the sisters," he ordered. "Billy and I will see what they want."

Charlie One Eye left them, and Billy pulled out his Colt and whirled the chamber, clearly full of nervous excitement. Almost breathless, he said, "Why do you s'pose only three of 'em is ridin' in?"

Holt put his hand out to steady Billy down some. "Put that dern gun away," he said. "This ain't some dern scene out of one of your ten-cent books." He casually started rolling a smoke as he watched the approaching Indians.

Billy's hand rubbed his sidearm, which he'd reluctantly reholstered. His face was red from Holt's remark. With an impatient gesture, he said, "What in blazes you rollin' a quirly for at a time like this?"

Holt put the smoke to his lips and lit up. "Why, hell, Billy. It's times like this when a smoke feels dern near as good as a woman," he said.

Billy would have carried on the discussion further, except the three Indians had nearly reached them. They rode up so close that Spotted Pony's horse had stepped between Holt and Billy's mounts. The animals' heads were almost touching. Spotted Pony stared, first at Billy, then at Holt, saying nothing.

Holt let them sit there a moment, then blew out some smoke so that it swirled around Spotted Pony's face. He said, "Did you come to make peaceful medicine, or to git yourself shot?"

Billy nearly fell off his horse. He pulled his eyes away from the Indians for a second to stare anxiously at Holt. In all his life, he had never heard such bravado from a man. He licked his lips nervously.

Spotted Pony was smiling at Holt, but it wasn't a friendly gesture. His voice came, harsh and biting. "You speak foolish. You have not heard of Spotted Pony, or you would choke on your words," he said.

Holt took one final pull on his smoke, then squelched the fire with his fingertips, a gesture not lost on Billy or the Indian. He said, "I have heard your name. They say you steal cows while people sleep and that you murder women and children."

A funny groaning sound came from Billy, while Spotted Pony's eyes blazed with hatred. A vein popped out above his temple, and his jaw worked angrily. "You speak like one who wishes to die," he hissed, "but I will kill you later. Today, I will only take the four horses that you have no need of." He glared challengingly into Holt's eyes. "What do you think of that, man of big talk?"

Holt leaned back in his saddle and grinned. "Why, hell, Spotted Pony! I think we might be fixin' to have us a powder-burnin' contest, and you're gonna be the big prizewinner!"

The Indian's body trembled. He yanked his horse's reins and raised his rifle into the air.

By this time, Billy was so nervous, his bladder was about to explode. When the Indian acted, Billy reacted by pulling leather. Before anyone could bat an eye, he'd put a bullet into the middle of Spotted Pony's forehead. The Indian's head pitched backward, and he fell dead from his horse.

The sudden shot surprised everyone, especially the skittish stallion under Holt. It whinnied and reared high in the air, and only the fact that Holt had shifted his weight kept him from being flung to the ground. As it was, he hung on as the stallion lit out, bucking and running toward the other seven Indians. Holt had ridden halfway to them before he was able to right himself and turn the horse in another direction.

The two Indians with Billy came out of their confusion. One turned to follow Holt, while the other moved forward toward Billy. With a whoop and a holler, Billy fired off two more rounds that dropped the Indian from his horse.

Holt was racing back to Katy and the others when he saw a puff of smoke issue from the other Indian's rifle. The bullet missed, and Holt fired in return. Up ahead, Billy started emptying his Colt at the Indian who pursued Holt, but without taking the time to aim accurately.

Holt hollered as he neared, "Git your ass back with the others!" He raced past. Billy kept firing as he backed away and then followed.

Charlie One Eye and Nikki had just reached the dry creek bottom and were dismounting, but to Holt's dismay,

Katy was still lumbering along, pulling the string of horses. Behind him, the sounds of gunshots were getting louder as the Indians charged.

He yelled to Billy, "Git over there with Charlie One Eye and start sending some hot steel their way. I'm goin' for Katy."

Billy nodded and took off. His face was shiny red with excitement.

Holt studied the situation. Katy was a sitting duck, with all those animals in tow. He got up close to her and pulled the stallion to a position between her and the Indians, then dismounted with his Winchester. The Indians were fast approaching. Holt dropped to one knee and began rapid-firing. The lead horse fell, and the Indian leaped to his feet.

Behind him, Holt heard Billy, Charlie One Eye, and Nikki open fire. He was just about to empty the Winchester when the Indians abruptly pulled up. The Indian who was afoot quickly jumped up behind another Indian, and they all silently retreated to their original position.

Holt watched them a moment, then turned to look behind him. Katy and the horses, along with his own mount, were just entering the creek bed. He stood up and started toward them, just as Billy stood up and began firing his Colt at the distant Indians.

Holt broke into a run, hoping the outburst wouldn't bring the Indians right back before he could get to the others.

"Put that dern gun away!" he yelled breathlessly to Billy.

Billy did as he was told, but he was so worked up that Holt was afraid he might start shooting again at any minute.

He reloaded the Winchester and pulled Katy next to him against the creek bank, which wasn't much more than two feet high. The setting sun beat down on them, causing sweat to drip across his face. Katy wiped it off with her handkerchief and said, "That was a mighty gallant thing you did, putting yourself between me and those Indians."

Holt gave her a smile. "Didn't want to lose you, Katy. This whole dern trip would be a wash if that was to happen. But"—he frowned—"I thought I told you to leave them dern horses if shootin' broke out! That was kinda silly, you know."

"Why, I wasn't about to let them thievin' redskins get off with my clothes and everything," Katy said.

Holt grinned. "Why, I reckon a lady does need to keep up her appearance."

Nikki was still clutching her rifle in her hand. She pushed back her hair with a dusty palm and peered out. "Is that good-for-nothin' Spotted Pony dead?" she asked.

"Dead as a tree stump." Billy beamed.

"Well then, let me shake your hand." Nikki held out her hand to Billy.

Holt watched their carrying on and commented, "You'd better hold that dern handshakin' until you see if we're still alive come mornin'." He said to Billy, "That was a dern fool thing you did out there. Why in hell did you up and shoot 'im for?"

Billy's eyes blinked at the criticism. "I thought he was goin' for us. 'Sides, you said there was gonna be some powder burnin'," he said.

"Bluff, Billy Boy. Pure and simple. Why, I 'spect if Spotted Pony had a mind to kill us, he'da done it right away. Thanks to you and them dern ten-cent books, we'll never know," Holt said. He grimaced as Billy shook his head stubbornly. No use arguing with him, he thought. Being a gunhand carried too heavy a load in the young man's esteem.

Charlie One Eye said, "What you reckon those Indians are up to?" He peeked over the bank. The Indians were still sitting a ways off in the distance.

"They're makin' plans, Charlie. Makin' plans," Holt answered.

"You mean, you don't think it's over yet?" Nikki asked him in a worried voice.

Holt rubbed his neck. He was starting to feel a soreness from when the stallion had reared up on him. He shook his head. "Nope, I don't imagine any self-respectin' Injun is gonna watch us kill two of 'em and just let us ride away. No, we'll hear from 'em soon enough."

"Let 'em come on, then," Billy said.

"Now, there you go," Holt spoke up. "In case you ain't counted, there's eight of them and just three of us."

Nikki looked wounded. "Wait just a minute!" she said. "What about Katy and me? We can handle ourselves."

"All right then," Holt agreed. "But that still makes it eight to five."

Nikki pulled her rifle up close and said, "Well, if you're afraid to fight, I reckon the rest of us ain't."

Katy sprang to her feet and faced her sister. "You shut up, talkin' to Holt like that! If it wasn't for him, I'll bet some of us would already be dead!"

Holt grabbed Katy and pulled her back down, looking at her longingly. If the situation hadn't been so dangerous, he'd kiss her right then and there, he thought. "Let's quit fussin'," he said. "I'm sorry, Billy Boy. What's done is done. Now, we best try to keep alive."

They sat there and kept watch until just before dark, when a low rumbling sound started in the distance. The Indians were coming at them, crouched low over their horses' necks. When they were within fifty yards, both sides started firing.

"Their horses!" Holt shouted over the deafening noise. "Shoot their horses!" He and Charlie One Eye promptly dropped two. The Indians pulled up and dismounted into tall grass.

The gunshots were so heavy, the smell of gunpowder filled the air. It seemed to Holt like they'd been held in that dry creek bed forever, when something happened.

At first, Holt couldn't figure out what had drawn his attention away from the Indians, what with all the shooting and the cries of the braves. Suddenly, one Indian fell into the grass, face first, then another and another. One Indian turned around a full time in confusion, then fell dead.

Off a few yards, behind the Indians, Holt spotted a saddled horse standing sideways. A man with a Winchester was standing behind it, using the saddle to rest his gun. The man continued to fire until the remaining Indians had scattered in all directions.

All went silent. As Holt and the others slowly climbed out of the bottom to see who it was that had run the attackers off, the stranger climbed atop his horse and rode toward them.

Billy whistled. "Hot damn! What shootin'!" He slapped his leg with his hat. "That cowpoke is a lead-pushin' dandy!"

Holt studied the figure riding their way, his eyes vacant. His mind had gone back—back to a time when he and Walter had robbed banks and trains. He gently nodded his head. "That, Billy Boy, ain't no cowpoke," he said. "That's a gunny. The kind you find in one of your ten-cent books."

8

STONE-FACED, THE STRANGER RODE ON IN. HE SHOWED neither excitement nor curiosity. His eyes slid across the group and rested on Katy and Nikki. He tipped his hat to the women.

"Anybody hurt?" he asked simply.

Billy took off his hat and stepped up to meet the stranger. He tried to look as important as possible. "Not a soul," he said. "My name's Billy Cordell. I got two of 'em." He grinned.

The stranger seemed disinterested in what Billy had to say. He was staring, first at Nikki, then at Katy. "It'll be pitch dark before long," he said, seemingly to Katy. "Best move on down this bottom a few miles, then make camp."

Billy, still holding his hat, stepped closer to the stranger to try to get his attention. "Think they'll be coming back?" he asked.

"Most likely, but it'll be a spell."

Billy tried again to stir up a conversation. "Like I said, my name's Billy Cordell. What's yours?"

The stranger said, "It ain't important that you know my name."

Holt spoke up then from where he was still sitting. His voice was steady and deliberate. "Why, Billy Boy, you're talkin' to Joe Harbin."

"Joe Harbin!" Billy repeated loudly. "Did you hear that, Charlie? This here's Joe Harbin! Can you beat that?" Billy was so impressed, he forgot himself and stared at Harbin openmouthed.

Harbin at last pulled his eyes away from Katy and fixed them on Holt. A smile hit his face from the mouth down, but it didn't hide the hardness in his eyes. "Holt Flynn! Well, I'll be damned! You still thievin' your way through life?" he asked.

"Nope. That's behind me. What about you? Is your height of ambition still livin' off the blood of others?" Holt answered.

The two stared at each other without batting an eye. Harbin's smile was gone. He said, "I'll forget you said that"—he paused—"this time."

"That's right charitable of ya. I'll keep that in mind," Holt said. He turned to the others. "Let's git."

They moved a little over two miles farther down the dry, sandy bottom and made camp. With the possibility of another Indian attack, there was no campfire made. They all took their blankets next to the bank to bed down. Katy broke out some jerky, and the hungry men ate just like it was a fat, juicy beefsteak they were enjoying.

Holt was somewhat surprised when Joe Harbin joined their camp. He had said very little, but stared hard at Katy when she offered him some of the jerky. It clearly unnerved her, so much so that she hurried back to sit next to Holt.

Talking was done in whispers by everyone but Billy. If there'd been any Indians within a quarter mile, they could easily have heard his voice as he relentlessly plied Harbin with questions. Harbin wasn't saying much in the way of answers, but that fact didn't deter Billy one bit. Harbin put up with it for a spell, but when he saw that Billy wasn't going to tire out, he yawned several times and turned his back on him. Billy finally gave up, and the steady whispers died down.

From the creek bed, they could look out and see a good ways in every direction. Still, Holt stayed up to keep watch. All was quiet, except for the light breeze that rustled the leaves of the trees that lined the creek. Katy decided to stay up with him, and had cozied up against his shoulder. They sat together in silence, watching the stars and listening for any distant sounds.

All was peaceful, though. Holt doubted if there would be any problems with the Indians, at least until morning, and maybe not even then. For one thing, the biggest Cheyenne camp that he knew of was located a good day or day-and-a-half ride away. It was doubtful whether the Indians they'd run off would try anything without reinforcements. And even Indians, he supposed, slept. He relaxed, enjoying the feel of Katy sitting next to him, and let himself think about the gold in Georgia. He smiled to himself when Katy's breathing deepened, and he felt her head drop on his shoulder.

A good hour passed before Holt heard the moaning. It was coming from close by, a low, painful sound. He looked around at the camp. Charlie One Eye was off by himself, rolled up tight in his blanket. Billy had taken himself a respectful distance from Harbin's bedroll, and was sleeping soundly. Holt zoned in on Harbin, whose head was jerking backward as his hands clutched his chest. Suddenly, Harbin yelled something unintelligible, loud enough to wake Katy with a start.

"What's that?" she said.

"Nothin'," Holt whispered. "Go back to sleep."

She ignored him, sitting up and rubbing her eyes. She caught sight of Harbin and watched him awhile, then turned to Holt and commented, "My word! He must be having a terrible dream. Maybe we should wake him up."

Holt shook his head. "Better let 'im be," he said. He'd

seen other men like Harbin struggling in their sleep. It wasn't a pretty sight, but then again, the lives these men had chosen weren't pretty, either. Making a living by killing other men had to take its toll on even the most hardened of men, one way or the other. Holt watched Harbin as the night wore on. Katy eventually fell back asleep, and still Holt saw Harbin tossing in his bedroll. Though he'd seen other men in this condition, Holt didn't recall ever seeing one with such a bad case of nightmares. The way Harbin winced and moaned and clutched at his chest made Holt wonder if he was in some sort of physical pain, too.

It was close to three o'clock in the morning when Harbin suddenly shot up to a sitting position. The Colt in his hand shook as he pointed it at some imagined foe. Even in the faint campfire light, Holt could see Harbin's eyes. They were opened wide and full of fear. His breathing was short and gaspy. Holt kept his hat brim pulled low so that Harbin couldn't tell he was watching. Harbin didn't seem to notice, or care, though. He sat there, holding his chest and gasping for five, then ten minutes. He didn't even look Holt's way.

It surprised Holt, then, when he suddenly heard a hoarse, raspy voice.

"You got the watch, Holt?"

"I do."

"Go to sleep, then. I'll take it from here." Harbin stretched and rubbed at his neck, then sat back with his Colt rested on his knee.

Holt didn't answer, but laid his head on top of Katy's. He closed his eyes and tried to go to sleep, but Harbin and his nightmare kept coming back to him. His mind turned over the sight he'd just witnessed, wondering what might be haunting the man so bad. It was something he obviously kept well-hidden by day. Maybe he didn't know himself. Holt thought, and thought some more. It was close to five o'clock before he finally rested in sleep.

Morning came, and no sign of the Cheyenne. Nikki

surprised everyone by quickly unloading one of the packs. She gathered up the makings for a fire, and soon had bacon and coffee ready for breakfast.

Charlie One Eye was particularly apprehensive about Nikki's fire. He worriedly kept a close eye on the horizon, in case the smoke signaled in any Indians who might be bent on revenge. He would, no doubt, stand up and fight if there was no other alternative, but when it came to Indians, he held about as deep a fear as could be had. Indians made him all nervous inside. He couldn't get near one without worrying about losing his scalp. It made no difference that, up until now, he had never even seen an Indian fight. The fact was, he was just scared of them, plain and simple. He took his concerns to Holt.

"Don't you think we oughta move on before them Cheyennes come back?" he asked.

Nikki spoke up impatiently. "Charlie, you just sit down! I ain't goin' nowheres without my mornin' coffee."

Charlie One Eye turned to look at the others. They all ignored him, and Holt just smiled as he chewed his bacon. Sighing, Charlie One Eye sat down where he could still keep his eye over the creek bank. He was mumbling nervously to himself when Nikki handed him some bacon and coffee. She stood there and waited for him to take a drink.

"That's good coffee," he finally acknowledged. "Black as a panther and as strong to boot."

Nikki smiled. Charlie One Eye had been making that comment about her coffee ever since she had met him, six years before. She had never understood why the men liked their coffee as thick as molasses, but she'd grown accustomed to it. At least she'd taken his mind off the Indians for a short spell. Satisfied, she left him and went back to the fire to get breakfast for herself.

Joe Harbin had finished eating, and was drinking his coffee, staring off in deep thought. He was so intent in his thinking that even Billy had given up any hopes of conversation with him. Harbin had a deep burden on his mind, and everyone could see it. The only time he would pull his eyes away from their fixed spot in the distance, it was to stare intently at Katy, who was busying herself with helping Nikki get things repacked.

Meanwhile, as much as Harbin was keeping an eye on Katy, Holt was keeping a watch on Harbin. Holt had noticed Harbin's unusual interest the evening before, but he hadn't stopped to reason out the agitation that was stirring up inside him. Generally, it wasn't Holt's way to be jealous, especially since he'd just barely courted Katy. He'd seen her only every three to six months. Harbin's open stares, though, made him angry to no end. He knew better, but the emotion of the moment finally overcame him.

"I see you still can't seem to keep your eyes off of things that don't belong to you."

Holt's sharp remark brought the camp to a sudden stillness. Everyone stared at him, for his words seemed to come right out of the blue. Nikki and Katy turned and eyed Holt, then followed his gaze to Harbin. A knowing look passed between the two sisters as they went back to work and let the two men have at their argument. Women were scarce, especially unmarried ones, and Katy and Nikki were used to such goings-on at their establishment. The fights seldom came to anything more than a halfhearted fistfight, followed by a reunion at the bar. This time, though, Katy's face held a shine, to think that Holt might feel a spark of jealousy over her.

Harbin pushed his hat back and leaned against the bank. He kept his eyes deliberately focused on Katy for a while, before he slowly turned them to Holt. "She belong to you?" he asked.

The hair rose along Holt's neck. Harbin's question had caught him off guard, turning his irrational anger into frustration. He wasn't about to answer such a question in front of the likes of Billy and Charlie One Eye, but all ears in the camp were waiting. All other thoughts had died out, and the silence was filled with the dangling question. Holt glared at Harbin. The longer he sat there, the more he realized that he really didn't want to answer such a thing in front of Katy, either. Finally, he spoke, a bit of the sting missing from his voice. "She belongs to herself."

Harbin's eyes moved back to Katy. Solemnly, he said, "That's what I thought."

Up until that point, Katy had been enjoying the goings-on. She spun on her heel and shook off Nikki's warning hand from her arm, then blurted out, "Now wait just a doggone minute! I don't rightly take to someone assessing my life for me!"

Harbin pulled his hat back to its rightful position, tipping it to Katy in doing so. "If I've offended you, I apologize," he said gravely.

Holt stood up and brushed the sand from the seat of his britches. He knew everyone expected a fight. In fact, there was probable cause to have one. Holt felt too confused to know just what he really wanted to do. "We need to git movin'," he said to Billy and Charlie One Eye. Then he turned deliberately to Harbin and said, "I reckon we're obliged for what you did last night. 'Course, I guess that sort of thing is kinda routine to you. Now, if it's all the same with you, we'll say good-bye."

Harbin also stood up and took a drink of coffee, then threw the remainder in the cup at Holt's feet. "I'll be leavin'," he sneered, "because I want to, not because of anything you've got to say about it."

"Just so you're gone. I don't give a good dern why," Holt answered.

The two men glared at each other awhile, then Harbin slowly walked over to Katy and handed her the empty cup. He let his hand touch hers, a little longer than necessary, glancing once at Holt, then back at Katy. She couldn't stop the shudder that went through her, having those dark, mysterious eyes boring into her own—eyes that had long since lost any tenderness. Her voice trembled as she said softly, "Please go now."

Harbin's lips formed a smile. He started to turn, but paused first. "Holt has a fancy for you," he said. "I reckon a lady could do worse."

9

WILFORD JAKES SAT WITH HIS WHITTLIN' IN THE straight-backed chair, which he'd hauled outside for that purpose. He was working on the figure of a cowpoke. The head was already done, with a hat and a hard face staring out. He held it up and admired his work, all the while checking his piece of wood and calculating down to the nub if he'd have enough for the cowpoke's horse.

The hot Kansas sun felt good beating down on him. He contentedly let the shavings fly. The sun made him sweat, and any time he sweated, he felt like he was accomplishing something. A fly buzzed around his hands, and he batted it away. Except for the flies, this was a perfect day for whittlin'.

He held up the piece again and was making plans on how to start on the rest of the cowpoke's body, when he noticed the rider coming in on a big gelding. He slowly lowered the wood and squinted to see better. There was something about the man that made his breath catch. Then he recognized the face and manner of Joe Harbin.

As Harbin drew nearer, Wilford put away his whittlin' and stood up from his chair. An anxious feeling crept over him. As sheriff of Leland Flats, he feared no man the way he feared Joe Harbin. The man simply made him jumpy, even though he couldn't think of any good reason why. Harbin had never given Wilford any cause for worry, treating him cordially enough and never breaking the law any. Still, Wilford would get the willies whenever Harbin was around. Of course, Harbin did have a reputation that could be envied by most every other gunhand. There was a coldness in him during gunplay, the likes of which Wilford had never seen in any other human. Once, Wilford had seen him feed hot steel to a pair of murderers before Wilford could even find the handle to his own gun. That had occurred right after the war, back when Wilford himself had hired his own Colt out to collect a few bounties, and before he'd settled down as sheriff of a relatively peaceful Kansas town.

Another time, Wilford recalled, he and Harbin had caught up with each other in San Antonio, then ridden north together to Fort Worth. There, in a dusty saloon, three brothers had recognized Harbin as the man who had caught their cousin and seen him off to prison. In their drunken state, they waited for Harbin to leave, then spilled out of the saloon and called his hand. For their efforts, Wilford remembered, those three brothers had ended up six feet under.

He smiled, trying to act as natural as possible. "Howdy, Joe. It's sure been a spell," he said.

"You're right, Wilford. It has been a spell," Harbin answered. He pointed at the wood chips. "I see you're still a-whittlin'."

Wilford felt embarrassed that Harbin had caught him sitting there in broad daylight whittlin'. He didn't want him to think that was all he had to do. "Oh, just passin' time," he mumbled as he shook Harbin's hand. He gestured. "Come on inside. I got some good whiskey. Ole boy down toward Chelsey made it, more'n a week ago."

Harbin nodded agreeably and followed Wilford inside the little jail. It was tidied up, but a layer of dust seemed to cover everything, as if there hadn't been any need for incarceration in a long time. Only Wilford's desk showed any signs of activity. He reached inside a drawer and pulled out a bottle, pouring for himself and Harbin. He then reached for a stack of papers and rifled through them until he came up with two. He shook his head. "Poor pickin's, I'm afraid," he said as he laid them out for Harbin to see. One of the wanted posters offered one hundred fifty dollars for a Herbert Smiley, convicted of stealing cows. The other held a bounty of one hundred dollars for the capture of Simon Brune, who had embezzled at a bank up in Wichita.

Harbin barely glanced at the two posters. "Not this time, Wilford. I'm about to retire," he announced. He raised his glass and took a drink of the whiskey. Surprised, Wilford followed suit.

Suddenly, Harbin began to gasp for air. He held up the glass and stared at the whiskey. "You tryin' to poison me?" he managed to say.

Wilford's eyes widened. He took another sip. It tasted fine to him. "Tastes just like always," he said, deep concern on his face.

Harbin put down his glass and coughed. "Well, then, you've plumb lost the taste for good whiskey," he said. With a hint of amusement in his voice, he asked, "What about women, Wilford? They say both senses leave a man at the same time."

"Why, I never heard such a thing before," Wilford said seriously.

Harbin smiled, then did something totally unexpected by pulling out a chair and throwing his feet up. Wilford was so surprised that he forgot his manners for a moment and stared openmouthed.

Harbin commenced to talking, so Wilford shut his mouth and sat down to join him. They stayed there, drinking the whiskey and making small talk, until early evening. Wilford kept expecting Harbin to jump up and go at any minute. For all the years he had known him, Harbin had never been one for sitting around and exchanging pleasantries. It seemed like he had never cared what other folks had to say in life.

Drinking that much whiskey in the afternoon had given Wilford a sizable headache, and on top of that, he was getting hungry. He usually started thinking about supper around mid-afternoon, when his lunch had finally settled. By five-thirty sharp, he was always seated at his table at Slowpoke's, eating.

Wilford glanced at his pocket watch. Suppertime had come and gone forty minutes ago, but he and Harbin had gotten on the subject of San Antonio, and he didn't feel the urge to break in on Joe Harbin, hunger or not. His stomach, upset over this change in schedule, began to gurgle.

It was finally Harbin who, much later, patted his stomach and brought up the subject of eating. Wilford felt as grateful as he could ever remember being over such a simple suggestion. His headache had grown, and Wilford was sure it must be a message his brain was sending to him that he needed food. He felt even more relieved when Little Black Bob came knocking on the door. The eleven-year-old colored boy had been orphaned as a baby, and he would stop by most evenings to see if he could run any errands for a cent or two. Pressing some money in the boy's hand, Wilford sent him off to Slowpoke's to pick up some food.

Little Black Bob returned with two plates right away. Both held a strip of liver that resembled black shoe leather, and fried potatoes that had the looks of being a day or two old. There were patches of cooled white grease on top of them. Wilford stared at his plate as he bit into the liver and chewed. It seemed like he'd have to chew all day and still wonder if he'd get it down. He chewed awhile more, then swallowed hard, grimacing at the way the meat stuck there in his throat. The potatoes were no better. They had an odd taste Wilford couldn't identify. The grease hung in the top of his mouth. He looked over at Harbin, who was leaning over his plate. Suddenly, he felt put out at this intrusion in his life. Wilford hated to be late for his supper, because this was what always happened. Slowpoke's cook was a man by the name of Gentry, who had been pulled off a cattle drive that was passing through. The angry cowboys had dern near started a war over losing their cook, and only when Wilford had swayed a seventeen-year-old local boy to hire on with the outfit did things settle down. The boy had no cooking experience whatsoever, but Wilford was able to convince the men otherwise.

Nowadays, Wilford wondered if the boy might not have been the lesser of two evils. Gentry was definitely not his idea of a good culinary artist. Mostly, though, it was Gentry's attitude. Whenever a person was late for supper, he'd set the evening fare on the corner of the cookstove, where the meat would dry and the potatoes harden. Wilford had complained to Gentry about this, but Gentry didn't seem to care. Come to think of it, Gentry didn't seem to worry about much of anything, not even the ruckus he'd caused by ditching those cowboys and hiring on at Slowpoke's.

Wilford tossed Little Black Bob a one-cent piece and sent him on home. No need to pursue the issue, he thought. He attacked his plate again, cursing Gentry with each bite. On the other hand, he noticed that Harbin didn't seem to realize what a sorry meal this was. He was eating his vittles without comment. Wilford was wondering over the fact when Harbin looked up and spoke.

"Did you ever think about retiring to a little ranch, Wilford?"

Between chews, Wilford answered, "Who hasn't? But on twenty-eight dollars a month, a feller don't amass much in the way of a fortune."

"Well, that's what I'm a-fixin' to do. Gonna retire. Maybe on a piece o' land I seen once north of San Antone," Harbin said.

Wilford nodded. He knew without asking what land Harbin was talking about. They had discussed that land once before, after the war. He was surprised, though, to hear Harbin mention it in such a serious tone. "That would be nice. Real nice," he said as he took his last bite of hard liver.

Harbin was still watching him closely. Leaning in a bit, he said, "You doggone right it would. Come along with me, Wilford. We'll retire together."

Wilford was so stunned by Harbin's suggestion, it made him gasp. As he sucked in air, the meat went with it and hung in his throat. He coughed for nearly two minutes before he could regain himself. What a curious statement, he thought. Why, when a man retired, it was usually with a wife, and maybe a passel of children. In fact, he'd had such an offer from the Widow Klemme who lived up north of town. Her passel of younguns numbered ten, and Wilford had shuddered to think of all of them jabbering and screaming at once. He said, "Why, Joe, I don't guess a man can just up and do such a thing! Why, to be truthful, I ain't got a cent toward such a project, even if I wanted to."

Harbin had pushed back his plate, scraped clean, and was using his knife to pick his teeth. "Don't need no money," he said. "I've got enough to cover things. That is, I will, soon as I catch up with Jesse James."

The whiskey was having its effect on Wilford. He couldn't help the snicker that escaped over Harbin's words. He blinked when he saw Harbin's eyes harden. "No disrespect a-tall! But Joe, there's been a whole mess of fellers tryin' for years to catch up with Jesse James! You heard somethin' about his whereabouts that the others haven't?" he asked.

By now, Harbin had gotten used to the awful-tasting whiskey, having drunk nearly half of the bottle himself. He took a swallow and stared off. "No," he said, "I'll just catch 'im, is all." He turned his eyes back to Wilford. "And you can go to the bank on that."

Wilford grew serious. He had no doubts about Harbin's abilities to claim a bounty, to be sure. The man was like a hound dog his daddy had had, back on the farm in Tennessee. That dang dog had been able to stay with a varmint, come rain or sunshine, with nothing on God's earth to deter it. Every time he was around Harbin, Wilford would get to thinking about that hound.

"Doggone it! Jesse James! Well, I'll be! I'd see where a man could do right well on that kind of reward money," he commented.

Harbin nodded. "That's right, and I want you to come with me."

Wilford said, "Why shucks, Joe! You don't need me to help catch ole Jesse!"

Harbin looked irritated. "Hell, I know that! I'm talkin' about goin' with me to retire!"

Wilford was sorry he'd made such a hasty remark without thinking. If there was one thing for certain, it was that Harbin didn't need any help in catching an outlaw, once he found him. No matter how big a reputation Jesse James had for being elusive, Harbin had a reputation, too. Then Wilford thought of something else.

"Why, I can't just up and retire!" he said. "Who would they get there in Leland Flats for a sheriff?"

Harbin gave an unconcerned shrug. "The first feller they could talk into takin' the job. Hell, I don't know!" he said. "Besides, what are you gonna do when the day comes and they put you out to pasture? You think they'll give a damn about you then?"

Wilford started. He'd thought those same thoughts many times himself. Already he was at the point where a cattle drive coming through could make him near sick with worry that some of their drinking would turn into gunplay. Once, he'd even gone to Mr. Simpson, the bank president and the town's mayor, with the idea of declaring the town off limits to the free-drinking cowpokes. At first, Simpson had thought Wilford was trying to be funny, but then he'd given Wilford a tongue-lashing for having such a stupid thought. "Who do you think pays your salary?" he'd yelled. "Why, if it wasn't for the money spent by those cattle drives that pass through, Leland Flats would dry up in a heartbeat!"

Wilford momentarily closed his eyes, and his mind went longingly back to the cowpoke he'd been whittlin'. Such thoughts were easier for him to reckon with then, when real decisions had to be made. Wilford hated to think about things that made him worry, but the problem was, he was a natural worrier. Even if some stranger were to pass through town and idly remark that there had been a jailbreak some three or four hundred miles away, Wilford would set to worrying that the escapee would end up in Leland Flats. He could sit and fret over a problem for days at a time, whether it was justified or not. Such goings-on could ruin a man's effectiveness, Wilford realized, but it was something he had no control over. Right now, he just wanted to be back to his whittlin', with Joe Harbin never showing up to lay this heavy burden at his feet.

When he opened his eyes, they were met by Harbin's own, direct and waiting. Wilford poured the last of the whiskey and quickly drank it down. He took in a deep breath and said, "You and me, well, we're just different. I don't understand why you would ride up here and want to retire with me. It just don't make no sense."

Harbin thought a moment, rubbing a finger around the rim of his glass. He picked it up and stared into it, wide-eyed, like it was some crystal ball. He sat there so long that Wilford began to wonder if the conversation was over. Then such a look crept over Harbin's face, Wilford realized that Harbin had a burden on his mind, too.

Harbin looked up. "I need," he said slowly, then paused, seemed to choke on his own words. "I need someone to help take care of me."

Wilford nearly dropped the glass he'd been fidgeting with in his hands. He felt a mild shock at the statement, and couldn't hide the fact. He wondered at first if it wasn't the whiskey they'd been drinking, or maybe if he hadn't been daydreaming while Harbin was speaking. He had a habit of doing that. He could be watching a person speak with the most serious of expressions, all the while letting his mind drift off on its own. He had done it so long, he'd even learned to nod at the proper times so as not to give himself away.

He said, "Why, Joe, I just can't believe my ears! Not you! Why, I 'spect you're just funnin' me." He knew that Harbin had a different sense of humor than most men.

Harbin, however, was shaking his head. "I'm not funnin' you, Wilford. I can't sleep. I've been having sickness in my gut and I get dizzy," he said.

"Well, then," Wilford said thoughtfully, "you oughta see Doc Roth. He ain't much, but he's got a little know-how, I guess. You know, there was a man fell from his horse once. He hurt his back. Gets dizzy spells, too. You fall from your horse?"

"I ain't fell from my damn horse. Whatever it is, it's on the inside," Harbin answered.

Wilford thought Harbin looked healthy as an ox, and the two talked further on the matter. Harbin had little else to tell, however, and Wilford had no medical knowledge at all. He asked all the questions he could think of, while they drank more whiskey from a new bottle. Finally, Harbin went off to bed in one of the cells. Wilford decided to take the bunk in the other cell.

Long after Harbin's light snoring filled the room, Wilford lay awake, worrying about this new situation. He thought first about Harbin's sickness, then about the fact that another man needed him. Harbin had certainly brought him a headful of worrying.

By the time he finally fell asleep, Wilford still hadn't sorted out any more than when he'd first lay down, except for one thing. It wasn't easy to turn down someone in need, especially when that someone was Joe Harbin.

10

IN CLELL MILLER'S EYES, THE DAY WAS GETTING OFF TO a questionable start. As he rode along behind Jim Younger, he had a feeling of dread or anxiety. He wasn't sure which. There was one thing for certain. He didn't feel right, and this concerned him greatly. For one thing, his hands held a quiver to them. He was sweating, and it was still the cool part of the day. Embarrassed to think that he might be discovered, he quickly glanced up at the other men who rode before him. At the front of the group, almost blocked from Clell's view, rode Jesse James, with Cole Younger riding alongside. Behind them was Sam Wells and Bob Younger, followed by Bill Chadwell and Frank James, then Jim Younger, then himself. The group had ridden silently for some time, giving Clell plenty of time to think about his worrisome feelings.

Off in the distance, they could hear faint sounds, sounds that could only come from a town full of people. It was morning, but Northfield, Minnesota, was apparently wide awake and well into the day's dealings. The group rode quietly toward the town. They would split up at the outskirts. That way, Cole had said, they could keep suspicions down among the citizens. That, he added, should make their job of robbing the First National Bank of Northfield a lot easier.

They drew nearer, reaching the point where they could see the tops of the taller buildings. Cole began to go over the details of the bank job once again. The other men listened tolerantly; Cole had dern near driven them crazy with his details. It was obvious that Cole was anxious over the job himself, and that fact was clearly having an effect on the others.

What surprised Clell the most was the behavior of the group's leader. Jesse James, who usually liked to call the shots himself, was being deathly quiet. At first, Jesse had raised objections to robbing the bank. He didn't feel right about it, and he'd said so. Cole, however, would hear none of Jesse's oratory. Hadn't the Younger brothers always dropped everything whenever Jesse had a job to do? The guilt tactic had worked, but only in the sense that Jesse agreed to take part. He was still sulking over having to give in to Cole Younger.

Such disagreements were not uncommon, but this silent battle between Cole and Jesse had made the other men fidgety. Frank James, Bob Younger, and Sam Wells had bought up a supply of whiskey and, despite Cole's warning glances, had drunk during most of the trip. It was plain that none of them was holding his liquor very well, but at least, Clell thought, they weren't sitting there shaking and sweating like he was.

Whether he felt any apprehension or not, it didn't register with Cole Younger. Any dissension in the group was also lost on him. Cole had a score to settle, and he intended on seeing it through. One of the First National Bank's most prominent officers was a man by the name of J. T. Ames. Ames's father-in-law, General Butler, had been the only man in the war to use the Gatling gun with any real results at the Battle of Petersburg.

Now, if there was any passion to be found in Cole Younger, it was a deep hatred for any man who had worn the color blue during the war. He hated every last member of the Union cause, especially those who had done anything that made them stand out in any way. Butler's devastating use of the Gatling gun certainly qualified. Robbing the Northfield bank meant money for the other men, but to Cole Younger it meant something more. It was a chance to repay General Butler what was owed him and all the other men in blue.

At the edge of town, Cole sent his brother Bob on ahead, along with Frank James and Sam Wells, while the others stayed back. The three were to ride to the town square and look things over before they entered the bank. Cole and Clell would then join them inside, while Jesse, Jim Younger, and Bill Chadwell waited outside with the horses.

Clell watched the half-drunken trio ride off without a word toward the square. The uncertain feeling in his stomach caused it to revolt. He leaned over and lost his breakfast, retching loudly. A startled Cole Younger turned around.

"I'll be hanged, Clell! What's wrong with you, boy?" he said with a smile. Cole always smiled, especially during the most challenging of times.

Clell wiped his mouth, and his gaze froze on Jesse James's face. There was a hard look in Jesse's eyes. Clell had seen that look before, but never directed at himself. He almost felt like throwing up a second time over the fact. As Jesse's cold eyes stayed fixed on him, he swallowed and held his breath. It wasn't like Jesse to be this hard. Not that Jesse didn't have a mean streak in him, especially when it came to his practical jokes. But Jesse only got nasty to those outside of the gang. Except for Cole, Jesse kept a fairly civil relationship with all of them. He and Cole had very little like for each other. In fact, about the only thing that could be held in common between the two was that they were perhaps the two best inside bank robbers ever to be found. Which led to another of Clell's causes for concern. This was the first time in all of their days together that Jesse was going to stay with the horses instead of ramrodding things inside. Clell had robbed with others, but no one took control like Jesse James did.

Cole was smiling at him again. "You git your nerves settled some, Clell?" he asked.

Clell coughed and lied, "It was just somethin' I et. I'm fine."

"Well then, let's git to robbin' the Northfield bank," Cole said. He spurred his horse.

Clell moved forward to join Cole, riding past Bill Chadwell and Jim Younger. As he passed Jesse, he felt fear tearing at his insides. There was a sadness on Jesse's face that clutched at Clell's soul, so intense that Clell was unable to contain the feeling. He blurted out, "So long, Jess," as he pulled his eyes away and rode on. Jesse said nothing.

At Cole's urging, the two quickened their horses' gait. Ahead, they could see Frank James, Bob Younger, and Sam Wells just entering the bank. Clell felt the sickness in his stomach move up to a tightening in his chest. The three seemed to stand out too much in the long dusters they wore to hide their Colts. There were several men standing around, chatting with one another. In fact, the whole street seemed to be busy with citizens. Clell swore he could see several men look at the trio with interest as they entered the bank. He glanced at Cole to see if he had noticed, but Cole was, as always, wearing his smile as he tipped his hat to the ladies they were passing.

They made it to the bank, and Clell dismounted, hoping his rubbery legs wouldn't give him away. Cole remained on his horse, smiling at the men who were standing around, chatting. "Go on in," he said to Clell. "I'll be along."

Clell tried to hide his confusion as he obeyed. Jesse had never changed their plans in mid-stream. Cole was supposed to be going in with him, but he was sitting there smiling. Reluctantly, he started for the front steps. Just then, the door was flung open and a figure burst through. Without thinking, Clell ordered the man to "git," but the man waved his arms and shouted, "They're robbin' the bank!" before he took off at a run down the street.

Cole fired a shot into the air, and all hell broke loose. Bob Younger and Sam Wells came running from inside the bank, nearly knocking Clell off his feet. He started for his Colt, but he was shaking so badly, he thought he would wet himself. A heavy rain of gunshots came from all directions. He remembered the sad look that had been in Jesse James's eyes just moments before as he groped blindly for his horse.

Frank James ran out of the bank then, and stopped beside the blinking Clell. "You all right, pardner?" he asked.

Frank frowned when Clell blankly stared back at him.

A bank teller appeared at the door, and Frank dropped him dead with a bullet to the neck. He then grabbed Clell and flung him toward the street where Cole Younger was firing at anything that moved. Frank lifted Clell to his horse, then took off on his own mount, riding low and firing his pistol at running figures. Clell was barely in his saddle when he saw an old man running toward him. The man stopped and fired a blast from his shotgun. Stinging pellets ripped into Clell's face, neck, and shoulder. His horse bolted under him and took off at a run after Frank James. Behind him, Cole Younger followed, still shooting.

They were all mounted now, riding hard to escape the hostile townspeople. The shooting seemed to be coming from everywhere, as if the town had been lying in wait for them. Ahead, Frank James and Sam Wells were firing indiscriminately at the armed crowd. Sam Wells shouted as his horse was shot from under him. He quickly jumped up behind Frank James. Bill Chadwell was taking aim at a rifle barrel that was pointed directly at Frank and Charlie when an unseen shooter's bullet exploded into his own heart. He was dead instantly.

Within seconds, the gang had regrouped and were nearing the outskirts of Northfield, still riding hard. Behind them, a posse was quickly being formed.

Clell Miller wiped the blood from his face with the sleeve of his coat. His sense of something being wrong had been accurate, but now that feeling was replaced by desperation to escape the angry citizens.

It was at the end of town, and the last building to be seen, that he glanced up in time to see the barrel of a Winchester peering out of a second-story window. The word "mama" escaped silently from his lips, just before a puff of smoke issued from the pointing Winchester. The bullet ripped into Clell's shoulder, then into his heart. No one in the gang noticed him fall dead from his saddle. His foot hung momentarily in the stirrup, and he was dragged several feet by one leg, until finally his body bounced in the dust and lay still in the street for the curious to study.

11

THE GANG ESCAPED THE ANGRY TOWN AND RODE HARD for thier lives, aware of the posse that would be in hot pursuit. Jesse rode at the lead, while the others followed, and not a word was spoken. They were two miles out of Northfield when Cole Younger raised up from crouching over his horse's neck and noticed that his brother Jim was slumping in his saddle, weaving from side to side.

"Hold up a minute, boys!" Cole shouted. "Somethin's the matter with Jim."

Even though the threat of a posse was growing by the minute, the group came to a halt. Protests died from their lips when they saw Jim's limp form fall from his saddle. Cole leaped from his horse and was instantly at his fallen brother's side.

Jim was spitting up mouthfuls of bright red blood. A close examination showed that he'd been shot in the mouth. The slug had gone through one cheek and out the other, taking three teeth along with it. Cole poured some water on his brother's face from his canteen, but that was all he could do.

Bob Younger had taken a hit in his right elbow. He sat atop his horse, holding his arm while it bled through his fingers. He was in pain, but hadn't mentioned it to anyone.

Cole looked at his brothers and told them to hang on until they could find a doctor whose silence could be bought, or at least a farmhouse where they could get some treatment. He had just gotten Jim pushed back atop his horse when the pounding of horses' hooves could be heard. The gang took off at a run, with Cole and Bob Younger riding on either side of Jim to keep him in his saddle.

Only the fact that the gang had superior horseflesh helped them to escape. Once they lost the posse, however, other problems got the situation looking as black as any man could endure. Bob's elbow pained him so bad, he had to stop every little ways to rest from the bouncing gait of his horse. Jim Younger was fighting hard to keep conscious. His mouth wound was getting worse. After a while, the bleeding slowed some, but he was so weak, Cole had to tie him to his saddle and let him lean on his shoulder as they rode side by side. The gang wandered through that country with no townsites or homesteads coming into view.

After five days of riding, they finally realized that they were only fifty miles outside of Northfield. It was a wonder the posse hadn't caught up with them. Must have turned halfhearted and given up the chase early, Frank James suggested.

That evening, they camped amid some bushes. There was no fire for cooking. The food was getting sparse, and the men longed for some coffee, but they had to settle for the water from a small stream that wound past them. Jesse, who hadn't said more than a dozen words since the failed holdup, straightened his hat and cleared his throat.

"Cole," he said, "we're in a terrible fix, and there's only one way out." Jesse exchanged glances with Frank, then turned back to Cole. His stare was cold and bitter. "We're leavin' a trail of blood that a blind woman could follow. It'll soon be the rope for all of us if we don't do something."

Cole's eyes narrowed as Jesse sucked in his breath and went on. He said sharply, "Your brother Jim ain't gonna live. Not with all that blood pourin' from him. We can't keep goin', and we can't hide. I suggest we dispose of him here and now. He can't make it, anyway. Then we might have a chance to get back home."

There were a few seconds of shocked silence. Bob Younger, who was holding his stiff right arm and nursing Jim the best he could, glanced quickly at Cole to see what his reaction might be. Sam Wells, who was afraid of both Jesse and Cole, stared down at the ground as if he hadn't heard a thing. Frank James stood outside of the group, waiting silently. He liked the Youngers, especially Cole. Jesse was his brother. It was a ghastly situation to be in, and his face showed pity for the gang.

Cole's face, however, had flushed a deep red that ran all the way to his balding head. He was so enraged, he rose and spat at Jesse's feet.

"You're a coldhearted devil of a dog, Jesse James," he said loudly. "If that's the way you think, then git the hell away from me and my brothers. And if I never look at you again, it'll suit me fine." Cole stomped around in a circle, kicking at the rocks at his feet. "To kill my own flesh-and-blood brother! Just go, damn you! Go! I'll stay with 'im till my Maker comes!" He turned and stared at Jesse with eyes that burned with a wild anger.

Jesse was silent. He took Cole's raging with a cool stare.

There were no more words spoken, as the decision seemed to have been made. The next morning, there was no fanfare, except for Frank James offering his hand to Cole. Then he and Jesse mounted up and headed west, leaving Cole with his two wounded brothers and Sam Wells, who had opted to stay behind.

As he watched the two ride away, Cole spat again and muttered, "Good riddance," but his voice had lost the anger from it as he thought about their hopeless situation.

True to his word, Cole stayed by his brothers, nursing them as best he could. They rode at a laborious pace, managing to avoid crossing the path of any posses that might still be out. Then, after a week had passed, they neared the town of Madelia, where they were spotted by a farm boy who was out checking on his father's cattle. Luck ran out on the four, and within hours a posse was headed their way.

The gunfight that ensued could have rivaled any scenario from the war. When the posse reached them, the four had already holed themselves up the best they could. Still, they were no match. Sam Wells was killed almost instantly, but the Youngers kept fighting. Bob had to use his left hand to shoot, balancing his gun over his useless right arm. Jim Younger lay propped on his side, shooting with little accuracy. His mouth wounds had opened up again, and he was gasping through the blood.

Bob Younger took a bullet to the chest and collapsed, clutching himself. Jim, who was so weak he could barely move, suddenly gave an angry cry and, like a madman, began to raise himself up, shooting blindly at the posse. Five bullets pummeled his body at once.

Cole Younger remained fighting, keeping low and aiming accurately, but one man was no match for an entire posse. When the shooting at last stopped, the head of the clan lay with eleven bullets in his body.

When the posse members approached to claim the corpses, they were surprised to find that all three Youngers were still alive. It was a miracle, they mumbled to one another. One man pulled his mustache thoughtfully and said, "They weren't like any humans I ever saw." He nearly jumped out of his boots when Cole Younger opened his eyes.

"Mister," Cole replied, "it ain't how many bullets you stop, it's where you catch 'em that counts."

More than one posse member wondered out loud if the Youngers might not be something other than human, to live through such a savage shooting. The townspeople agreed that they had done something historical with the shooting of the three.

A legend was beginning to grow on that day, and Cole Younger made that legend even stronger when the posse took him and his brothers into the town. As the three Youngers rode in a wagon down the street of Madelia, people stared in amazement when Cole raised his shot-up body and stood, waving to the crowd and bowing to the ladies.

12

WHEN HOLT RETURNED HOME WITH THE TRAPP SISTERS, he'd expected Walter to take one look at the women and pitch a good-sized hizzy. Walter, however, watched the group ride in, and without saying a word to anybody, grabbed up his saddle and horse, mounted up, and rode away. He had stayed gone all day and through the night.

Holt wasn't surprised by Walter's leaving. The man could be as cantankerous as a Missouri mule, but still he was worried that Walter might have met up with some bad luck. For one thing, there wasn't another place anywhere close for him to go. Besides, his horse wasn't likely to hold up for much of a ride. Riding out alone wasn't of much risk, but staying out all night could get mighty nasty. Holt was led to worry that something had happened. Maybe the Cheyenne had picked up their trail home, followed and found Walter. Whatever, it just wasn't like Walter to do without the pleasantries of their home, such as it was.

Holt was tired from their ride and the struggle with the Indians, but he still kept to his practice of rising early. He got up before daylight and, after picking up his Winchester, went out to the corral.

He watched and waited for any thirsty deer to come wandering up to the pond. He really didn't know what he'd do with a deer. The Trapp sisters had brought along enough food to feed a small army, but old habits were hard to break. It was nice and quiet there, and Holt reckoned he had enough important things to think about so he didn't have to worry about shooting a deer.

He leaned back comfortably with one foot resting on the rail of the corral fence, laid the Winchester across a post, and pulled out his fixin's. He had just lit up, when he saw a lone figure riding in. From the wearisome gait of the horse, he knew it had to be Walter long before he was close enough to be recognized. Holt felt a sudden relief come over him, but he held back from saying anything.

Walter dismounted and unsaddled his horse in silence. Holt watched and waited for him to say something in the way of an explanation, but Walter was either unwilling or unable to say anything. Finally, Holt threw down his smoke and said, "Where in hell have you been off to?"

"Never mind that." Walter frowned. "I wanted a private word with you, and I reckoned you'd be the only one up at this hour."

Holt pretty much knew what Walter was about to say. He looked at the condition of Walter's clothes, and could put together a fair scenario of what he'd done. Walter had obviously ridden out with no supplies and slept on the hard ground. He looked tired, dirty, and hungry.

"Walter, them Trapp sisters is gonna be our grubstake to Georgia," Holt started to explain.

Walter's head started to nod as he said, "I shoulda known it was somethin' this crazy! Well, I'm tellin' you, them sisters ain't gonna stake me to nothin'!"

"What are you gonna do, then? Stay here by yourself? 'Cause I'm dern sure goin' to Georgia," Holt said.

Walter said matter-of-factly, "Go on, then. Go. Ain't nothin' stoppin' you. Make a fool outa yourself."

Holt bit his lip and turned to stare at the pond. Walter's statement irritated him. After fighting off the Indians, he was in no mood to put up with Walter's sour outlook on everything. Walter had grown bitter in prison, and when they'd gotten out, there wasn't hardly a day gone by that he didn't have something negative to say about something. On those rare days when he couldn't think of a thing or person to gripe about, he always managed to feel sick until a new subject would come up.

Holt said, "Hell, Walter! There ain't a dern thing to stay here for! We're a total wash as ranchers. Why, we don't do a thing but sit here and wait to grow old. Well, I'm not gonna let that happen to me! I'm gonna do it."

Walter reached out and took Holt's tobacco from his shirt pocket and rolled a fixin'. "You don't really think there's a dang cave full of gold, do you? Why, I've sat here and watched that old Indian. He ain't right in the head. That's for sure," he said.

Holt remembered that Katy didn't believe in the gold story, either, but somehow it didn't bother him. "Hell, Walter, supposin' there ain't no gold! Lookin' for it dern sure beats stayin' here and half starvin' to death," he said. He motioned toward the half-dried pond and the run-down house. It had needed a new roof when they settled there, and now it leaked like a sieve when it rained. Not only that, but the flies and mosquitoes could find their way in through the holes just like they'd been invited. Holt added, his voice softer, "Come on, Walter. Surely you don't want to die out here in the middle of nowheres! Let's put some excitement in our lives."

"Like I said. You can go by yourself, 'cause even if I had of decided to go, I ain' doin' no travelin' with the Trapps," Walter said stubbornly.

Holt smiled at Walter's comment. "Now there you go! Hell, ain't you looked at them sisters? Why, they're prettier than a Fort Worth whore!"

"I got eyes, but that dang Nikki wants to rope a man into marryin' her," Walter protested.

Holt had to laugh. "Why, hell, Walter! You're puttin' up a purty high opinion of yourself! Why, I reckon if Nikki wanted to find her a man to marry, there's plenty that comes and goes that has a lot more to offer than you do!"

Walter started to say something back, but he looked past Holt and stayed silent. His eyes glistened suspiciously as he watched Nikki coming their way from the house.

"Why, there you are," she said in a loud voice. "We thought you'd fallen in a hole or something." It was plain that Nikki was delighted to have Walter back. She walked right up to him and stood so close, Walter had to take a half step backward. He shrugged his shoulders and gave her a disgusted look.

Nikki didn't seem to notice his unfriendly attitude, or at least she didn't show it. "That sure is the snoringest bunch I've ever been around," she commented. "But I guess their snorin's about over for another night. I need me some wood to cook breakfast with."

Holt grinned and gave Walter a pleased look, but Walter was standing with his hands stuck in his back pocket, leaning backward a little to distance himself from Nikki's smiling face. He stared off at any object he could latch on to, hoping to avoid her eyes.

"Why," Holt said, "wood we have! Seems like I've been gatherin' up every scrap o' wood I could find for six years, and my labors are about to pay off! You gonna make biscuits?"

Nikki nodded. "Sure am. Bacon 'n coffee, and I got some good sorghum. Bought it off a peddler from Kansas City." She spoke to Holt, but was still eyeing Walter.

Holt said, "Did you hear that, Walter? Nikki here is gonna make us some biscuits. With good sorghum."

"I heard," Walter broke him off. He ducked his head and marched off toward the pond.

Three days passed, with everyone in the group trying to think of a way to convince Walter that he should go along to Georgia. Holt had met with no success at all. For every reason he could come up with why Walter should go, Walter could answer with an equal reason why he shouldn't.

Billy was clearly getting impatient with the whole issue, and his comments served to irritate Walter rather than encourage him. Even Charlie One Eye, who never had much cause to say anything directly to anyone, had prodded Walter a time or two.

Surprisingly, it was Nikki who brought about the first favorable reaction from Walter. Instead of appealing to his mental reasoning, she aimed in another direction. During those three days, meal after meal, she heaped the table with such feasts as the men had never seen. In fact, after a couple of trips to the table, Walter and Charlie One Eye had developed stomach problems, brought on by the sudden rich foods. Instead of complaining, though, both men were back at the table for more at the next mealtime.

It happened on their third night, when the men had finally pushed themselves away from the table and their empty plates. All were relaxing, except for Billy, who seemed unusually agitated. He was up and pacing when he broke into their small talk with the announcement that it was time to get on with the trip to Georgia, and that any person who wanted to go along had best be ready by morning, because, come hell or high water, he was going. That afternoon, Billy had watched the old Indian napping on the floor, and had noticed that his breathing pattern had changed. This alarmed him so much that he'd told Charlie One Eye about it. Charlie One Eye had watched the Indian sleep for about twenty minutes, and even though he couldn't be sure if the breathing was irregular or not, he nonetheless agreed with Billy's observation. When Billy made his announcement to the others, Charlie One Eye nodded his head in approval.

The conversation around the table had stopped as everyone looked at Billy in mild surprise. "Well?" Billy said.

Walter suddenly spoke up. "With all these supplies you brought, what we need is a wagon."

Everyone in the room froze and grew silent. They looked at each other expectantly. Walter had spoken in a purely conversational tone, but his words had hit the room like a small explosion to everyone but the old Indian, who had fallen asleep on the floor again.

They were all relieved when Holt broke the silence. "Well, hell's bells!" he said calmly. "Where do you think we're gonna come up with a wagon?"

Walter was picking his teeth with his pocketknife. "At Greasy Abe's," he answered.

Holt laughed. "Greasy Abe's? Why, that turd wants an arm and a leg for his wagons! We ain't found the cave yet!" he added, glancing at Katy.

Greasy Abe Penny had once been a trapper in the Rockies and beyond. He had moved to the plains, where he gained his reputation by killing more buffalo in the Territory than most white men could ever have thought of. He was a big man with wild, close-set eyes that would make one think he could be dangerous if talked to the wrong way. Greasy Abe always wore a long buffalo coat, except when it was hot. Then he'd put on a buffalo vest. He was never without one or the other, and they were both so full of grease and grime, they glistened under the sun. It was hard to get too close to Greasy Abe because of the smell. He'd established a trading post in Indian Territory, and along with his reputation for being filthy, he was also known for making a good dollar off of anything he traded.

Walter had propped his feet up on the table and was picking his teeth while everyone stared at him. He was making little sucking noises as he looked up at Nikki. "I thought this trip was going to be grubstaked," he said.

Nikki's eyes twinkled at him. "Why, Walter, if you think we need a wagon, then a wagon it will be! Greasy Abe owes me and Katy a hundred dollars, anyway. But why do you think we need us a wagon?"

Walter gestured toward the door. "Why, you're sure to kill those horses before you can make it out of the Territory! To look at all the stuff you got packed, a body'd think you was movin' the entire household on those dang two horses! Besides, where you gonna sleep if we get in some heavy rains? With a wagon, you women could sleep inside whilst the men sleep under it."

Nikki nodded solemnly in agreement, but Holt could detect the slight smile that played on her lips as she turned away to tend to the dishes.

That evening, Holt and Katy took a walk down by the pond. Katy felt glad to have a chance to talk alone with Holt, but he had further intentions that had been building inside him ever since they'd eaten breakfast together. Besides being one of the prettiest women he'd ever laid eyes on, she had a way of moving in her clothes. It was like they clung to her body in just the right places. He'd even had trouble concentrating on enjoying Nikki's cooking skills, what with watching Katy moving around the table.

Katy put her arm through Holt's and asked, "What do you s'pose changed Walter's mind?"

Holt smiled. "You ever hear that saying, 'The way to a man's heart is through his stomach'?"

Katy looked confused. "I don't understand."

"No, but Nikki sure does. Why, I 'spect Walter hasn't had a steady diet of good cookin' like this in twenty years. I imagine that got to workin' on his mind, thinkin' about being here all by himself and eatin' catfish and rattlesnakes. No, Nikki knew what she was doin', all right."

Katy frowned and started to say something, but Holt put a finger to her lips. "Hold it right there," he said softly. He took off his hat, bent over and kissed her, then pulled her down to the ground.

Overhead, the stars twinkled in the sky, and the still waters in the pond reflected their light. A catfish splashed, causing the gleam on the water to break into undulating waves. The flickering lamplights in the house could be seen in the distance, and the creatures' nightsongs had begun.

Holt Flynn, however, was aware of none of them. He and Katy were in San Francisco, in a big four-poster feather bed. He could feel the bay air drifting through an open window to refresh him as he was carried away.

13

ONCE THEY GOT TO GREASY ABE'S, NIKKI DECIDED THEY weren't as well-stocked as they should be. She not only purchased a wagon and team, but also added two Dutch ovens and more supplies, mainly in the way of potatoes, salt pork, flour, and eggs. None of the men said anything to her, though they did comment to one another that they'd never seen so much food at one place in their lives. (Charlie One Eye remembered seeing a considerable amount of food on the two cattle drives he'd joined up with, but that had been for feeding a dozen men or so.) The men were amazed at how much Nikki had been able to load up on those two packhorses in the first place, and now their supplies had grown even more.

They also remained silent when, after the supplies had been loaded and the deal struck with Greasy Abe, Nikki climbed atop the wagon and took the reins herself. She ordered a quick inspection to be sure everything was properly tied down.

At the door, Greasy Abe was leaning to the side, rubbing his chin with a curious look about him. There were three other scrubby-looking men sitting on the porch, silently watching the strange sight.

As Nikki gave rein to the team, Greasy Abe called out,

"Californee and Oregon be in the other direction."

Nikki paid him no mind. She was already irritated from having to do business with Greasy Abe in the first place. They had paid too much for everything. Besides the hundred dollars that he had owed her for two years, Nikki had traded him the two packhorses, and had still ended up paying him as much cash as she would have charged for all the supplies in her own store. It pained her to be taken in such a way, especially by the likes of Greasy Abe.

As they began to move out, the three scrubby men's tongues loosened, and they began to talk back and forth with Greasy Abe. They started to laugh.

Greasy Abe raised his voice and hollered, "You Trapp sisters be sure 'n protect those menfolk, now!" More laughter filled the air.

Charlie One Eye, riding next to Holt, let the last comment go by. He was still worrying over the first one.

"What did Greasy mean about Californee and Oregon?" he asked. "Where'd he get such an idee? Why, we'd be goin' way out of our way, goin' that way."

"Why, hell, Charlie!" Holt said. "Don't you ever read any books? Ain't you ever looked at a map?" He knew Charlie One Eye was about as dull-minded as a man could be and still manage to get around, but sometimes one of his remarks could still catch Holt off guard with its absurdity.

"Can't," Charlie One Eye said.

"Can't what?" Holt asked.

"Can't read." A sad expression crossed Charlie One Eye's face.

Holt said, "Well, you oughta get Billy to teach you. He's always readin' them there shoot-'em-up books."

Just then Billy rode up next to them. He was looking behind them, a scowl on his face. "I'd like to put a load of steel in that Greasy Abe! Where's he get off sayin' such a thing? Why, ain't no woman goin' to protect me!" he said.

"Wouldn't serve nary a purpose, Billy Boy," Holt said.

"Why, I guess some self-righteous bastard that never dealt with Greasy Abe would just hang you for it."

Billy shrugged and let the subject drop. He was too excited about finally being on the way to Georgia to let anyone as low as Greasy Abe dampen his spirits. Georgia was a long way off, he knew, and the faster they got there, the better. He looked worriedly at the Indian, who rode along by the wagon at the rear. He was keeping a close watch on the old man. It was going to be a close call whether he would make it all the way or not, and Billy had every intention of seeing that he did.

He rode up close to Nikki, and after considerable haggling, talked her into letting the Indian ride in the wagon. Nikki thought it was a ridiculous request, since the Indian was managing a horse well in spite of his age. She gave in, but it was more to silence Billy than in agreement with his arguments.

Billy took great pains in making the old Indian a comfortable pallet in the wagon. Of course, the supplies had to be reorganized in the process. While the others waited, Walter, who'd ridden along in silence during the whole trip, started complaining to no one in particular.

"We might make it to Arkansas by Christmas, at this pace," he said.

Nikki looked at Walter, then turned impatiently to Billy, who was still fussing over the Indian. "He's all right," she said. "Let that Indian be, and let's go."

Once they got started again, the group rode without stopping until the sun behind them was offering its last flash of light before slipping under the horizon.

They found a spot next to a little group of blackjack oaks. Nikki and Katy quickly broke out the Dutch ovens, and Walter built them a fire. The men took care of the animals, then sat down to wait for their supper.

Nikki brought out the makings for sourdough biscuits, potatoes, and some nice beefsteaks that she'd purchased from Greasy Abe. She gave the meat to Katy to flour.

Katy looked at all the food Nikki was getting ready to prepare. "We're making way too much food," she said.

Nikki paid her no mind. "Just hurry up with those beefsteaks," she said.

The talk of Georgia gold and the smells of the food cooking built up a hearty appetite in the men. When the meal was over, Nikki stood up and, with a knowing look at Katy, gathered up the empty plates. There wasn't a bite of food left. "Why, as lank and lean as these fellers are, you'd never guess they could eat this much," she remarked. "Why, I'll bet they could win an eatin' contest without even workin' at it!"

Katy shook her head at the men and got up to help Nikki. They scoured the plates clean with sand, then sat down around the fire with the men.

Most of the group were feeling too tired to offer much conversation. Billy, though, felt like talking. He put them all asleep, except for Holt and Katy, who had managed to take themselves off to a spot just outside of the glow of the campfire.

Billy had protested loudly when Nikki refused to let the old Indian sleep inside the wagon with the sisters. He had fussed over the Indian like a mother hen before he was satisfied that he had made things as comfortable as possible. Walter and Charlie One Eye threw their bedrolls down close by the Indian, hoping that might reassure Billy some.

When Nikki had finally climbed inside the wagon and pulled the flaps shut, Billy, who was still up and looking for more conversation, called out, "Holt! Yo, Holt! You awake?"

Holt held a finger to Katy's lips, and neither said a word. After a moment, Billy gave up and, with a heavy sigh, lay down close by the Indian. Soon, the camp was filled with heavy snores.

Off by themselves, Holt and Katy lay in their secluded spot until well past midnight. They counted the stars and talked, whispering and giggling like youngsters. Everything they said seemed funny. Holt couldn't remember ever feeling so good.

He was just snickering at something Katy had said when he noticed the shadow in the firelight. At first, he thought his eyes might be playing tricks on him, but then he saw it again. Katy was still whispering, but Holt had stopped listening. He put his finger to her lips and stared. The first shadow was joined by another. Holt tensed when he saw the first black silhouette cross in front of the fire, approach the wagon, and climb inside. A third shadow appeared then and stood waiting at the wagon's steps.

Holt motioned for Katy to lie still. He grabbed for his gun, but his hand clutched at an empty hip. He remembered that he'd taken the gun off after supper. His eyes slid to the wagon wheel he'd been propped up against. There it was, the Colt's pearl handle, shining out at him. He cursed to himself. Beside him, Katy's breathing was low. He felt her body tense as she realized what was happening.

One of the shadows was moving around to the other side of the wagon. Holt felt like rubbing his eyes. The dim firelight gave it a floating, disembodied appearance.

There was a sound of movement by the blackjack where the horses were tethered. Holt felt his stomach lurch. Something had to be done, and quick. He looked over at the snoring men on the ground, and felt a stab of anger. Groping around on the ground with his free hand, he found a big rock. He pulled himself from Katy and raised to one knee. Aiming at the shadow at the end of the wagon, he threw the rock with all his might and at the same time hollered out as loud as he could, "Now boys! We got 'em!"

Holt began to scream the Rebel yell. The rock bounced off the shadow's shoulder, and the shadow cried out in pain and confusion as Holt waved his arms and ran toward the fire, still screaming.

The third silhouette fired a quick shot at Holt before he took off at a run. Holt let him go and went instead for the man who had gone inside the wagon. He barely noticed the sleeping men come flying from their bedrolls.

Billy, who always slept with his Colt in hand, jumped up and promptly put two slugs into the body of a dead blackjack oak. The others were still turning in circles, trying to make some sense of what was going on and stay clear of Billy's gunfire.

Holt started up the steps to the wagon, when he felt a sharp blow to the side of his head, knocking him sideways. He grabbed at the wagon for support, then another blow to his eye knocked him cold.

The next thing Holt knew, he was lying with his head in Katy's lap. The camp was quiet except for the murmur of familiar voices. He opened his eyes and tried to focus on Katy's face above him. Other faces would appear next to hers, gazing down at him with concern in their eyes. It was so hard for him to see anything, it felt like he was partially blind. His head ached, and his left eye and the bone around it were throbbing like they had a little heart of their own.

It was Walter's remark that finally brought Holt back to his senses. He shot up to a sitting position when Walter commented, "The bastards got away with four horses. Don't see nothin' else missin'."

"And that's because of Holt here," Katy said. "You shoulda seen him." She tried to push Holt back to a prone position, but Holt brushed her hands away.

"Shoulda seen nothin'!" he exclaimed angrily. "If I hadn't been so stupid, takin' my dern gun off!" His speech was ended abruptly when the pain in his head took over. It was then that Holt noticed that he couldn't see a thing out of his left eye. He reached up to touch it and found that it had swollen shut. His shirt, he also found, was covered with blood. He lay back down on Katy's lap and took a deep breath.

Billy, who was pacing back and forth, rubbing the handle of his Colt, stopped long enough to ask, "Holt, was it Indians?"

"Nope." Holt shook his sore head. "It weren't Injuns. It was that dern good-for-nothin' Greasy Abe! That's who it was, and when I git my bearin's I'm goin' after the sorry turd!"

Walter frowned. "Greasy Abe? He's sorry enough, all right, but I doubt he'd be this low."

"Believe what you want," Holt said, "but it was him, all right."

Walter still wasn't convinced. "How can you be so sure? Did you see 'im?"

"Nope, but I smelled 'im just before the lights went out," Holt said, rubbing his head.

Billy paced up close to where Holt was sitting. "Well, if you're goin' after him, I'm goin' too," he said.

"Me too," Walter said.

Holt looked at them, then at Charlie One Eye, who was sitting on his bedroll with a solemn look. "What about you, Charlie? I guess you're gonna want to go, too."

"Yes." Charlie One Eye nodded. "I believe I will."

Holt shook his head at the group. "That's what I figured. Not a one of you is thinkin' of stayin' here to look after the wagon and the women. 'Course," he added, glancing slyly at the Indian, "I guess we could just leave Chief, here, propped up against a wagon wheel with a Winchester in his hands."

Walter was getting irritated at Holt's attitude. "Well, just what do you have in mind, then?"

"Well, I'll just tell ya, Walter," Holt said. "I'll take Billy Boy here. There are four of 'em. I suspect it's Greasy Abe and those three turds that was with him this mornin'. We oughta be able to handle 'em, easy enough."

Billy's chest pushed out. In all his adult life, which hadn't been too long, no one had ever put so much confidence in him and his gun. To keep from letting his excitement show, he hurried off to fetch two of the remaining horses. When he returned, he was leading Holt's stallion and Charlie One Eye's mount.

The gesture wasn't lost on Holt. He knew Billy's lust for adventure all too well. The fact was, he hated to take Billy along with him, but someone had to stay with the women, and Walter could handle things just fine with a little help from Charlie One Eye. It was safer to keep a watch on Billy. Besides, he might come in handy. If he hadn't proven anything else to Holt, he'd proven that he could handle his Colt, the way he'd dropped Spotted Pony. But, Holt realized, that fact was a double-edged sword. He sure didn't want Billy to start up another shooting match, like he had with Spotted Pony, right out of the blue. Such actions could get a man killed, and Holt knew it. Billy was a mite too young and too eager to be a long-lived gunhand, and Holt intended to exert his own caution.

Once their plans were laid, Holt was ready to get started. Billy was about to have an anxiety attack before they could get on Greasy Abe's trail, but Katy had her own announcement to make. She would hear none of their plan to leave in the night, she said, what with Holt's injuries still fresh. He needed a night's nursing to get his strength back before he could go.

Knowing that there was no use in arguing with a woman of Katy's nature, Holt saw no alternative but to wait. He calmed Billy's protest with a warning look and put his head willingly enough back onto Katy's lap. She sat up next to him as he slept, holding a wet cloth over his head.

It was almost four o'clock in the morning when Holt awoke from a fitful sleep. Katy had fallen asleep and was lying beside him. The camp was again filled with the sounds of men snoring. It almost amused Holt, to think that a group of grown men could sleep as peacefully as babies, when only hours before they'd been robbed, and could have been killed just as easily. He shook his head, and it occurred to him that he could include himself in his amusement.

The campfire was down to a few dying embers. Holt sat up slowly, but the pain shot through his head with such intensity that he had to fight the urge to lie back down. He couldn't give in to the pain. But let a man steal your horse, and the next thing you knew, he'd be after your woman, too. In this country where men were as hard as the times, a man rarely owned much more than a horse, and very few men could lay claim to a woman. Holt himself had never enjoyed the permanent company of a female, but the last few days with Katy had made him feel like a man who did. In any event, she had made him start thinking about such things, and a man's need to protect what was his.

Holt sat there a moment and rolled a fixin'. He felt like kicking Walter awake, but he knew he'd better not, unless he felt like killing the man. Walter was venting his disapproval of the trip by any little means he could devise to get Holt's goat. Right now, sleeping soundly under the risk of robbers and murderers was Walter's plan to get Holt's rile up, and it was working. Holt shook his head and let the matter be.

When he had satisfied himself with the smoke, he nudged Billy awake.

"Come on, Billy Boy. We best go if we're figurin' on gettin' our horses back," he whispered.

Billy sat up like a shot, his eyes wide, clutching his Colt. He stared blindly for a second, but when he realized it was Holt who had interrupted his dreams, he just nodded importantly.

Holt woke Charlie One Eye by nudging him with his boot.

"What's up?" Charlie One Eye said, trying to focus his good eye.

"Hell, Charlie!" Holt said in a loud whisper. "Some Injuns just carried off the women!"

The word "Injuns" brought Charlie One Eye flying from his bedroll. Still groggy, he said, "They did? When was that? I didn't hear a thing!"

"I don't imagine you did," Holt remarked. "The way this bunch sleeps, a herd of buffalo could wander into camp without disturbing a soul." He turned away with a half grin on his face, and was going to say something to Billy, when Charlie One Eye broke in. He was starting to wake up, and Holt's words were beginning to make some sense.

"Hold it!" he said. "What about the Trapp sisters? You goin' after them, or the horses?"

Holt rolled his eyes. "I was just foolin' you, Charlie. The Trapp sisters are just fine."

Charlie One Eye rubbed his hand across the top of his head, then put his palm to his nose. He said in a voice loud enough to wake the entire camp, "I know tell of a woman who got carried off by Comanches down in Texas. They never got her back, last I heard."

Holt shushed him quiet, then shook his head. "That's nice to know, Charlie." He bent over the campfire, and soon had a fresh fire going. "Now, you best keep that good eye open till mornin'."

Charlie One Eye nodded, his eye roaming over the sleeping forms in the firelight.

Holt climbed atop the big stallion, and soon he and Billy were riding off into the darkness. Overhead, the sky was alive with a million twinkling stars.

14

AS HE RODE EAST THROUGH THE DARKNESS WITH HOLT, Billy thought about his shoot-'em-up novels. He could remember every one he'd ever read, and could almost recite page by page each gun battle or fight. That was how he wanted life to be, and this was the moment he had lived for. It was, he thought, his moment of truth. To all outward appearances, he was as cool as morning dew. The real truth, though, was that inside, Billy felt as nervous as he could ever recall being. He couldn't stop the anxious feeling that gnawed at him.

To make matters worse, Charlie One Eye's mount had an uneven gait. The horse was bouncing his insides to the point where it felt like something must be shaking loose. That, along with his nervousness, was getting Billy worried that he might get sick. He tried to think about something pleasant to get his mind off being churned to death by the horse, but it was hard to do. He hoped Holt wouldn't glance over and notice what a hard time he was having. It was still dark enough that Billy couldn't see Holt's face, but he was sure that Holt could see his.

Daylight began to approach, and the two continued to ride. Holt was silent, keeping his own thoughts. Billy had shifted his mind to his childhood. It always brought on a feeling of inadequacy, followed by anger, when he remembered how much he'd hated his growing-up years. His father had been an Illinois dirt farmer who never seemed to care whether he had a son or not. Billy had been born to a sickly woman. He had never seen his mother get out of bed, even once. She had died when he was eight, and now his only remembrance of her was lying in that bed, reaching out to him and murmuring, "Come here, baby." Billy could sometimes wake up from a dream about his mother holding out her hand, and the image would remain with him, so strongly that he would lie there, tears filling his eyes, and cry in the safety of the dark night.

When Billy's mother died, his father found himself saddled with raising the boy by himself, a job that he couldn't have cared less about. Determined to make quick work of turning the mama's boy into a man, he had forced young Billy to do man's work, belittling him when he couldn't always perform as well as a man. Billy had retreated from the disappointment by burying his nose in books—any books he could get his hands on, from the old catalogues his mother had kept, to his novels. Other children made fun of his bookish ways. His father had never understood how a person who read books all the time could amount to anything, and told him so countless times.

It didn't take long before Billy decided to leave. At fourteen, he ran off to become a cowpoke out West. Above all else, he was determined to be a gunhand. Taking odd jobs here and there, Billy managed to use up nearly every cent he earned on his ten-cent novels and on the ammunition spent while practicing with his Colt.

Before the ordeal with Spotted Pony and the Cheyenne, Billy had thought life was surely going to pass him by. Now, to have a chance to hunt down four horse thieves was almost more excitement than he could control. In his mind, Greasy Abe and his three comrades were no less than the fanciest gunnies in the West.

They rode steadily through the rest of the night. Once

daylight was full, Billy looked down and found that they were right on Greasy Abe's trail. The fact surprised him. He believed Holt's theory that Greasy Abe was the culprit they were after. It just amazed him to think that they could ride at night in the dark, then end up smack dab in the middle of his tracks the next morning. He regarded Holt with new feelings of awe.

They had ridden no more than an hour into daylight when they spotted a thin rise of smoke in the distance. It was coming from behind a small hill that was barren except for some scattered sagebrush. They pushed toward it, and in moments their nostrils caught the alluring smell of coffee. Right away, Billy felt his stomach start to grumble. He could almost taste a good breakfast of coffee and bacon already.

"Whoever that is, I hope they ain't et yet. I'm starvin'," he said, and started to put spur to his horse.

Holt put a finger to his mouth and pulled rein on the stallion. Startled, Billy quickly followed suit, but he frowned just the same. He was almost too hungry to be careful about who they were riding up on. Just above a whisper, he asked, "What's the matter?"

Holt slowly pulled his tobacco pouch from his pocket and rolled a smoke. He licked it tight, then put the cigarette between Billy's lips and lit it. Billy, who wasn't a smoker, took in a short breath and had to suppress a cough. He held the cigarette gingerly between his fingers and squinted. The drifting smoke burned his eyes. Wondering why Holt would do such a strange thing, he sat silently and waited while Holt stared at the hill and rolled another fixin'. On his own, Billy would never have hesitated so long over seeing about having a free breakfast. What if the folks ate it all up before they finally rode in, or got everything all packed up before they'd made enough to go around? He sat there with his unwanted cigarette and wished Holt would resolve whatever it was he was pondering.

Finally, when he'd lit up and taken a few pulls of the

cigarette, Holt blew out a puff of smoke and said, "We best tie the horses and go by foot from here."

Billy's face grew serious as he pulled his glance from Holt's face and stared at the rising campfire smoke. Suddenly the smell of coffee had gone bad. "You don't reckon that's ole Greasy Abe, do ya?" he asked.

"I figure it is. Let's go take a peek."

Somehow, the idea that this could be Greasy Abe's camp hadn't entered Billy's mind, even if they were still following his tracks. He had assumed that Greasy Abe and his friends had ridden straight back to his trading post, and that the smoke was coming from the campfire of some friendly cowpoke.

Billy followed Holt up the small rise to a clump of sagebrush, where they knelt to peer down at the scene below.

Holt had been right as rain. There, crouched beside the fire, Greasy Abe had his big head bent over the flames. He was waving the smoke away from his face while he tended to the coffee and whatever else he was fixing.

Lying nearby to his left were the forms of two sleeping men, still in their bedrolls. Off by the horses, they spotted the fourth man, who was taking his daily constitutional. He squatted on the ground, smoking, with his pants down around his ankles.

Billy's heart raced as his sweaty palm rubbed the handle of his Colt. He tried hard to calm himself as he leaned next to Holt. He'd just as soon die as have Holt see any signs of nervousness. Bracing himself for a showdown, he turned to watch for Holt's signal to run for their horses and ride on in. To his surprise, though, Holt just seemed to relax even more.

Holt turned away from Greasy Abe's camp and rested back against the sparse prairie grass. "Bring up the horses," he ordered casually, "and try and keep 'em quiet."

Billy's wide eyes blinked. "What's your plan?" he whispered frantically.

Holt pulled out his tobacco and rolled another smoke. A small smile crossed his face as he shrugged lightly.

"Hell, Billy," he said. "We're gonna ride in, and I reckon we're gonna see about gettin' our horses back."

Billy's blinking stopped. He stared hard at Holt and shook his head. Even though he'd never been in very many situations that could be considered the least bit dangerous, Billy was quite sure of one thing. A body always needed a plan. Barely keeping his words to a whisper, he hissed, "What kind of plan is that?"

Holt was still wearing his amused smile. "Just git the horse, Billy Boy," he said.

Billy shook his head again and fetched the horses, pondering the possibility that Holt might be leading him into a no-return situation, not having a plan of attack and all. In the books he'd read, there had always been some way to surround the bad guys and take them, easy enough. But this was real life. Billy suddenly wished there was some book he could read to tell him how to handle the situation he and Holt were in right now, and without any plans to guide them.

They climbed atop their horses and, true to his word, Holt spurred the stallion over the top of the little hill. Together, he and Billy rode right into Greasy Abe's camp.

Greasy Abe was so busy with his breakfast he didn't see them right away. They were right on him when he looked up. With a grunt, he grabbed for his gunbelt and strapped it on. Besides his Colt, the belt held a big skinning knife. The knife was as much a part of Greasy Abe's appearance as the matted buffalo vest he wore. Greasy Abe wasn't wearing a shirt, and Billy stared at the bulging arms and barrel chest. They had nearly as much hair on them as the buffalo vest did. Billy was reminded of the big grizzly bear he'd seen once on a ranch in Kansas. A cowpoke had found a motherless cub up in Montana, and had taken it home to the ranch in Kansas to raise. The bear had grown to be so big and mean, the ranch owner had built a cage to keep it away from both man and livestock.

According to the outfit's cook, the bear had gotten loose once, and even after the cook had fired three bullets into the bear, it was still unfazed. Since hearing the story, Billy had kept a respectable distance away from the bear's cage, giving it a wide berth whenever he was forced to walk by. Even now, remembering sent a shudder through him as he stared at Greasy Abe.

Greasy Abe pushed some hot coals toward the center of the fire and waved the smoke from his face with his hat. "You fellers lost? Or did those Trapp sisters run you off?" he asked.

Billy rubbed his back, keeping his eye on the two men who were waking up in their bedrolls. They rubbed their eyes, then sat up abruptly when they saw the two visitors. Off by the horses, the man who had been squatting was struggling to pull up his britches.

Finally, Holt said, "Listen, fatso. I been ridin' dern near all night. Now, I'll make this simple enough for you to understand. We came for our horses." He stared calmly at Greasy Abe and waited for an answer.

Holt's statement surprised Billy nearly as much as had his brashness in dealing with Spotted Pony. His confident tone, though, did have a calming effect. Even though he didn't realize it, Billy was no longer quivering as he waited for whatever lead Holt threw his way.

Greasy Abe's eyes looked menacingly at Holt. He pulled out his big shiny knife and stuck it into a half-done piece of fatback, which was cooking over the fire in a rusty skillet. He pulled the meat from the knifepoint with his teeth. "You ain't takin' none of my horses, less'n you want to buy some. Seein' as I got four extras, I could cut you a deal on them," he offered slyly.

Billy's mouth fell open. He started to say something, but instead turned to Holt for his reaction.

Holt's expression had not changed. He said, "Maybe you

didn't hear me, fatso. Or would you rather have me and Billy Boy here do a little target practice on that big gut of yours?"

Greasy Abe shook with rage. He turned his attention to Billy. He growled menacingly, then a deep laugh rumbled out of his mouth. He pointed the skinning knife at Billy. "Why, this boy's still got baby shit behind his ears! I think I'll just skin 'im," he added, waving the shiny blade in the air.

Billy rose up and spat. "You try that and I'll plug you good."

Greasy Abe growled and showed his yellow teeth. "Why, you little scrawny sprout!" He stepped toward Billy, his arms outstretched, cursing his threats.

Billy didn't flinch, but pulled leather, putting a round into Greasy Abe. The big man charged, and Billy thought he must have missed. He fired again. The bullet struck Greasy Abe in the chest, but still he kept charging. His big hand grabbed Billy and pulled him from his horse with ease. With a grunt, Billy stuck the barrel of his Colt into Greasy Abe's stomach and fired twice more at the raging beast of a man. At the same time, a sharp pain ripped through his side. Greasy Abe's knife came away bloody. Billy knew he'd been cut deep, even though the pain wasn't as bad as he would have expected. He gave out a last effort and emptied his Colt, but still the big man held his death grip.

The two men who had just stepped from their bedrolls stood there, frozen spectators of the battle of death. They made no effort to help Greasy Abe or themselves. The fourth man, having done with refastening his britches, made a sudden move. He was tall and lanky and of middle age, and as he drew his Colt, he was awkward in his decision as to who his target should be. Holt shot him dead, then let his gaze slip over the two men who held up their hands in surrender, to the twisted forms of Billy and Greasy Abe.

Taking aim, Holt squeezed the trigger, and sent a shot that took a chunk off the top of Greasy Abe's massive head.

Greasy Abe's eyes glazed over as he looked his last into Billy's eyes. His grip still held, and Billy's shirt was torn away with the weight of his fall.

Billy blinked wildly as he stared down at the behemoth figure at his feet. His heart was pounding in his chest, but it wasn't from the joy and excitement he had always anticipated would be there. He had tangled with a bear of a man who could have sliced him in two. Somehow, living through such an experience had a sobering effect. He took a shaky breath and felt a streak of pain in his side.

Holt, who still held his Colt trained on the two remaining horse thieves, gave Billy a moment to come to his senses, then said, "Git two ropes."

Billy's head shot up, and he gave Holt a quizzical look. "What for?" he asked.

"We're gonna hang 'em, Billy Boy," Holt said.

"Hang 'em?" Billy could hardly believe his ears. He suddenly felt weak inside. In all his days of wanting to be one of the finest gunnies in the West, he'd never once thought of hanging a man. He and Charlie One Eye had seen a hanging down in Texas once, and the memory wasn't a pleasant one to his way of thinking. Hangings were for lawmen, and he couldn't fancy seeing himself ever getting involved in one. "What you wanta hang 'em for?" he asked, hoping to dissuade Holt from his intentions.

Holt eyed the two horse thieves for a moment, then said in a loud voice, "For stealin' our horses, for starters. And for dern near killin' me in the process."

Holt and Billy stared at the two men in silence. Up until then, the two thieves had stood there mute, with their hands waving in the air. At the seriousness in Holt's tone, and the somber way he and Billy were staring at them, they both began to gibber at once. Their words ran together, but Billy and Holt could understand enough to hear that both men were claiming that "it was Greasy Abe's idea."

Holt glared at the men for a long time, so long that they both started to shake where they were standing. Billy started to shake himself, waiting to find out just what he and Holt were going to do. Finally, Holt said in a cold voice, "You boys went along with it. Anyhow, I reckon you know that horse thievin's a hangin' offense." He turned to Billy, but kept his stern eyes on the two men. "Git those ropes, Billy," he said.

One of the men fell to his knees and sobbed like a child trying to escape a whipping. "Pl-pl-please, mister! Don't hang us! Don't you have no feelin's?" he cried.

Holt's face turned angry. "I got feelin's, all right, but not for some bastard that dern near kilt me." He glared at the sobbing man. The other thief kept his face lowered, but Holt could see the tears streaming down his face. With a grin, he turned to look at Billy, who still stood frozen in the same spot as if he were afraid to move, too. Suddenly, he let out a loud laugh. "Hell, boys! I weren't gonna hang you, but I'll dern sure make you wish I had, if'n I ever lay eyes on you again. Now, git on outa here while I'm feelin' charitable." With a wave of his gun, he watched with disgust as the two men tearfully thanked him for sparing their lives, then took off at a run. Holt shook his head at the fact that they had left behind all their belongings, commenting on their foolishness. Then he calmly bent over Greasy Abe's body to search through the dead man's clothing.

Billy watched openmouthed as Holt retrieved over a hundred dollars from Greasy Abe's pocket. Satisfied he'd done a thorough search, Holt rolled the body back over and stuffed the bills into his own boot. When he stood up straight, he saw that Billy hadn't moved an inch from the same spot, and that his side was oozing blood.

"Why didn't you speak up, Billy Boy?" Holt pulled up Billy's shirt to expose a deep cut about four inches long just above the belt line, and let out a low whistle. "Derned if that fat SOB didn't slice you, but good."

Billy smiled. Since Holt had let the two horse thieves go without hanging them, he had felt his bravado slowly coming back. "I'll be all right," he said, pulling his shirt away from Holt's grasp.

"Maybe so, but we better try and stop some of the bleedin'," Holt insisted. He took out his canteen and washed the wound, then mixed dirt and water and packed the mud mixture over the cut. Billy nearly called out in protest when Holt cut away the shirt of the dead man by the campfire. He held his breath in revulsion when Holt cut off a wide strip and tied it around Billy's waist. It did feel some better, but wearing the clothes of a dead man didn't seem too appealing.

Holt insisted on helping Billy back onto his horse, and, with the four stolen horses in tow, they rode back to their own camp. Billy pondered the events that had just taken place. The long ride gave him time to think. He began to feel better about the whole experience, realizing that he had taken his first step toward his life ambition, and lived through it. He wondered if the two horse thieves they'd set free knew what his name was. He wished somehow he could have given it to them. After all, Greasy Abe had carried a fair reputation as a man not to be crossed, and he and Holt had done just that.

Billy's spirits picked up considerably, and the pain in his side seemed to go away. When the mare under him gave a sudden jolt, the stab of pain it brought made him feel even better. He would forevermore carry a reminder of his first real gunplay. Not that killing Spotted Pony was a joking matter. Killing a white man in a fight, though, was something that could gain a man some real respect. Even if Holt had done the shooting that finished off Greasy Abe, Billy's own bullets would soon have done the job if Holt's hadn't, and that was what counted.

15

WILFORD JAKES AND HIS HORSE HAD BARELY SET FOOT out of Leland Flats when he started feeling his regrets. He was more mad than anything else, to think that he had let himself get talked into retiring with Joe Harbin so easily. Oh, the idea of settling down on a nice spread in Texas would be a pleasant enough experience, he knew. It was the getting there that pained him most. They'd been gone just four hours when his back started to ache, and the thought of something to eat was starting to gnaw at his fast-emptying stomach.

Wilford was still smarting over the ease in which the town had let him go. Leland Flats's leading citizen, the banker Simpson, had accepted his resignation without so much as a word to dissuade his leaving. Even if he wasn't the most ambitious lawman in the world, Wilford had expected his sheriffing would merit just a little recognition. It was a humiliating experience, and Wilford was glad Harbin hadn't gone with him to see it. He hated more than anything to admit it, but Harbin had been right about the town's complete lack of appreciation for all the years he'd given to them.

Disappointing as all that was, those thoughts were secondary in Wilford's mind as he rode with his protesting stomach. He thought about the man he had cursed every day of his recent life. The times he had complained about Slowpoke's cook, Gentry, and his lack of cooking imagination, now seemed distant and foreign. In fact, Wilford was thinking, he'd give a month's wages right now for one of Gentry's beefsteak and cornbread dinners, along with a big glass of buttermilk. His mouth watered at the thought, hard meat and cold grease aside. Sighing, he pulled a hard biscuit from his saddlebag and chewed on it sadly while they rode. The leftover biscuits were all he had managed to persuade Gentry to give him on such short notice. Gentry's biscuits held a bitter taste to them, and Wilford had pointed this out many times, commenting that he couldn't see how anybody could manage to make a biscuit that tasted bitter, even if he tried. Gentry, of course, didn't care, and the fact had nearly driven Wilford crazy. Today, though, as he rode along with his sore back and unhappy stomach, he bit into the biscuit, and paid no attention to its bitterness at all.

The first day went by, and the men rode steadily, without so much as a brief rest for the horses. This irritated Wilford, to the point where he mentioned to Harbin that a man ought not to push an animal that long without stopping. It wasn't something a man should do if he expected to make it all the way to Texas on one horse. Of course, if the truth were known, Wilford couldn't have cared less about his horse's welfare, but it made for a good excuse that suited and justified his irritation.

They rode, barely speaking a word between them. Wilford had a lot of questions about what their future plans might be, but he guessed that Harbin must have talked himself out on the subject for the time being. The silence was enough to make him want to complain, and with not so much as a piece of wood to whittle on as he rode. He hoped he wouldn't fall asleep from boredom, if he didn't die of hunger first.

When Harbin finally chose a spot to make camp, Wilford's aching back and tender rear were consuming his thoughts nearly as much as his hunger pangs were. He climbed down from his horse's back and dropped gratefully to the ground, lying flat on his back. Sharp rocks and hard clumps of prairie grass cut into his back and legs, but he didn't care. To him, that ground felt as good as a feather bed in the finest hotel in Kansas City.

Joe Harbin fried up some fatback, and when he offered the skillet to Wilford, Wilford took a handful of the greasy meat, mindless of the fact that it was nearly burnt. Normally, after he'd been riding all day, a bill of fare like this would have put him in an uproar, but not this evening. Wilford wolfed down the meat like a hungry dog.

He lay back and fell into a deep sleep, unaware when Harbin threw a blanket over him. Even in the night, when Harbin began to twist and holler, and came awake in a sweat, Wilford slept peacefully.

The next morning, a wordless breakfast of coffee and more fatback was waiting for him when he awoke. Wilford stood up slowly and stretched, realizing that the hard ground hadn't helped his soreness any. The thought of riding all over the country, chewing on burnt fatback, sent him into despair. Absently, he looked off to the west, in the direction of Leland Flats, as if doing so would somehow transport him back there and away from this nightmare.

The next two days turned out to be exact replicas of the first. It was on the fourth day and late afternoon when they came upon the woman. Wilford was getting more tired of the relentless pace by the minute. Fearful as he was of Joe Harbin, he was seriously considering what he thought would be taking his life into his own hands by challenging Harbin to slow to a more comfortable pace, when they came upon a wagon. A weeping woman was nearby, kneeling over a pile of rocks that had been heaped and stacked in the shape of a grave.

Both men studied the unusual scene as they rode closer. The woman looked to be approaching the latter stages of middle age. Her long black hair held slivers of gray, and her bronze skin gave her the appearance of being a squaw.

There was something about her, though, that made Wilford know better. Most remarkable about the woman was the fact that she was naked as a jaybird, and her body was so filthy it was plain that she had been without clothes for a long time.

The sight was so overwhelming, Wilford rode his horse to within a few feet of the woman and stopped, staring with disbelief. Harbin rode on past her and around the wagon. He peered carefully inside, then surveyed the surroundings with a frown.

The woman seemed to be oblivious of the two men. She continued to kneel over the pile of rocks, while Wilford continued to sit on his horse, his eyes still fixed on her.

Harbin rode back to the two and climbed off the big gelding. He looked down at the woman. "Your man?" he asked.

There was no response, so Harbin said to Wilford, "Climb on down and see if you can find some clothes in that wagon."

Wilford did as he was told, forgetting all about his angry stomach and aching body for the first time since he'd left Leland Flats. He held his eyes glued on the strange woman, and nearly tripped over the wagon's tongue as he backed away from her. This brought a hard stare from Harbin.

Wilford fetched a worn dress from the wagon and handed it to the woman, but she wouldn't take it, so he just tossed it on the ground beside her. He didn't know what else to do, so he stood back and stared. There was no need to feel like he was being rude, since she wasn't paying attention to them anyway. Still, he was glad when Harbin spoke up.

"Here, ma'am. Put some clothes on."

Still, the woman ignored them, so Harbin reached down and pulled the woman to her feet and nodded for Wilford to retrieve the dress. Wilford held the dress out at arm's length toward the woman, who stood there with her head lowered, her face hidden from them.

It was then that Wilford noticed her hands. They hung at her sides, torn and bloody, raw to the bone. Frowning, he diverted his eyes to the pile of stones. There were smudges of blood smeared on several. Wilford searched for some kind of digging tool, but could find none. Then it dawned on him that the woman had buried whatever it was with her hands and hauled up enough rocks to cover the grave. Some of the rocks were mighty big ones, too. Wilford felt a sudden envy. This was no more than a slip of a woman, and she certainly didn't look hearty enough to be toting such a sizable pile of rocks.

The woman's feet were black and bloody as well. More envy ran through Wilford, to think that she had managed such a job by herself. Such feelings of jealousy over a hard day's work came over him often. It seemed that a lot of the folks in Leland Flats considered him to be lazy, and few kept that opinion to themselves. Wilford, of course, thought it was totally absurd on the citizens' part. After all, he was a lawman, not some common laborer. Still, it bothered him to be so misunderstood, and he would often daydream about some outlaw coming to town, tearing down the street, and shooting up everything in sight. In the scenario, he would visualize himself arresting the outlaw in some heroic fashion. Then the fickle townspeople would come to understand just what a lawman's job was all about. They would stop making jokes about his laziness. He would be treated with new respect.

Wilford was reliving that scene as he stared at the woman's tattered feet. Now, he thought, there was no sheriff left in Leland Flats to handle any destructive outlaw that might wander through. He almost wished such a thing would happen to the town. Then, maybe the banker Simpson and his friends would reconsider their position. They could come and rescue him from this situation, and beg him to be the sheriff once again. Of course, Wilford didn't want the outlaw to be of the dangerous variety, but the townspeople didn't have to know that. After he had dealt with the outlaw and put him away, Wilford could once again sit in his chair and whittle, and eat three squares a day.

But those were only the hopeless wishes of a man who had given up the right to them. Wilford sighed, and impatiently shook the dress for the unresponsive woman to take it.

She was still being supported by Harbin, but when Wilford shook the dress at her, she seemed to jump back to life. Suddenly, her head shot up, and she stared at Wilford. He gave an involuntary gasp as his heart jumped in his chest.

The woman's face was streaked with dirt. Tears had left white circles around her eyes, and there were dirty tracks down her cheeks. The long hair was tangled with dark rats' nests, hanging against her cheeks like spiderwebs. Wilford thought of the drawings of witches he had seen as a boy. This woman looked just as spooky, and crazy on top of that. He had pretended not to believe in such things, but deep inside he had always nursed a fear that there were, indeed, such evil beings on the lurk.

Wilford had to keep himself from crying out when the woman pulled herself away from Harbin's grasp and jumped toward Wilford. She stared hard at him, then at Harbin, her eyes so wide you could see the whites all around. In a high-pitched tone that should have come from a little girl, she said, "You didn't kill Papa. Who killed Papa? You tell me that."

Wilford felt chills running down his back. The little-girl voice gave him the creeps like he couldn't remember since he was a scared child. What's more, the filthy, tearstained face wasn't one of sorrow or fear. It was the face of one who has gone mad.

In a trembly voice, he said, "Someone kill your pa?"

The woman's eyes widened even more at Wilford's question. Her lips worked silently. She stepped up close to him, so close that he could smell her odorous breath. She said in a scolding voice, "You don't know who killed Papa! But you do hunt other men! You do not like this hunt," she added, nodding to herself.

"What's that you're sayin'?" Wilford said. But before the words had left his lips, she had turned away from him and taken a step toward Harbin.

The woman looked Harbin up and down. She started to move closer to him, but stopped. Her mouth curved into a sneer.

"But you—you enjoy the hunt," she said, and gave a guttural laugh. "You have the blood of many on your soul."

Wilford's mouth dropped at her strange statement. It was enough to raise the hair on the back of his neck. What made him downright scared, though, was the look that had crossed Harbin's face.

Joe Harbin, who was usually as emotionless as a horned toad, was blinking in total bewilderment. That got to Wilford just about as bad as the crazy woman did.

"You stop that kind of talk, you hear?" he said in an uncertain voice. The belief that she was some kind of witch was becoming more of a reality, from the effect she was having on both of the men. The way she stood there, staring at them with those wild eyes, and the things she was saying, certainly hit the mark, as far as he was concerned. The thought suddenly entered Wilford's mind that whoever was buried under those rocks might have been killed by the woman herself. Maybe she had given the sting of death to the unfortunate soul, or worked some kind of evil magic on him.

The woman turned from Harbin and waved a hand at Wilford, like she was shooing away a fly. "You think I'm crazy," she said. Then, widening her eyes and twisting her mouth into a snarl, she leaned forward and, with a jerk, cried, "Boo!"

The move unnerved Wilford so much, he took a big step backward and let his hand go to his holster. "You stop that!" he said, irritated that he had let Harbin see him lose his composure.

The woman began to laugh in that high-pitched little-girl voice.

Wilford couldn't stop the hair from standing out on his neck again. He was at a total loss as to what to do with this woman. He looked to Harbin for some kind of response or decision—he wasn't sure what he expected to see. But Harbin was still standing there as before, with no responses to give. Frowning, Wilford again held out the dress. "Here," he said in a voice that was far from strong, "put on this dress. It ain't decent, standin' out here buck naked." He avoided the gaze of the woman who might be a witch. Instead, his eyes involuntarily slid down her naked front. He realized with dismay that he really didn't care if she covered herself or not.

The woman began to laugh. Wilford lifted his head and saw that her eyes were burning deep into his own, reading his mind, ripping deep inside him. When she pulled herself erect and threw back her head to laugh even harder, he wanted to turn and run. He might have done just that, if Harbin hadn't acted.

Like a snake snatching a mouse, Harbin reached out and grabbed the woman by the hair at the back of her head. He yanked so violently, Wilford flinched. Holding her head back, Harbin lowered his face until it almost touched her own. His eyes had gone cold, his face was granite. In words that were measured and full of bitterness, he said, "Shut your mouth and git your clothes on."

The two stared at each other a moment, her eyes blazing with surprise and contempt, his eyes allowing nothing. Then, as deftly as he had grabbed her by the hair, Harbin flung the woman at Wilford's feet.

She lay there a moment, breathing deeply, her dirty hair spilling loosely into the dirt. Wilford thought she must have started crying again, but when she looked up at the men through her hair, he was amazed to see that there was not an ounce of fear to be found on her face. Slowly, she sat up and reached out to clutch the dress to her body.

"We will leave Papa now and go kill the ones who killed Papa," she said, as if the decision was hers to make.

Harbin's sharp voice cut into the woman's words. "We'll see that you git to the next town. Now git your clothes on," he said.

The dirty witch woman stood up and smiled. She was still clutching the dress, but it was so wadded up that it did little to cover her. She glanced slyly at Wilford, then held the dress away from her body. She shook it at him and laughed.

Most of the fear had left Wilford by now, but the fact that he couldn't pull his eyes away from her naked front disturbed him just as much. In truth, underneath all that dirt there was a fair-looking female, formed in a way that was more than pleasing to him. She seemed to be enjoying the effect she was having on him, too. Wilford glanced at Harbin, who was paying no mind whatsoever to her condition. Surely, he thought, this naked woman was just as curious a sight to Harbin as she was to him. In fact, Wilford could recall that Harbin had always had a healthy appetite toward females. But, instead, Harbin seemed to be impatient with the whole situation, or disgusted, or both. Wilford wiped his sweaty forehead with his sleeve. It was all too confusing for a simple sheriff from Leland Flats, he thought.

When the woman's fun with Wilford had played out, she stopped laughing and turned to walk to the wagon. She was toying with the dress in her hand, letting it drag on the ground, and talking softly to herself in a sing-song voice.

Wilford watched her, his eyes fixed on her buttocks as they moved up and down with each step. Except for a few of the better whores he could remember, this woman was made as fine as he'd ever seen. Of course, he'd never had a chance to look at a woman this long before, except for the time when he and his cousin had swum naked in the pond behind her house. They were both eleven at the time, and even though she hadn't started sprouting yet, Wilford had still been instantly aware of what parts of her anatomy would draw the most attention. Now, he couldn't help feeling the pleasure, getting to look at a full-blown woman, even if she was crazy.

He watched her backside until she had climbed all the way inside the wagon, then turned guiltily away. Harbin was staring at him with a dark expression Wilford couldn't read.

"You best tie your horse to the wagon and ride with the woman," Harbin said. He swung atop his horse and looked down at Wilford expectantly.

Wilford was still standing there uncertainly. Even though he had certainly enjoyed seeing her nakedness from a distance, he felt spooked at the thought of riding on that wagon, alone with the witch woman. What if she cast a spell on him? He wanted to protest to Harbin, but he knew better. Instead, he said, "What about supper? We ain't et since mornin'."

Harbin answered matter-of-factly, "We got a couple hours of daylight left. We'll eat then."

Wilford searched for something else to say that might get him out of the wagon with that woman, but Harbin was already riding out. Left with no say in the matter, he tied his mount and climbed atop the wagon seat. There was no sound from inside the wagon, so Wilford carefully peeked in to see what the woman was up to.

She was sitting in the middle of the wagon floor, her arms wrapped around her knees. Wilford swallowed hard. she was still naked, and the dress was gone. She had put it away somewhere, or maybe even thrown it out. Just then, the woman looked up and met his eyes, and smiled that eerie smile.

He turned away as quickly as he could and whipped the team. He would try to stay as close to Harbin as possible, in case she tried something. In the meantime, it would be best if he tried not to look at her, at all. Then she started to laugh. Goose bumps crawled up his back and down his arms and legs as the woman's high-pitched laughter grew and grew, until it filled the air.

16

AS THE TRIO RODE EASTWARD TOWARD MISSOURI AND the land of Jesse James, Joe Harbin was feeling worse than he could ever remember feeling. The cold sweats that he had come to expect in the middle of each night were now finding their way into the daytime hours as well. He would be wringing wet, then the chills that would follow would get so bad he found it hard to stay in his saddle for the shaking. By mid-afternoons, he was tired and worn out from trying to hold himself up. To make matters even worse, Harbin was finding that everything he put to his mouth made his chest burn. He'd found temporary relief when, at a couple of friendly farmhouses, he'd gratefully accepted the offer of fresh buttermilk. But the indigestion soon crept back into his sour stomach to get it all churned up again.

He was riding along, thinking about how good another glass of buttermilk would feel, even if it was temporary. It occurred to him that this hunt was certainly different from any other he'd been on. Usually, when Harbin set out for a man with a price on his head, he would feel a straightforward enthusiasm that would divert his attention from any discomforts to be found along the hard trail. This time, though, there wasn't any enthusiasm to be had, and he couldn't understand why. He thought about it until he grew tired of the subject, then thought about it some more. The one thing he didn't consider, though, was giving up the hunt. It was something he would see through to the end, no matter how many nightmares or sour stomachs he might have to endure. Men who lived on the edge seldom changed, even when their usefulness had passed.

Most likely, Harbin figured after careful study, these new ill feelings had been brought on by the "witch woman," as Wilford called her. They hadn't managed to find a place to leave her, and her presence was having an unsettling effect on the men. She nearly scared Wilford half to death, for one thing. Even Harbin was puzzled by her odd behavior. Why, even after two days' riding, she was still sitting in that wagon, as naked as before.

He didn't believe, as Wilford did, that the woman possessed any kind of magical power, but some of the things she said could, indeed, sound convincing. Just the night before, she had come out of the wagon to sit by the campfire, staring into the flames with those white-ringed eyes for so long, Harbin wondered if she might go blind. He was just starting to say something about it to Wilford when the woman turned to him and peered into his eyes. With a nod, she said, "This hunt will be your last."

Harbin started at her statement, but Wilford broke in by saying that she wasn't making any great predictions, since this was, in fact, Joe Harbin's last hunt. Besides, he added, they were planning to retire.

The woman stared at Wilford, then began to giggle like a taunting child. She pointed at Harbin. "You will not retire," she said, "but this will be your last hunt. I tried to warn Papa, too. Now Papa is gone."

Her words hung in the air like a promised threat. Wilford shook his head and went to his bedroll mumbling. For Harbin, though, sleep was elusive for most of the night. Her words kept coming back to him, adding fire to the misery that was already being caused by his burning chest. Not until long after the flames of the campfire had died did he find the solitude of sleep, brief as it was. The nightmare started at once. His weakening spirit tried to fight it off, but it had become too much to handle. When he awoke with a moan, he heard a faint, high-pitched giggle. It unnerved and so enraged him, he pulled his Colt and fired a round into the wagon. The giggling suddenly stopped, and Wilford sat straight up, shouting something unintelligible. He looked at Harbin, and went back to sleep. With a sigh, Harbin lay back down and closed his eyes, trying to tell his body to relax and ignore the foolish woman's words. He had nearly fallen back asleep when the faint giggling had resumed.

Now, as he rode in the comfort of the warm sun, Harbin nursed his aching chest. The witch woman's words were starting to haunt his thoughts. He felt so tired, he thought he could sleep sitting up in his saddle.

Up ahead, he knew, lay the town of Crawford. Come hell or high water, Harbin intended to deposit the woman there. It disturbed him to see the effect she was having on Wilford, too. He had been jumpy as a grasshopper since they had come across her, and besides that, Harbin had noticed how Wilford had let his eyes linger over her nakedness. He couldn't understand it—the woman was dirty enough to have wallered with hogs. But then again, he never could remember Wilford ever having much luck in attracting a decent female. It used to amuse him, years ago when they had ridden together, that Wilford would spend so much of his earnings on any whore that would accept his offer. Not that Harbin begrudged the man a whore. He himself had, at times, laid down hard cash for relief from a hard day's ride. Mostly, though, money hadn't been necessary in acquiring that necessity in life.

A mile outside of Crawford, they came to a shallow creek. Harbin pulled up, letting the big gelding drink.

"Best water the team, and git that damn woman in the crick," he said.

"What if she don't wanta git in the creek?" Wilford said in a worried voice. He glanced backward into the wagon as if he was afraid she might leap on him at any second.

"I don't give a good damn whether she wants to or not," Harbin said. He turned back to the gelding. His eyes searched ahead toward Crawford. He had been through the town before, and remembered that it wasn't much more than a one-saloon affair. Behind him, he could hear Wilford's weak voice trying to coax the witch woman out of the wagon. Harbin hated to repeat himself, and rarely did. He stepped down from the gelding and walked to the wagon.

"You gonna git her out of there or not?" he asked. When Wilford looked at him helplessly, he added, "Crawl on in there and see if you can find some soap."

"You mean, inside?" Wilford said, fiddling with his hat.

Normally, Harbin could get irritated at such behavior, but now he was suddenly amused at Wilford's reluctance to be in such close proximity to the witch woman.

"Now, git on in there, Wilford, and find some soap. Or do I have to do it myself?" he said. There was a lightness to his usually hard tone.

Wilford took in a deep breath and held it. He disappeared inside the wagon. It reminded Harbin of someone diving into deep water for the first time and wondering if he was going to make it back to the surface.

Wilford reappeared a moment later, carrying a large bar of lye soap in one hand, and pulling the witch woman behind him with the other. He had such a perplexed look about him, Harbin had to keep himself from laughing out loud. Wilford struggled with the witch woman, who didn't seem any too anxious to cooperate, before he finally managed to drag her into the middle of the creek. There, he pushed her down into a sitting position and tossed the lye soap in her lap. That done, he wasted no time in moving clear of her and putting in a safe distance away. At the water's edge, he turned and said gruffly, "You git to warshin' that grime off, less'n you figure on stayin' here."

His threatening words lacked any real sound of authority, but the woman silently picked up the soap and soon had a good lather going. Wilford tried to keep his eyes averted from the sight. Instead, he watched the creek water carry the white soap bubbles downstream. Every now and then, though, he would find his gaze wandering back to the woman, thinking that the loss of dirt was leaving some fine results to be enjoyed.

The witch woman seemed to know just the right things to do that would irritate a man. She took a long time to wash in the creek. When Wilford would steal a glance her way, she would hold a leg high out of the water and rub the bar of soap slowly up and down. The sight had an overwhelming effect on him. He finally gave up trying not to look, and stood there with his eyes fixed on her efforts.

The same could not be said for Harbin. He soon lost his patience with the goings-on, and said, "We can't sit here all day. Git on in that crick and scrub 'er down good."

Wilford jumped as if he'd been bitten. He pulled his eyes away from the witch woman, who gave one of her little-girl giggles at Harbin's words.

"Why, surely you're pullin' my leg!" Wilford said. "I don't reckon that would be a proper thing, a-tall!" His body shook at the thought.

Harbin answered, his voice again hard and without emotion, "I guess the only one doin' any leg-pullin' around here is that crazy woman. Now, Wilford, if you're plannin' on comin' along with me, you best git on in that crick and start scrubbin'. And scrub 'er down good!"

Wilford's shoulders slumped. He clearly didn't want to be left out there, all alone, with a crazy witch woman. The very idea set his heart to racing. He tried to move, but his feet were rooted to the spot.

Harbin's temper flared at Wilford's reluctance. He said, "For cryin' out loud! As filthy and crazy as she is, it's more like scrubbin' down a dirty hound than some damn female!"

Harbin turned abruptly away from the pathetic look on Wilford's face. He thought about what he had just said.

If the truth be known, he didn't really have the right to order Wilford to wash the woman up. He could do the job, himself, by rights. After all, he had talked Wilford into quitting his job and retiring with him. But it had always been Harbin's nature to take charge of the situation, even when he knew it was no more his business than anyone else's. He couldn't change the fact, even if he wanted to.

It wasn't his nature to linger on such deep thoughts, though. Instead, Harbin unsaddled the big gelding and led it downstream from the woman. He took off his hat and dipped it into the water, then washed some of the sweat and surface dirt from the horse's back.

Wilford reluctantly pulled the soap free from the witch woman's long fingers. Looking down at her, he felt a mixture of emotions run through him. Just the fact that she had gotten about half of the grime washed away added new appeal to her nakedness. One part of him wanted to run in revolt at his own lustful feelings, while the other wanted to stay and be overwhelmed by them. He slowly took the soap and started to wash the back of her arm, when she suddenly pulled free and leaned back on both hands, allowing him a full, close-up view. Wilford swallowed hard.

The sight momentarily took his breath away. As he had suspected, under the dirt was the looks of a fine female form. A small giggle issued from the woman. Her eyes smiled wickedly into Wilford's. She was reading his innermost thoughts, and he knew it. He took her by the arm and said, "Now, you stop that foolishness and let me scrub ya."

The woman threw her head back to where her stringy hair dipped into the creek water. She pulled it free and tossed her head. The hair flew, spraying tiny drops of water in all directions. Wilford had to blink his eyes to shake a single drop that had caught on his eyelash.

He said, barely audibly, "Wet your head in the water, you hear, and let me scrub it."

The witch woman, smiling at Wilford, slowly dipped her head and, just as slowly, pulled her hair from the water.

Wilford took the soap and began to lather her head, trying his best to think of a hound in a washtub. He even tried whistling between his teeth, but the stirring inside him told him this was not a hound he was washing. He had her hair in a good lather when he felt something between his legs. At first, he didn't grasp the sensation. It was only when he started to grow in his pants that he looked down and saw the witch woman taking his privates out of his britches.

Wilford wanted to protest, but there were no words to be found inside him. He whistled faster and scrubbed harder on the woman's hair, trying to take his mind from what was happening down below. The faster he scrubbed, the faster the witch woman's hands moved, following his pace. Finally, Wilford just closed his eyes and gave in to her willowy fingers. He had forgotten about the hound, and about washing her hair, for that matter, when Joe Harbin's words cut into him like hot steel.

"What in the hell you doin' in there, Wilford? You gonna take all day?"

Wilford's eyes shot open. The sky was blue. He didn't even remember letting his head fall backward. Guiltily, he looked around him.

Harbin was leading the gelding along the bank. Panic shot through Wilford, as he realized that Harbin would soon be in full view of the goings-on of the witch woman and her magical hands.

With a yank, he pulled himself free of her tight grasp. He turned his body away from the bank where Harbin was approaching. His heart was beating so loud, he could hear it knocking against his chest.

Below him, the witch woman threw her head back and laughed. "What's wrong?" she asked. "Don't you wanta finish washing me up?"

Wilford said through clenched teeth, "Just shut up and dunk your head and rinse off. Let's git the hell outa here."

It wasn't until the witch woman had gotten out of the water and was walking toward the wagon that Wilford was able to adjust himself and rejoin the others on the bank. He avoided looking Harbin's way—instead he climbed straight atop the wagon seat. He was giving the horses rein before Harbin had even finished cinching his saddle.

On the short ride to Crawford, an array of feelings ran through Wilford. He even glanced back into the wagon a time or two, letting his eyes linger over the witch woman's naked body. The stirring that was going on inside him was something that Wilford had never experienced—not with all the Texas whores of his younger days or the few that had drifted through Leland Flats over the years. He wanted so much to possess some magic of his own, where he could wave a wand and suddenly make her become normal. The truth was, though, Wilford didn't possess any magic at all. In his mind, she was a witch. And that was that.

17

THOUGH NIKKI TOOK IMMEDIATE CHARGE OF BILLY AND the wound Greasy Abe had sliced in his side, Billy was less than gracious about it. First of all, it took some doing to clean away the mud pack that Holt had applied to stop the bleeding. Even though Billy was of medium height, and so skinny his ribs showed through, he was strong and wiry. It took a sizable effort by Holt and Charlie One Eye to hold him down while Nikki worked on him. She clucked and scolded him like a mother hen for all his howling and protesting. After she had the wound washed and rinsed clean, she doused it with kerosene, and then commenced to sewing the gash shut. She worked with painstaking care, so slowly that Charlie One Eye commented that it was starting to hurt him, too, having to hold on to Billy and listen to him complain.

When Nikki had made the last stitch, she sat back and admired her work. She had, she figured out loud, sewn up nearly as many cowpokes as she had dresses since she had settled in Kansas. That fact did little to impress Billy, though. He quickly replied that she had better stick to making dresses and such, for her nursing abilities were certainly wanting. That brought on more scolding from Nikki, who declared that Billy was just plain ungrateful.

As the group moved further across the Territory, more effort was made to keep night watches. Even Walter had given up his demonstrated stand, and had volunteered to take his share of the rotation. White thieves and murderers were about as common in the Territory as Indians were, and all agreed that being cautious was more important than nursing any differences they might have.

Billy, who had been in such high spirits over his first real gunplay, grew a bit sullen when it didn't bring him the glory and attention he'd thought it would. In fact, everyone seemed to be slapping Holt on the back for killing Greasy Abe and bringing back the horses. That was largely due to the fact that Katy was singing Holt's praises night and day, citing him as some sort of hero. She never missed an opportunity to talk about it. Oh, Charlie One Eye had mentioned to Billy that he had been courageous in his acts, but Charlie One Eye just didn't talk enough about Billy's bravery, or anything else for that matter, to impress anybody. In fact, the only time Billy did get any special attention was when Nikki started mother-henning him, and that only meant another dousing of kerosene on his stitched-up side.

As they progressed across the Territory, the days remained pleasant. The moon was making its monthly rotation and was now full in the sky. To most cowpokes, this meant better night vision under the cool light. To Charlie One Eye, though, it was the time of the month he hated most. There was something about the bright, pale yellow ball and its shadows and images that made him worrisome. As a boy growing up in Arkansas, he had sat on his grandpa's front porch in the evenings, listening to the old man tell tales. One of his grandpa's favorite stories told of how there were giants living on the moon—great beasts with tiny heads that were taken up with huge, grasshopper eyes. When the moon was full, the giants would step down to earth. They would sneak through locked doors and windows, taking people from their beds and devouring them. Then before daylight struck, they would disappear to take refuge on the yellow ball and wait until it turned full again.

Charlie One Eye had believed his grandpa's story with all his heart. He believed it so much, he rarely got any sleep on the nights of the full moon, for lying there with his eyes glued to the windows. In the spirit of friendship, he'd even related the story to some fellow cowpokes while he was working on a spread in Texas. They were seated around the supper table at the time, discussing the day's work and how best to spend their free time that evening. Charlie One Eye had been hesitant to go riding out under the full moon, such as it was, and when they queried him about it, he told them about giants that lived on the moon and came down to prey on humans. The other cowpokes had teased him so severely, he had never mentioned the story to anyone again—not even Billy. From that day, he had never completely believed any of his grandpa's stories—not as much as before, anyway. On nights of a full moon, though, he still found himself anxious and unable to close his eyes for fear that the story of big giants with grasshopper eyes was true.

Now, as the moon shone down with all its intensity, Charlie One Eye was having a double case of worries. Not only was the moon lighting up the sky like a big cat's eye, but the group had ridden smack dab in the middle of Indian Territory. Indians and full moons together were a heavy load for Charlie One Eye to handle. If it weren't for his and Billy's visits to see Holt and Walter, he would never set foot in Indian Territory. Not that Indian Territory was the only place where you ran into Indians, but at least Kansas and Texas hadn't been named after them. That had to mean something significant, to Charlie One Eye's way of thinking. In any case, ever since he'd heard what this new land was called, he had steered clear if he could.

He was staring upward at the source of his worry, ready to run at the first sign of Indians or giants, when Holt's voice made him jump.

"What you see up there, Charlie?" Holt stood beside him with his hands propped in his pockets, staring in the same direction.

Charlie One Eye's good eye danced nervously back and forth until he had regained his composure. "Up where?" he asked. "In the sky?"

"Why, hell, Charlie! What else is up there to look at this time of night? Everything that flies is asleep,'cept for the owls, of course."

The mention of owls sent a chill through Charlie One Eye. He wasn't afraid of them as much as the Indians and the moon giants, but the mere fact that owls hunted at night made him feel skittish. "Weren't lookin' at nothin'. Just thinkin' is all," he said. He took off his hat and rubbed his head, then smelled his hand. "How long you reckon it'll take us to clear the Territory?"

Holt was still staring up at the moon like it held a fascination for him, too. "At our pace, I'd say a week or two," he said.

"That long, huh?" Charlie One Eye said disappointedly.

Holt pulled his eyes away from the sky, rolled a fixin', and lit up. He nodded his head. "We got a fair piece of travel before we hit Georgia. You ain't gettin' discouraged already, are ya?" he asked, squinting over the glow of his smoke.

"No more than anybody else. Just wonderin', is all." Charlie One Eye shrugged.

Holt seemed satisfied and bade him good night. Charlie One Eye volunteered to take the first watch. The solitude of being the only soul awake played on his nerves. He didn't bother to wake Walter when his time came, keeping his good eye trained warily on the moon. He watched through Walter's turn, then Billy's, until he finally fell asleep. He dreamed about big-bodied men with tiny heads, and he was just looking terrified into a par of horrible grasshopper eyes when Holt nudged him awake with a sharp rebuke. He had fallen asleep with his jaw full of chewing tobacco. The suddenness of being jolted awake at that moment caused him to jump and swallow his chew. He was embarrassed and angry at himself for falling asleep in Indian Territory, leaving the camp, and himself especially, unprotected. He wanted to say something that would lay blame in Holt's direction for not having better range manners than to waken a man suddenly. Trouble was, though, the chew stuck in his throat so bad, he found his immediate concern was to keep from choking to death. By the time his gagging spell ended, he had forgotten all about covering up his falling asleep on watch.

The next day, they rode into an area of low rolling hills that were covered with bright yellow wildflowers and soft prairie grass. The constant wind had lessened to a gentle breeze that made traveling pleasant enough. Here and there were scattered groupings of blackjack and cedar trees, and mixed among them was an occasional jujube. Nikki took delight in riding off to pick the ripe fruits for snacking after the evening meal. Holt teased her about making a jujube pie, which Nikki replied she just might do someday. That gave Charlie One Eye something different to think about, wondering what a jujube pie would taste like.

The horses' gaits began to pick up as they sensed water nearby. They approached a large group of trees, and soon saw the low-lying draw that led to a sizable pond. On the other side was a clearing, where there sat a little cabin next to a cornfield. A man was dozing on the porch, and in the cornfield, a plump young Indian woman was hoeing weeds. They rode in toward the cabin, trying to make enough noise so as not to startle the man.

He appeared to be a heavy sleeper. His eyes were still closed when the group rode right up to the edge of the porch and stopped. Holt cleared his throat and was about to speak, when the man opened his mouth.

"Howdy. The name's Arthur Crumb. You have reached a place of rest, brothers," he said, his eyes opening to slits.

"Howdy yourself," Holt said, looking the man over. Must be close to sixty, he thought. Gesturing toward the plump woman in the cornfield, he asked, "Your woman?"

Crumb's eyes widened. "Why, brother, you are an observant soul. She is, indeed, my woman. Not by the marriage of man, but by God Almighty Himself," he said.

There was a shuffling in the doorway of the cabin, and Holt looked up to see a second young Indian woman standing there. Behind, another set of eyes peered over her shoulder. Neither woman appeared to be out of her teenage years. Crumb smiled as Holt studied the situation thoughtfully.

"Yes, brother. Before you ask, they, too, are my women in God's eyes," he said.

Holt said, "I didn't ask."

Arthur Crumb's face softened, and he nodded his head graciously. "So you didn't. But, if you'll pardon me for saying, I knew your thoughts. The one working the fields is, indeed, too young to have grown children. And, like so many other men who do not understand the written Word, you have questions in your heart." He spread his arms. "But not to worry. My women will serve you and your fellow travelers. You look hungry and tired from your journey, brethren."

"Like I say, I didn't ask," Holt repeated.

"I know, brother. You didn't, but out back we have plenty of good water. You and your brethren would surely like to wash away the dirt of your travels. Let us serve you some good corn and fried prairie chicken," Crumb offered. "Just this morning, eleven of them were sent to us by the Almighty. You see, He provides for all who believe." He made a wide gesture toward Nikki and Katy. "The ladies would surely enjoy the comforts of a clean bath. Please, brother, there is nothing to fear."

Holt said through a sardonic grin, "That's comforting to know." He turned to the others. "It's up to you-all."

At first, no one offered any comment on the matter. Charlie One Eye had his one-sided gaze set on the two young Indian girls who stood in the doorway of the cabin. He hadn't heard ten words that Arthur Crumb had spoken. Instead, he was thinking about how amazing it was that this old man had managed to acquire three wives. One was too many, in his estimation. And these were Indian wives, at that. He shuddered to think of such a fate. It would be dern near impossible to close his eye and rest under such conditions. It suddenly dawned on him that there might be more wives, hidden away somewhere. He twisted around in his saddle to scrutinize the place for more female forms.

Billy, for his part, was hungry, and the two Indian maidens were nice enough to look at. Where Charlie One Eye was afraid of them, Billy was fascinated by Indian women. He'd been so ever since the day he'd ridden up on one in Texas. She had been bathing in a creek and had never noticed he was there, so he watched until she rose out of the water and casually dressed herself. It had been an enjoyable surprise to him, and even though he had never been with an Indian woman, it was something he liked to consider from time to time.

Not wanting to appear eager, Billy said, "I guess Chief here could use the rest."

Nikki simply shrugged her shoulders as if it didn't matter to her one way or the other. Katy did likewise. Anything they decided to do was fine with her, as long as Holt was involved.

Walter broke the deadlock with his observations. "Just as well," he said. "We gotta eat somewhere. Just as well be here as down the trail."

Arthur Crumb stood up and, with his thumbs, popped his suspenders. "Good enough, brethren! Step down and join us in our humble dwelling."

18

THE INDIAN WOMEN JUMPED TO LIFE AT THE NEWS THAT they had guests for dinner. At Arthur Crumb's signal, the two younger women stepped into the darkness of the cabin and returned shortly to the doorway. One was holding something in her hands. The woman who had been hoeing corn came directly in from the field and stood before Katy and Nikki. As she wiped the sweat from her forehead, she spoke in near-perfect English.

"Come and take of our water. I've soap and cloths to dry yourselves with." She gestured to one of the younger women, who tossed her a bar of soap and some rags.

Holt, who was still perched atop the stallion, threw a leg casually over the horse's neck and rolled a fixin'. He was slightly surprised when Katy and Nikki exchanged glances and, without hesitation, hurried to fetch some clean clothes from the wagon and followed the Indian woman around back of the cabin. When the women had disappeared, Crumb made a gesture to the two younger women in the doorway. Immediately, one stepped forward with another bar of soap in her hand, while the other moved back inside the cabin.

When the girl tried to hand the soap to Charlie One Eye, he pulled back and shook his head. Walter turned away from her with a low grunt. Billy scoffed at them and took the soap. He climbed down off his horse and headed in the same direction as Katy and Nikki.

Arthur Crumb shook his head. "No, brother," he said. He nodded to the south toward a group of trees. "Yonder. You must show the ladies privacy."

Billy stopped in his tracks, his face turning red. "Shoot fire! I wasn't goin' to watch them women," he muttered as he stomped off toward the group of trees. He turned his head to avoid seeing any amusement that might show on Holt's face.

From inside the cabin, the smell of cooking was already filtering out the door, giving the men a pleasant aroma to enjoy. Walter and Charlie One Eye moved themselves to the shady side of the wagon and sat down. Arthur Crumb had handed out all his orders to the Indian women from the same spot on the porch where he had been sitting. He returned to his chair and propped his elbows, hands folded across his stomach.

The Crumb household seemed friendly enough, but Holt still couldn't justify climbing down from the stallion and relaxing. He waited until all had returned from bathing before he dismounted. He couldn't quite understand why he felt so uneasy. He thought about it as he listened to the idle chatter among Crumb, the older Indian woman, Nikki, and Billy. Company was apt to be rare in these parts, and Holt felt certain Crumb hadn't entertained anyone as talkative as Nikki and Billy for a long spell. He couldn't begrudge a man some decent conversation. Still, he had to wonder over Crumb's peculiar manner. He had never heard such a way of speech before, and for a man to have three wives was beyond his comprehension. Holt wondered if there wasn't some law against that.

But Crumb neither did nor said anything to arouse any further fears, and when he asked Billy and Charlie One Eye to fetch a table from behind the cabin, Holt put away his worries.

The table was soon set up, and the two young Indian girls brought out heaping platters of fried prairie chicken, along with corn on the cob and loaves of fresh-baked bread. There were even fresh tomatoes and a plate of butter.

It was a meal fit for a king. Arthur Crumb smiled at each of his guests before he bowed his head and offered a lengthy blessing, thanking the Lord for each person at the table and for the bountiful meal before them. When he had finished, he bade the visitors to eat their fill. The sight of such a feast was overwhelming, and the travelers dug in with enthusiasm. They ate and overate, with very little conversation in between. Even Katy and Nikki had to finally push themselves away from the table, complaining that they were too stuffed to move.

The older Indian woman was just rising from the table when she looked up and suddenly gasped, holding her hand over her mouth. Everyone turned to see the old chief climbing gingerly out of the wagon. He managed to get himself down, and stood there, crouched over, with a hazy look in his eyes.

Arthur Crumb spoke out, his voice full of surprise, "Where in tarnation did he come from?"

Billy, who had grease smeared over his hands and past his wrists, was still chewing on a prairie chicken leg. "That's Chief. He's with us," he said. He threw down the meat, wiped his hands on his pants, and hurried over to help the old Indian to the table. "He's been sleepin'. Come on, Chief. Eat somethin'." He offered his plate to the old man, refilling it with corn and bread. The old Indian slowly picked up the chicken leg and took a tiny bite, his head bent wearily over the plate. Billy cheered him on with each bite.

Holt pushed himself back from the table and crossed his legs. He rolled a fixin' and sat back, keeping a watchful eye on Arthur Crumb and the three Indian women. He half expected at least a question or two about the old chief, but the women averted their eyes and sat down to wait for the meal to be finished. Crumb let the old man be and turned his attention to Holt.

"Brother." He waved his hand gracefully over the table. "There is still plenty to eat. Are you sure you've enough?"

"I have."

Holt gave Crumb a brief nod and moved from the table to the wagon. He crawled underneath and lay down to do some smoking and thinking. He hardly noticed when Katy crawled next to him. She lay beside him on her stomach, resting her chin in her hands, and tried to speak, but he wasn't listening. He only grunted when she commented on the fine food they'd eaten, and how good it felt to get into some clean clothes.

The afternoon turned out to be a pleasant one for most of the group. Everyone laid himself out to let the rich food digest, while Crumb's Indian wives hovered nearby to tend to any of the travelers' needs. Holt stayed in his secluded spot under the wagon, Katy at his side, and Charlie One Eye kept a safe distance off to himself, but the rest of the group were more than struck by the fine hospitality they were enjoying. They even agreed among them that they would stay for supper, then make camp for the night in front of Crumb's cabin. As Billy had pointed out, old Chief, and everyone else for that matter, could use the rest.

Billy, Walter, and Chief took a nap, and when Walter awoke, he headed south toward the group of trees for a bath. Charlie One Eye was sitting up in the wagon seat where he could chew and think in peace. He was thinking mostly about the old man with his three wives. It was certainly an oddity that a man would even consider such a thing. His eye searched the clear blue skies. Days were safe and warm, but when the sun went down, it meant another long night. Charlie One Eye wished they could be on their way. It was too much for him, getting stuck with Crumb and his three Indian wives on a night with a full moon. To him, it was a spooky affair indeed.

Nikki sat on the porch, talking with Arthur Crumb. They made small talk, something that Nikki could do almost as well as her younger sister. Whether she thought Crumb was a bit unusual or not, it didn't seem to matter. She talked to him all through the afternoon as if they were friends.

Around five o'clock, Crumb's wives went inside to prepare the evening meal. Nikki, glad to be on the receiving end of the supper, leaned back contentedly against a porch rail to enjoy more conversation.

Holt, who had remained in deep thought since the noon meal, crawled out from under the wagon and looked slowly around the farm. Katy quickly jumped up to his side. Her eyelids were heavy from dozing in and out all afternoon. Smoothing down her tousled hair, she followed him like a sleepy puppy to the porch of Arthur Crumb's cabin.

Holt stood there a second before he spoke. "If'n you got some more of that soap, I'm goin' to wash myself off," he said in a low tone.

Arthur Crumb smiled. "Why, certainly, brother! Whatever thy wish, we are here to serve!" he exclaimed. He called inside the cabin, and a wife quickly appeared with soap and cloths. Holt thanked her and started toward the water with Katy at his heels.

Inside the woods, they quickly found a little stream. There were flat rocks along the banks. Katy found a nice one and sat down to warm herself in the sunlight that filtered thinly through the treetops. Holt laid the soap and cloths on one of the rocks, but instead of undressing, he crossed the creek and kept walking. Frowning, she jumped up and tiptoed through the water behind him. She grew more perplexed as Holt walked farther into the woods.

"Where in the world you goin'?" she asked.

Holt didn't answer. He walked another twenty or so paces, brushing the low branches from his face, careful not to let them slap back in Katy's face.

They came to a small, bare spot. Holt stopped, tilting his head upward. When he spoke, it was almost to himself. "Something's not right. Just not right," he said.

Katy giggled. "Why, Holt Flynn! Don't tell me you're jealous of that old man,'cause he's got him three wives!"

Holt still studied upward. "I don't give a dern how many wives he has." He paused and rolled himself a fixin'. "You smell that?" he asked.

"Smell what?"

"That dead smell."

"I don't smell a thing." Katy held her head up, imitating Holt's gesture, and sniffed. She shook her head, not even trying to suppress her smile.

Holt drew in hard on his smoke and blew out. "Well, it's there." He bit the inside of his lip. "Did you notice those wagon tracks going up the hill by the side of the cornfield?" He turned and looked at her. His eyes were serious.

"No, I didn't, but what are you gettin' at?" Katy said.

"You can go on and think I'm crazy if you want," Holt said, peering deeply into her big doe eyes. "But I was through this very spot not more than two years ago. I was on my way to Fort Smith on business. And there weren't no cornfield, and there weren't no cabin, and there weren't no Arthur Crumb and his three wives." He turned away and let his eyes sweep through the trees before them.

Katy's grin grew bigger. "You sure you got your bearin's right?"

Holt nodded. "I got my bearin's right. I remember the stream through the woods that emptied out into the pond. I thought to myself at the time that it would make a good spot to settle into. I camped here, in fact. And don't you think it a bit queer that a wagon would go up that hill, when there's two ways around it? And I'll tell you another thing. That weren't no prairie chicken we et. Those were domestic."

Katy shrugged.

"Well, they were, I tell ya." Holt insisted. "There weren't no wild taste to 'em. Besides that, I noticed some chicken crates by the side of the cabin. You know, them crates they haul chickens in. Had fresh droppin's in 'em. Now, why would a man lie about that?" Holt said thoughtfully. "Hell, if a man lies to you about something trivial, he'll lie to ya about anything."

Getting no response from Katy, Holt started walking deeper into the woods. He stopped every few steps and held up his nose. "There!" he said after a ways. "You smell that?"

Katy sniffed and wrinkled her nose. "Yeah, I smell somethin'. Probably a dead varmint of some kind. I declare! You get somethin' on your mind, and you won't let it drop, will you?" She laughed at her own words.

"It ain't no varmint. That's human. I've smelled it before," Holt said grimly.

They walked farther. The heavy smell of death grew thicker with each step. Occasionally, Holt would tip his nose up, using it as a guide. By now, Katy was holding her hand over the lower half of her face. They had gone nearly a mile, when they reached a point where the smell was so overwhelming, they could barely breathe. They stepped into little knoll, and found themselves staring into a swarm of buzzing flies.

It was a shallow grave, dug crudely in the earth. The bodies were barely covered. There were so many of them, Holt couldn't count the number. Body parts protruded. An arm had been gnawed on by the vultures that hopped about the foul earth. The top of a head poked through, picked and half eaten. The big birds were fighting among themselves over the exposed flesh, which seemed to be everywhere.

Katy cupped her hand and tried to suppress the sickness that rose to her throat. In a strained voice, she moaned, "Oh, my God! What is this? I think I'm gonna be sick!"

Holt paid little attention to her words. He studied the huge grave. He could tell that some of the victims had been buried for a long time. Some of the mounds were fresh. He thought of the wagon tracks and the chicken crates. There had been something nagging at the back of his mind ever since they had ridden up to Crumb's cabin that morning. Something hidden deep in his memory that he knew would best stay hidden.

But the sight of the mass grave brought it all back to the surface. The mind being like a dam when it springs a leak and comes gushing forth, the puzzlement that had nearly driven him crazy for the past few hours suddenly became clear. The face—the bodies—it was all too familiar now. Except the name was not Arthur Crumb.

It had been more than twenty years ago, in a small town east of Austin, Texas. A man by the name of Arthur Salter was caught murdering folks that happened to be passing by his place. Only he had not stopped there. It was soon discovered that Salter was cannibalizing his victims. The headlines had created a sensation across the country, even reaching the streets of world capitals such as London and Paris. This had happened before Holt had hooked up with Walter. He had just begun his first stint in jail for public disorder. Holt had been taken to his cell, and soon after Arthur Salter was brought in. Holt remembered that Salter had been the main topic of discussion among the prisoners. The man had actually fed off the flesh of those he murdered. No one had dared to go near the cell of the crazy man. Later, he escaped and was rumored to have drowned.

For a few years after that, Holt had thought about the man and his horrid crimes from time to time, but, like anything else, his memory had faded with the passing years. Now, as Holt stood at this gruesome scene and smelled the stench of death, the horrible incident came flooding back. He pulled Katy in close to his side and held her.

"We better get back and warn the others," he said after a moment.

A voice called out, sharp and sudden, "Not so fast!"

Holt's hand dropped with deftness from Katy's side and reached for his Colt.

"Now, brother, that would not be a smart thing to do," the voice said.

Holt relaxed his hand. He turned slowly and peered into the twin barrels of a shotgun. Not a dozen paces away stood Arthur Crumb.

Crumb's eyes were wide. "How naughty. You have spoiled my little surprise. But no matter," he added, nodding his head. "He has sent you to me, and I will carry out His justice for your wicked ways."

19

THE ODOR OF ROTTING FLESH IMBEDDED ITSELF IN THEIR nostrils. Holt and Katy made their way back to the cabin with Arthur Crumb's gun pointing close behind. Even when they had reached a point far enough away from the mass grave that the odor should not be noticed, they could still smell it.

When they reached the small clearing where they had stopped before, Crumb's oldest Indian woman was standing there, waiting. She watched them approach, then nodded her head and took off at a run.

Holt cupped his hands around his mouth and hollered out as loud as he could, "They're gonna kill us! Run!"

Katy gasped as Arthur Crumb grunted and stepped forward, but there was no time to warn Holt before the barrel of the shotgun was slammed against the back of his head.

Holt dropped to one knee. His eyes closed shut, then opened, but they were glazed over. Pain went all the way from his head to his feet. In that instant, he didn't even know where he had been struck. His hand involuntarily grabbed the back of his head. He could feel warm blood, sticky against his fingers.

"That, brother, is just a reminder not to be so foolish," Crumb said. "Soon, you'll face the Almighty. You must cleanse your soul. Do not fight this."

Holt had trouble registering what Crumb was saying. The words all seemed to be coming together from someplace far away. He clutched at his head and blinked wildly, fighting to stay conscious. He let Katy take his head in her arms and pull him against her, hardly aware of what she was doing.

Crumb indulged this for only a minute, then ordered Holt to get to his feet. "It will be your woman companion who feels the wrath of the Almighty if you try such a foolish thing again," he warned.

Holt's head was still reeling, but he pulled himself to his feet. Katy held on to his arm, and he leaned on her for support until he found his legs. Slowly, they walked back toward the cabin, with Crumb offering his spiritual retributions and poking them with his shotgun. Holt wished his head would clear. He could jump the man and wrestle away the shotgun. He had planned on making that very move when they had reached the creek, but then the Indian woman had shown up. Now, besides the fact that he had lost the element of surprise, his throbbing head would not allow such an action.

When they reached the cabin, they saw that the three Indian women had gathered everyone together. They were sitting in a huddle between the cabin and the wagon. All three Indian women held Winchesters pointed at the stunned group. Billy was nervously biting his bottom lip, and Walter looked angry.

"Aw, my wives." Crumb smiled. "You have done His work. He will be well-pleased."

"What in hell's goin' on?" Walter demanded when he saw Holt.

Arthur Crumb lifted his shotgun and fired into the air, just over the group's heads. The shot struck the wagon seat, sending splinters of wood flying. "We will have none of that devil talk!" his voice boomed.

The warning shot had its effect on everyone in the group but Walter. Nikki and Katy screamed. Billy ducked his head, while Charlie One Eye grabbed his hat and pulled it down low over his ears. When things had settled down some, Walter again opened his mouth.

"Like I said," he said to Holt, "what in hell's goin' on here?"

Holt's eyes gazed at each member of the group, one by one. He said grimly, "Our host, Arthur Crumb—or should I say, Arthur Salter—is gonna kill us and eat us."

"What?" Nikki screamed. She looked frantically back and forth from Holt to Crumb.

Billy, who had been at a loss since the three Indian women had drawn on them with the Winchesters, blinked wildly. "Eat us? What kind of talk is that? Why, he's a religious man!" He turned to Arthur Crumb, his eyes blinking more rapidly. "You're a religious man!" he said, as if he needed to remind Crumb of the fact.

"Religious man, my ass!" Walter retorted. "I knew he was full of horseshit the minute he told us them three savages were his wives!" He glared at Crumb.

Arthur Crumb's face flushed red. He stepped close to Walter, so that they were face to face. "Shut your trashin' devil mouth," he growled. He drew back, then struck Walter square in the nose with the butt of his shotgun. The impact of the blow echoed through the air like a pistol shot as the bone in Walter's nose snapped.

Nikki screamed again and dropped down to where Walter had fallen. She hovered over him, forcing his hands away from his face so that she could see what damage was done. His nose had been laid open with a big gash that split his left nostril. Nikki had seen many a cowpoke get his face busted up in a saloon fight, but she had never seen a nose get so distorted. She lifted the hem of her dress and pressed it to his nose. In seconds, blood was flowing through the material and onto her hands. Tears began to roll down her face as she realized there was nothing she could do to stop the bleeding.

Arthur Crumb made a kicking motion with his feet. "Git

up, sister, and leave the heathen be," he ordered impatiently.

Nikki paid him no heed. Instead, she continued to nurse Walter's bleeding nose, talking softly to him. She was just starting to tear away the fabric of her petticoat when Crumb nodded to the older Indian woman and pointed at Nikki.

The Indian woman stepped forward and, with considerable strength, grabbed Nikki by the hair. Nikki's hands grasped futilely for the air as she was yanked onto her back. Anger raged up inside her as the Indian woman stepped over her, and, with a wild scream, Nikki reached for the woman, flung her to the ground, and climbed on top of her chest. She drew back a fist and, before Crumb could react to the goings-on, landed a perfect right against the Indian woman's jaw. The woman groaned, and lay still. Nikki was about to land another punch when Crumb's voice interrupted.

"There'll be no second warning. You will meet the Creator on the ground you occupy," he said.

The twin barrels of the shotgun were trained just inches from Nikki's face. She glanced briefly at the barrels, then stared past them to see the rage of Arthur Crumb. His fingers were squeezed white against the trigger.

"Git up, Nikki. I'm afraid he means it," Holt said.

Slowly, Nikki stood. Her legs were weak and her chest was pounding as she tried to shake off the fury and come back to her senses. She glanced down at Walter, who was sitting with his hand over his nose. Blood ran through his fingers and down into his shirt sleeve.

Crumb backed away from her then, still pointing the shotgun. When everything had quieted down, he gestured to the entire group. "Now," he said, breathing deeply, "I want all of you to take your clothes off down to your underthings."

No one moved a muscle or said a word, but stared at Arthur Crumb as if they doubted what they had just heard.

Crumb's hands shook at their disobedience. "I swear by the Almighty Himself," he bellowed, "that my patience is about exhausted. Now, start undressing, or you'll surely die right here and now."

Nikki pulled her dress over her head, then dropped down and helped Walter. His eyes were already starting to puff up. They would surely swell shut, she thought. His chest was bare, and he wore long-handle bottoms. The blood dripped onto his naked chest through the small patch of hair in the middle and quickly found its way to the dingy white underwear. His red eyes looked into her face, and, for the first time, Nikki found warmth in them, even if they were half-seeing. For a tiny instant, she forgot about Arthur Crumb and the hunt for gold. She wanted to take him into her arms, but she resisted that urge.

Billy, his face still a mixture of disbelief and concern, peeled down to his underwear, leaving on his hat and boots. His only conscious awareness came when he glanced sideways at Charlie One Eye, who stood there in dirty long-handles. Doggone it, he had warned Charlie about buying him some new underwear, he thought. It had always disgusted him how Charlie One Eye would let them rot off his body before he'd spend a nickel on such necessities. When he caught Charlie One Eye's attention, he motioned his head toward the frayed and holey underwear and raised his eyebrows with a scolding look.

Charlie One Eye had no idea what Billy was carrying on about. He was praying, with his good eye bouncing from one Indian woman to another. The thought of being eaten by an Indian made the situation that much worse. He wondered where you started eating on a human—whether it was an arm or a leg or someplace in the middle. He remembered how, on the trail, cowpokes had talked once about the Tonkaway eating other Indians. They hadn't ever said anything about eating white folks. It didn't matter, but he hoped these three women weren't Tonkaway. He wished someone would have thought to have asked, back when

Arthur Crumb was being friendly. It also occurred to him that the noon meal had sure tasted like fowl. He tried hard to remember every little detail about the meal. He couldn't recall anything that looked like human parts. Surely, Holt must be pulling their legs. That didn't really matter, though. Just the thought of being captured by Indians, whether they be Tonkaway or not, made him want to drop down and cry. He would have, too, but his legs wouldn't bend.

Katy waited until Holt was undressed, then quickly pulled off her dress and turned toward him, pressing against his body. She was naked to the skin.

When Nikki saw, she blurted out, "I told you to put on some blamed underwear!"

"Hell, Nikki, I don't see where that makes any difference anymore," Holt commented, pulling Katy closer. "They're gonna kill us, anyway."

"He's a religious man, I tell ya!" Billy repeated, his voice high-pitched.

"No, Billy Boy, he's not a religious man a-tall," Holt said. "He's just sick, that's all. A lot of men distort God's word and twist it to fit their own silly notions. I reckon if you added it all up, Jesus has been used more to help men justify their wrongdoings than anyone else." He shook his head sadly. "It's turds like Arthur Crumb that put a bad taste for religion in a whole lot of folks' mouths that shouldn't be there."

Arthur Crumb sent one of the younger Indian women into the cabin, and she returned with a cloth that she held out to Katy. "Put this on your female," he said to Holt. Then he turned and looked at Chief. "Does he speak the English language?" he asked.

Holt said, "To tell you the truth, he speaks it right well."

Arthur Crumb, still staring at Chief, shouted, "Then you heard my words, brother! Take off your clothes."

The old chief looked past Crumb and at the sky. At first, his words were just mumbles. Then he addressed Arthur Crumb, "If I must die before I reach my home, then I choose to die like a man. I will look you in the eye and spit in your face, but you will kill me with my clothes on."

The oldest Indian woman whispered into Crumb's ear. Crumb's expression did not change, but he said, "You do not know the word of the Almighty. You can keep your clothes, but you must perish, just the same."

Crumb and the three women got behind the group, and headed them toward the cornfield. They walked slowly as the rocks and hard earth cut into their tender feet. Holt looked at Billy and wished that he had kept his boots on, too.

Crumb didn't push them to a faster pace. He didn't speak until they reached the cornfield, then he briefly guided them to the east, and soon they were engulfed by cornstalks. Suddenly, they came to a clearing where, built close to the ground, was a roof that measured some eight by six feet. The roof was lifted a foot off the ground by logs that had been driven vertically into the earth. There were six-inch spaces between the logs.

As one of the younger Indian women hurried to open a small door in the roof, Holt heard Billy murmur, "It's a damn jail in the middle of a cornfield!"

20

AFTER HE'D HERDED HIS PRISONERS INTO THE EARTHEN jail and locked them up, Arthur Crumb pulled out a Bible and read scriptures for nearly fifteen minutes. He read slowly and with feeling, pausing occasionally to highlight a particular passage with reproachful stares at Holt's party. When he had finished, he closed the book, and he and his three wives bowed their heads.

Crumb began, "Almighty Father, this is surely a blessed day, for six of Satan's travelers have come here to make retribution for You and Your cross. With them is one old redskin. He is ignorant of Your kingdom, Lord, and I reckon he can be sorted out of Satan's lot on the other side. We thank Thee, Holy One, for allowing us the privilege to serve Thee at this hour. Amen."

Crumb opened his eyes and looked down into the jail. Holt pulled Katy as tightly against him as he could, as they all waited silently for the inevitable. Instead, though, Crumb and his wives turned away and left, disappearing through the cornstalks.

No one said anything at first. Holt took a look around. The little structure they were in had been occupied recently by hogs. The droppings were fresh enough that the stench was still very prevalent.

Charlie One Eye had started digging furiously with his fingers the moment Crumb was out of sight. Holt watched him for a bit, noticing that the walls of the dirt cell held several claw marks already. It was plain that the place had housed other unsuspecting guests. He started to explain to Charlie One Eye how futile his efforts were, scraping his fingers over the hard clay, but thought better of it. As jumpy as Charlie One Eye already was, the spent energy might settle him down some.

Billy was rubbing his hand over where his gunbelt should have been. "You think he really intends on killing us?" he asked.

Holt looked around. Walter, who had spent the better part of the last few years cussing the Trapp sisters—Nikki in particular—was lying along the north wall with his head in Nikki's lap. His eyes were turning purple and had swollen to slits. In fact, that whole part of his face was ballooning out. Nikki sat with her head against the earth wall, cradling Walter's. Her face held a mixture of fear and, oddly, contentment. Charlie One Eye was busy with his digging and clawing, while Billy paced and rubbed his side. Katy's body shook as she held on to Holt. She wasn't crying, but Holt knew she could start at any time.

His eyes met Billy's solemnly. "He's gonna kill us, all right."

As they waited for their executioner to return, the time passed without sign of Crumb or his three wives. Sundown was approaching when the wind started to blow, just a good-sized breeze at first, then picking up to the point where it was whipping the cornstalks back and forth. The northwest sky quickly turned to a dark gray, then the storm clouds rolled in like a black curtain. Lightning began to flicker in the distance. The winds blew harder, ripping whole stalks of corn from their roots, and the lightning came nearer, growing into sharp bolts that cut across the sky. The harsh winds were short-lived, but the lightning remained, followed by horrible booms of thunder that shook the earth.

As Holt watched the storm through the rough-hewn logs, he felt big wet drops against his face.

When the heavy rain came, it came in torrents. Sheets fell to the ground, too much for the earth to handle. Streams of water flowed through the rows of corn, cutting ruts into the soil. Soon, the winds had started up again, and it seemed like the world was going to be picked up and washed away.

Storms in the Territory were like this. They would come suddenly, and with a fury that only Mother Nature could deliver. To a sporty man like Holt, they were not altogether unappreciated. In fact, he'd grown fond of them, whereas most men hated storms as much as they hated anything. Maybe it was some sort of excitement he needed to stir up his mundane life. Walter had scorned him as being a little crazy for finding enjoyment in such a nasty affair. Whatever the reason, Holt had always felt a sort of anticipation when the weather turned bad.

This time, though, there was no enjoyment to be had, real or imagined. Holt realized that the storm might be giving them a brief delay of Crumb's intentions, but it was posing a new problem as well. As he stood there with the wind and water lashing against his face, he noticed that the storm was sending rivers of water into their earthen cell at an alarming rate. Already Nikki, who had helped Walter into a sitting position, was pulling him to his feet.

Charlie One Eye cursed as he continued to dig. His fingers were bleeding, but he couldn't seem to stop from tearing away at the wall. Billy had joined him, but the two were making little headway against the earth that had hardened with time.

Usually, bad thunderstorms in the Territory would come with a blast of wind, drop bucketfuls of water, and then leave as quickly as they came. All-day rains were casual affairs, with some heavy rain mixed intermittently with a lighter drizzle. Holt had seen such rains go on for days at a time, only occasionally causing any flooding. It was the hard rains that left floods, with no place for the water to run off to. One man had told of such a rain going on for five hours straight, flooding out a whole Cheyenne village and killing a passel of Indians. Holt had doubted the story at the time, but now he wondered. Water was past his knees and was rising by the minute.

The rain didn't let up for the next half hour. Soon, the water was up to Holt's chest, and there was no sign of the storm breaking. Behind him, he heard a scream over the noise of the wind and rain. He turned to see Charlie One Eye thrashing about wildly. Charlie One Eye held up a long black object and flung it desperately across the cell.

It was a snake, and it landed so close to Holt he reached out and grabbed it. He tossed it out between the logs, and watched it being washed away. When he turned back inside, he saw two more snakes, their bodies writhing in the swirling water. He grabbed one and threw it out, then yelled to Billy, "A snake!"

Billy, who was holding Chief's head out of the water, nodded and quickly removed the snake, then hurried back to the old man's side.

The rain was no longer coming down with the ferocity of before, but it was still hard and steady. The cell was now filled to ground level, with water flowing between the logs and the roof. Holt had to stand on his tiptoes to keep his nose clear. His head was touching the roof. He looked at Charlie One Eye, who was the tallest of the group, standing a good inch or two taller than Holt. Charlie One Eye's head touched the roof when he stood flat-footed. Nikki had managed to wrap one arm around a log, and was holding Walter and herself high enough out of the water to get frequent breaths of air.

The rushing water beat against their faces, submerging and receding, as they fought to help one another. Holt had pinned his arm around Katy's waist, holding her head up as high as his own. He looked at her face. She was scared, but she said nothing to complain.

All thoughts of Arthur Crumb left him as the threat of death hovered just inches away. He pulled Katy closer and kissed her, long and deeply. Words that he had never spoken to another human being since his ma had died came pouring out from inside him. "I love you," he said, not softly, the way such things were supposed to be said. The roar of the rushing water made that impossible. Instead, he had to yell it out above the noise of the storm. Soft or not, though, the words were heartfelt and sincerely meant.

Tears that she had hidden away for the man she loved came gushing down Katy's cheeks. She cried, half in fear and half in joy. She shouted out, "I love you, too!" as loud as she could. They kissed again, their heads bumping against the roof of the cell.

They held each other close, lost in their own world, waiting for the end to come. They stayed that way, even when the rains had stopped and the flowing waters had receded. It wasn't until the others began to talk and move cautiously about in the watery enclosure that Holt and Katy loosened their embrace and let the joys of love subside.

Billy and Charlie One Eye managed to evict four more snakes that churned up out of the water. All the while, Billy kept a firm grip on the old Indian.

It was late when the rushing waters quieted down, leaving pools glistening under the moon, which had reappeared when the heavy, dark clouds moved on in a southwesterly direction. Water filled the earthen cell, almost reaching the top rim. By now, each person had wrapped an arm around one of the logs for support. Some managed to doze, but until deep into the night when fatigue overtook them, their efforts to rest were mostly futile. Every so often, one would nod off, only to be awakened when his face dropped into the water. Unable to sleep, Holt studied the situation all night. Katy napped on his shoulder, waking from time to time.

When the first signs of daylight began to appear on the distant horizon, Holt nudged Billy out of a light sleep.

"Take your hat and start dipping out some of this dern water," he said.

Billy looked around at the others, then whispered, "I can't."

Holt frowned. "What the hell you mean, you can't? We need to git some of this pissin' water outa here." He was in no mood to be argued with. He reached up and pulled Billy's hat from his head. Even in the semi-darkness of the early morning hour, Holt caught the glint of something in the crown. "What's this?" he asked, staring into the hat.

"It's a derringer," Billy said. "That's why I kept my hat."

"Well, I'll be derned! You mean to tell me you had it all along, and didn't say nothin'?" Holt said. He reached inside and took the derringer from the straps that held it inside the hat, pulling it free. "For once, Billy Boy, I'm glad you have such a fascination with guns. Even if it is just a little bitty ole pop gun!" New blood rushed through Holt's veins as his mind turned over the situation. He broke open the derringer and squinted. "Why, damn, Billy!" he exclaimed, loud enough to wake Katy. "Ain't but one bullet!"

Billy's eyes blinked. He stared down at the water. "Bought it off a cowpuncher in Kansas. He didn't have no bullets exceptin' the two that was in the chamber. Had to shoot it once to make sure it worked." His head shot up. "What are we gonna do?" he asked. "We only got one bullet and they got four guns between 'em!"

Holt said, "Well, it ain't a very enviable position we're in, but it sure beats the fire outa where we were before!" He handed the hat back to Billy. "Now, start bailin' some of this water outa here."

Soon, everyone had joined in scooping water out of the cell, all but Billy using their hands. Even Walter was working, although he could barely see. The old chief still clung weakly to a log, staring blankly at the others.

As the water level began to drop in the cell, a discovery was made that gave new hope to the group. On the northwest corner, the water had washed some of the earth away from the logs, exposing them. Right away, Billy and Charlie One Eye went to yanking on the posts. They didn't move, but Charlie One Eye could swear that he felt them give a little. Furiously now, the group worked to empty out all the water, while Charlie One Eye went to digging more earth away from the posts.

Billy eased up to Holt and whispered, "Where'd you put my derringer?"

Holt nodded toward a spot in the corner of the roof, where he had wedged the derringer between two logs. Billy started for it, but Holt held him back. "Leave it be, Billy Boy."

"Why, it's mine!" Billy protested.

"What's yours?" Nikki asked.

"Nothin'," Holt said. He whispered to Billy, "Just shut up, Billy Boy, and let's git this dern water outa here."

"Well, it is," Billy whispered between clenched teeth.

Holt stuck his finger in Billy's chest. "I'll take care of this. We got one chance, and one chance only. Ain't no room for mistakes."

Billy looked hurt, and Holt added, "Look, Billy. I know you're a good gunhand, but this is somethin' that calls for experience. I figure I got us into this mess. I didn't like the looks of things from the start, but I let it happen. Hell, Billy, with this little pop-shooter and only one bullet, our chances of escapin' are between slim and none. Our best bet is to get a couple of them logs out and hightail it outa here, without havin' to rely on that little pop-gun a-tall."

There was a commotion as Charlie One Eye gave a whoop. "By damn, it's a-comin'!" he said, his voice rising.

"Shhh!" Holt hissed. "You wanta tell Arthur Crumb about it?"

Sure enough, once Billy and Holt joined Charlie One Eye in pulling on the log, it came free from the muddy earth.

They immediately set to work on another exposed log. It came out much more easily. Charlie One Eye dug some more at the earth, and before long he was able to wriggle his shoulders through the hole. He slid back inside. "By damn, we're outa here!" he said, a big smile crossing his face.

"Get on back up there, and let's pull these ladies out first," Holt said.

Charlie One Eye pulled himself up again through the hole. With his shoulders through, he dug in his elbows to pull the rest of his body out. He was promising to the Lord that, once he made it out of this mess, he would never return to the Territory again; that is, except for maybe an occasional trip to the Panhandle to see Holt and Walter. Of course, even that might not be necessary, once they found the gold.

He was almost completely out of the hole when a voice behind him stopped him cold.

"Oh, brother! I was afraid such a thing might happen!" Arthur Crumb said. He stood there with the two young Indian girls on either side of him, their Winchesters pointed at Charlie One Eye. "Now, back down in there with ye, brother. Join your heathen friends, for the kingdom of heaven is nigh, but so is Satan's fire for the wicked."

Inside, the cold, wet group slumped against the walls. So close to escaping, only to have it all end. Holt looked up into Crumb's round face. The way the man's eyes burned, Holt knew that he had come not just to check on his prisoners, but to kill them.

"Brother Crumb." Holt held up his hand. "We've talked it over, and if we're to die, would you at least help us set ourselves at peace with God?" he asked solemnly.

Arthur Crumb's face twisted into a smile. He said, "That would be pleasing to the Almighty. It's too bad you had to wait until the end to mend your devilish ways." His voice had softened.

Walter jerked his head from side to side, trying to see through the swollen slits. "By damn if that son of a bitch is prayin' for me!" he declared. "I always did think you was crazy, Holt! Now I know!"

"You just shut up, Walter. Let's let Brother Crumb cleanse us of our sins," Holt said. "Why, there's abundant water right here where we stand. He could baptize us right here!" He pointed at their feet.

Walter growled, "Why, you stupid SOB!" He swung in Holt's direction.

Holt quickly sidestepped him and said sternly, "Settle down, Walter. I'll handle things." He turned back to Crumb. "Come on in, Brother Crumb, and baptize those of us that will allow you."

Arthur Crumb's smile disappeared. "You think I am some fool, don't you? You want me to come in there so you can jump me." He nodded bitterly. "You almost had me believing. Well, I'll show you! You will be the first to die!" His stubby finger waved at Holt.

"No, no!" Holt said earnestly. "Listen, brother! I thought about it all night! You don't have to come in here! Look, look!" he said. "You can just reach in and take water to pour over our heads, one at a time. The others can stand back! I just want salvation. I wish to leave this world with my soul cleansed."

Arthur Crumb stood there, his face not revealing what he was thinking. Finally, he said, "Forgive me for not believing that even the most vile can come home to God." He stepped forward and waved his hand. "You others, get back!"

No one budged. Holt turned and talked to the others through clenched teeth. "Do as he says. That includes you, hon," he said to Katy.

The group stared at him in disbelief. "I reckon you'll be the only one saved," Nikki commented dryly. " 'Cause he ain't touchin' a hair on my head. And from the looks of things, he ain't touchin' no one else, either."

"That's fine with me," Holt said. "Now, like I said, git back."

Arthur Crumb waited until they were a safe distance back in the cell, then walked slowly to where Holt stood. He relaxed his shotgun, but still kept it trained on Holt.

"Step back a bit, brother." He peered down at the remaining water and shook his head. "Why, brother, I cannot reach down that far." He stood erect, looking around. "But we'll not let that stop us." He walked over by a row of corn and scooped up a handful of water, then returned to the earthen jail. "Lean your head forward, brother, and ask God for His mercy."

Holt leaned his head, staring at Crumb's boots. He felt the water trickling over his head and down around his ears. When he saw Crumb's feet start to move backward, he said quickly, "Would you put a hand on my head and pray over me?" He bowed his head, and felt a hand touch it.

Crumb cleared his throat and opened his mouth to speak. The only word to escape from his mouth was "Dear," before Holt pulled the derringer up and fired.

The bullet struck Crumb in the forehead. A small round hole appeared. Arthur Crumb's eyes widened. He stumbled back a pace, then started walking erratically toward the cornfield. His body had stiffened. He reached out as if trying to grab at something, and then fell dead into the mud.

"All right," Holt snapped at the Indian girls. "Either one of you bitches move, and I'll drop you where you stand. And if you don't believe me, just give it a try! Now, drop them damn Winchesters!" His eyes blazed. "Now!"

The two young Indian girls' faces had taken on a dazed look as they stared at Arthur Crumb's fallen figure. They turned at Holt's command. There was neither fear nor bravado in their eyes.

Everyone both inside the cell and out was silent for what seemed like forever as Holt carried out his bluff to the fullest, with the tiny, empty derringer against the two Indian girls who held fully loaded Winchesters.

Holt finally broke the silence. He had bluffed his way this far, and there was no turning back. He tried to read the two women, but couldn't. His voice was still full of anger, rage, and, above all else, authority. "I ain't waitin'," he said. "You two best make up your minds what it'll be."

First one, then the other, the girls laid their Winchesters in the mud. Charlie One Eye was the first out of the cell. He started for their guns, but stopped. They were, after all, Indian women. He turned to fetch Crumb's shotgun instead.

Once the group had all climbed free, they went back to the cabin. The top of the wagon was gone, and everything inside had been removed. Utensils and food lay stacked on the ground. The place where they had left their clothes was now bare. They crept up close to the corner of the cabin and huddled together. Slowly, Holt peeked around the corner, with Billy doing likewise below him on his knees.

There, on the porch, was their clothing, neatly folded. Holt could tell with one glance that all of their pocket goods had been removed.

They looked all around. There was no sign of the oldest Indian woman. Holt figured she must be inside the cabin. He could swear he'd heard some kind of movement. He whispered down at Billy, "I'll go in the front. You go around and come in the back."

Billy gave Holt a toothy grin. It pleased him that Holt had the confidence to send him, instead of one of the other men, into this dangerous affair. After all, if the woman was inside, she surely had her hands full of a Winchester.

When he figured Billy had had time enough to reach the back of the cabin, Holt raised his foot and kicked through the front door.

The Indian woman started in surprise. She was seated at thc tablc and was going through the goods that she had taken from their clothing. On the table lay scattered pieces of jewelry and coins, along with the men's pocketknives. There was a wad of money. Holt recognized it right away as the money he had taken off of Greasy Abe and stuck in his boot. Also on the table were the men's six-shooters. The woman's initial look of surprise quickly turned to one of contempt and anger. Almost as quickly as a gunhand would have done, she grabbed for one of the Colts.

Holt warned, "Don't. I'll drop you dead where you sit."

Holt's words were not as quick as the woman's deft hands. She grabbed a Colt and swung it toward him.

Holt fired the Winchester from his hip. The bullet struck her high in the chest. Before she hit the floor, Billy pumped another round into her back. The powder from the smoking Winchesters filled the room.

Holt had never before shot a woman—Indian or white. The realization had a sobering effect on him, even if this one was a murdering thief. His mouth was as dry as cotton. He stepped back outside and sat down on the porch, suddenly feeling old and tired.

Billy appeared at the doorway behind Holt. His face broke into a wide grin. "Well, it's over! We got 'em!" he boasted. "Now, by dog, we can git down to business and git on to Georgia!" he said. He looked around at the others, who were just now coming out from the side of the cabin. He frowned.

"Where's Chief? We gotta keep that old man alive. After all, it's still a far piece to Georgia!"

21

IT TOOK MOST OF THE MORNING TO GET THE WAGON loaded and the top put back on. Everyone worked quietly, with the exception of Billy. He went on like a magpie about the events of the morning, hoping to stir up a word of praise here or there about his own heroics. No one paid him any attention, though, except for Holt and Charlie One Eye, who occasionally gave a tolerant nod in his direction. Instead of going into a sulk, Billy just talked some more and entertained his own notions of bravery.

Once the wagon was fixed, Nikki brought up the fact that the two young Indian women should be taken to a lawman somewhere. After all, they had been a party to the whole affair. If Holt hadn't killed Arthur Crumb and carried out his bluff, the women would have been just as guilty as Crumb for the group's demise.

But not one person would agree with Nikki. Charlie One Eye, who didn't care to be in the same country with Indians, let alone riding with them, spoke right up against the idea of taking them anywhere. "Leave 'em here," he insisted, his eye wide and serious.

Katy thought about it, but decided she'd rather just leave and get on with their trip. "Let 'em go. It ain't worth the effort," she said.

Holt, who discovered that the Indian women were of Kiowa blood, stated that it was an unwise and dangerous idea. "We can hang 'em or shoot 'em ourselves, but ride with 'em all the way to Fort Smith? No," he said, firmly shaking his head.

After much discussion, they finally set the two girls to walking on foot, with orders to find their people the best way they could. With not so much as a word or a change of expression, the two young women quickly disappeared.

Holt felt relieved when they had gone. He took a deep breath and went inside the cabin to gather up their belongings from the table. He took up the wad of money that he had lifted from Greasy Abe's body, then let his eyes slide slowly around the room. As an afterthought, he decided to search the cabin, and called for Billy to help.

Together, they uncovered over six hundred dollars that had been hidden away. Holt counted the money. "You know, there's probably a lot more stuck away someplace," he said.

Billy shook his head and said, "Well, I ain't stayin' to find out. No siree! Georgia's my next stop!"

Holt said, "I hope you're right, but the way this dern trip has started, it leaves a man to wonder." He took out a hundred dollars and added it to the hundred he'd taken from Greasy Abe. Then he held the remainder out to Billy. "Split this up amongst you and the others," he said.

"Why, that money don't belong to us! Some poor folks lost their lives over it!" Billy said, disturbed by Holt's gesture. He refused to touch the money. Besides that, he was still smarting over the way Holt had one-upped him in the killing of Arthur Crumb.

Holt gave him a stern look and pushed the money in his own britches. He shrugged. "Whatever suits you, Billy Boy. But I'll be derned if I'm leavin' it here for some other turd. Besides," he added, "when did you git so righteous? Or does it have anything to do with what happened this morning? Is that what's in your craw?"

Billy's jaw stuck out, and his temper snapped. "It was my derringer! I shoulda got to take 'im!" he said. The truth was, Billy felt frustrated. Holt had one-upped him not just once, but every time they had run into trouble. Why, he had seen more gunplay in the last few days than most men did in a lifetime, but Holt had managed to outshine him on every occasion. Even the Indian woman, who still lay in her own dark blood at their feet, had been felled first by Holt's bullet.

Holt slapped Billy on the back and scooped up the pieces of jewelry from the table before he headed for the door. "You're right, Billy. I shoulda let you take 'em both," he said. He left Billy standing there, breathing hard with his jaw dangling.

Outside, everyone else was gathered around Walter, talking. Holt heard the last of a remark that Nikki was making that there was "no sense in turning back now."

He walked up and handed the jewelry to Nikki, then pulled the money from his britches and held it up. A hand reached over his shoulder and grabbed the first share.

"Give me my hundred," Billy said gruffly.

Holt grinned and handed the money out to the others.

Walter felt the money in his hand and said in a bitter tone, "By rights, it oughta go to the sisters. Weren't it them that grubstaked us on this here leisurely trip we're enjoyin'?"

"By dern, ain't you the ungrateful one," Holt commented. "Why, I reckon you'da bled to death if it weren't for Nikki here."

Walter's face turned toward Holt, but only by habit, for his eyes were swollen shut. It made him look even meaner and angrier than he sounded. "I don't need any of your smart talk," he said. "Now, if you all will just listen a minute to someone with a little sense! I say we turn back, right now! This here trip is gonna git us all killed, and for what? Some cockamamie story from some old fool Indian!"

Pushing the remainder of the unclaimed money into Nikki's hand, Holt said, "All right then, we'll vote on it. Billy, it all started with you. You vote first."

"I'm goin' to Georgia," Billy said simply, staring hard at the others.

"Charlie?" Holt asked.

Charlie One Eye dropped his head and swallowed, causing his Adam's apple to roll up and down. He flat hated to get involved in a dispute among friends. Right now, all he wanted was to get as far out of Indian Territory as possible. He didn't care which direction it was.

Holt said, "Well, Charlie? You gonna vote or not?"

Charlie One Eye glanced at Billy. "Georgia, I guess."

"Katy?"

She shrugged her shoulders and gazed into Holt's eyes. Her pretty face still held a glow, even at this point, and the near disasters they had faced couldn't change her feelings. True, it was crazy to go on. She had never believed that there was a cave full of gold in the first place. Back home, her life would be safe, but simple. The only promise of excitement would be in the form of drunken cowboys who were eager to drink away their monthly wages. Out here, though, every moment was spent with Holt, exciting or otherwise. And that was worth any amount of hardship, she decided. She turned to the others and said, "We've gone through all of this." She waved her hand around them. "And for that reason, I say we go on."

Holt held Katy's eyes for a moment, then said, "Nikki? Last vote's yours."

Nikki looked at Walter and bit her lip. "I vote with Walter," she said.

Holt nodded curtly and said, "Okay. It's four to two, or five to two if you wanta count Chief, there. We go on."

Walter barked out a short, harsh laugh. "You can vote all day for all I care. I'm goin' back."

Holt turned to him. "Well, Walter, first of all, you'll have to wait till those eyes go down and you can see. I 'spect by then, those Kiowa bitches will be back with their kin to lift your hair."

Holt's remark caused all the blood to rush to Charlie One Eye's head. "Well, hell!" he blurted out. "Let's git movin'!" He moved close to his horse and fidgeted with his saddle, keeping his eye watchful in the direction where the two Indian girls had disappeared.

No one paid him any attention, but watched to see Walter's reaction. Walter clearly had no real choice in the matter, and he knew it. Angrily, he threw up his hands.

Quickly, Nikki ordered Chief out of the wagon and guided Walter in instead. This new arrangement pained Billy, who was certain that all the excitement was bound to weaken the old Indian. Nikki, though would hear none of Billy's arguments on the subject.

When they pulled away from Crumb's cabin, Billy rode close to Chief, cursing Nikki's obstinance under his breath. The wound that Greasy Abe had slit in his side was burning like fire, and he attributed part of the pain to her irritating behavior. Soon, though, as they moved along under a fresh new sky, his heavy feelings began to lift. They were again on their way to a cave that was filled with more gold than fifty men could spend in a lifetime. That gold carried with it the promise of more excitement from every direction. Maybe, Billy thought to himself, there was still a place in life where he could carve his name. When they got to Fort Smith, he would use some of his share of the money to buy him a saddlebag full of dime novels. Only this time, he would read them as a man of experience.

22

"I DON'T MIND TELLIN' YOU, IF I LIVE TO BE A HUNDRED, I'll never eat tortillas and Mexican beans again," Jesse James said to his brother, Frank.

After the two had left the Youngers in Minnesota, they had headed south, riding hard until they hit Mexico. They had originally planned on passing through Mexico and riding all the way to South America, if that was possible. But, as on most ventures, Jesse had grown tired of the idea of staying in a country where both the weather and the food were too hot for his liking. They had holed up in a tiny village that was just deep enough inside Mexico to keep them hidden. The village was surrounded by farming land. Jesse thought all the farmers looked alike with their sombreros and loose clothing. Lacked imagination, he commented.

The little village wasn't anything more than a church with a cemetery next to it, an empty adobe building that was used by the area residents for meetings and such, a few dwellings, and a small cantina.

Jesse and Frank were the only paying customers who had visited the cantina for days. A few men had come in for pails of beer and an occasional bottle of tequila, but there had never been any money seen changing hands.

Jesse and Frank sat at a small rickety table, drinking warm Mexican beer.

"Hey, Pedro!" Jesse hollered. "What's for supper tonight?"

The little man behind the counter frowned. "Senor, my name is not Pedro. It is Fedencio. Fedencio Rojas. And tonight we have tortillas and beans," he said.

Jesse looked at Frank and said solemnly, "It's tortillas and beans for supper."

Frank didn't share Jesse's enjoyment in teasing Fedencio Rojas. In fact, there was nothing about this place that Frank did enjoy. He wanted more than anything to be back in Missouri, where he knew both the land and its people. Now, though, Missouri was the last place they could go. No, they would have to wait a good long spell before things settled down and they could return home. Mexico was just one of the unpleasant aspects of a bank robber's life that had to be endured.

"Pedro!" Jesse hollered again. "What about a whore? You got any dollar whores in this place?" He winked at Frank, who blew out a breath and shook his head.

Rojas hurried out from around the counter, eager to please this paying customer. "Senor, there is no whores here! You must go to a bigger place. I try to tell you, these people are poor, senor. They are just hardworking peasants."

Jesse leaned back in his chair. He reached into his vest pocket and pulled out a twenty-dollar gold piece and placed it on the table.

Fedencio Rojas stood frozen, staring at the coin. He had not seen so much money in a long time—never in this tiny village. He put his hand to his face and rubbed the back of his finger over the fine hair that grew above his lip. "Senor, I will return in a moment. Please help yourself to some more beer." With that, he disappeared outside.

Frank's beer hit the table with a loud thud. "Shit fire, Jess!" he said. "Why'd you go and do that for? He's liable to come back with a mob of farmers, and no tellin' what they might do! Why, they could rob 'n kill us!"

Jesse waved him off. "You worry too much. Like Pedro said, they're poor people. Hell, I ain't seen a gun since we've been here. What are they gonna do, rob us with a few hoes?" He laughed at his joke.

"Well, just the same, I wish you'd keep your head about such things," Frank said. He had a lot of bothersome things on his mind, and wasn't in the mood for any of Jesse's foolhardy ideas. "What do you think about headin' for Kentucky?" he asked.

Jesse blinked his eyes. He'd blinked them so much that day, it had given him a sizable headache. The blinking was caused by a granular eye condition that Jesse had had since childhood. Often, it would make his head start to ache, and that would affect him one of two ways. He would become either quick to anger, or silly-minded. Today, he was obviously in a jocular mood. He tilted his head and considered Frank's suggestion.

"Well, I guess we could go to Kentuck, all right. But that's a lot of ground, and a whole lot of lawmen to dodge before we get there," he said.

Frank would not be talked out of his idea so easily. Adair County, Kentucky, was where their cousin Wood Hite lived. Trust was the highest compliment that could be paid a man in Jesse's estimation, and the James brothers trusted Wood almost as much as they did their own mother. Besides, Frank was getting more wishful by the day to be back in familiar surroundings. "I say we leave right away. We got us some fine horseflesh. We'll stay off the main trails. What do ya say?" he asked anxiously.

They were talking over the idea when Fedencio Rojas returned. He held a young Mexican girl by the arm. She was wearing a loose cotton dress but no shoes. The hair that rimmed her face was still wet where he had washed the sweat of working in the fields from her face. Rojas brought her directly to their table.

"Senor, this is Rosetta, the daughter of my sister. She is seventeen and still fresh. None of the muchachos have yet touched her. In fact, she helps Father Juan in the church when she is not in the fields." Rojas watched Jesse hopefully.

Jesse was taken aback. The girl was small, and her face was as beautiful as he had seen in some time. She was much more than a man who was seeking a companion for a frolic could expect. She stood there before him, staring down at the dirt floor. Jesse looked her over good, enjoying that simple pleasure in itself. Then he pursed his lips in thought before he turned to Rojas and shook his head. He said slowly, "I've done a lot of things I ain't exactly proud of, but payin' for a virgin ain't one of 'em."

Rojas was distressed. "But senor! It is all right, for when the landlord comes from the city for his crop, he barely leaves enough for her family to feed themselves. Your gold money, senor—it will mean many good things for her and her family." He nodded encouragingly and pushed Rosetta closer to the table, until her body was almost touching Jesse's arm.

Still, the girl did not look up, but neither did she pull away. Jesse took another long look at her beauty, then reached into his vest and pulled out another gold coin. He picked up the other coin from the table and placed them both in her palm. "Tell her to take this to her family," he said as he folded her hand over the money. "And Pedro, tell her to stay fresh till love comes along. Don't give herself away to any old scoundrel with money jinglin' in his pockets."

The girl raised her head and gazed questioningly into Jesse's eyes as her uncle explained what Jesse had said. Then she smiled at him, not in a friendly way, but more out of politeness. "Gracias, senor," she said softly.

Rojas quickly shooed her away. "Vamoose!" he said, turning her toward the door with a pat on the head.

Jesse glanced at Frank, who had an amused look on his face.

"Don't say nothin'," he warned.

Frank shrugged. "You're all heart, Jess. You know that? I 'spect them tortillas and beans is gonna taste a mite more palatable tonight."

"What are you gittin' at?"

"You're a much better giver than a taker, is all," Frank said. "Hell, these Mescans are gonna think you're some kinda saint."

They both laughed.

That evening, after one more supper of tortillas and beans with warm beer, Jesse and Frank wordlessly saddled their horses, then bade farewell to Fedencio Rojas.

"Adios, amigo," Jesse said as he reared the muscular chestnut mare under him. As they passed the little church, they saw Father Juan handing a bowl of goat's milk to a small boy for his sick mother. Jesse suddenly yanked on the reins and doubled back to the church. From his vest pocket, he dug out the rest of the gold coins and tossed them at the father's feet.

In seconds, he had rejoined Frank, and they rode hard for the border. They had quickly put all thoughts of tortillas and beans out of their minds, but there was one remembrance that would not leave them. It was of a good girl, young and still fresh, yet she had been willing to give all she had to help her family. That was a quality in a person that the James brothers could, and did, appreciate.

23

"IF YOU COULD LIVE YOUR LIFE OVER, WHAT WOULD you do different?" Joe Harbin asked.

Wilford had a mouthful of beefsteak. He chewed hard, then said between gulps, "Why, I don't know, Joe. I reckon I'd change a lot of things." He quickly went back to work on his plate.

"Oh, I know that," Harbin said. "That stands to reason. What I mean is, what other line of work would you have pursued?"

Wilford was sorry that Harbin had taken this time to want to talk, just as he was sitting down to the best meal he could remember ever eating. The big beefsteak in front of him was cooked just the way he liked—real pink and moist on the inside and burned to a crisp on the outside. There were also potatoes, peas, and a bowl of stewed onions. Why, this was the sort of food they served in the finest restaurants in Kansas City, and there he was enjoying it in a two-dog town like Crawford. The idea pained him. He'd never had this kind of luck with the food back in Leland Flats, and he felt jealous. Why, there wasn't even a sheriff here—just a youngster by the name of Quinton Rakestraw, who wasn't anything more than a night watchman with a badge. Yet this town had ended up with a fine eatery. It didn't seem fair.

Finally, knowing he'd have to answer Harbin's question before he could get back to his food, he said quickly, "A barber."

"A barber?" Harbin replied, leaning back slightly. "Well, I'da never thought!" He was talking to the top of Wilford's head, which had already bent back over his plate. "I'll tell ya what I would of liked to of been," he said. "A schoolteacher."

Nothing obsessed Wilford Jakes more than eating, but Harbin's statement made him nearly choke on his beefsteak. His knife and fork fell to the sides of his plate as he stared at Harbin. A teacher? Why, that was about the silliest thing he'd heard in his life. He couldn't tell whether he should laugh. Instead, he just said, "You woulda wanted to be what? A teacher? Why, that's a bit queer, ain't it? I mean, all the schoolmarms I ever known was little ole ladies, or some young thing that went to school back East and come out here to teach our younguns whilst she tried to find her a man. You ain't tryin' to put me on, are ya, Joe?"

Harbin stared past Wilford in thought. "Well, it may seem a bit queer to you and everybody else, but, by golly, if I had it to do over, that's what I'da done. Instead of killin' 'em, I'da taught 'em." He laid down his fork and pointed at himself, then Wilford. "I mean, look at us, Wilford. We spent damn near all our life gettin' shot at, and what have we got to show for it?" He shook his head sadly.

"You've done pretty good, if I do say so myself. Ain't nobody better at it than you, Joe," Wilford said as he resumed his feeding.

"That's just the point. I'm good at killin' men for the prices on their head. Think of the absurdity of that," Harbin said.

"Don't seem absurd to me. Somebody's gotta do it."

The conversation had played out for Wilford. He was back to being totally occupied with the plate in front of him. Besides, what was the use of using up so many words on something that couldn't be changed in the first place?

Thinking about such things could give a man a headache, and he certainly didn't want a headache. Not with this fine plate of food in front of him, and especially since they'd gotten rid of the witch woman.

When they'd ridden into Crawford, there hadn't been a hotel to be found, but they did run into a Mrs. Beavers, who operated a boardinghouse. After they had put down the money, she had agreed to take the woman in. The mere fact that Wilford didn't have to ride in the same wagon as the witch woman anymore had lifted a heavy burden from him, and once again his thoughts were able to turn to more pleasant subjects, like potatoes and beefsteaks and such. Now there he was, enjoying such a meal, and Harbin wanted to spoil it with conversation. Wilford thought about all the miles they had ridden in total silence. Now Harbin had gotten the urge to talk. It didn't figure.

"A barber?" Harbin persisted. "Now, that's a job I wouldn't have thought of."

Well, maybe Harbin would never have thought of being a barber, Wilford thought, but he himself had contemplated it several times over the years. He studied his fork, which held a sizable piece of the pink-centered beefsteak. "I reckon it would be a doozy of a job," he said. "They don't do a blamed thing but stand there and cut hair and shave faces." He leaned forward to where his chin was just inches above his plate. His eyes grew to slits. "You take ole Royce Johnson, back in Leland Flats. Now, that ole buzzard ain't even friendly. Nicked my damn ear a dozen times. But, when it's all over, he sticks that money right in his britches! And a man's gotta have a haircut ever so often. The way I see it, Joe, is you git 'em in there and git 'em out. Outside of what money you spend on toilet water and a pair of scissors, the rest is yours. Don't have to work on Sundays, neither."

"I don't know," Harbin said. "Most barbers I know are combination cooks and hair-snippers on cattle drives."

"I ain't talkin' about no cattle drives. I'm talkin' about town barberin'," Wilford said. The mere thought of Royce

Johnson set him into another melancholy mood. He used to sit across the street from the little barbershop, whittling and watching Royce cut and chew the fat with his customers. To him, it looked like the easiest job on earth.

Wilford was still thinking about Royce Johnson when Mrs. Beavers burst into the room, holding a handkerchief over her mouth. She marched right up to their table.

"Git that hussy out of my boardinghouse!" she yelled.

Wilford leaned away when she pulled the cloth from her face and showed them a fat lip.

"Wh-wh-what happened?" he stammered.

"That hussy hauled off and socked me right in the mouth, is what happened!" Mrs. Beavers said. "Ain't nobody tried that since the late Mr. Beavers, and he's out at the family cemetery!" She propped her hands on her ample hips and glared at them.

"Did you do something to provoke her?" Wilford asked hopefully, knowing well that it was a futile question.

"No, I didn't provoke a blessed thing, but you're gonna provoke me if you don't get her out of my house! She's touched!" Mrs. Beavers said.

Wilford looked into the eyes of Joe Harbin, and the blood drained out of his face. He knew what the man's thoughts were, and they surely included some plan whereby Wilford would be the one to fetch the witch woman out of Mrs. Beavers's house.

Harbin gave him a nod. "You best go check on her. See what that crazy woman is doin' now," he said.

Easy for him to say, Wilford thought. It always rankled him how some men could just give out orders and expect others to take them. Normally, Wilford would offer his two cents' worth, right quick, but with Joe Harbin, it was best to let his two cents' worth slide, and he knew it.

The young town constable, Quinton Rakestraw, walked up behind Mrs. Beavers and patted her on the shoulder. It was clear that Mrs. Beavers was a respected citizen in Crawford.

"I heard what happened, Mrs. Beavers," he said, then turned to Wilford and Harbin. "You two better get over there, right now, and take care of that woman," he said, "and be quick about it."

Wilford might have to take orders from Joe Harbin, but this young whippersnapper was a different matter. He kicked his chair back and stood up. "Boy, you hold on, right there. You know who you're talkin' to?" he asked.

"I don't, and furthermore, I don't care." Quinton Rakestraw sniffed.

"Well, we'll just see," Wilford said. "I'm Wilford Jakes, and I been the sheriff over at Leland Flats for years." He pushed out his chest and twisted his face into an important grimace.

The fact that he was sheriff of Leland Flats had little swaying on Quinton Rakestraw. "This ain't Leland Flats," he said.

Wilford was miffed. "Well, this here feller"—he pointed to Harbin—"is Mister Joe Harbin!" His eyes squinted at Rakestraw. "Maybe you heard of him?"

Quinton Rakestraw quickly looked at Harbin. It was obvious he had heard, all right. He pulled his hat from his head. "I sure have heard of you, Mister Harbin. I don't reckon there's a feller in Kansas that ain't heard of you." His face had turned a bright red. "I reckon I could get her out of that room for you."

"That's okay," Harbin said. "We don't even know the wench's name."

Quinton Rakestraw's red face drew into a smile as he burst out with the news. "Why, that there's Alfie Nicholas. She's batty. We wondered what had happened to her. Couple of fellers over in Coffeyville got to braggin' about killin' her man. I guess they took some leisures with her, too." He raised his eyebrows.

"You don't say?" Wilford said. His mind was somewhat relieved that she hadn't killed her husband herself. "How do you know all of this?" he asked suddenly.

" 'Cause I just got back from Coffeyville. Two ole boys—I think one of them was named Burns and the other feller was Cheyenne Bob Calloway. They got drunk over there and killed a deputy sheriff." Quinton Rakestraw pulled his face into a serious posture. "They won't be killin' nobody else, though, 'cause they done hung 'em good."

Wilford knew Cheyenne Bob Calloway all too well. Once, Calloway had gotten drunk in Leland Flats and shot a man in the kneecap for speaking to the whore that Calloway had singled out at the bar. He had laughed at Wilford and even taken a shot at him. Luckily, Cheyenne Bob was more noted for his quick temper than his fine shooting abilities. He had missed Wilford by a hair, and by the time Wilford had gained his composure and fired two shots of his own, Cheyenne Bob had gotten away. Mayor Simpson had been angry, scolding Wilford severely for not going in pursuit of the outlaw. Wilford had explained that Calloway had only shot the man in the leg and hadn't killed anybody. Mayor Simpson had complained about the incident for days, but Wilford didn't care. Now, hearing the news that someone had finally caught up with Calloway and hanged him made Wilford feel good.

Mrs. Beavers stamped her foot. "If we're through goin' over the family tree here, I want that hussy out of my boardinghouse, right now!"

Wilford shot a quick glance at Harbin. He grimaced and patted his belly. "I'll go along with you, if you'd like," he offered to Quinton Rakestraw.

As they walked across the street, Quinton Rakestraw said, "How long you been travelin' with that Nicholas woman?"

"A few days," Wilford said.

"She's batty, you know. Her and her husband did some kind of fortune-tellin'. I had to run 'em out of here three months ago. Found out they were stealin' on top of tellin' fortunes. I'm surprised they didn't hit Leland Flats. Folks up in Coffeyville were real familiar with 'em." Quinton Rakestraw leaned toward Wilford confidentially. "You know, they say she buried an axe in the top of her first husband's head? Feller by the name of Long."

Wilford wished he would shut up. It was bad enough having to come face to face with the witch woman again, without having to hear any more about her wicked ways. He remembered bathing her in the creek, and wondered how God could make a woman's body so inviting and let her mind go bad. To think that he had actually thought about dallying a time or two with her gave him the creeps.

When they reached her room, Alfie the witch woman sat on her knees with her hands on her hips. They were clenched into fists. Wilford had put a coat around her shoulders before presenting her to Mrs. Beavers. Now, the coat was lying in the corner of the room, and she was once again naked as a newborn.

Wilford stopped at the foot of the bed. His eyes couldn't help taking in her nakedness again. He said, almost wishfully, "Now, don't give us no trouble. Young Rakestraw here told us what happened to you and your man. We're gonna put this coat back around ya." He motioned for Rakestraw to retrieve the coat. "And we're gonna go downstairs, real nice."

Alfie gave that now-familiar high-pitched giggle. "Ain't gonna tell, ain't gonna tell. You and the world ain't gonna make me tell," she said, giggling some more.

"Tell what, ma'am?"

"Ain't gonna tell, ain't gonna tell," she repeated. "What's gonna happen? Ain't gonna tell."

Wilford, who was approaching her with the coat, stopped. He got to pondering what Quinton Rakestraw had mentioned about fortune-telling. He remembered how her earlier statements had had such an unnerving effect on Joe Harbin. He had never seen another human being have that kind of power. He said, "You shut up that crazy talk. Now come here and put this coat on." To his surprise, she got up, walked close, and looked up at him while allowing him to slide the coat over her shoulders.

They went downstairs with Quinton Rakestraw leading the way. Alfie followed, with Wilford in the rear. Just before they got to the bottom step, her hand reached back and clutched Wilford's crotch. He jumped and almost hollered out.

"You stop that, you hear?" he hissed through clenched teeth.

Instead of letting go, she squeezed his member. She turned toward him, moving close to where her hot breath touched his face. "I ain't gonna tell what's gonna happen to the tall one," she said softly, "but you!" She giggled. "We both know what's on your mind!"

She continued to hold him, and when Wilford slapped her hand away, she just reached back and took hold again. "Come. Go with me in the wagon. I will satisfy your wants. Leave the tall one, for he soon will be face to face with the devil," she said.

Wilford yanked her hand away from his privates. "You git on out and climb into that wagon, till I can figure out what to do with you," he said.

Crawford was a small town, and the street was mostly deserted, but Wilford had no intention of letting anyone see the witch woman fondle his member, or do anything else crazy, like taking off her coat in full view of everyone. He hurried her along.

Once they had got her inside the wagon, Quinton Rakestraw made a face. He leaned close to Wilford. "Can you imagine her asking you to leave with her, in that wagon? Whew! They say she buried an axe in her first husband's head!" he said.

"Yeah, yeah," Wilford shushed him. "You done said that. I best git on over and talk to Joe." He hurried away, leaving Rakestraw cautiously peering into the wagon.

When he got to the eatery, he found Harbin standing on the porch with Mrs. Beavers. She marched past Wilford with a huff.

"I put her in the wagon. I didn't know what else to do," Wilford said. "I guess we can try to drop her off in Coffeyville."

"Now listen here," Harbin said. "I'm for leavin' her right here. We got a lot of ground to travel."

"I couldn't agree more," Wilford said. He wanted, also, to be rid of her once and for all. He looked over at Rakestraw and Mrs. Beavers. "But shucks, Joe! That boy ain't dry behind the ears. What's he to do with her? Believe me, I don't fancy ridin' on that wagon, not knowing what she's doin' behind my back. But I'm game, if you are."

"Come on," Harbin said, motioning for Wilford to follow.

They walked up to the wagon and joined the others. Harbin wasted no time.

"Look here, Rakestraw. I got a twenty-dollar gold piece if you'll fetch this woman over to Coffeyville. I reckon it's a big enough place that somebody'll take her off your hands."

The twenty dollars amounted to almost a month's wages. Without hesitating, Quinton Rakestraw said, "Yes, sir, Mister Harbin. I'll git her there for ya. No problem."

Harbin nodded. "Good. Wilford, if you're ready, I'd just as soon make a few miles tonight."

Wilford eyed the eatery. "You know, we could stay all night here at the boardinghouse. Maybe catch a bite to eat in the morning." His mind rolled over a big platter of fried eggs, along with biscuits and gravy with some good ham or sausage.

Mrs. Beavers lost her huffiness over the idea of paying customers. "I got a room. Just two bits a head," she offered.

"What do ya say, Joe? It would be nice, sleepin' in a bed for a change," Wilford said.

Harbin said, "That's fine, Wilford." He tossed Mrs. Beavers a half dollar.

Wilford felt good at once. He could taste that breakfast already. He said, "Just let me git my stuff out from under the wagon seat."

He was still smiling when he groped under the seat for his Winchester. Suddenly, Alfie appeared. She reached out and released the brake, then grabbed the reins. "Giddup!" she yelled.

The wagon team bolted. Wilford, whose arm had become caught under the seat, stumbled alongside the wagon, trying to free himself. "You give me those reins!" he shouted.

Alfie whipped the team harder. As they picked up speed, Wilford grew desperate. He reached up with his free hand and grabbed for the reins, but caught her arm instead. His feet gave way under him, and as he fell, he pulled her with him. Alfie fell headfirst, striking the wagon tongue, and then falling to the ground.

As he tumbled on the ground, Wilford could see the front wagon wheel roll over her legs. Her body bounced. He tried to holler out, but there was no time. The rear wheel rolled over her back, then the team and wagon raced on. She screamed once and then lay silent.

Behind, Joe Harbin had mounted his horse and taken off after the runaway wagon. Wilford pulled himself to one knee. His arm felt like it had been wrenched from his shoulder, and his legs were weak and bruised. He saw Quinton Rakestraw race past him toward the woman's still body. With an effort, he pushed himself to a standing position and slowly walked to where she lay. He knelt down beside her.

Rakestraw had rolled her onto her back. Blood was streaming from the corners of her mouth. Her eyes, open wide, found Wilford's. When she smiled, her white teeth were ringed in red.

"I ain't gonna t—" she started, but couldn't finish. A deep gurgling sound came from her throat, as bloody bubbles formed on her lips. She touched Wilford's cheek, and died.

24

A BREEZE BLEW IN FROM THE NORTH. IT ENTERED THE open window, causing the curtain to rise and flap gently. It was a perfect sleeping condition, with the wind coming in clean and refreshing, cool enough to dry away the sweat. Such breezes were common on the Kansas prairie.

Under normal conditions, Wilford Jakes would be feeling like he was in heaven to be in such a fine sleeping atmosphere. The bed under him was almost too soft—he was used to sleeping on the hard ground or, at best, a hard cot in one of the jail cells. As he lay back on the thick pillow and breathed in the sweet night air, though, sleep wouldn't come. He had lain awake through the early nighttime hours, thinking about the witch woman.

The grisly scene of her death had had a terrifying effect on him. It was worse than any death he could recall. Wilford couldn't help but shudder over the way the crazy woman had worked on his lustful nature. In a way, he thought, it was good that she was gone. Still, she had been a human being and deserved better.

He had just about worked that problem through, and was attempting to fall asleep at last, when Harbin's large, muscular form began to thrash about in the bed. Under the cool night wind, Harbin was perspiring to the point where

Wilford thought he might have caught himself a cold and a fever. Wilford lay there, not knowing what to do, while Harbin tossed back and forth and moaned. He had never seen such carryings-on before in a man. Rather than disturb him, he decided to stay clear on his side of the bed.

Harbin awoke suddenly, clutching at his chest. When he cried out, it nearly scared Wilford to death. Then Harbin reached over and grabbed Wilford by the collar with one of his strong hands and yanked him so close, they were almost eyeball to eyeball.

"I can't breathe," Harbin said in gasps.

Wilford was near panic. He thought Harbin must be out of his mind, maybe gone crazy like the witch woman. He remembered the woman's words about how the "tall one" would come face to face with the devil, and swallowed. Carefully, he pried himself loose from Harbin's grip, but his shirt was torn in the process. Once free, he leaped to his feet and started for his boots.

"Don't go!" Harbin said, sucking for breath. "I can't breathe. Help me!" he pleaded.

Wilford realized then that Harbin's troubles were real. He felt ashamed for thinking that he might be out of his mind. He hurriedly lit a lamp and peered closely down. Harbin's hands were holding on to his chest as sweat poured down his face. His eyes were shut in a grimace of pain. It didn't take a second look to know that Harbin was, indeed, a sick man.

He thought back to all the previous nights when Harbin had suffered from the nightmares. He seemed to be getting more and more tired, too, as the dreams kept robbing him of a decent night's sleep. As he stood next to the bed, Wilford remembered that night at the Leland Flats jail, when Harbin had told him he needed his help. It hadn't really registered with Wilford that Harbin had meant just what he said. It was a load of responsibility to take on, and thinking about it sent his head to spinning. As he watched Harbin lying there, suffering with pain, Wilford grew confused. His head started to ache, starting at the base of his neck, then moving on to the top of his skull.

He didn't know what else to do, so he took a cloth and dipped it into the basin on the washstand. Ever so tenderly, he dabbed the cool cloth over the beads of sweat on Harbin's face. Harbin didn't complain, so he wiped the cloth over Harbin's chest. Nothing seemed to have much of an effect, but Wilford kept rinsing the cloth and dabbing Harbin on the face and chest, over and over, through the night. Harbin didn't protest, but he didn't relax any, either.

By the time morning came, Wilford was bone-tired. His body ached from the fall he'd taken from the wagon. Still, he kept up his vigil beside the bed. He was as nervous as he'd ever remembered feeling, for, as the daylight crept into the room and cast its glow across the bed, he'd taken his first good look at Harbin.

Harbin's face was twisted in pain, and looked the color of ashes in a campfire. His bloodshot eyes stared up at the ceiling. The puffy circles under them were dark, almost black. His breathing was short and uneven, his chest rising with each attempt to suck in air.

Wilford was so uncertain, he grew even more nervous. It was hard for him to conceive how a man like Harbin could be this sick and look so ghostly. Harbin was bare to the waist, and Wilford studied the long, powerful arms and the hands that were big and strong. The chest was thick with muscle. Where a lot of men used their pistols to knock a man unconscious, Wilford had seen Harbin put a man to sleep with just one thunderous blow from the powerful upper body, and on more than one occasion. In all of his years, Wilford guessed that Harbin was the only man he knew who had few, if any, peers when it came to using his gun or his fists.

The morning wore on, and Harbin was becoming more and more difficult to arouse. Wilford tried talking to him, but Harbin had stopped trying to answer and seemed to be slipping in and out of consciousness. His breathing still came in short gasps. Wilford knew that he had better find a doctor, and fast. He didn't know if he could be heard or not, but he leaned down anyway and said, "Joe, I'm gonna see if I can rustle up a sawbones."

There was no response, so Wilford got up and moved to the window to take a look out in the street. Searching for some sign of a doctor's shingle, he caught the aroma of breakfast cooking. His stomach responded with a loud gurgle. He swallowed hard. It suddenly made him angry that Harbin had to pick a time like this to get himself so sick. He turned back into the room.

"Joe," he said, "I'm gonna grab a bite of breakfast across the street."

Harbin didn't respond. His hands were again clasped tightly together over his chest. Wilford took in a deep breath and grabbed his hat. His statement had satisfied the guilt he was feeling over leaving a fallen friend. It was only temporary, after all. He would hurry back with a doctor just as soon as he had eaten.

He went downstairs and was just reaching for the door when Mrs. Beavers appeared. She was wearing a full apron over her dress, carrying a broom and dustpan, and her hair was falling out of the bun at the back of her head.

"You boys gonna sleep the mornin' away? I wouldn't of figured you for the type," she said.

"No, ma'am," Wilford said. "We ain't doin' such a thing, a-tall. My friend is upstairs sick. I been sittin' with 'im most of the night. I reckon he needs to have a doctor look at 'im." He pulled on the door handle. "Where's the closest sawbones at?" he asked, pulling on his hat.

Mrs. Beavers shook her head and looked sorry. "Coffeyville is the closest town with a doctor for humans. All we've got is Doc Chandler, and he's strictly for the livestock."

"Coffeyville." Wilford's headache pounded harder in his head. He was just taking a step out the door, when Mrs. Beavers headed in the other direction, up the stairs. "Well, come on," she said, holding her skirts and talking over her shoulder.

Wilford hesitated. "Well, I just thought I'd get a bite to eat, 'fore they close down breakfast," he said.

"There'll be plenty of time for you to feed your face," Mrs. Beavers said. "Let's have a look at your friend first."

Wilford held on to the doorknob and stared out across the street at the eatery. His mouth watered at the thought of all the fine vittles he'd tasted the evening before. He sighed as he removed his hat. Life never seemed to balance out right, he thought.

When he reluctantly turned back inside, Mrs. Beavers had already cleared the top step. She turned and looked down at him with her hands on her hips. "Well, are you comin'?" she hollered.

Wilford cast a final glance at the eatery and cursed to himself. His legs felt weighted down as he climbed the stairs. He didn't want to go back into that room, because he didn't want to have to look at a powerful man gone sick. It troubled him too much. Big men like Joe Harbin, who lived on the bold and dangerous side of life, didn't get waylaid by sickness and such. That was for women and children and weak, cowardly men.

When he entered the room at last, Mrs. Beavers was bent over Harbin. She studied him briefly, then straightened up and turned to Wilford. Her eyes were serious.

"This man is as sick as the late Mr. Beavers was the night he died," she stated.

Wilford's eyes opened wide. He felt dizzy, and his heart started pounding along with his head. The thought that Harbin might be dying had not occurred to him. It was impossible, he thought.

Mrs. Beavers wiped the sweat from her forehead. The room felt close, in spite of the breeze coming through the open window. She noticed the wet cloth, which Wilford had dropped on the nightstand beside the bed. She picked it up and gave him a scolding look.

"You dumb jackass!" she said. "You should of woke me when he got sick! Looks like you mighta waited too long." She stared down at Harbin a moment longer, as if she were trying to make some sort of decision. Then she turned to Wilford. "Now, you git on over to Hap's Eatery and fetch Doc Chandler," she ordered.

Wilford felt too stunned to move. He was shocked at Mrs. Beaver's assessment of Harbin's illness. Surely she was just a babbling old hen of a woman. Joe Harbin wasn't going to die, just like that. And her derisive tone confounded him even more. Where did she get off, talking to him like that? he wondered. Still, he jumped when she spoke again.

"Now git!" she said, raising her voice. "And don't you be stayin' and eatin' first! You can fill that face of yourn later."

Why, if she wasn't a female, he'd backhand her for talking to him like that. Wilford muttered the fact out loud, but only when he was out of Mrs. Beavers's range of hearing. He walked across the street to the eatery and inquired after the doctor.

Doc Chandler was seated at a table by the window. He was a dirty little man wearing round spectacles and a dusty derby hat. When Wilford approached him and explained the situation, he nodded silently. He pushed his last bite of egg onto his fork with his finger. Wilford noticed the dirt that was caked under the man's fingernails and wondered how a doctor could be so filthy. Then he remembered that this was an animal doctor, and figured none of his patients noticed or cared one way or the other how clean he was.

The doctor took the last bite and washed it down with coffee, then threw some money on the table and walked straight to Mrs. Beavers's house. Wilford followed silently, feeling like he ought to be saying something to Doc Chandler, but unable to think of a thing.

Upstairs, Doc Chandler entered the room and nodded at Mrs. Beavers. He had no bag, no instruments. Harbin was flat on his back, still sweating and working hard to take each breath. His eyes were tightly shut, and his hands gripped the sheet that Mrs. Beavers had pulled over his chest.

The doctor knelt beside the bed. He felt Harbin's head and took his pulse, then pulled open his eyes and examined them. It took some effort to pry Harbin's hands away, but he finally did, then laid his head on Harbin's chest and listened. He frowned, then listened some more.

Wilford had little enough faith in this animal doctor, but he was the only hope to be had in the small town. He stood there, watching anxiously, while Doc Chandler repeated his examination one more time. At last, he straightened up and shook his head.

"Got an irregular beat. I'd say an attack of the heart," he said simply.

Wilford was dumbfounded. He twisted his hat in his hands. "You sure?" he asked.

"Well, not a hundred percent, but that's my guess," Doc Chandler said, pulling the sheet back up over Harbin's chest. He pushed his greasy spectacles up on his nose.

"Is he gonna live?" Wilford asked, his voice unable to hide his worry.

"I'm just a stock doctor, but I'd say he'll never leave that bed alive," Doc Chandler said matter-of-factly.

Wilford took a deep breath and hung his head. He stared down at the floor, trying to shake away the shock of what the doctor was saying. He glanced at Harbin, who still seemed so strong and alive. Harbin, who had always been in charge of every situation. Surely he was going to jump up at any minute, and things would be back to the way they were. But, the truth was, Harbin wasn't moving or going anywhere. Wilford felt a helplessness unlike anything he'd ever felt before.

Mrs. Beavers said, "He can do his dyin' here, but it'll still be two bits a day per head."

Wilford stared at her. "Ain't you the kind one?" he said.

Mrs. Beavers shrugged. Life was a day-to-day affair to her, and two bits was two bits, any way she got it.

25

WITHIN HOURS, WORD THAT JOE HARBIN WAS DYING IN Mrs. Beavers's boardinghouse had spread throughout the small town of Crawford. The news soon reached Coffeyville, and by the third day, it had spread across the wires like a raging fire.

The little town was bursting at the seams with curiosity-seekers. Wilford believed that half of Coffeyville must be there. At times, he felt important, answering questions. Just finding out that he had been Harbin's riding companion had somehow given folks the general view that he, too, had been some kind of fancy gunhand. It was these thoughts of admiration that sustained him, for at other times, like when he was sitting alone with Harbin in the room, he could nearly go crazy with worry. The thought of his future would make him want to cry. What was he going to do without Joe Harbin and his ranch to retire on? He had sent a wire to Mayor Simpson about his old job, but hadn't heard a word back. He had no money, except for a few dollars. He was too old, he thought, to find another job that was as comfortable as the one in Leland Flats. Some other town would most likely want him to prove himself, anyway, and he had passed his proving stage years ago.

Then there was Alfie the witch woman. Her body still

lay in the funeral parlor, unclaimed by any relatives, which wasn't surprising. Wilford had been approached by the undertaker regarding who was going to pay for the woman's burial. Wilford knew he shouldn't let that eat at him, too, but it did. Then he had had a run-in with Mrs. Beavers and Quinton Rakestraw, along with the undertaker, over Alfie's wagon and team. The team had been removed to the livery, but the wagon still sat in front of the boardinghouse. Earlier that morning, Wilford had looked out his window to see the three rummaging through it. The wagon didn't belong to him, but still, he'd felt a rage go through him. He evicted the trio from the wagon at gunpoint, swearing to shoot any soul that was caught disturbing it again.

These new responsibilities hit Wilford as hard as a roaring bear. There was no one to help him sort things out, so he had taken to talking to Joe Harbin about it. In his youth, he had heard his father telling stories about how he and Wilford's grandmother had once talked an uncle back from death. Wilford didn't know whether the story was true or not, but he was ready to try any kind of answer to his problem. He talked, even though Harbin gave no signs of listening. There had been no change in Harbin's condition at all. He simply lay there, breathing in gasps. Occasionally, his eyes would open. But, for the life of him, Wilford couldn't say whether the man was seeing anything or not.

Doc Chandler paid an occasional visit whenever he didn't have to be out on a ranch somewhere, doctoring cattle. There was nothing he could do, though, other than confirm what he'd already diagnosed. Mrs. Beavers was the only person who seemed to know what to do. She would come in every hour or so to bathe the sweat from Harbin's face and neck. Twice a day, she would force a little soup and water down his throat. When Wilford protested that she was likely to choke him, Mrs. Beavers said in that scolding tone, "In his condition, I don't see where that matters any, but I'll not have him dying of starvation."

Wilford had to admit that she made a good point, so he let her be.

There was a knock at the door.

"Come in!" Wilford hollered.

The door opened and a head poked through. "Excuse me. My name is Martin Diel. I'm with the newspaper over in Coffeyville."

Wilford was unimpressed, looking into the red face of the young reporter. "Well, have a look-see," he said. "I guess that's what you're here for." He turned back toward the window and gazed outside.

Meanwhile, Diel stepped inside, brushing his hands absently over his ill-fitting suit. He walked close to the bed and eagerly stared down at the nearly lifeless form of Joe Harbin. He watched Harbin for a long time, staring as if he were already dead and lying in repose. Finally, he turned to Wilford, who still had his back to the room as he studied the street below. "They say you were his riding partner. You're—" Diel looked at his notes. "Willard Jakes?"

"Wilford. It's Wilford Jakes."

"I'm sorry, Mr. Jakes," Diel said, making hasty scratches with his pencil. "Mr. Jakes, I'm gonna be honest with you. The paper sent me over here to do a story, but I'd like to do more than that. I'd like to write a book, sort of a tribute to your friend here."

Wilford eyed him curiously. "Now, what makes you think Joe would want a book written about him? He's a private man, you know. Besides, as you can see, he ain't in the right state of mind to be tellin' you his life story."

The young reporter's enthusiasm wasn't dampened a bit. He pulled up a chair next to Wilford, catching a look of annoyance in the process. "Mr. Jakes, it wouldn't be much, but I'd be willing to pay you a little fee if you'd give me the story. Why, I'd even cut you in on any profits that would be made," he offered.

Wilford's initial feelings of irritation changed into a mood of interest. He was low on funds, and no prospects of a good job lay ahead.

"First off," he said, "I don't know what kind of story I could tell about Joe. But, say I could. You reckon a book like that would sell?"

Martin Diel's face widened into a big grin. "Why, I hear that your friend there has killed over fifty men! You can bet his story would sell, and sell fast!" he said. "People back east in New York and Boston and Richmond—why, they would eat a book like that up! It might even make London and Paris! You never can tell!"

"Fifty men!" Wilford repeated loudly. "Where'd you hear a blamed fool thing like that?"

"Why, sir, that's what everybody's saying," Diel said.

Wilford rubbed his chin. The number fifty seemed an impossible number, he thought. His mind drifted back over the years, to when he and Harbin had ridden together. Before long, he had easily counted fifteen men who had fallen at Harbin's hand. He swallowed hard. This young cub reporter just might be right, he thought. He remembered hearing, over the years, about other men that had been killed by Harbin's gun. One here, two there.

"I don't know about that number fifty," he repeated, but with less certainty. He leaned forward, almost touching Diel's face. "But I must admit, he killed him a passel of 'em."

The two talked through the morning, becoming so engrossed that Wilford took to running off anybody that turned up at the door. He even lashed out at Mrs. Beavers, using the argument that Harbin needed privacy. Young Diel plied him with questions, his pencil working furiously in his notebook. If Wilford didn't know the answer to a question, Diel wrote something anyway. They talked until the scent of the noonday meal rose up to greet their nostrils, all the way from Hap's Eatery across the street.

Wilford rubbed his belly. "I could talk better with a full

stomach," he said. "Meals would be part of my fee, you understand."

"Why, certainly, Mr. Jakes. I'd be glad to buy your lunch," Diel said.

"It's Wilford, son. Just call me Wilford."

When they rose to leave, Wilford stopped at the foot of Harbin's bed. He cleared his throat and said, "Joe, we're gonna go on across the street and git somethin' to eat. By the way, this here young feller is Martin Diel. He's from a newspaper over in Coffeyville."

A deep moan came from the bed. Harbin's eyes opened halfway, blinked a couple of times, then closed. This caused Martin Diel to get excited.

Once they were outside the door, he leaned close and whispered to Wilford, "I thought they said he was unconscious. He is going to die, isn't he?"

"I only know what that animal doctor said," Wilford replied.

Diel was not satisfied with the speculative answer, but it was the best Wilford could do. They went across the street, where Wilford ate three bowls of the daily special, beef stew. Diel tried to ask more questions, but he found it useless as long as Wilford had food before him.

After they had eaten, they returned to the room and picked up where they had left off on Harbin's story.

"Who was the last man he killed?" Diel asked. "It would make a nice touch to go back to the scene and talk to some witnesses, don't you think?"

Just then, a noise exploded in the room as a bullet ripped through the lamp that sat on the table between them. Fragments of glass sprayed through the room. Wilford jumped, nearly losing the three bowls of stew. Martin Diel shrieked and jumped out of his chair. The two were stunned, when a low voice sent chills up their spines.

"I ain't reached numbers fifty-one and fifty-two yet, but I'm a-fixin' to," Joe Harbin said. His voice was weak, but his words were plainly understood.

Both men turned around slowly. To their surprise, Joe Harbin had his right hand filled with his smoking Colt.

Wilford's voice was down in his throat somewhere. He grunted and coughed and spit before any words would come out. "Damn, Joe! You scared the hell outa us."

"I'm gonna do more'n that," Harbin said. "If I don't git some peace 'n quiet."

Martin Diel stepped toward the bed, holding his hands up in front of him. He said, "My name is Martin Diel. Your friend and I were just talking about doing a story about you." With his hands raised, he moved backward to retrieve his pencil and pad. He started for the bed, when Harbin thumb-cocked the Colt.

"You got exactly ten seconds to clear this room," Harbin said. His left hand moved up to clutch his chest. Still, he kept the Colt leveled at Diel.

Wilford looked into Harbin's eyes. They reminded him of something straight out of hell—all yellow with red streaks running through them. "You best git movin', son. He means what he says."

"But, Mr. Harbin—" Diel began, but was stopped by Wilford.

"Look, boy. You better git, and git now."

Diel fumbled for a second with his pad and pencil, then marched out of the room.

"I would've thought better of you, Wilford," Harbin said in a weak voice.

Wilford felt ashamed to think that he had betrayed a sick friend. The fact that this sick friend was holding a cocked Colt on him didn't make matters any easier to reckon with. "I'm sorry, Joe. I really am," was all he could manage.

Joe Harbin slowly let the hammer down on the Colt, and his hand fell to the bed. Soon, he was back asleep.

As the days passed, Harbin continued to drift in and out of consciousness. Some days, he seemed better. He eventually was even able to sit up and drink a little of

Mrs. Beavers's soup. His face stayed an ashen color, and his hands would fumble with the soup spoon.

Outside of trying to watch over Harbin, Wilford had Alfie's funeral to deal with. He managed to wait until Harbin had fallen into one of his deep sleeps, then retreived enough money from his britches to bury the witch woman properly. The small town was still crowded with the curious who waited to hear news of Harbin's life-and-death struggle. Many of them attended Alfie Nicholas's funeral—not out of any kind of respect, but in the hopes that they could somehow be a part of the excitement.

Looking around him at the mass of people in the funeral parlor, Wilford was saddened for Alfie the witch woman. He didn't think he'd ever been to such a funeral, where not a soul even knew the departed one. Even Martin Diel covered the event, with his pad in hand. He had tried to strike up a conversation with Wilford by asking about Harbin's health, but Wilford dodged him with the comment that he'd best tear up everything he'd written in his little notebook, if he knew what was good for him.

After the funeral, Wilford walked slowly back to Mrs. Beavers's boardinghouse. Mrs. Beavers had volunteered to sit with Harbin while he was gone. He felt reluctant to return to that room where Joe Harbin lay. He wished more than anything that he could be back in Leland Flats, whittlin' and waiting for an occasional sheriffing duty to call. It was the waiting that bothered him the most. That and the wondering what was going to happen next. He just wished that, if Joe Harbin had to die, he wouldn't have to find out about it until years later.

As he stepped into the room, it wasn't Mrs. Beavers who rose to greet him. Instead, a small man with round eyeglasses, holding a black bag, turned to give him a smile and a nod.

"You must be Wilford Jakes. I'm Doctor Nelson from over in Coffeyville," he said.

Wilford looked past the man. Harbin was half awake.

His face was turned toward the window, as if he was paying no attention whatsoever to the doctor. Wilford's eyes narrowed.

"You ain't another one of them animal doctors, are ya?" he asked.

Dr. Nelson straightened his shoulders and said sternly, "My good man! I assure you, I have the proper credentials."

Just then, Mrs. Beavers appeared, pushing her way past Wilford into the room. She had heard Wilford's question, and it put her into one of the huffy moods that Wilford found so irritating. She put her hands on her hips and retorted, "Why, you dumb jackass! Don't you be wastin' the doctor's time! He's real, all right. I sent for him."

Wilford stared ahead. He didn't want to look at Mrs. Beavers. She was a pain of a woman who always seemed to be looking for a way to humiliate a man one way or another with her foul words. Wilford had known other women like her. Man-haters, he called them. He would often get the urge to put such women in their place, but, through a few embarrassments, he had learned that it was best not to tangle with them, for they always ended up managing to make him look like the fool. He swallowed a harsh reply and, with his jaw jutting out, strode past the doctor to the foot of the bed. He said, "What do you think, Doc?"

Dr. Nelson, who was clearly a man of few tender feelings, said matter-of-factly, "Well, your friend's a sick man. Should have been under a doctor's care, but I'm not so sure that would've done him any good, either."

Wilford looked down at his friend, whose eyes were opening and closing. Not very gently, he grabbed the doctor by the arm and pulled him outside of the room. "If you don't mind, I'd just as soon do our talkin' out here," he said.

"Whatever," said Dr. Nelson. "What exactly is it that you want? Do you want me to tell you if Harbin's going to live or not?"

Wilford blinked at the doctor's bluntness. "Well, uh, I guess—well, yes."

Dr. Nelson took off his glasses and wiped them on his sleeve. "One can never be sure, but your friend is a mighty sick man," he said. "My educated guess is that his chances of ever leaving his bed are slim. Now, understand that with the heart, one can never tell."

Wilford took a step away from the doctor and turned toward the stairs, his eyes not really focusing on anything. He had come to the same conclusion himself, but hearing it said by a human doctor somehow had a more sobering effect. His future passed before his eyes—a vast blank. He still hadn't received a reply from Mayor Simpson. He thought of the young reporter, Martin Diel. Maybe there was still a chance that he was willing to pay something for Harbin's story, even if Wilford only knew bits and pieces.

Dr. Nelson interrupted his thoughts. "If you have no further questions, I'd like to look in on Mr. Harbin once more before I leave."

Wilford grabbed his sleeve. "How much time are we talking about?" he asked.

"Again, you're asking a question that I can't rightly answer." Dr. Nelson shrugged. "He could die at this very moment. Could be tomorrow, or next week. 'Course, I've seen them pull out of these things and live on for years."

Wilford's face brightened at the doctor's last statement.

"Now hold it! I didn't say he'll pull through." Dr. Nelson held up his hand. "I just said it's happened before."

With that, the doctor returned to the room. Wilford waited until he and Mrs. Beavers had left before he went to Harbin's bedside. He sat next to the bed, watching Harbin doze in and out, until the aromas of supper started drifting up to him from Hap's Eatery. Drawn to the window, he searched his pockets. The best he could tell, he had enough money left for one more supper and a breakfast. As hungry as he was, he waited until Joe Harbin had fallen back into a deep sleep. Then, like some petty thief, he reached into Harbin's pockets and took out twenty dollars in gold. He took the money, even though he felt as shameful as a man could be. Joe Harbin could cut a man down with his steely-eyed gaze, or drop a gunhand before the man could draw leather, but Wilford knew that this was also a man who would not begrudge a few meals to a friend who sat by his deathbed.

26

FORT SMITH WAS BUSTLING WHEN THE GROUP RODE in. Holt had remembered the town as being quiet and peaceful. He stopped a man on the street and asked him what had brought out all the people.

The man looked excited. He said, "A hangin'. Tomorrow mornin' at ten o'clock. Gonna hang two of 'em."

Billy had made it clear more than once that he cared nothing about hangings. Still, he was interested enough to ask everyone he came across what had happened to bring about such an event. Had there been any gunplay? he wanted to know. To his disappointment, he found out that the two to be executed were a rotten pair of locals who had robbed and murdered a minister and his family. Word was that a posse had found them just a few miles from the murder scene, hiding out along the Arkansas River. The two had gotten themselves drunk senseless, and they screamed like banshees when the posse rode up on them with their guns drawn.

Holt nodded knowingly when he heard the story. He said, "Billy Boy, let that be a lesson to you. You'll find in life that those who care so little about other folks' lives usually holler the loudest for their own." He got nothing more than a blank look in return from Billy.

They rode on into the center of town. The streets were so congested that Nikki had her hands full with the wagon, trying to keep from running over folks. She had insisted when they first got there that she was going to make Walter see a doctor. His nose was still swollen, and he had difficulty breathing. Walter had protested, but very little. In fact, to everyone's amazement, especially Holt's, Walter had settled quite nicely into letting Nikki tend to him.

Nikki pulled the wagon to a halt in front of a building that held a doctor's shingle. An arrow pointed to the rear. The front of the building was taken up by a small saddle shop.

"I reckon this is good enough, right here. We're not going any further until we get Walter's nose checked," she announced.

"How long you think it's going to be?" Billy asked. He was already worrying about the prospect of spending the night in Fort Smith and being a witness to a hanging the next morning.

"Why, I don't know. What's your hurry? I thought we might spend the evening. Wouldn't do none of us any harm, sleepin' in beds for a change. I'd like to work out some of these kinks in my back," Nikki remarked.

Holt said, "Sounds all right by me. I'm gonna visit that barber across the street. Git me a bath and a shave. What about you boys?" he asked Billy and Charlie One Eye. "Wanta come along?" He stepped down off the stallion. "I reckon a body could smell us, upwind or down."

Charlie One Eye quickly dismounted. "I believe I will have me one of them baths and a shave."

Billy rubbed the soft, fine hair on his chin. It pained him that he still hadn't developed a respectable beard yet. All he had ever grown was a spattering of fuzz, with a couple of coarser hairs popping up once in a while. He climbed down off his horse. "Well, I reckon I wouldn't mind a good bath and a shave," he said, "but why do we have to spend the night? There's still a lot of good daylight left."

"Why, hell, Billy," Holt said. "That cave'll still be there. Nikki's got a good idea. Wouldn't mind laying these old bones on a soft feather mattress." He grinned at Katy, who smiled her agreement.

Nikki disappeared into the rear of the building, Walter in tow. Katy went off on her own, heading for a mercantile store that boasted a couple of ready-made dresses in the window. Billy checked to make sure that old Chief was all right, seated safely inside the wagon, then he, Holt, and Charlie One Eye made their way together to the barbershop.

At the rear of the shop was a bathhouse. There was no one seated in the chair. They found the barber hurrying toward the front. There was sweat running down his temples. He wiped his face with his shirt sleeve and said, "You boys here for a cut or a bath?"

"Both," Holt said.

The barber shook his head and said, "Well, the haircuts are no problem, but you'll have to give me a little time to heat some more water." He took a deep breath. "Those hangings tomorrow have sure kept me running, ever since I opened up this mornin'! Seems like everybody and his brother wants to get cleaned up." He shook his head and grinned. "I'm not complaining, you understand. But it sure does seem peculiar." He nodded for Holt to take a seat in the empty barber's chair. "I'll be right with ya."

Holt turned to Billy and Charlie One Eye and said, "One of you boys go on ahead. I'm gonna take a nice long bath before I git clipped."

When Billy didn't move toward the chair, Charlie One Eye stepped forward. "Well, if it's all the same, I believe I'll go on and git a cut," he said, and seated himself. "Ain't in no hurry for a bath, anyhow."

"I'll be with you in a jiffy," the barber said. He scooped up a handful of wood and headed out back.

"Don't hurry none," Holt called after him. "Charlie ain't got nothin' but that stringy lot o' hair over his ears. Ain't none on top. Shouldn't take no time to finish with him."

"I use to have lots of hair," Charlie One Eye said. "But that was before I started wearin' a hat all the time. Blocks out the sun, you know."

"Why, hell, Charlie! That's just an old wives' tale!" Holt laughed. "I 'spect I've worn a hat near as long as you have, and I've managed to keep most of mine." He pulled off his hat and bent the top of his head toward Charlie One Eye to show him.

Charlie One Eye didn't have an answer to counter Holt with, but that fact did nothing to change his mind about what wearing his hat had done to his hair. He wiped his hand across his head and sniffed. He thought a moment, then added, "I mostly slept with my hat on, too. Bet you didn't do that."

Holt smiled. "Right you are, Charlie. I never much did."

They took their baths and got shaved. The barber kindly took as much time on Billy's peach fuzz as he did with Holt's full, thick beard. He left Billy's hair a little more on the long side, while Charlie One Eye stepped out with a neat fringe of closely cropped hair around a shiny crown.

By the time they returned to the wagon, Walter and Nikki had been to the doctor and back. They found Chief leaning against a wheel, which meant that Nikki had once again pulled him out of the wagon and replaced him with Walter. Billy spat and kicked at the ground. All this upheaval wasn't doing the old man any good, he worried to himself. He wished they hadn't tried so hard to talk Walter into coming along. Folks seemed to be getting their priorities mixed, as far as he was concerned. He glared at Nikki, who paid him no mind.

Katy, who had been sitting on the wagon seat, jumped down and moved close to Holt when he returned. She was holding a package in her arms.

"What's that in the package?" he asked. "Somethin' pretty, I bet."

Katy nodded. "I think so." She added, softly so that only he could hear, "I got it to wear just for you."

Just then, Nikki appeared from inside the wagon. "That dern doctor had to rebreak Walter's nose," she said. "He said it was one of the worst busted-up noses he's ever seen. Told me it's a good thing we stopped when we did. Walter's hurtin' a-plenty." She looked off down the street with concern. "I went down to that hotel," she said, pointing at a large building two blocks away. "They're all filled up. Said there wasn't a room to be had anywhere. I guess that minister and his family had lots of friends," she added unhappily.

"Maybe," Holt said, "but I reckon folks will come to see somethin' morbid faster than a herd of buffalo."

"Well, then," Billy spoke up hopefully, "I guess that means we'll be movin' on."

Nikki shook her head adamantly. "Nope. Walter needs some rest. I thought we could camp down by the river. Maybe even fish a little. We brought some hooks and some good stout string along, you know." She turned to Holt for support.

Holt thought a moment, remembering how they had all practically duped Walter into coming along on the trip in the first place. A broken nose was not a pleasant matter, he knew from experience. But he'd never known a man to let it stop him from going on about life. Why, he reckoned broken noses were about as common as the wind. Still, he had to admit that Walter had as severe a case as he had ever seen. Nikki was looking at him like everything in the world depended on his answer. He said, "Hell, Billy. Nikki's right. I'm for stayin,' myself." He ignored her sudden smile and pulled himself up on the stallion. "Come on, Katy Bug. Grab your reins. Let's take a ride," he said.

Billy asked, "Where you off to?"

"Can't rightly say," Holt answered. "But we'll either see ya down by the river tonight or"—he smiled as he gave spur—"in the mornin'."

Katy mounted up. She followed Holt down the street a ways, to where Holt had noticed a fair-sized livery stable. There, Holt paid the man six dollars to care for the horses and to rent the small loft above the stable for the night.

Upstairs, Katy opened the package and held up a pretty new dress. "You like it?" she asked. Her smile was almost shy.

"Why, I love it," Holt said. " 'Specially when I think of you wearin' it."

"Well, turn your head then." Katy took off the old shirt and britches she was wearing and pulled the new dress over her naked body. She hadn't worn a dress since the day they'd left Arthur Crumb's. The crisp new cloth made her feel pretty again.

That evening, they ate steak at the fanciest eatery in Fort Smith. Then, walking back to the livery, they passed a theater with a billboard that promised a fine fare of entertainment. Holt snatched Katy's hand, and inside they went.

The stage was full of music and songs that were foreign to their ears. The acting troupe was from London, England. They did a fine job, but Katy paid little attention to what was happening on stage. Just sitting there and holding Holt's hand was enough for her.

For Holt's part, while the music may have been lost on him as well, he sat like a wild-eyed boy, full of fascination with the goings-on. The exuberance he felt was exactly what he had always anticipated it would be. As a boy, his mother had read stories to him and his brother, never missing an opportunity to point out the niceties that went along with a good education and breeding. Of course, the breeding was purely wishful thinking on her part, as they had been as poor as church mice. Any discussion of the theater was based solely on her active imagination. Holt's father, a Tennessean, had been a wanderlust. He had gone with Davy Crockett to the Alamo when Holt was just an infant. Shortly after, word reached his mother that his father had been killed in the battle. His mother had taken Holt and his older brother to Texas, which was a strange thing to do, considering the fact that there was nothing for her there. But his mother had always chased after her husband like the faithful soul that she was. As the boys grew, if a visitor should ever ask, she would make up stories about their father, saying what a fine and decent Christian man he had been. It wasn't until the summer and winter of his thirteenth year, when Holt had gone back to Tennessee to work for an uncle, that he learned the truth. His father had, in reality, been a man of ladies and drink who enjoyed a good fight as much as a parson enjoyed a good sermon. Holt never betrayed his mother and her stories about his father, but his viewpoint on such things as drinking and sermons had been changed forever. He had confided the information to his brother once, but his brother was either unwilling or unable to accept the truth about their father. He had gone into a rage and bloodied Holt's nose, and ever afterward a bitterness had grown and festered between them.

When the play had ended, Holt and Katy walked to the Arkansas River. There they sat until after midnight, past the time when any noise could be heard from the people who camped along its banks. Only the lights that flickered off in the distance gave any indication that there was another soul within miles. The city was asleep. Even the excitement of the upcoming hangings had been put to rest until morning. Holt and Katy had the world to themselves. They talked about life, its failures and disappointments, and about a future of growing old alone. They held hands and counted the stars and listened to the soft kerplunking of the rocks that Holt tossed into the river. Finally, they strolled back to the livery and climbed the stairs to the loft.

27

BY NINE-THIRTY THE NEXT MORNING, THE AREA AROUND the gallows was so crowded, people were standing shoulder to shoulder. Those with strong backs held children aloft, while some even carried their womenfolk. All along the street, the tops of the buildings were lined with dangling legs. Every window was filled with curious faces. Dogs and children ran in and out among the legs of the adults.

It was almost like a carnival. Some had even brought picnic baskets and spread them out along the ground, albeit at a safe distance and out of sight of the gallows.

Nikki had pulled the team and wagon in among the picnickers. She stood atop the wagon seat and looked, but only the top of the gallows was visible. Satisfied that she wouldn't actually see the men hang, she settled the horses, then went inside the wagon to tend to Walter. Their conversations were strictly one-sided, but she didn't seem to care. The fact that Walter no longer protested her being in such close company was encouraging.

Charlie One Eye had taken Chief, and together they had managed to get within a few yards of the gallows. Charlie One Eye wasn't particularly interested in seeing the men hang. That curiosity had been satisfied years before. He was just excited to be in among so many people. It was good, hearing them talk and laugh like they were going to see a circus act instead of a hanging. His good eye searched the crowd, taking in the oddities of mankind that a crowd has to offer.

For the old Indian, this was just another example of the white man's foolhardiness. He had given up trying to understand the ways of the paleface. He stood next to Charlie One Eye, weary and stoop-shouldered, staring at the back of the man that he was pressed up against.

Holt and Katy still had not emerged from the loft at the livery. They had decided to stay right where they were, rolled up in each other's arms, until the spectacle was over.

Billy had taken himself off to the farthest saloon he could find. He didn't even want to hear the crowd noise, let alone the sound of the gallows when the platform fell away from under the men's feet. Thinking about the squeak of the rope and the sight of the men with their necks broken, feet swinging in the wind, made him feel weak and flushed. He walked up to the saloon door and stopped.

As were most of the businesses in town, the saloon was closed. Billy stood there a moment, then started to pound his fist on the door. He banged until a man finally appeared.

"What in tarnation do you want, cowboy?" the bartender asked while pulling on his suspenders. It was obvious that he had been awakened, and he didn't particularly like the interruption.

Billy shuffled his feet, looking down at them. He mumbled, "I want a whore."

"You want a what?" the bartender exclaimed. "Why, I oughta git the sheriff." He turned away and waved his arm angrily. "To think you woke me up for such a thing."

Billy's head flew up. He was desperate, and the money he'd taken from Arthur Crumb was burning a hole in his pocket. He wanted a whore, not just because he wanted to get as far away from the hanging as possible, but because he knew that there wouldn't be another chance to get away from the others in a town that had sporting ladies. At least, he thought Fort Smith had whores. Every town along the trail from Texas to Kansas had boasted at least one. Those in the smaller towns were usually either past their prime or, if they were young, they tended to be on the plump side. But cowboys, who often went for weeks or even months at a time without even seeing a female, weren't much interested in looks, so it didn't matter one way or the other. In a town the size of Fort Smith, Billy reasoned, there had to be at least one pretty whore to be bought. He hoped so. He had been traveling with the Trapp sisters, who were as fine-looking a pair as he had ever laid eyes on, especially Katy. He had even gotten a few quick peeks at her, and now he wanted to find himself a woman with such fine features. The idea rushed through him like a hot flame. Without thinking, he grabbed the bartender by the arm.

"Here! I got ten dollars to spend!" He shoved the money in the bartender's face.

"Uh! Ten measly dollars? Listen here, cowboy! My girls did enough business the last few nights that ten dollars won't even git you a smell!" The bartender sniffed, staring at the money.

Eyes glued to the bartender's face, Billy reached into his pocket and pulled out another ten dollars. "Here's twenty dollars. Now, do I git a whore or not?" he demanded.

The bartender's face softened as he stared down at the money. He scratched his head. "I don't know. It's awfully early," he said.

"Look, dern it! This here's nearly a month's pay for punchin' cows," Billy said. His voice was almost pleading. He couldn't understand himself why he was going to such trouble for a whore. He just knew he had to have one.

The bartender hesitated a moment, considering. He said slowly, "There's one. Betsy. She doesn't work much. I mean, she has a friend, Texas Dan Simon. He's a mean one. The men around here are afraid to buy her. They're scared he might drop in at the wrong time." He stopped and looked around, rubbing his head some more. He noticed the gleam in Billy's eyes and his eager red face. Suddenly, he reached out and grabbed the money from Billy's hand, faster than a frog would grab a fly. "Go to the top of the stairs. First door on your right," he said.

Billy hurried past him, trying to straighten his clothes as he walked toward the stairs. It was hot in the saloon. He smelled himself and hoped that yesterday's bath and dousing of toilet water still had their effect.

The bartender called out behind him, "She may or may not be awake. Knock twice, then twice again. And, cowboy, don't say I didn't warn you about Texas Dan Simon."

Billy touched his hat, turned, and patted his holster. "Let me worry about Texas what's-his-name," he said.

The bartender shrugged and pocketed the money. "It's your funeral if you git caught," he said.

At the foot of the stairs, Billy took off his hat and wet his fingers. He tried to touch up the hair around his ears. He had a cowlick that refused to be controlled, and it irritated him. He remarked, "If you're so worried about this Texas hand, why do you keep her around in the first place?"

The bartender went behind the bar and poured himself a drink before answering. He swallowed it in one gulp, set the glass down, and said, "She used to be my best, before she got hooked up with Texas Dan Simon. Since then, I ain't rightly had the heart to ask her to leave." He poured another drink and, as with the first, gulped it down. He sucked in a breath and blew it out. "I was young and foolish once, but as a man gets older, his pride is replaced. It becomes an instinct for survival. I myself have no hankerin' to cross Betsy's Texas friend. The way I see it, when she wants to leave, she'll leave. Till then, her business is her own decision, long as I get my share."

Billy laughed at such silly notions. Young or old, he didn't think the bartender had ever been the type who would stand up to very many cowpokes. If the bartender's views were commonplace, then this Arkansas, he thought, must be different from the Territory, or Texas and Kansas. He studied the door at the top of the stairs for a moment, then turned and gave the bartender a smile before he climbed the stairs.

At the door, he adjusted his clothes one last time. He took off his hat and smoothed down his hair. Feeling so nervous that his knees were starting to shake, he knocked twice. In the morning quiet, the knocks sounded like thunder. He knocked again, but with less force.

His heart raced when he heard a faint voice from the other side of the door. "Come in."

Billy nervously fumbled with the doorknob, trying at the same time to think of what he would say. He tried to think of other whores he'd talked to, but nothing special came to mind, and there was no time to stop and come up with something witty.

He had planned to open the door and step calmly inside, but when he turned the knob, he felt himself bursting into the room in the same motion.

The woman was startled. "Who are you?" Betsy said. She was sitting at a mirror, brushing her dark blond hair.

Billy's hands worked at the brim of his hat, curling it into a tight roll. "My name's Billy Cordell, ma'am," he said, licking his lips.

Betsy turned her chair around to face him. She was in a state of half-dress, and her exposed shoulders and legs were smooth as silk, milky-white. "Well, Billy Cordell! How'd you get in here?" she asked, somewhat amused.

Billy was taken in by her beauty. She was, in fact, the most beautiful woman he'd ever met. Her beauty made him feel more awkward than he already was. His sweaty hands twisted even harder on the brim of his hat, so tightly that he mashed the crown together. He motioned back toward the door. "The man downstairs let me in."

She turned back around, brushing her hair and glancing at him in the mirror. "Well, I'll have to have a talk with Horst. He knows better than to send a customer this early in the day. And a young sprout like you, to boot!"

Billy said defensively, "I ain't no sprout! I reckon I'm near old as you." He wished he looked older, anyway.

"Well, just the same, you don't look too experienced. Believe me, I can tell," Betsy said. She took a good long look at him in the mirror. "Look," she said, "I didn't mean to get your dander up about being a sprout. But you young ones are all awkward and about as gentle as a buffalo. If you wait around till evening, we've got some older women that cotton to you young bucks."

Billy shook his head at the offer. "No, ma'am. I ain't got till this evenin.' 'Sides that, I done paid for you," he said, his heart sinking at the idea that she might not accept his business. That would be an embarrassment he couldn't live down. "You're young yourself," he pointed out. "Why would you prefer them old men, instead of men your own age?"

Betsy laid down the brush and gave him an exasperated smile. "All right. Get undressed and wash yourself over there in the basin."

Billy felt relieved and overjoyed. His knees again shook. "I had a bath just yesterday," he said as he tore out of his clothes.

Betsy stood up and laughed. "I'm not expecting you to take a bath!" She laughed again. "Just wash your thing."

Billy was embarrassed that he had misunderstood and shown his ignorance of such things. He washed as fast as he could, but when he turned around, he was surprised to find that Betsy was already waiting for him in bed.

"You'll have to take off your boots, and leave your gun over there by the basin. I don't cotton to having it go off accidentally," she said.

Billy started for the basin, then stopped. He remembered what the bartender had said about Texas Dan Simon. "I'll hang it on the bedpost, if you don't mind," he said.

"Well, I do mind," she said. "If you're planning on getting in bed with me, you'll put the gun over there."

Billy stood there, frozen between his fear of being caught by Texas Dan Simon and his deep desire for Betsy. Lust won out, and he reluctantly laid his Colt down on the stand next to the basin. Moving close to the bed, he hurriedly removed his hat, boots and underwear, then dove under the covers next to Betsy.

When their frolicking was done, Billy laid back against the soft pillow and closed his eyes. It was the best twenty dollars he'd ever spent, he thought. He even considered offering to buy her for the rest of the day, but down deep he knew that they'd be pulling out of town just as soon as the hanging was over and Nikki had picked up more supplies.

The two lay there for a long time, staring up at the ceiling. Billy felt exhausted, and he was still sweating, even though his heart had slowed back to normal. He replayed the last few minutes over and over in his mind, and wondered if Betsy was doing the same thing, or if he was just another dollar to be made and forgotten. It surprised him, then, when she reached out and rubbed the back of her finger gently across his cheek.

"You're hot with the fever," she said. "I hope it ain't something I can catch."

"I ain't got no fever," Billy said. He felt his head. It was sweaty. "I reckon you just got me all steamed up."

Betsy rolled over and felt his chest. "No"—she shook her head—"I noticed it right away. What's this?" she asked, examining the scar in Billy's side where Greasy Abe's knife had left its mark.

Billy grinned, full of brag. "That's where a feller cut me, over in Indian Territory," he said. "But I shot 'im."

Betsy frowned and bent closer to look at his side. "But have you had a doctor look at it? Why, this thing's all full of pus!"

Billy lifted his head and twisted his body to examine the scar. The area was swollen, making it hard to get a close look. He could see that Nikki's stitches were still in, and there were little round dots of pus around them. The scar was sore, all right, but he'd just figured it took that long to heal. "It ain't nothin'," he said, but without much conviction.

Betsy lay her hand over it, then lifted her eyes to meet his. They were filled with genuine concern. "It's all hot and infected. I'm tellin' you, you best see a doctor," she insisted.

Billy saw the compassion on her face, and a feeling welled up inside him and raced through his body. He knew he was in love, and the fact that he loved a whore didn't bother him in the least. This was love. He knew, because he'd felt it before. It had been a year ago, when he met Bernice Loucks, a ranch foreman's daughter up near Ellsworth, Kansas. She had had blond hair and wide blue eyes that smiled every time she looked at him. Billy had taken to volunteering for every errand that had to be run, hoping to get sent to the big house and catch a glimpse of her. He knew that she liked him, too, by the way she smiled at him. Once, she had even made a comment to him about the weather. Billy had made plans to ask her to marry him, but then she had up and married another cowpoke. He and Charlie One Eye had quit the next day, and it had taken some time before he had forgotten. Now, though, even the most loving thoughts of Bernice couldn't compare to the way he felt about Betsy. He felt a sudden urge to propose to her, right then and there, but, in truth, he knew that she would just laugh at him. Still, her concern over his scar made him feel all the warmer inside.

"I'm all right, I tell you," he repeated, pulling her close against him. He closed his eyes, enjoying the softness and warmth of her body, and held his tongue until the urge to ask her to marry him had passed.

Finally, Betsy sighed. "Well, I guess it's your life," she said. "Where are you headed when you leave Fort Smith?" she asked. "Texas?"

"Nope. Goin' to Georgia," he said.

"Georgia? Well, I would of never guessed! I wish I was going somewhere," she said, staring around at the drab furnishings in the little room.

"Too bad I can't take you with me to Georgia."

Billy was shocked himself at his sudden boldness. He gave a small nervous laugh. Maybe, he thought, she would take it as a joke.

Betsy smiled ruefully and said, "If I ever get out of here, Georgia ain't exactly where I want to go. No, maybe Chicago or Denver, or maybe New Orleans. You ever been to any of those places?"

Billy searched for an answer. He felt embarrassed at not having one handy. It always worried him that he might look young and inexperienced in life. "I got close to Denver once," he said.

"Well, someday I intend on getting more than just close," Betsy said wistfully. She suddenly pulled free from Billy's embrace and sat up in the bed, tucking her legs under her. She gestured with her hands as she talked, growing more excited. "You take Chicago. They have fine restaurants and big, fancy homes." She gazed dreamily at Billy, her face all lit up and happy. "I mean, lots of fancy homes. Not like here, where most people live in shanties while only a handful of folks have nice houses. And the theater! I've heard they've got several of those. And the men," she added, "they wear suits with fancy gold watches and chains."

Billy watched her as she rattled off every reason she could think of for living in one of those faraway cities. The shops, the eateries, the entertainment, the crowds of people. None of them sounded like very good reasons to him, but just seeing how her pretty face got to shining as she talked made him fall in love all the more. As he listened to her explain the allure of big-city life, he found it hard to place himself in such a situation and appreciate it the same way she did. It just plain didn't make any sense to him. What would a person want with a big house, lined up next to another big house? It sounded too crowded for his taste. Still, the idea of being in such a place with Betsy made him want to stop and consider.

"Why don't you just up and go?" he asked. "Why don't you pick out a big city, and maybe even git you one of those big houses with the picket fences." Billy couldn't help smiling to himself. He'd seen pictures of houses with picket fences, and the knowledge of such things made him feel worldly.

Betsy smiled and touched his cheek. "You're sweet. You know that? But"—she sighed—"the truth is, I couldn't buy one of those big houses anyway. Even if I made it to one of those places, I wouldn't have the money to do much more than rent a room . . ." Her voice trailed off. She stared past Billy and out the window. Her eyes grew wide and wistful as she realized the futility of her situation.

Billy couldn't stand to see her look so sad. He blurted out, "Well, I'm gonna have enough money to buy a whole city—lock, stock, and barrel, if I've a mind to." He nodded firmly. "And it won't be long, neither!"

Betsy pulled her eyes away from the window. They were doubtful but amused. "What are you gonna do, cowboy? Rob banks?"

"Nope," Billy said, and slid his hands behind his head. "I ain't gonna rob no banks, nor nothin'. And I'll tell you what. If you're still here when I come back from Georgia, I might just buy you the whole dang town of Chicago," he stated.

Betsy held herself back from Billy and watched him closely. "You seem awfully sure of yourself. If you ain't a bank robber, where are you gonna get that kind of money?" she asked. It was apparent that she was starting to take him more seriously, if only to find out more about his braggings. She'd heard this kind of talk before. Too many men would take a small truth and turn it into a mountain of a lie, especially when talking to a sporting woman. She had learned long ago to put on her artificial smile and pretend to be greatly impressed with the tales of grandeur that passed over her bed. Men somehow thought they became more appealing if they told lies about themselves. It didn't even seem to matter that the women they were trying so hard to impress were whores. The bigger the lie, the better. She had reached the conclusion that men were an insecure lot, for the most part. There was something different about Billy, though. Something in the way he talked. The confident gleam in his eyes. She wanted to believe him.

Billy felt her intense stare as she waited for an answer. Her cheeks were flushed a light red. The close attention filled him with pleasure. "In Georgia, you see, I know a place—" he began, then caught himself. He remembered how Holt had scolded him about keeping his mouth shut unless he wanted the whole country in on the hunt. "Well," he said slowly, "let's just leave it at this: I'm fixin' to have more money than you or me or a dozen like us could ever spend."

Betsy leaned over and kissed Billy. She rubbed his forehead and twirled a lock of his hair around her finger. "You cowboys are all alike," she said. "And I was just beginning to like you."

Billy started to say something, but she put her finger over his lips. "Don't lie to me," she said. "Like I say, I was beginning to like you. Let's don't spoil it." She pressed her body close to his.

Billy squirmed free. "I don't reckon I'd be lyin' about such a thing. I don't know about other customers, but you can bet anything that what I tell ya is the truth. And I am goin' to have that much money. More than you'll ever find in Fort Smith," he said, half angrily.

She climbed back on top of him and said, "Whatever you say, cowboy." She kissed him again. "I like you. Let's frolic some more. This one's on me."

Once again, Billy freed himself. He did, indeed, want another frolic in the worst way. In fact, he wanted to spend all of his life holding and frolicking with Betsy.

But it disturbed him deeply that she wasn't taking him seriously. He thought about Holt and his words. Then he remembered that Holt had Katy hanging all over him. And Walter! Why, any fool could see that Nikki had her clamps on him. Suddenly, he felt annoyed at Holt and Walter. Their feelings about women and such were no more important than his. He said, "You don't believe me, do ya?"

"Well," Betsy began, "a cowboy can come in here and say anything. No disrespect, Mister Billy Cordell, but what would you say if I was to tell you that I was fixin' to have more money than I could spend? Now, would you believe me?"

"Well, it's true!" Billy said defensively. His face grew red as the words burst out. "In Georgia, there's a place. Why, there's gold chunks as big as your fist in it! More gold than any banker in Chicago has ever seen. I'll tell ya that!" he added sharply.

Betsy sat up. "I declare! You ain't chasin' some gold story? That one's as old as the hills!" She laughed. "I've had more customers that knew about some lost gold mine, or some friend that knew about one! I reckon if all those stories about Spanish gold and treasures was true, then we'd all retire!"

"Laugh all you want. Everybody else has. But, you see, I've got this Indian chief with me. He was born there. He found this cave, lined with gold. He and his people kept the cave a secret, and then they were forced to leave Georgia. He knows it's there, all right. 'Sides that, he done showed me a sizable chunk of it. Been carryin' it around for years. Now he's an old man, and ready to die, but he wants to go back home to Georgia to do his dyin'. The way I figure it, it's his way of gittin' back at the white man for runnin' 'em off in the first place." Billy shrugged. "But then again, who knows how Injuns think? Anyhow, we're a-takin' him to Georgia in exchange for leadin' us to the cave."

Betsy's eyes widened, and the smile disappeared from her face. Her parents had come from Ellijay, a small town in the mountains of north Georgia. Her father had spent years looking for a so-called cave of gold that the Cherokee had found. She had heard the story all of her life. Suddenly, goose bumps ran up and down her body. "Where in Georgia?" she demanded.

"I don't know where. Just somewhere in north Georgia. Old Chief's gonna show us when we git there." Billy shrugged.

She covered her mouth with her hands, unable to hide her emotions. "My Lord."

Billy wouldn't look at her. He was still smarting over the fact that she doubted him. He said, "I didn't expect you to believe it. But that's all right."

"No, no! You're wrong! I do believe you." Betsy stood up and paced around the room, nervously biting her finger. She swung around to face him. "Take me with you!" she blurted out.

Billy couldn't believe his ears. His heart raced up into his throat as blood rushed to his brain. "I-I don't reckon as how I can do that. You see, there's others," he said. He tried hard to calm himself, biting on his lip until it almost drew blood. He sure didn't want Betsy to think he was some stammering boy. More evenly, he said, "But I will come back for you, and that's a promise."

"What others?" Betsy asked. "I want to go! Please let me go!" she pleaded.

Billy sat up on an elbow. "I thought you didn't believe my story. What changed your mind?"

"I'm from there, Billy. Georgia. When I was a kid, I heard a story about a cave of gold that was found by the Cherokee. Please take me!" Betsy stared at him as if that would make him change his mind.

Billy wanted more than anything on earth to walk out of that room with Betsy in tow. He rubbed his eyes, thinking hard. "Look, I promise, I'll be back." He looked away from her. "I knew the minute I walked in here that I would be back. But it's a long, hard trip, and I've already got my hands full with Chief." His eyes strayed up and down her body, and his resolve weakened. She was, after all, built much like Katy, and Katy certainly didn't seem the worse for wear. "Can you even ride a horse?" he asked doubtfully.

"I'm a fair rider," she said, encouraged by his question.

"What about this Texas Dan what's-his-name?" Billy asked, cocking his head. "That bartender downstairs—Horst? From what he allowed, your Texas friend wouldn't take too kindly to your up and leavin'."

"He's off somewhere in Texas, robbin' banks, I reckon. He only comes here to evade the law over there. But"—Betsy paused—"he's mean and ornery, and he could be a problem for you."

Billy glanced at his Colt, which still lay by the wash basin. "Ain't gonna be no problem for me, less'n he catches me sleepin'."

Betsy leaned one knee on the bed. "You better be good. I mean, real good, with that gun of yours, 'cause Dan Simon is. He'd as soon shoot you in the back while you're sleepin' as look at you."

Billy felt put off by what appeared to be her lack of respect for his own abilities. But then, how was she to know? "Look, that hand of yours couldn't be much of a gunny, 'cause I ain't even heard of 'im. You let me worry about Texas Dan." Billy's chest rose as he spoke. "You got a horse?" he asked.

"No, but I've managed to save a little money," Betsy said.

Billy took her hand and squeezed it. "This is crazy. I don't know what the others are gonna say." He took a deep breath and held it.

Betsy raised an eyebrow. "Why, from the way you talked, I thought you were the boss of things."

Billy said, "There ain't no boss, but, by golly, it was me and Charlie One Eye that found Chief in the first place." He slapped his hand on his leg. "And I reckon if I wanta bring you along, it's my business!"

28

HOLT WAS THE FIRST TO SPOT BILLY RIDING TOWARD them with a fancy-dressed young woman on a sorrel horse beside him. Nikki had just restocked their supplies and packed the wagon. Everyone, including Walter, was ready to leave Fort Smith and the gallows behind. For all of the prehanging excitement that had filled the town, it had quickly turned back into a sleepy little town. As soon as the two men's necks were broken, a silence had fallen over everything. The spectators disappeared, gone back to their homes and day-to-day lives.

"Find yourself a wife there, Billy Boy?" Holt asked, peering at Betsy.

Billy leaned on the saddle horn, nervously looking up from the ground at each of them. "This here's Betsy, and I reckon she's goin' to Georgia with us," he announced.

Holt looked hard at Billy, but only for an instant. "The hell you say? Walter was right. We're apt to turn into a circus troupe before we're done!" He turned his attention to Betsy. "Don't believe I caught a last name," he said.

She said, "Betsy Legg."

Billy couldn't help blushing. He felt stupid for not finding out something as simple as her last name. After all, he had as much as asked her to be his girl. Why else would a man invite a woman to travel halfway across the country with him?

Nikki, who was already in a bad mood from having to wait for Billy, said from her perch on the wagon seat, "Where in blazes did you pick her up at?"

Billy shifted in his saddle. "We met this mornin'," he began.

Nikki broke in. "And I bet I can guess where, from the looks of her! Well, she ain't goin' with us!" she declared.

It was Betsy's turn to blush. She spoke up angrily. "Look here, woman! You'd better watch what you say. You don't know me!"

"I don't know ya, honey, but I've known others like ya. Now, we ain't movin' nowhere"—Nikki looked at the others—"till Billy gets rid of his little saloon tramp!"

Billy had seen plenty of men go to blows before, but the thought of trying to control two fighting females made him even more jittery. "Just hold it a dang minute!" he said, frowning at Nikki. "I reckon she's as much right to go with me as anybody else."

Unfazed, Nikki shook her head stubbornly. "I say we vote on it, and my vote's no!" She glared at Betsy.

"You can take your vote," Billy said, "but she's ridin' with me and Chief. Look, the only reason you sisters wanted to come along was 'cause of Holt and Walter. And don't you deny it. Any dang fool could see that! I mean, Katy spends every spare minute with Holt. And Walter up in that wagon with a broken nose! Why, you'd think he got a leg shot off or somethin', the way you make over him!"

That made Nikki even more angry. She put a hand on her hip and opened her mouth to say something, but Holt jumped in between them.

"Whoa!" He held up his hand. "Now, let's hold on here a minute! Why, I reckon Billy's got a right to bring along a lady friend if he'd like. But I think we'd better set some rules down, right now. He turned to Charlie One Eye with a poker face. "You need a lady friend, Charlie?"

Charlie One Eye, who had been as surprised as anyone about Billy's impetuous move, gave Holt a blank look.

"Hell, Charlie, say something! Let's work this out, right now! Do you want to find you a lady friend to bring along?" Holt persisted.

"You mean, to ride with us to Georgia?" Charlie One Eye took off his hat and rubbed his hand over his head.

"Why, hell, Charlie, what do you think we're talkin' about here, anyway? If you need a lady companion, right now's the time to speak up," Holt said.

Charlie One Eye glanced first at Nikki, then at Billy. What would he want a female riding companion for? If was the most absurd idea he'd ever heard. "I'd vote with Billy," he said finally, "but I don't reckon that I need one for myself."

"Fine. Charlie One Eye's out of the way. What about Chief, there? Whoa! Chief! You need a squaw to ride back to Georgia with?"

The old Indian's eyes twinkled. "No. When I meet the Great Spirit, I will meet Him alone. I am old. Too old to do a squaw any good."

The old man had been silent for so long, his words seemed to jolt everyone out of their thoughts. They all stared at him for a moment. Holt pulled his eyes away from him and said to Nikki, "There we have it. Everybody's had their chance. The woman can go. Now, maybe we can drop the subject and move on."

Nikki wasn't satisfied with the situation one bit. Angrily, she whipped the team, and would have run Billy and Betsy over if they hadn't yanked on their horses' reins and hurried out of the way.

Holt and Katy followed the wagon. Charlie One Eye, who rode with Chief alongside him, wordlessly waited with Billy until he had calmed down Betsy's sorrel horse. Billy held the horse's bit. "You think you can handle your horse now?" he asked Betsy.

"Better than I can handle that woman in the wagon," she said dryly.

"We better git along, then," Billy said softly.

When they passed the saloon, Horst the bartender was standing inside the door. He waved, but there was a sadness about him. He, too, had fallen in love with Betsy, but the wisdom of age had taught him how to let go of such things. It would be nice, not having Texas Dan Simon scaring his customers anymore—that is, if the outlaw didn't take a shine to another one of Horst's sporting ladies. He tried to think of Betsy's leaving as a relief, but that didn't stop the deep pain that pierced his heart. He stood there and watched her until she was just a dot at the far end of the street.

Very little conversation was made for the next few days as the group traveled east out of Fort Smith. There seemed to be a need felt by everyone to have a moment to think about all that had happened to them, and to consider the possibilities that lay ahead.

Nikki wasn't concerned about any cave full of gold in her future as much as she was about Betsy. It made her mad, plain and simple, to have the woman along. She realized that her feelings didn't make much sense. After all, she had gotten closer to Walter than she'd ever dreamed of being. Something about Betsy, though, filled her with jealousy every time she looked at her. Betsy wasn't just any female; in fact, she was about as handsome a woman as Nikki had ever seen. It turned her stomach sour to think that Walter might take a shine to Betsy, even though Walter never shined much to any females at all. She didn't say anything about it that might irritate Walter, but kept a watchful eye to make sure Betsy didn't get too close to the wagon.

Riding among such mute company for the last couple of days was suiting Walter just fine. It gave him time to think without having to be interrupted by someone else's bull. Nikki was as attentive as ever, but she said very little, and that suited him also. He was getting a bit tired of riding in the wagon. It was stuffy, and the ride was far from smooth, but the truth was, he just couldn't talk himself into leaving it. He had gotten used to lying back out of the sun, and not having to hold himself up in a saddle all day. Besides that, the back pain he'd suffered from being on horseback was now gone. No sense, he decided, in giving up the pleasures just yet.

Holt and Katy maintained the silence, but there was no brooding feeling between them. They didn't seem to have a worry in life at all. Often they would exchange friendly glances, and, when they got bored, they would put spur to their mounts and lope ahead of the wagon. Sometimes they would put miles between them, then sit and wait for the others to catch up. Holt had taken along a small-bore, single-shot rifle, and he would grab it when he and Katy went on their forays. They had ridden into squirrel country, and each evening when the group would find them, Holt would have a half dozen or so hanging from his saddle. No one had a word of complaint for such a supper.

Charlie One Eye could skin a squirrel as quick as a barn cat can cat a mouse. He passed the meat on to Nikki, who would fry up the whole lot, then make a big pan of gravy and Dutch oven biscuits.

Although everyone had settled into his own world of thought since leaving Fort Smith, nothing had dampened their appetites. They ate Nikki's evening meals appreciatively, until not even the tiniest scrap was left.

Billy was the only exception. He stopped Nikki at half a plateful, then only picked at his supper. He was too deeply in love with Betsy to think about food. He could hardly pull his eyes from her. His stomach didn't help matters any. It had such a case of the flutters, he was afraid it would reject too much of Nikki's rich cooking. The only thing he could concentrate on was this woman who had surprised him by asking to go along with him, all the way to Georgia. Each night, while the others sat quietly, sipping their coffee, Billy would take hold of her hand, and they would slip off by themselves. As the two figures left the dim glow of the campfire, the others would watch them disappear into the darkness, but no one said a word.

29

WILFORD HAD FOUND HIMSELF A GOOD PIECE OF WOOD. He sat in front of the open window, whittlin', with the breeze cooling his face nicely. At his feet was a pile of shavings. As he carved at a fair pace, the head of a longhorn steer was already visible, perfectly shaped with the horns curving at just the right angle. It was the first peaceful moment he could recall enjoying for what seemed like weeks. He let his mind stray to pleasant subjects like settling down on a nice, quiet spread in Texas. Maybe things would work out, and he could still retire, like he and Harbin had planned. Or there might be some other sleepy little town that could use a sheriff. He could find him a place that wasn't bothered by outlaws and such, and volunteer his services. It wasn't as good a notion as retiring in Texas, but at least he could make a living and still enjoy his small pleasures.

He was just starting to think about lunch when there was a movement in the room. He nearly jumped as he realized that someone had walked up beside him. That someone was Joe Harbin.

"My goodness! What are you doin' out of bed?" Wilford said, startled.

Joe Harbin looked for all the world to Wilford like walking death. He had lost so much weight, his ribs poked through his skin and his cheeks were sucked in. His color was still ashen, and his eyes were sunken with big black semi-circles underneath.

"You best git back in bed," Wilford said. "That doctor from Coffeyville said you need all the bed rest you can git."

Harbin stood there a moment, staring down at Wilford. He finally said, "A man could die in bed, and I ain't fixin' to. 'Sides, I feel pretty good." The effort of speaking, however, left him breathless. "If you don't mind," he began, then took in a deep breath, "I'll borrow your chair. And pull that night table over here in the light."

Wilford moved swiftly. He kicked aside the shavings and retrieved the table, placing it closer to the window. He stepped back and glanced curiously at Harbin, who stood with his face toward the window. Thinking maybe Harbin was waiting for him to do something else, he pulled out the chair. Still, Harbin just stood there, staring. After waiting a bit longer, Wilford said, "Here you go, Joe. Let me help ya into the chair."

"I don't need no help," Harbin said. With an effort, he moved slowly to the chair and sat down. His body shook a little. "That's a lie. I guess I am pretty weak," he admitted. A coughing spell overtook him for a moment. When he had recovered, he wiped his watery eyes on his sleeve and pointed. "Over there, in my shirt, there's a pad and pencil. Would you git 'em for me?" he asked.

Wilford found the paper and pencil and placed them on the table. Harbin nodded, then said, "Now, go on downstairs and ask Mrs. Beavers for an envelope."

When Wilford returned, Harbin had a piece of paper folded in his hand. He struggled trying to put it inside the envelope. Wilford knew that Harbin was a very sick man. So sick, in fact, that the doctor had told him that his friend would most likely never make it out of the bed. Still, it was shocking to see those once-deft hands fumbling with the envelope. They were hands that once could pull leather and squeeze a trigger before most men had time to blink. Now they reminded Wilford of his grandma, whose hands had curled up in her old age and shook when she tried to use them.

"Here," Harbin said, handing Wilford the envelope.

"Who do you want me to give it to, Joe?" Wilford asked.

"You keep it. If somethin' happens to me, open it."

"Sure, Joe," Wilford said, puzzled, as he shoved the envelope into his pocket. It was a strange request, he thought, but even in Joe's sick condition, Wilford was not about to question him.

Harbin spent the rest of the day sitting beside the window. He even managed to run Mrs. Beavers out of the room when she scolded him for being out of bed and complained about Wilford's wood shavings. The same routine followed the next day. On his third day out of bed, Harbin walked around the room several times. He would sit for a while, then get up and walk some more. On the fourth day, he managed to walk downstairs and sit out front on Mrs. Beavers's porch. For the next two weeks, each day brought more activity, and Harbin began to regain his strength.

Each bit of progress that Harbin made was a source of amazement to Wilford. But none of that prepared him for the next amazement to enter his world. He and Harbin had walked across the street to Hap's Eatery. They had just sat down to dine on beefsteak and potatoes. Harbin hadn't said much that day. He seemed to be heavy in thought about something, so Wilford had let him be, intending to enjoy his dinner instead of any conversation.

Harbin ate awhile in silence, then suddenly put down his fork. "I'm gonna give you some money. I want you to pay up our bill at the livery and Mrs. Beavers's. We're gonna ride out in the mornin'," he said.

Wilford had just started to put a big bite of beefsteak in his mouth. He stopped with his fork in mid-air. "Move out? Where?"

"I still got that reward to collect on one Jesse James," Harbin said, digging his fork back into his plate.

Wilford, who had attempted to commence eating, pulled the bite of meat back out of his mouth and stared. He couldn't believe what he was hearing. He had assumed that, if Harbin did somehow recover well enough to travel, they would just move on down toward that ranch in San Antone. He'd completely given up on Harbin's chase after Jesse James. Anything that ambitious would be impossible. And dangerous.

"Why, Joe, I reckon that would be a foolhardy thing to do, what with your bad heart, and all," he said with a worried frown.

"Foolhardy or not, I intend to catch 'im, then retire. We'll ride over into Missouri and try to pick up a scent there," Harbin announced.

The next morning, the men paid Mrs. Beavers and the livery what they owed. Then, true to his word, Joe Harbin climbed atop his big gelding. Wilford watched him, carefully trying to detect any weakness in the man, but couldn't. Outside of the fact that he moved a little bit slower and his frame was several pounds lighter, Joe Harbin, once he'd strapped on his big Colt, looked for all the world to be the same fearless bounty man that Wilford had always known.

They were just fixing to give spur to their mounts when a voice behind them called out.

"Hold on! Don't leave yet!"

They turned around to see Quinton Rakestraw running toward them, waving his arm. They glanced curiously at each other.

When Rakestraw reached them, he gasped, "Boy, am I glad I ran into Mrs. Beavers when I did! She told me you two were fixin' to leave!" As he spoke, he handed up a small box to Harbin.

"What's this?" Harbin asked.

"We found it among Alfie Nicholas's personal belongings," Rakestraw explained.

Harbin opened the box and stared inside for a moment, then looked doubtfully back at Rakestraw.

Rakestraw nodded. "Yes, sir. There's more'n two thousand dollars in that box."

"Two thousand dollars?" Wilford cried. "Where'd that crazy woman git that kind of money?"

"Your guess is as good as mine," Rakestraw said. "I guess Cheyenne Bob Calloway and that other feller they hung missed this box. We found it in a little compartment under the wagon. It was dang lucky, too. Anyway, I figure her horse and wagon will cover any funeral expenses. Mrs. Beavers took the clothing and personal belongings. Said she could make quilts outa the dresses. As for the money, I sent telegraphs out, and, far as I can tell, she didn't have any relatives to be found. So, I guess it's rightly yours as much as anybody's."

Wilford's spirits turned from excited to sad. He thought about Alfie, sitting in the creek and teasing him with her naked body looking so inviting. He remembered how he had run Mrs. Beavers and Rakestraw away from the wagon, only to find it gone the next day. He'd been angry over the fact that they had been so nosy about the wagon. But then, the thought occurred, what would he have done with it? He may have driven the wagon for several days, but in truth it didn't belong to him any more than anyone else. He watched Harbin turn the box of money over in his hands. This sudden windfall made him feel more kindly toward Rakestraw. Even Mrs. Beavers, who Wilford had thought didn't have a kindly bone in her body, might deserve some reconsideration. It suddenly occurred to him that maybe she wasn't so kindly. Wilford's eyes narrowed. He wondered how much money she had taken out of the box before it reached Rakestraw's hands.

His thoughts were broken when Harbin held out the box and said, "This money's not ours. We didn't do nothin' more than bring her into town. You sure she doesn't have any family anywheres?"

Rakestraw shook his head. "You got more of a right to it than anybody else," he insisted. "The sheriff over in Coffeyville wired me that he never knew of any family. So take it. It's yours."

"Well, we're thankin' you, then," Harbin said. "Here"—he turned to Wilford—"I reckon you earned this." He tossed the box to Wilford, nodded to Rakestraw, then gave spur to the big red gelding.

Wilford caught the box high on his chest. He nearly fell off his horse. He was so stunned by this turn of events, he sat there, frozen in his saddle, clutching the box up against him. He sat there so long, in fact, that Quinton Rakestraw looked up at him with a puzzled expression.

"You're not going with Mr. Harbin?" he asked.

Wilford's head jerked to attention. He looked east, where Joe Harbin was putting distance between them. He grinned at Rakestraw. "Are you kiddin'?" He kicked his horse, and was nearly at full gallop when he turned back around, waved his hat, and hollered, "We got us an outlaw to catch, by the name of Jesse James!"

30

WILFORD AND HARBIN RODE FOR DAYS WITHOUT SEEing another soul. The solitude suited them both; so much so, in fact, that they kept their conversations to a minimum. Harbin knew that Wilford still had his questions about the ranch in Texas to be answered, but he was too busy thinking about the job that had to be done first.

They had just barely crossed into Missouri when they came across two men on horseback. Harbin spotted them while they were still a ways off in the distance.

They were riding straight toward Harbin and Wilford. As they drew closer, the men's hands edged carefully toward their revolvers, which were shoved into their britches.

It was the man in the lead who first recognized Joe Harbin. He pulled up and waited until they were within twenty paces, then said, "Why, Joe Harbin. I do believe you're out of your usual huntin' grounds, ain't ya?" His words had a friendly tone, but there was a noticeable nervousness in his eyes.

Harbin recognized the two. Simmie Yoakum and Harley Boren had once ridden with Jesse James. "Is that you, Simmie?" he asked. He casually reached into his pocket for a fixin'. He rolled the smoke with his fingers, keeping his gaze fixed on the pair.

"It's me all right, Joe. Me and Harley Boren. You remember Harley, don't ya? You should, seein' as how you're the reason he spent better'n three years locked up like a dern animal," Simmie said with a dry grin.

"I remember," Harbin said. He slowly licked his fixin', paused, and lit it. The big gelding under him pranced a step or two as he took a deep draw, his steely eyes locked on the men. "You boys can relax. I ain't got no reason to be callin' on you at this time."

Simmie Yoakum's eyes flickered at Harley Boren and back. He said, "Why, we are relaxed, Joe. We were just moseying along. Ain't got a thing to hide."

"I doubt if that's true," Harbin said. "Why else would you ride up with your hands on them revolvers?" He looked down at their waists. Both men had not one but two revolvers stuck in their britches. "Don't you boys ever worry about your horses gettin' skittish? Hell, if they was to buck, you'd likely shoot your blamed peckers off."

Simmie Yoakum gave a small laugh at the comment, but Harley Boren puffed up and glared sullenly at Harbin. He found nothing funny about the situation. He didn't like Joe Harbin one bit. He didn't care who knew the fact, but at the same time, he also knew better than to cross the man. He sat on his horse and hoped his silent stare would say enough.

"Now, we ain't done nothin', mind you, but if it ain't us you're lookin' for, what brings you to Mizzou?" Simmie Yoakum asked.

Harbin drew on his fixin' and squinted through the smoke. "Like I said, I ain't got no business with you two, but I reckon I could haul you in, and I'd bet there'd be somebody willin' to pay a dollar or two for a couple o' scamps like you. I'm sure there's some charges pendin' somewheres," he said, then added, "You men could give me some help, though. We're lookin' for Jesse."

Simmie Yoakum laughed at that. "Why, hell's fire, Joe! I would imagine there ain't a lawman west of the Mississippi that ain't looking for Jesse and Frank!" He relaxed, feeling better knowing that Joe Harbin had no interest in himself or Harley Boren.

"When did you boys last see the Jameses?" Harbin asked.

"To tell you the truth," Simmie Yoakum said as he tucked a plug of tobacco in his jaw, "it's been part near a year since I seen any of those boys. I can tell you for sure, ever since that ordeal up in Minnesota, they've been scarce around these parts! Those detectives from Chicago have fanned out all over Mizzou, looking for Jesse and Frank." He shook his head and spat.

"What ordeal in Minnesota are you talkin' about?" Harbin asked with a puzzled look.

Simmie Yoakum's eyes widened. "You must be puttin' me on! Why, Jesse and the Youngers robbed some dern bank up there! Hell, they got all shot up by the town! Killed three or four of 'em and caught Cole and his brothers!" He wiped his mouth with his hand and gave a disbelieving look. "Can you imagine, a bunch of blamed farmers catching the Youngers and killin' the rest of the gang?"

"What happened to Jesse?" Harbin asked, unable to hide his concern.

Simmie Yoakum shrugged. "I guess they got away. 'Course, ain't nobody proved they were there in the first place. I was talkin' to one of their cousins about a week ago. He just got back from Texas, and claimed he saw Frank and Jesse headin' toward Nashville."

Harbin looked hard at Simmie Yoakum, so hard he caused Simmie to look away. It was inevitable that someday, someone was going to catch up with the gang, but it was still difficult to believe that the Youngers had been captured. It was no surprise that Jesse and Frank had slipped away from the law once again. Harbin felt selfishly glad. Jesse's being seen in Texas? That was hard to figure. Maybe it was the threat of the Texas Rangers, or maybe it was the existence of men like himself, but for some reason the James brothers hadn't tried many dealings in Texas.

Finally, he repeated, mostly to himself, "Nashville, you say?"

"That's what his cousin said." Simmie Yoakum nodded. "Said Jesse was goin' to Nashville, then on up to Kentuck."

"You shut your stinkin' mouth!" Harley Boren shouted angrily. He was clearly mad at Simmie Yoakum's loose tongue. "Ain't none of your business to be tellin' Jesse's whereabouts to a blamed bounty man!" His eyes refused to meet Joe Harbin's gaze, but his words were full of harsh meaning.

"Relax," Simmie Yoakum said. "Ain't no bounty hunter from Texas goin' to catch Jesse!"

"Never mind that," Harley Boren said as he finally looked at Harbin. "Look. I done my time on account of you. I don't owe you a dern thing. 'Sides that, people around here wouldn't take too kindly to us siccin' the dogs on Jesse's trail."

"Put your mind at ease, Harley. You ain't responsible for nothin' I do. Come on, Wilford," Harbin said as he pushed his big gelding right between the two men, splitting the pair as he rode through. The men let them pass through, too surprised to comment.

They rode northeasterly, until they were completely out of the two men's sight. When he was sure they weren't being watched or followed, Harbin pulled the red gelding southward, then gave it spur. Wilford wondered what crazy thoughts must be going through Harbin's mind, but he followed anyway. They rode hard for about ten minutes, before Harbin slowed to a lope. When Wilford had worked his horse alongside Harbin's, he hollered.

"You surely didn't believe them fellers back there? Why, they're more'n likely sendin' us on a wild goose chase!"

Harbin just smiled without answering. They rode on for another two hours before they stopped at a farmhouse. There, Harbin made arrangements to stable the horses and bed themselves down in the barn for the night. Then he tipped his hat to the farmer's wife, and soon she was offering them an evening meal. She proved to be an excellent cook, and the men ate until they could barely walk away from the table. It was well after they'd eaten and bade the farmer and his wife good night, when Harbin finally decided to answer Wilford's question. They had spread their bedrolls and were lighting up a final smoke, when Harbin leaned back with his head on his saddle.

"Simmie Yoakum told us the truth all right," he said softly. "He owed me a favor or two from way back. That's not to say that his information was accurate. He told me the truth as he knew it. You can count on that."

Wilford scratched his head. He was sleepy after eating such a fine big meal. Besides, Harbin had let the subject of Jesse James hang there all day, so long that Wilford had lost interest. Now, he just wanted to forget all about this Jesse James business and head on down to that ranch near San Antone. "Why do we have to go after Jesse at all?" he asked. "This here money"—he reached out and patted his saddlebag—"I want to throw it in on the ranch. Pay my share of the load." He felt good about his newfound wealth and the fact that he could help pay their way to retirement. Chasing after Jesse James just wasn't necessary.

Harbin looked at Wilford's hopeful expression. He knew the man was right. He, too, would have liked to just ride on down to San Antone, buy the ranch and run a few beeves. Forget about chasing down outlaws. In that moment, many thoughts raced through Harbin's mind at once. For one thing, the ordeal he had just gone through back in Crawford had brought his own mortality to the front. For another, getting right back on the trail was showing him just how weak the sickness had left him. Part of the reason he had refused to talk to Wilford was that he just didn't have the will or the energy to talk and ride at the same time. It worried him to the point that he was having self-doubts. He started to wonder whether he could even stand up and make an account of himself if he did ever find the elusive Jesse

James. Still, he carried the doubts with him as a driving force. It was the final chance for a man who had spent his life perched on the thin line between life and death. He would fill the final chapter with one last great effort before he closed the book. It occurred to Harbin that he might be losing his sanity, wavering between such thoughts. Maybe he had been too successful for too long, in a trade where only the elite survived. Maybe, but it didn't really matter.

He squashed his smoke and said, "Look, Wilford. I want to play out this one last card on Jesse. Maybe Simmie Yoakum did give us some bad information. If he did, we might just come up empty. Then maybe—" He stopped, looking off into the dark corners of the barn. He was having a difficult time saying what came next. "Hell, if we come up empty, then we'll head toward San Antone." Abruptly, he turned away from Wilford and closed his eyes.

The promise seemed to have a soothing effect on Wilford, for soon after he was sleeping like a baby. He dreamed about a house with a porch and a rocking chair. Nearby was plenty of wood for whittlin'. In his dreams, they even hired a cook who filled the table with heaping platters of the finest food Wilford had ever eaten.

Sleep came early for Joe Harbin, too, but it was not restful. The nightmare was waiting. In it, Harbin fired his Colt at the faceless foe, and felt the sting of lead rip into his own body. Again, he lay wounded in the dusty street. This time, however, there were no townspeople. It was only the two of them. Then the foe came to stand over him, and began to reload his revolver. Harbin could only lie there and wait helplessly. As he watched, the face slowly began to come into focus. The lips were curved into a sneer. Harbin lifted his stunned gaze and stared into eyes that blinked constantly. The gun was reloaded, and pointed at his face. The shot echoed through the streets of the nameless town.

When he came violently awake, sweating and clutching at his chest, Harbin knew he had just looked into the face of Jesse James.

31

TEXAS DAN SIMON HAD WORN OUT TWO HORSES RACING to Fort Smith. In fact, one of them, a gray mare, had just collapsed and died a few hours before. It annoyed him to have to track down a replacement when he was in a hurry. He was running from a posse that was pursuing him for robbing a bank and killing three people inside. It hadn't been necessary. They were just cruel-hearted, non-felt killings.

When he rode up to the front of the saloon on the sore-footed chestnut, it was nearly closing time. Texas Dan pulled his Winchester from its scabbard and strode inside. At the bar, he flung a dollar at Horst, the bartender.

"Have your boy take care of that sweaty chestnut outside, he said, and headed for the staircase.

Horst let Texas Dan get to the third step before he got the nerve to stop him. "Betsy's not up there," he said. Quickly, he reached behind the bar, poured himself a drink, and swallowed it down.

Texas Dan turned and gave Horst a look that all the whiskey in Fort Smith couldn't soften. "Well, then, where's she at?"

"I-I don't know. Sh-she left with a feller a few days ago," Horst faltered.

The anger in Texas Dan's face could have heated the room in the coldest of winter. He whirled around at the sound of a chair scraping across the floor. There was only one customer left in the saloon at the late hour. A young, broad-shouldered farmer who lived on the outskirts of town had been nursing his last beer. Earlier, he had challenged several men with his big fists, and he was still feeling smug about it. At the sight of Texas Dan's glare, though, the big farm boy quickly recovered from his drunken stupor and made a fast exit, knocking over a table and several chairs as he did so.

Texas Dan climbed back down the stairs and walked to the bar. Horst stood behind it, clutching the bottle he'd drunk from and hoping that Texas Dan wouldn't blame him for Betsy's leaving. Texas Dan had wicked eyes that showed through, even when he smiled. There was no smile now, though, and in Texas Dan's angry state, Horst felt like he was looking at the devil himself, and that scared him even more. As he raised his glass to his lips, his hand was shaking to the point where he had to steady it with his other hand to keep the rye whiskey from splashing over his arm.

Texas Dan planted himself directly in front of Horst and laid a hand menacingly over his Winchester. "Now, then," he said, "where did the bitch go, and who did she leave with?"

Horst shook his head. There were beads of sweat forming on his forehead. He said, "I swear, I don't know his name. Just some young cowboy who come in here. Looked like he might be from Texas. H-h-he was just a cowboy. A young one, at that."

Horst was holding on to the top of the bar to keep himself from shaking so badly. His grip was so tight, his knuckles showed white. He had just finished speaking, and didn't even have time to blink, let alone pull his hands free, before Texas Dan, like a sudden bolt of lightning, raised his fist and smashed it onto Horst's hand.

The pain that shot up Horst's arm was terrifying. He looked, disbelieving, at the big knife that Texas Dan had buried into the back of his hand. He felt as if he might faint from the pain and the raw fear that gripped him. Blood trickled out onto the bar from around the edges of the knife where it protruded from his flattened hand. Soon, there was a red pool around his hand, which was growing numb.

Texas Dan said through clenched teeth, "Now, don't make me ask again. Where'd she go?"

Horst was so frightened, he didn't know if the words would come out or not, but he knew he'd better make an effort. He said, "I swear on my mother's grave! All I know is she left with the cowboy and headed east, like they was goin' to Little Rock!"

Texas Dan yanked on the handle of the big knife. When the point came free from the wood under Horst's hand, he pulled on it again. The blade sliced forward, splitting the flesh all the way through the back of Horst's hand, and exiting between his middle fingers. Blood spewed, splattering huge drops across the bar as Horst screamed in pain.

Texas Dan walked to the door, turned, and gave Horst a disgusted sneer. He said, "I should kill you. In fact, when I come back, I'm gonna do just that." He turned back around and stared out at the street.

Horst stood there mute, cradling his hand and holding his fingers together. Blood ran down to his elbow, then dripped to the floor. At his knees, under the bar, was a sawed-off double-barrel shotgun. He wanted so badly to have the nerve to reach under and get the gun and blow Texas Dan Simon to kingdom come. He wanted to do it for Betsy and for himself. Maybe that was what Texas Dan wanted him to try, he thought. Maybe that would give Texas Dan an excuse to kill him, even though Texas Dan didn't seem to need a reason for any of the things he did. Whether Texas Dan was baiting him or not, though, Horst flat didn't have the nerve to go for his shotgun.

Texas Dan pushed through the saloon's swinging doors and climbed back atop the beaten chestnut. He dug his spurs into her bloody flanks. The chestnut tried to run. It panted and dug at the earth under it. The poor horse had no way of knowing what impatience and anger sat atop it. Not more than a hundred yards from the saloon, a pair of horses was tied in front of another saloon. There Texas Dan pulled violently on the chestnut's reins, the bit cutting deeply into its already tender and bleeding mouth. He dismounted, taking only his money-laden saddlebag and his Winchester. He flung his saddlebag across a roan horse and climbed atop. The roan reared and started to buck, but Texas Dan slammed the handle of his Colt as hard as he could, catching the roan between the ears. The confused animal settled down some, but Texas Dan was not satisfied. Before he left Fort Smith, he gave one final show of his wrath. Drawing his Colt, he turned and fired a round of hot steel into the eye of the chestnut. He briefly let his eyes sweep over the empty street before he galloped away.

The roan's gait was rough, causing Texas Dan to keep a constant curse going. He felt so angry, he wanted to ride back and shoot the chestnut again for pulling up lame on him. If he didn't have Betsy to find, he would also like to return to Fort Smith and kill Horst. He was angry at himself for letting the man live, but he decided he could take care of that matter later.

He rode through the night, spitting and cursing. His body was tired, but Texas Dan wouldn't allow it to interfere with his mission. The morning dew was heavy, and a light fog crept down from the sky, almost mingling with the moisture on the ground.

It was in the silver wetness that Texas Dan rode up on a farmer. The man was working at repairing a fence. A couple of fine horses grazed on the lush pasture grass.

"How do, neighbor?" the farmer said when Texas Dan had ridden within speaking distance.

Texas Dan gave the man a cold stare. "I'm hungry," he said.

The farmer smiled. "Ain't got nothin' but cornbread and buttermilk, but you're welcome to it," he said. "Come on and follow me up to the house."

Texas Dan climbed down off the roan. Walking behind the farmer, he fixed his eyes on the two horses that stood grazing.

At the house, the farmer's wife hurried out to greet the visitor. She was young, probably young enough to be the farmer's daughter. She studied Texas Dan with an openness that surprised him. Her eyes carried a lean and hungry look to them. For all of his evil ways, Texas Dan was considered handsome by the ladies.

He dispensed with any exchange of pleasantries. Instead, he stepped over a chair and wolfed down the cornbread and buttermilk. He accepted second helpings of both before he had had his fill. All the while, his eyes continued to roam over the young woman's curves. She didn't seem to mind, and the farmer didn't notice, but Texas Dan wouldn't have cared regardless.

Finally, he pulled his eyes from the woman and looked at the farmer, who sat across the table from him, sipping a cup of coffee. He said, "I'm lookin' for a woman. About the size of yourn. Got blond hair and pretty features. Goes by the name of Betsy. She's travelin' with a young cowpoke."

The farmer scratched his chin. "Well, to tell you the truth, I can't say I didn't see her. A while back, there was a lady that fit that description, all right. She was with a cowboy, too, but they was travelin' with a couple other females and some other cowboys. Had an old Indian with 'em, too. They spent the night here. Don't recall nobody bein' called Betsy, but there was one gal who sure fit your description." Glancing to see that his wife's back was to them, the farmer turned and winked at Texas Dan. "Fact bein's, all three of the ladies was purty ones."

Texas Dan gave him a cold stare. "They say where they was headin'?"

"Not rightly. Said somethin' about goin' to Georgia, or maybe it was Alabam. Don't rightly recall. Nice folks, though. Well"—the farmer drained his coffee cup and stood up—"the chores ain't gonna do themselves." He walked outside.

Texas Dan looked into the eyes of the young wife. She held his gaze for several seconds. Finally, he rose from the table and went to the door.

The farmer was walking across his front yard. Slowly, Texas Dan pulled his Colt and walked to the edge of the porch. The farmer turned and smiled, and was just about to speak, when Texas Dan raised his arm and fired.

There was a scream behind him, and Texas Dan turned to the young wife, who stood in the doorway. The gleam that he had noticed in her eyes was gone, replaced by dark fear.

"You shut up," he said. He grabbed her by the arm and flung her back inside, then dragged her to her bed. She said nothing, but cried silently as he had his way.

When he had finished, he fell asleep, still sprawled atop the woman. He awoke to a warm afternoon sun, and found the woman outside, weeping over her dead husband.

"I'm hungry," he said crossly. When he got no response, he walked over and grabbed her by the hair, pulling her face to his. "I said I'm hungry."

The woman slowly got to her feet and went to the house. Texas Dan wanted meat, so she fried bacon to go along with the cornbread and buttermilk. He forced her to sit at the table with him while he ate heartily. When he had finished, he ravaged her once again.

He left her there on the bed alone, to deal with her suffering. Outside, he unsaddled the roan and threw a rope on the finer of the farmer's two horses.

He didn't look back. The farmer and his wife were easily forgotten by Texas Dan Simon as he rode east. There was a pretty woman to be found, and a cowboy that needed to die.

32

THEY WERE A FEW MILES OUTSIDE OF LITTLE ROCK WHEN Holt began to notice that something was wrong with Billy. He and Betsy had spent most of the time alone, riding off by themselves, and no one had noticed how wavery his riding had become. Besides that, Billy was usually so cocksure and full of himself, the others had learned not to pay any attention to him. It surprised Holt, then, when he got his first close look at Billy that evening.

They had just made camp for the night, with plans to ride into Little Rock at mid-morning the next day. Billy seemed to take longer than usual dismounting. He sat atop his horse and watched the others for a moment, then slowly pulled a leg over and climbed down. It took such an effort, he started breathing hard, and his leg buckled under him. Betsy had to grab his arm to give him support.

The mere fact that Billy, who was a fine horseman, had trouble mounting and dismounting concerned Holt deeply. He said, "You're not lookin' well, a-tall."

Billy said, "I'm all right," but his words lacked any strength or emotion behind them. He tried to brush aside Betsy's efforts to help unsaddle his horse. Betsy, though, took the animal firmly by the reins and pulled it over to where she could work by herself.

Holt put his hand to Billy's head. "Why, hell, Billy Boy! You're burnin' up with fever!" he said.

"Ain't nothin' wrong with me," Billy insisted. He pulled himself away and sat down against a tree. He looked thoroughly upset with the situation that had left him helpless and dependent on a woman. Betsy tended to his horse, then hurried to sit close by his side.

Holt decided to let the subject drop for the time being, since Billy was too stubborn to admit that he wasn't as strong as a bull. All during the evening meal, though, he kept a close eye on Billy. Tomorrow they would find a doctor, he decided. Like it or not, Billy was going to get some medical attention.

The next morning, Holt tried without success to get Billy to ride in the wagon. Chief had once again taken to occupying it, since Walter had improved to the point that he was back on his horse. Billy would have none of the wagon business, however. But, with Little Rock being only a few miles ahead, Holt allowed Billy his stubbornness and said nothing more about the matter.

As they neared the town, Holt kept a watchful eye on Billy and Betsy. Billy looked weaker than ever, if that was possible. His pale skin was red and chafed, and he was sweating much too heavily for such a cool morning. As he rode, it was apparently becoming harder for him to hold up his head. Betsy kept having to reach out and steady him. Finally, it got to the point where Betsy had to leave her mount and ride double with him. Billy didn't even utter a word of protest. He was too sick to show any embarrassment.

Holt had to admit that he was feeling a lot better about Betsy. He was glad, too. It wasn't his nature to be judgmental about people's feelings and their dealings with each other. The truth was, in the beginning he had shared Nikki's skepticism. Why else would a beautiful sporting woman take up with Billy so quickly? He had suspected one of two things. Either Betsy was looking for a way out of Fort

Smith and had happened upon an able and obliging sort in Billy, or he had told her about the gold, and she was looking to get her share of the take.

After they had left Fort Smith, though, Holt had had a lot of time to observe Betsy and do some reconsidering. There was something warm and genuine in the way Betsy cared for Billy—the way she looked at him like her heart was in it. He hated to let his guard down, especially where females were concerned, but Holt had to give Betsy her due. Granted, some of this might have something to do with the way his own feelings were changing. Since his youth, Holt had always attracted females. He had managed to keep his senses about him; that is, until Katy Trapp had come along. Early on, he had been strongly attracted to her, but his visits to the Trapp establishment had been so few and far in between, his feelings toward Katy had always had time to cool. Now, he didn't know. Every time he would look at Katy, funny things would happen to his insides. The word "love" had formed on his lips only once, but it was starting to etch itself into his heart. This scared him some, but these days, the way he felt when he was with her, he didn't care if he was falling too deeply or not.

When they reached Little Rock, it took little time to locate a doctor. Holt ordered everyone except Betsy and Katy to stay outside. He didn't want to have Betsy and Nikki together in the same place any more than he had to. His worries, however, proved to be unnecessary. Nikki wanted to do some shopping on her own, and Walter, Charlie One Eye, and Chief quickly set out for the nearest place to buy themselves some good whiskey. Together, Holt, Katy, and Betsy got Billy into the doctor's office.

Dr. Elmore Hobbs was a young man, and a talkative sort. He led Billy to a long, draped table and helped him lie down, but instead of beginning his examination, he just kept talking. The four waited patiently while he made his introductions.

Dr. Hobbs was a Philadelphia man. He had once had every intention of hanging his shingle in Colorado. "I've been told that nights in Colorado are cool in the summertime," he said. "Good sleeping weather. And even though the winters are cold, I hear it's a dry cold. Now, I could tolerate that. Those Pennsylvania winters, on the other hand"—he shivered—"they're a wet, bitter cold that can drive a man indoors and ruin his ambition for days."

He paused in his speech long enough to pull Billy's shirt away from the wound in his side, and peered down at it. "No, I haven't made it to Colorado yet." He laid his palm on Billy's swollen wound and shook his head. "Came here to Little Rock to visit my Aunt Esther, and derned if they haven't had me here practicing ever since! Don't know exactly what happened, but I guess that's just the way of things."

"What about Billy here?" Holt said.

The doctor looked again at Billy's side. "Who stitched him up?" he asked. "Was it you?" He looked at Betsy.

No one said a word. The doctor paid no attention to the fact. He wasn't really listening, anyway. "Well, whoever it was did a very good job indeed. But, good sewing job or not, this young man has a nasty infection! Nasty infection," he repeated. "Don't know if I've ever seen a worse-looking one, to be honest. It's a good thing you brought him in to me," he added. "Otherwise—well, let's not think about that right now." He reached out and started to probe and poke the wound with his fingers. The wound had swollen to a large, deep purplish-red mound. Billy moaned each time the doctor touched him.

"Yes, it's a good thing you came to see me," the doctor repeated. He glanced at Holt, then Katy and Betsy. "Where you folks from?"

Holt didn't answer. He was staring at the wound in Billy's side and wondering how it had gotten so bad without anyone noticing or Billy letting on.

"From the looks of you, I'll bet you folks are from Texas," the doctor added.

"We ain't from Texas," Holt said, clearly irritable with the doctor's chatter. "What do you propose to do with Billy here?"

"Well, there is only one thing we can do," Dr. Hobbs said, poking his finger into a soft spot in the wound. "We could try to drain some of this infection out and see how he reacts to that." He turned and picked up an instrument that resembled a small, shiny knife. "New Mexico," he said suddenly. "You folks must be from there if you aren't from Texas."

Holt didn't answer the geographical inquiry. Instead, he stared at the little knife in Dr. Hobbs's hand and said, "Are you gonna slice him open, just like that? Is that the idee?"

"Not exactly. Here, on this soft spot." The doctor poked it again. "I'm hoping I can cut him right here and a bunch of that infection will drain out. If it doesn't, then yes, I'll have to open this wound completely back up and see what we can get out. Then I'll pack it." He raised his head and widened his eyes at the women. "Of course, from the looks of him, with his fever, the poison could have already spread through his body. So, is it New Mexico you're from?"

Billy raised his head up. The effort made him tremble. Sweat dripped from his face. "Will you just shut up and do what you have to do?" he gasped.

Dr. Hobbs nodded and looked at Holt. "You might want to hold your friend down. This shouldn't hurt, with the fever and all. But I wouldn't want him moving around. He might jump, and I could cut right into his gizzard!" He laughed at his own joke.

Holt took Billy by the arms. "I'm gonna hold on to ya, Billy Boy. You just relax," he said.

Billy closed his eyes and silently nodded.

"I hear that, out there in Colorado, a doctor could make good money," Dr. Hobbs said, tapping the shiny side of the blade against his finger.

Holt stopped him short. "Would you git to cuttin'? I don't want to have to stand here and hold him all day."

Dr. Hobbs took one final probe with his finger into the soft tissue at the center of the mound. He placed the point of the little knife where he wanted it, and pushed it in. A thick, grayish liquid spurted out, spraying the front of the doctor's shirt. "Just what I thought," he said. "We might have been lucky." He then widened the incision to a full inch with the blade. The thick infection poured down Billy's side, onto the table. The doctor motioned for Katy to fetch a handful of towels to lay beside the open wound. Soon, the towels were soaked.

Holt found himself holding his breath at the awful smell. It was a repugnant odor, unlike anything he could ever recall. The whole room began to reek of it. The infection continued to pour out, until finally the doctor grabbed a tin can to catch the flow. He stuck it against Billy's side. The oozing soon filled the bottom of the can. Dr. Hobbs found another spot on the mound to push, and more of the liquid poured out. The liquid turned from gray to a reddish-gray, then finally changed to a light reddish-yellow, but did not slow up. The doctor worked for nearly an hour before the flow stopped.

Dr. Hobbs took a deep breath and sat back. "Well, we got a bunch of the infection out. Hopefully, it was isolated to this area."

By now, Billy had fallen into a deep sleep. Betsy took a washtowel and was wiping his face gently. "His fever's gone. In fact, he feels right cool." She smiled.

Holt took his hand and held the back of his fingers against Billy's cheek. "Well, I'll be derned. Fever is gone," he said.

"That's because we got all that poison out of him," Dr. Hobbs said.

"What do we do now? Think that's got it all?" Holt asked.

"What this young man needs now is a lot of rest, and two hot baths a day," the doctor said. "The hot water will soak the wound, and bring any more infection to the surface.

Now, you folks could put him up in the hotel across the street, but I'd suggest you leave him right here. Got a bed and a tub right in the next room. We can tend to his needs just fine. Now"—he glanced at the women—"which one of you is his wife?"

Betsy looked down at the floor, while Katy shot a glance at Holt. "Well, you see, Doc," Holt began, "ain't neither one. Betsy, here, is his companion, though. Reckon she could stay and look after him. After all, she's been takin' care of him since we left Fort Smith."

"Oh my." Dr. Hobbs sighed and stared out the window with a worried frown.

"Is there some kind of problem with that arrangement?" Holt asked.

"This here's Arkansas," Dr. Hobbs said, still looking cautiously out the window.

"So, it's Arkansas," Holt said. "What's that got to do with anything?"

Dr. Hobbs said, "Why, cowboy, it's got everything to do with it. You see, folks here in Arkansas are a bit on the prudish side, if I do say so. But"—he tapped his fingers against his lips—"she would be a great help to your friend, and to me."

"I'm stayin'," Betsy said adamantly. "Why, I've been living over in Fort Smith, and I reckon folks are just as ornery and cussed in Arkansas as the next place."

Holt had seated himself in the chair behind the doctor's desk. He rolled himself a fixin', lit up, and said, "Now that we've got that problem taken care of, how long do you figure it's gonna be before Billy's fit to travel?"

Dr. Hobbs shrugged. "That's hard to say. He's got so much poison out of him, he could come around pretty fast. Then again . . ." He trailed off and stared at Billy's sleeping form. "Why, I've seen men die with less poison in their bodies."

Holt stood up and grabbed Katy by the arm. "We best go and tell the others that we're gonna stay around in Little

Rock for a few days. You need anything, Betsy?" he said kindly.

Betsy's eyes filled. She smiled at his tone. It was the first time she had smiled at anybody besides Billy since they'd left Fort Smith. "I'll be all right." She took in a breath and wiped a tear away. "And so will Billy."

Outside, Holt said, "We best go and tell the others. Nikki'll be madder than fire about Betsy stayin' there with Billy."

"She can get mad all she wants!" Katy said firmly. "Ain't none of her business! Anyway, it's plain that Billy likes Betsy. That's good enough for me, and I reckon it'll have to be good enough for Nikki!"

33

BETSY TOOK TO HER JOB OF CARING FOR BILLY WITH A passion that only a mother could match. She hardly left his side for a moment. Everyone took notice, and several commented on the fact that Betsy was doing a fine thing for Billy. Nikki may have secretly acknowledged Betsy's good deeds, too, but it still hadn't softened her demeanor toward the other woman any.

This hostility was unsettling, and Holt was growing concerned. A man could only handle so much dissension before it got the whole group riled up. After a couple of days of hearing Nikki's criticisms and complaints about Betsy, he decided that it was time to air out their differences, now and forever.

It took a hard effort to coax Betsy away from Billy's side. She clung to him like she might not ever see him again, her eyes showing the betrayal she felt in leaving him all alone, even for a moment. Holt assured her that it was only for dinner, and then she could get right back to nursing Billy to health. Even Billy urged her to go, sensing the seriousness in Holt's manner. Finally, she bent down and kissed him sadly, promising to return as soon as she could.

Breathing a heavy sigh, Holt guided Betsy down the street to meet the others. He had chosen a place called the

Frog's Jump. It was called an eatery, but inside it was a wild place that served jars of liquor that had been stilled out in back of the building. The spirited drinkers kept the place filled with loud talk and laughter. It was rowdy, and reeked of sweat and fried meat, but the Frog's Jump also had the reputation of serving the biggest and best beefsteaks in Little Rock.

Holt had already had words with the proprietor over Chief. Holt had no sooner seated the old man at a table when a man wearing a full apron came running out and ordered the Indian to leave. Glancing worrisomely at Katy, Nikki, and Betsy, he said it would be trouble enough having ladies present, let alone an Indian.

Holt held his ground. The ladies and the Indian would stay, he said. If anyone wanted to start trouble, he assured the man that they would handle it.

The owner stared at Holt a moment, then shrugged his shoulders. "It's your funeral," was all he said.

As the rest of the group seated themselves, Holt thought to himself what a strange place Arkansas was. Here they were, in an eatery that was packed to the walls with customers, and there was not a female to be seen, except for the three at his table. Even the waiters were all greasy, straggly-looking men. Why, the eateries in Texas and Kansas all used females to serve the food; that is, if there were enough women in the town to do the work. For the most part, women were scarce in cowboy country. Here in Little Rock, though, the streets seemed to be filled with women. He studied the attitude of the customers. There were just as many men drinking as eating. He guessed it had to be the nature of the Frog's Jump that kept the women away.

Still, the meal went smoothly. They all enjoyed the fine food and overlooked the atmosphere of the place. Life in the West had made them all hard and tough to such behavior. Even Chief was undisturbed at the threat that had been suggested against him.

When Holt had finished, he wiped his mouth, then cleared

his throat. "The way I got it figured," he announced, "we're nearly halfway to Georgia. Now, we still got a ways to go, and I say it's time we put aside any differences, right here and now."

He turned to look meaningfully at Nikki. In return, she glared back at him, her lips set in a straight line. The rest of the group continued to eat their dinner, keeping a curious but cautious watch on the two.

Nikki was not one to be bashful. After a moment, she deliberately folded her hands in her lap and said, "Spit out what's in your craw, Holt Flynn."

Their eyes deadlocked for several seconds, until Holt pushed his plate to the center of the table and leaned forward on his elbows. His voice was calm and firm. "Hell, Nikki. I think you know what I'm talkin' about. It's Betsy, here," he said, gesturing at Betsy but holding his gaze on Nikki. "It's time we started accepting her as"—he paused, searching for the right words—"as Billy's companion," he finished.

Noisy talk and laughter filled the room all around them, but the group's table became suddenly still. The others held their eating utensils in their hands, glancing back and forth between Holt and Nikki, waiting for Nikki's answer.

It came. Nikki's face was flushing, just as it always did when anger was rising up inside her. She spoke only to Holt, but her words were searing to Betsy's ears and embarrassing to the others.

"If it's this whore that you're beatin' around the bush about—well, let me tell you something. If you expect me to sidle up to her, then you're crazier than I thought! Let her go back to her own kind, is what I say," she said with a bitterness that surprised them all.

Holt's eyes burned into Nikki's. He took in a breath to calm himself somewhat before he answered. "Nikki," he said, "you might wear your britches and shoot your mouth off like a west Texas cowhand, but I for one am tired of all the bickering and fuss made over Betsy here. Now, I can't speak for the others, but I got an idee that they've all pretty much accepted her. I mean, after all, ain't but about half the folks at this table thinks there's any gold in the first place. Don't you find that a bit queer?"

"Just what are you trying to say?" Nikki said through clenched teeth.

"Simply that most of us here have other reasons why we came along on this trip. And none is any more or less honorable than the others. Walter, there. He dang sure don't think there's any gold in Georgia. Do ya, Walter?"

Without waiting for a response, Holt went on, "And Katy, here. Why, she's told me she thinks we're all crazy! No, by damn, we're all here for a lot of reasons, and I'll be the first to say that, gold or not, I'm glad I come along." He shot a glance at Katy.

Nikki sat there, stewing. Finally, she said, "Well, I can see no one else is going to speak up about that—"

The word "whore" was forming on her lips when Katy broke her off. "Don't you dare call her that again, Nikki! I'll not have it!"

Nikki's eyes shot to her sister. "Don't you tell me what I can or can't say, young lady! The way you've been carrying on with Holt there! It's a disgrace!" she said, raising a fist and slamming it down on the table.

Katy shook her head scornfully. "You don't scare me. You just better not say that word again, and that's all I got to say on the matter," she said firmly. She put her arm around Betsy's shoulder. "Listen, honey, you're as welcome as anybody else is."

Holt had known this wasn't going to be an easy subject to discuss, but he hadn't expected the debate to get so heated. He said to Walter, "What about you? You got anything to say that'll shed any light on the subject? I've never known you when you didn't."

It was clear that Walter was irritated at being singled out. He grumbled, "I think the whole lot of us is crazy, if you ask me. Shoot, I don't care who Billy rides with, or anybody else for that matter. I just wanta get this damn trip over with."

The red in Nikki's face slowly drained away as she looked at Walter, openmouthed. It hadn't lately occurred to her that Walter cared absolutely nothing about the trip they were on. He had quit complaining, way back in the Territory, and she had let herself assume that he had turned favorable. Inside, she had to admit to herself that the biggest thing she disliked about Betsy was her threat to Walter. As she thoughtfully stared at him, though, she finally came to realize that Walter didn't really care about anybody, including herself. She bit her lip and looked sadly down at the table.

"Look," Holt said, a little more kindly, "let's make the best of this. I mean, I've been with Walter for a long time. I know him. I understand him. And Charlie One Eye, there. Hell, Charlie is a pleasant enough traveling companion. Chief hasn't been no problem to anybody." He pointed to the old man. "We been through a lot together. I mean, back there in the hole that bastard Crumb stuck us in? It made me do a lot of thinking. Sure, I hope we find that cave, and that it's so full of gold it'd choke an elephant. But you know what? Even if it ain't got a lick of gold in it, life ain't gonna change none. I can't speak for you all, but I have to say that this trip's added somethin' to my life that I've been needin' for a long time." He looked at Walter. His eyes had softened. "Hell, Walter," he said in a low voice. "Somewhere down inside that armor that you keep around you, this trip's been good for you, too. Don't you get it? Gold ain't what this trip's all about." He shook his head. "No, sir. Ain't about gold at all." He reached down beside him for Katy's hand.

No sooner had Holt finished talking, when a giant of a man in overalls walked up to the table. Chewing tobacco had left thick stains in his beard. When he spoke, his teeth showed, rotten and black. "How would you ladies like Big Al to buy you-'ns a drink? I see none o' these squirts have." He was standing directly above Holt's head when he spoke.

Three other men were standing behind him, laughing. One of them cackled and said, "I told you Big Al would do it!"

Another man stepped up toward Betsy and held out a jar. "Here, girl, have a drink!"

The other men bent over in laughter.

Holt leaned back away from the table and smiled at the big man. "That's mighty generous of you boys, but we done tried. These girls won't drink with ya. They won't even drink with us," he said.

The man who called himself Big Al growled out of the corner of his mouth, "Shut up, squirt. I wasn't talkin' to you."

Walter laughed. "Squirt?" He laughed again, looking at Holt.

Holt glanced at Walter and smiled. Since he was over six feet tall, the name was a new one on him, too. He tried to position himself in his chair, in case he had to take action, but movement was impossible. Big Al was pressed up against him, so close that Holt could smell him. There was no way Holt could stand up before Big Al could make a move and get hold of him. He couldn't remember ever being in such a tight situation. The wall was behind him, Katy sat to his left, and there stood Big Al on his right. "Why don't you boys let us buy you a drink?" he offered.

Big Al paid Holt no mind. Neither did the other three men, who had moved to where they were now surrounding the table. The man who had spoken to Betsy was rubbing her hair and grinning.

Big Al held out the jar that he had clutched in his behemoth hand, the long, thick fingers surrounding it. "Here!" he offered, shoving it under Katy's nose. Liquor splashed over her front.

Holt's pistol was in his hand and the barrel crammed into Big Al's crotch before anyone had seen him make any motion. Big Al tried to peer over his massive belly at the Colt, which was stuck into his privates.

Holt said slowly and deliberately, "Now, fatso! I've been polite, but this here pistol has a hair trigger, and I mean a thin hair, at that. Now, from the looks of you, I'd say you ain't seen that pecker of yours in quite a spell, and it probably ain't been put to no use in just as long, but I'm tellin' you, if you boys don't mosey on back to where you come from, I'm gonna geld your ass with a forty-four, right now!"

Big Al's eyes, so menacing before, blinked nervously. His mouth was opened to speak, but said nothing.

The man rubbing Betsy's hair grabbed a handful and jerked her head backward. With his free hand, he whipped out a pocketknife and pressed the blade against Betsy's throat. "I'll cut her! I swear, I'll cut her if you don't put that gun away!" he shouted.

Walter still sat there, smiling. He gave a harsh laugh, but said nothing.

"What's so funny?" the man with the knife said angrily. "I swear, I'll cut her good!"

"I'll tell you what's funny. I was just thinkin' about fatass, there, with his pecker blown off, and you sportin' a hole between your eyes," Walter said, his voice laced with cold sarcasm.

The Frog's Jump patrons, drunk and sober alike, were all watching and listening, so closely that one could have heard a pin drop. By now, Big Al had regained enough of his voice to mutter to the other man. "Put yer knife away," he said. A big drop of sweat rolled off the end of his nose and splattered on the table.

The knife in the man's hand shook with his impatience. "He's bluffin!' He ain't gonna shoot ya!" he told Big Al. He glanced at Holt. "It's all big talk," he insisted, then shifted his gaze to Walter. His mouth twitched nervously.

"Boy," Walter said, "if you got any money, I'll make a bet with ya, 'cause I been around this man for a long time, and if I don't know nothin' else, I do know that he surely means to shoot fatass's pecker off. And I'll double that wager with any takers in this establishment that he can put a hole between your eyes before they can blink."

There was a gleam in Walter's eyes that none of them, with the exception of Holt, had ever seen. Charlie One Eye swallowed, his Adam's apple bobbing up and down. Unaware even of his own thinking, he rubbed his head and put his palm to his face. It was wet with sweat. From his seat at the table, the old Indian watched the goings-on stone-faced. Betsy held her breath, her hands balled up tightly into fists. Nikki, who had grabbed hold of Walter's shirt when Holt first pulled his Colt, still clutched it tightly. Katy watched Holt, remaining confidently by his side, a look of satisfaction on her face.

Holt frowned and thumb-cocked his Colt. "My patience is about to run out, fatso," he said menacingly. "Now, you and your smelly-assed friends had better find somebody else to play games with. And I mean right now." His eyes were wide and full of hatred—eyes that could make a man's heart sink nearly as fast as the forty-four that he held in his hand. He pushed the Colt harder into Big Al's groin, causing him to stumble back into chairs and customers at the next table. Holt stood up then, and Big Al raised his hands.

"Please, mister! We were jus' foolin' around!" He glared at the man behind Betsy. "I said to put that knife away! Now!" he said roughly.

The man looked unsure. His eyes darted back and forth at the others around the table. He gazed into the nervous eyes of Big Al. Reluctantly, he slowly closed the knife and stepped away from the table.

Walter smiled at him. "I guess you'll live to see another day, but next time, you fellers oughta be leery of who you mess with."

Big Al and his three companions took little time in leaving, and the Frog's Jump returned to normal, with the room filled with conversation about what everyone had just witnessed. Several men stopped by and patted Holt's shoulder. One man commented that he had never seen anyone stand up to Big Al before. This seemed to amuse Walter, for it set him to laughing again. In a light mood, he ordered a round of drinks.

Holt quickly forgot about the incident. There were bigger things on his mind. He stood up, pulling Katy up with him. "I hope we can all travel the rest of the way in a civil manner," he said simply. "The important thing is to get Billy Boy fit to travel." With that, he took Katy's arm, and together they left the Frog's Jump.

Charlie One Eye was the first to speak. "That Holt can sure fool a feller," he commented, staring at the others with his eye wide. "Why, I think he woulda shot that man!"

"That he would've," Walter said, smiling into his jar. "That he would've."

34

When they rode out of Little Rock, a more relaxed atmosphere had, indeed, settled over the group. Holt and Katy enjoyed several of their long, philosophical discussions as they took the lead. Behind them, Nikki seemed somewhat subdued as she steered the wagon. She still wasn't speaking to Betsy, but she *had* taken to keeping her opinions about the woman to herself, and was no longer giving her hard, disapproving stares.

Walter, Charlie One Eye, and Chief were behind the wagon. Walter was still in a good enough mood to encourage conversation. He and Charlie One Eye were commenting to each other on the lush green countryside, when Charlie One Eye wondered aloud if Georgia was anything like Arkansas.

To their amazement, Chief spoke up. Shaking his head slowly, he said in a surprisingly strong voice, "This land is one of lakes and rivers. Georgia is a land of many mountains and trees, where strong warriors once lived in peace and harmony. Where the great forests protected my people from their enemies."

Charlie One Eye reached up habitually and took off his hat. His scalp glistened under the sun until he wiped it dry with his palm. His eyes stole a worried glance at the Indian.

"There ain't no more of them Injuns hiding in them Georgia trees, are there?"

Chief looked ahead and said no more. When Charlie One Eye turned questioningly to Walter, all he got in the way of a response was a shrug. "Guess we'll find out, won't we, Charlie?" Walter said with an amused grin.

Up ahead, Billy was bedded down in the wagon. He was so weak, Dr. Hobbs had tried hard to convince him to stay longer in Little Rock for observation, but Billy would have no more of his confinement. Holt had agreed to moving on, but only after he insisted that Billy stay in the wagon for several more days. It nearly killed Billy to give in, but the fact was, he was so weak he wouldn't have lasted half a day in the saddle. Besides that, he didn't have the strength to win any arguments with anyone, let alone Holt. It helped some that Betsy had tethered her horse alongside his behind the wagon, and was riding inside with him. She held his head in her lap and talked to him to help pass the time. Dr. Hobbs had prescribed a hot pack of wet towels be placed on his wound every evening, and Betsy made Holt promise to keep up an ample water supply, or to camp near water each night. It wasn't hard to see that Nikki resented having to pull Betsy in the wagon, but she kept silent on the matter.

Holt had commented that the wagon was getting to look like a field hospital, and that bothered Billy even more. After a couple of days, he rose up like a stubborn mule and demanded to be put back on his horse. Weak as a newborn kitten, he climbed atop his mount with the help of Betsy and Charlie One Eye, and announced that he was ready to ride. Holt started to protest, but instead let out a sigh, and signaled the group on.

It was all Billy could do to stay atop his horse. Betsy stayed constantly by his side while Walter and Charlie One Eye took turns helping her watch over him. He was stubborn about riding, though, and each day out of Little Rock he regained a little more strength. Days later, just when it looked like he was getting back to normal, Billy again took a fever. Betsy cried out to Holt with concern when she touched Billy's burning forehead.

Dr. Hobbs had cautioned them that this could happen, and had instructed Holt on what to do. He called the group to a halt and went to inspect Billy's side. Sure enough, there was a little swollen spot on the wound. Nothing like before, but a small area had risen up and was hot to the touch. Holt unpacked a piece of deercloth that Dr. Hobbs had sent along with them, and unrolled a shiny little knife. He prodded around until he found the center of the mound mount, then pushed in the point of the knife. The infection drained out, not as much as before, but still a goodly amount. In no time, Billy's temperature had dropped, just as it had in Dr. Hobbs's office. Billy felt better right away.

Eventually, traveling got easier for Billy. Soon, he was taking in the beauty of eastern Arkansas like everyone else. They were heading toward Mississippi. Nikki had wanted to go to Memphis, but a man in Little Rock had told them that Memphis was way up north and out of their way. Also, they would have a hard time negotiating the wagon through that area. He had told them they needed to take a southerly direction through Mississippi and Alabama instead of through Memphis and down through Chattanooga. "Stay out of them mountains a little while longer," he had said. At first, Nikki had been disgruntled at the advice. She had always wanted to see Memphis. After her run-in with Holt, though, she knew better than to complain. Besides, being a practical woman, she saw the logic in it, and quickly got over her disappointment.

Holt and Katy were back to killing squirrels and enjoying their riding forays on ahead of the others. They never seemed to run out of topics to discuss with each other, and even their quiet times were satisfying. Neither one had mentioned the word "love" again but it was becoming more of an unspoken feeling between them. They had been so caught up in each other the last few days, it came as a shock when Billy made his announcement as they were all gathered for the evening meal.

Billy and Betsy sat side by side with their plates balanced on their knees. The conversation had died down as everyone dug eagerly into Nikki's fried squirrel, potatoes, and good sourdough biscuits. Billy solemnly looked at the others sitting around them and then at Betsy. She smiled at him and nodded her head. Suddenly, he blurted out, "Soon as we get to Georgia, me and Betsy's gettin' married. In Ellijay. That's where Betsy's from, you know," he added, matter-of-factly.

The group sat there, dumbstruck, with their forks in their hands. Billy's words hung in the air like an unwelcome guest.

From where she sat across the campfire, Nikki sucked in her breath. She stared briefly at Billy, then her eyes slid suspiciously to Betsy and narrowed into angry slits.

Charlie One Eye couldn't hide his emotion. He looked sadly off into the distance, while loneliness crept over him like a cool wind on a damp night. He had ridden with Billy for a long time, and though he didn't like to think about such things, he wondered what life held for him without his riding companion. Billy was the only close friend he had ever had. As a boy, he had lost the sight in one eye in a bad fall out of a tree, and from that day, he couldn't remember a time when the other boys hadn't teased him about it. He had acted as if it didn't bother him, but in reality, it had cut some deep scars inside him. When Charlie One Eye had first come across him, Billy had been a young sprout, much younger than Charlie was, and full of cockiness. Billy had never noticed the bad eye, or at least, he gave no indication. Even if he had noticed, Billy had been kind enough to keep it to himself. Right away, Billy had just given Charlie One Eye a smile of acceptance and made him feel as important as the next person. That Billy called him by his nickname made no difference. It was a name that had stuck to him years before; in fact, it was a name that Charlie One Eye had taken to using himself. Billy's kindness had meant the world to him.

In that moment of sadness, Charlie One Eye suddenly wished he had married Gertrude Langley. It seemed such a long time ago. Gertrude had been unforgettably ugly. With her big nose dominating her face like a beak, she had reminded him of a buzzard. Their mothers had been friends, and had pushed the pair toward matrimony. It had seemed like a natural thing, with his long, gangly legs and cocked eye, and Gertrude's big nose. Charlie knew his chances of finding a more comely woman were nonexistent, but he hadn't had even the tiniest feelings for Gertrude at all, and had skirted the marriage issue forthwith. Since that time, besides an occasional sporting lady along the trail, he'd never run across a single female that took any real interest in him. Right now, he wished he had. Even the thought of a cave full of gold didn't sound so inviting without a friend to help enjoy his newfound wealth.

They all finished the meal in silence that night. It was while Nikki and Katy were doing the dishes that Holt said to Billy, "It's none of my business, Billy Boy, but I guess you've given this quite a bit of thought."

"Enough," said Billy, feeling irritated at Holt's question.

Holt, sensing Billy's defensive tone, said, "Just relax. I didn't mean anything. It don't take some folks very long to come to some conclusions, while it takes others a lifetime. I wish you two the best."

Billy smiled nervously. He himself was surprised at how quickly he had proposed to Betsy, and even more surprised that he had told the others about it.

That night, she nursed him as best she could, both mentally and physically. Billy seemed restless and more than a little upset. While she was packing his wound, he finally voiced what was on his mind. He said, "Well, I guess the whole blamed lot is mad at me now."

Betsy knew what he meant, but she acted as if she didn't. "Why's that, Billy?" she asked.

"Shucks, I reckon you know why." Billy gestured toward the others. "They think I'm just some dang kid who doesn't know what he's doin'. But they're wrong. That Nikki, with her superior attitude! Why, I reckon me and Charlie One Eye done as much business with them Trapp sisters as the next feller! Nope, they just don't think I'm man enough, and it bothers 'em," he stated angrily.

Betsy kissed him on the forehead. "I think you're wrong, hon. It's just unexpected, is all. I think I understand the way they feel, and what I don't understand—well, I still try."

Billy sat up and looked at her earnestly. "I love you. Do you love me, too? I mean, do you get all squishy inside when you're with me?" he asked anxiously.

Betsy suppressed a smile. She didn't want him to think she was laughing at him. "Of course I do. I didn't at first, though," she said, peering speculatively toward camp and the others. "Oh, I guess they were right about me at first. Especially Nikki." She smiled and rubbed her fingers through his hair. "Why, the way you came in that morning, all full of yourself! You made me feel good. All the other men"—she paused, shaking her head—"all the other men in Fort Smith were afraid to come around me. Afraid of Texas Dan. At least, that's what Horst told me. And he was probably right." Betsy frowned. "Texas Dan is a low-down snake, if I ever saw one. But you—there's something exciting and refreshing about you, Billy. Yes, I admit I did want to get away from Fort Smith and that dreary old life, but believe me!" She touched his face with her hand. "You have nothing to worry about, because I do love you, with all my heart." She pulled a blade of grass and tickled his nose with it.

Billy sat up on his elbows and asked, "Well, if you didn't love that Texas Dan feller, what in the world were you his girl for?"

"I don't reckon I was *his girl*, as you put it," she said, mocking his tone.

"Well, I reckon you was," Billy said. "The barkeep told me that. 'Sides, you yourself just said all the other men in Fort Smith was afraid to come around because of him. You don't have to deny it."

"I'm not denying anything," Betsy said. "He did think he had his say on me, but I never, ever felt nothin' in my heart for him. He gave me money, and that was all. 'Sides, you oughta be happy," she pointed out. "It kept all the other men away from me, just thinkin' that I was his! But let's not talk about Texas Dan Simon," she said coaxingly. "Let's talk about us. You know, my mama's still alive in Ellijay, and bein' as we're plannin' on gettin' married, I sure want you to like her. I want her to like you, too."

Billy took her hand. "I don't know how I can help but like her, if she's anything like you."

"She's old," Betsy said, "but she's a good woman. Lives on the side of a mountain, all by herself, and she's tough. Why, it gets so dark in the mountains at night, it used to give me the willies every time the sun went down. But I never heard Mother complain." She stopped and looked at him. "What are you gonna do about your friend Charlie?"

"What do you mean by that?" Billy asked, puzzled.

"I was watching him when you told the others about us. Billy, that man was hurt. Not mad, you understand, just hurt, like he'd lost his last friend."

Billy said, "Why that's crazy! Charlie One Eye will still be our friend, I reckon! I'm just wishin' the others weren't upset with me."

"Oh, I don't think they're really upset, Billy. You see, as far as Nikki was concerned, I was another hen in the henhouse. It's plain that she likes Walter. And Katy? Why, she hardly pulls her eyes from Holt," Betsy said. She patted his arm. "Everything's gonna be fine, you'll see. And as for Charlie, maybe you oughta just talk to him a little more. When you get to feelin' better, ride with him some—just the two of ya. Show him you're still friends."

That night, while everyone was still sitting around the fire and waiting to fill their bedrolls, Billy sat down next to Charlie One Eye and tried to warm things back up between them. It was a hard effort, though, for Billy was feeling weak and downright sick. Charlie One Eye was cordial, but he himself wasn't the same. He gave no effort to help make Billy's job any easier. Of course, Charlie One Eye had never been one to carry much of a conversation. When it came to talking, or anything else for that matter, he was strictly a follower. He sat there mutely while Billy tried to start up one conversation after another. He made no move to ease Billy's worries any. Finally, Betsy, sensing that Billy needed to heal a little more before rushing such things, took Billy on to bed. Billy gave a deep sigh as he stood up to move to his bedroll, but Charlie One Eye held his silence.

Soon, the camp was filled with snores. Charlie One Eye tried to relax, but he knew he was too upset to sleep. He huddled close to the fire, hugging his knees and staring into the flickering light. Twice, he thought he heard something move in the thick of the trees to the north, but even strange noises couldn't pull his eyes away from the flame, or his mind from the depressed state he was in. Under normal circumstances, he would get spooked at a bird whistling through the brush. But these were not normal circumstances, thanks to the heavy burden that Billy's words had laid upon him.

He was glad that the others had all fallen asleep around him. It was hard enough to think about normal, everyday things when there were other folks yakking all around. To think that he had to deal with this new and most upsetting problem was even worse. Charlie One Eye almost felt mad at Betsy for stealing his companion away. He glanced resentfully at her sleeping form as she lay with her head on Billy's shoulder. There was no way to compete with a female. He grabbed for his bedroll and flung it out over the rough earth.

Through the trees came the faint glow of a fire. Charlie One Eye looked at it absently, but the curiosity of the light didn't register. He lay down to think some more. Just when he fell asleep, he couldn't recall, but when he did, his heart was still as heavy as ever.

35

THE NEXT MORNING AT BREAKFAST, BILLY WAS AGAIN feeling poorly. The fever had returned during the night; besides, he was still eaten up by the thought that his friends might not think as highly of him as before. That idea pained him, for up until he had met Betsy, the most valued part of his life was centered around Charlie One Eye, along with Holt and Walter. To think that he may have dropped in their estimation, coupled with his sickness, was almost more than he could stand.

Betsy kept herself busy, wiping his forehead and hovering over him like a worried mother. She was planning to heat more wet cloths over the fire to treat his wound as soon as breakfast was out of the way. Everything seemed brighter in daylight, and Betsy found her spirits starting to lift. Everyone except Nikki seemed friendlier than usual this morning. Maybe they had all accepted Holt's view on the matter. Betsy hoped so. She found herself humming as she got up to fetch her water pail. Ever since she was a child, she had always hummed when she felt good. An old hymn that her mother had taught her suddenly popped in her mind. She grabbed up the pail and walked toward the woods. There was a little stream where she had gathered water the night before. As she stepped through the thick underbrush, her thoughts were on her mother in Georgia. Would she think Billy was handsome? Would she be proud to have him as her son-in-law? Betsy smiled. Nobody had ever been good enough for "Mother's little girl," as her mother had put it. She had been so proud to tell everyone about the money that Betsy had sent home on occasion. Betsy had told her that she worked at a bank. She wondered what her mother would have thought if she had gone to Fort Smith and found her little girl in the small upstairs room at Horst's saloon.

At the stream, she waded into the water and was dipping the pail when a shadow caught her eye. She suddenly glimpsed the front set of a horse's legs on the other side of the creek. Grabbing her chest, she almost hollered out.

"You startled me!" she said, smiling. She looked up to see who had ridden up on her so quietly, expecting one of her own party.

Her heart jumped in her chest. The world started spinning as she gazed into menacing eyes that were so full of hatred and anger. In the brief seconds, their eyes locked, and Betsy felt herself gripped with a fear like she had never known.

Texas Dan Simon's jaw was set, and the muscles in his cheek twitched. His lip curled into a snarl as he spoke.

"You stupid bitch. I've come to take you back, and to kill the bastard that took you."

His eyes bored into Betsy's. She shuddered, but tried to stand up to him. When she spoke, her voice was trembling. "What do you want?" she said.

"I just told you, whore. I've come to take you back, and I mean to kill the bastard that took you." Texas Dan touched his horse's flank enough to make it step into the water toward her. She stepped backward, dropping the pail of water.

"No, please!" she begged. "Please go away! I don't want to be with you!"

Texas Dan scowled and rode the horse right up next to her. Its powerful chest bumped into Betsy, almost knocking her off her feet. Before she could react, he drew back and slapped her hard across the face, knocking her to the ground. When she didn't move quickly enough to suit him, he reached down and grabbed her violently by the hair, yanking her upright.

"Now move, whore! We're gonna ride in, and you're gonna point out the bastard that took you," he said angrily.

"Oh, please, no!" Betsy cried desperately. She started to cry.

"Move!" Texas Dan said. "Right now, I'm just figurin' on killin' the bastard that took you, but if you rile me, I swear I'll leave a graveyard behind me." He pushed her forward with his horse. Betsy walked on weak legs, sobbing uncontrollably.

Texas Dan walked her right on into the unsuspecting camp. Billy was leaned against a dead tree stump. Nikki was busy cleaning up the breakfast plates, and Walter was helping her pack up the provisions. Charlie One Eye had gone off to relieve himself, and was just returning to camp. Chief was seated at his customary spot against the wagon wheel, lost in his musings. By the horses, Holt and Katy were getting their mounts saddled and ready.

At the sight of Betsy and the stranger, Billy climbed to his feet. He had no idea who this intruder was, or why Betsy was crying. Suddenly, she broke away and ran toward him, grabbing him in a desperate hug.

"What the hell's goin' on here?" Billy demanded as he tried to pull himself free from Betsy's grasp.

Texas Dan looked Billy over with an amused leer. "So, it's you?" he said. "Why, you're nothin' but a pup! Well, I'm gonna kill you, just the same."

The other members of the surprised camp fell silent. Holt handed his horse's reins to Katy and quickly moved to Billy's left, while Walter and Charlie One Eye sidled over to the right. All eyes held hard stares on the stranger who had ridden in, full of fighting talk.

Betsy pressed her tear-streaked face into Billy's shoulder. "Please!" she cried. "That's Texas Dan Simon! He'll kill you, Billy! He'll kill all of us!"

Billy took her by the shoulders and tried to free himself to where he would have a fighting chance against the outlaw, but he was so weak, he could only struggle with her.

Holt's strong voice called out, "I don't know who you are, mister, but you've got a lot of gall, riding in here with your threats."

Texas Dan acted as if Holt didn't exist, let alone acknowledge the statement. He kept an eye trained on Billy as he shouted at Betsy. "Move, whore! I swear, I'll put a bullet through both of you!"

Holt took a step toward him then, his hand hanging loosely beside his Colt. "You've been asked to leave this camp," he said, more deliberately than before.

Betsy stepped out in front of Billy and shielded him as she pleaded with Texas Dan, "Just leave! Please! None of these people has done anything!" She turned desperately to Holt. "This is Texas Dan Simon, and he'll kill us for sure! Please, don't upset him," she begged.

Holt dispensed with all cordialities. His face froze into a cold stare that meant only business. In words that were hard and measured, he again addressed Texas Dan, "Looks as if you got folks thinkin' you're some mean son of a bitch. Well, I don't know who you are, mister, and on top of that, I don't give a good damn. I guarantee, you buy yourself a fight here, and you'll never leave this place alive."

With all his effort, Billy suddenly shoved Betsy aside and stood as erectly as he could. His body quivered from the sickness he was suffering, but he managed to position himself to where he could pull his Colt. "Everybody back off," he said to the others sternly. "If this here Texas sumbitch wants to fight, then I'll do my own fightin', by damn!"

Texas Dan climbed slowly down from his saddle, never taking his eyes away from Billy. His face was twisted into a menacing leer, with not a trace of fear to be seen. He said, "You best get ready to ride, whore."

Betsy started to move, but Billy shook his head angrily for her to stay put. He brushed away the sweat that was forming across his forehead and planted himself in a fighting posture.

Holt looked at the situation. He had no idea what was going on, but there were times when a man had to fight first and ask questions later. He pointed to Billy and called out to the outlaw, "He's sick. You can see that for yourself. But if it's a fight you're wantin', I'll oblige you, mister."

The camp seemed to be the only place on earth for that moment. The sky closed in around them, bright and blue, and the birds that had homed themselves in the woods nearby were crisscrossing above. The beauty of the place was mocked by the threat of death that Texas Dan Simon had brought with him.

Nikki was still standing at the rear of the wagon. She was digging around desperately for her Winchester. Chief remained seated against the wheel. It was as good a place as any. He was too old and tired to worry about another white man's gunfight. In among the horses, Katy peered out over her horse's back. She gripped the reins tightly. She was nervous, to be sure, but at the same time, an excitement ran through her. The outlaw looked as menacing as any human she had ever laid eyes on, and the fact that Holt had called him out stirred her emotions even more.

To Billy's right, Walter and Charlie One Eye stood out in the open. They had both taken a similar fighting stance, hands ready and close to their sidearms. Charlie One Eye had already decided that he was going to kill Texas Dan Simon, just for talking to Billy in such a disrespectful manner.

"No!" Billy said, looking around the camp at his friends. "It's me he wants, and it's me he'll get." Sweat was popping out all over his face. His shoulders shook. He tried to straighten himself, but his legs were unsteady. For years, he had visualized himself in such a situation, yet in the back of his mind he had always wondered if he could muster up the courage it took. At this moment, though, courage was not a factor at all. He wanted, more than anything, to put a bullet into Texas Dan. He cursed his sickness for making him weak at a time when he needed his strength the most.

Texas Dan shrugged. "No use in you bastards arguing over it. I'll just kill the lot of you."

Texas Dan pulled leather. His reputation was not exaggerated. He was fast—really fast. Something happened, though, that would forevermore tarnish that reputation. Before he could squeeze the trigger, the morning air exploded around him.

Holt's hand was like an unexpected bolt of lightning. A bullet from his smoking forty-four ripped through Texas Dan's heart.

It was an instant later when Walter's bullet struck him high on the cheek, just below the left eye.

The third shot came from Billy's gun. The outlaw's body jerked violently as a piece of hot steel tore into his side.

With a deadly accuracy and a ferocity that the restless night had stirred up inside him, Charlie One Eye added a final shot to the outlaw's crumpling body.

Texas Dan Simon was dead before his eyes could blink.

36

JESSE HAD NEVER BEEN ABLE TO PASS UP AN OPPORTUnity, such as when a good horse presented itself to him. That was the case when they had ridden to just west of Little Rock. Frank James knew that they were riding good horses already. They had stolen a fine pair in east Texas, and he was getting really fond of the animal under him. Still, Frank recognized the change in Jesse's expression the instant they rode up on a young farmer.

The farm boy was riding bareback atop a big plow horse, with three mares tethered behind. They were beautiful horses, a fact that was clearly not lost on Jesse.

The young farmer was barefoot, wearing only a pair of patched overalls. If he was out of his teens, it was just barely. His hair was a bushy thatch of red that shone orange in the sun. He waved to them as they rode up, but the smile on his face quickly disappeared when Jesse started to query him about the tethered horses.

"I reckon I'd like to make a trade for two of them horses," Jesse finally said. "We've already got some fine horseflesh here, but we've been ridin' hard, and these two need a rest."

The young farmer said with a serious expression, "You fellers must be crazy! Why, my pap would skin me alive,

I reckon! He races these horses, and he sure wouldn't take too kindly to me swapping a pair of 'em."

"Well, I'm sorry as can be," Jesse said, "but I think we need them horses more than your pap does."

"Well, you ain't gonna git 'em," the young farmer snapped. His skin coloring had turned redder than his hair.

Jesse, who was sitting with one leg propped over his saddle, smiled at Frank. Even though Frank knew what he was up to and frowned a warning, Jesse unbuttoned his coat and pulled it back to reveal two holstered pistols. There were two more in shoulder holsters under his arms. He said, "Now, look here. You just tell your pap that two men rode up and stole those horses from you, if that'd save your hide. I expect a loving father would rather have you than a couple of racehorses."

The farm boy's eyes peered wide at the four pistols that were affixed to Jesse's body. Some of the red had drained from his face, but there was apparently still enough fear of his pap to make him argue. He swallowed hard and said bravely, "I don't want to die, mister, but like I said, my pap would skin me alive. I don't reckon you can have any of these horses. I got some others I'd swap ya, but to tell you the truth, they don't look as good as the ones you're ridin'."

Still smiling, Jesse dug around in his pocket and came out with a hundred dollars. "Now, these are some fine horses that me and my brother's ridin'," he said. "I'm gonna give 'em to ya, and this hundred dollars, too." He held up the money. "Now, I can tell you for a fact that there ain't no horseflesh in Arkansas that's worth a hundred dollars and these two horses! Now, you be sure and tell your pap that, and you can tell him, too, that the horse traders you done business with was Jesse James and his brother, Frank."

"Jesse James!" The young farmer's eyes shot up from where they had been glued to Jesse's hardware to his face.

He looked doubtful. "Why, I've read about you. Are you sure you're Jesse James?"

"The one and only." Jesse's chest stuck out. He gestured toward his brother. "And this here's my brother, Frank."

Frank James closed his eyes and shook his head dolefully at Jesse's indiscretion. Jesse had always had a contradictory nature. At times he would go to great lengths using aliases, and sometimes even wearing disguises. Other times, though, he could be as careless as a schoolboy with his showing off.

"I wish I knew for sure," the boy said, glancing back and forth between Jesse and his pistols and the clearly agitated Frank. "How can you be Jesse James? I heard that you robbed a bank with them Youngers up in Minnesota, and they were lookin' for ya up there. What would you be doin' in Arkansas, anyway?" he asked.

"Just maybe we didn't rob that bank with the Youngers," Jesse suggested, laughing as he looked at Frank. "You know, it seems like the blamed law in this country pins everthing on me." He looked back at the boy, his face turned serious. "But I s'pose it doesn't matter anyway. A person will believe what he wants. Now, you look to me like a fine feller," he said. He pulled out twenty more dollars. "I'm gonna give you this hundred, and these two horses. That's for your pap. This twenty here is just for you. Don't even tell your pap, you hear? Spend it on some pretty young girl in town. Now, if you don't mind, we're in a bit of a hurry." He slid down off the side of the horse and began to uncinch his saddle.

"I don't know," the boy said, now sounding more unsure. "You don't know my pap. Why, I reckon he dern near loves these horses as much as he does his own family!"

"I'm sorry to hear that," Jesse said, "and I wish I didn't have to do it." He glanced down at his waist. "But then again, we could have just stole the dang horses from you. And to tell you the truth, I would like to make this trade as uneventful as possible."

The boy wanted to protest, but he clearly understood Jesse's meaning. Besides, whether it really was Jesse and his brother, Frank, or not, it wasn't worth dying over. He resolutely lowered his head and said, "Molly and Ginger are the two best, I reckon. Piglet's got a bit of a sore leg."

Jesse handed him the money, then shook his hand. "I'm obliged to you. What's your name?" he asked.

"Jacob Petty."

"Well, Jacob Petty, I'd appreciate it if you'd wait a spell before you tell this part of Arkansas that you done business with me and my brother." With that, Jesse cordially tipped his hat.

Within minutes, Frank and Jesse were riding off hard with the two racehorses pounding the earth under them. They could easily see why Jacob Petty's father wouldn't want to part with them. Jesse decided it was as fine a horseflesh that he had ever been atop of.

It was days later when they saw the wagon that had stopped some distance ahead. There were people gathered around, and it looked like they were burying someone. Frank pulled up at once, fully expecting them to stay clear of any crowds. He had been lecturing Jesse ever since Jacob Petty's horse deal, warning that they shouldn't spread their names around so freely. He kept reminding his brother, even though he knew he was wasting his time. Jesse would do the oddest things. He always had.

Jesse whirled his horse around. "What you stoppin' for?" he demanded.

Frank gestured toward the wagon. "Ain't no use lookin' for trouble," he said.

Jesse rubbed his midsection and groaned. "You worry too much. Looks like there's some females in that group. I'm hungry, and where there's females, there's usually food. 'Sides, if they ain't friendly, I reckon ole Molly here could outrun a forty-four slug," he pointed out.

"I hope you're right on both counts," Frank commented as they both rode toward the group.

When the James brothers rode up, Charlie One Eye was just dumping the last shovelful of dirt on Texas Dan's grave. He, along with the others, stopped and looked up at the riders.

Holt stared a moment. "I'll be danged, if it ain't Frank and Jesse James!" he suddenly called out.

Jesse was surprised at the remark. His hard gaze softened as a grin crept over his face. "Is that you, Holt Flynn?" he said. He quickly scanned over the others. "And Walter!" He paused a moment, snapping his fingers. "Walter Kens!"

"Krenz," Holt corrected.

"That's right!" Jesse said. He waved his arm at his brother. "Hell, Frank! It's Holt Flynn and Walter Krenz!"

Frank nodded and tipped his hat while Jesse went on.

"Talk about a sight for sore eyes! What in the world you boys doin' over here in Arkansas?" he asked.

"I could ask you the same thing, Jess," Holt said. He caught Frank James peering over at the campfire. "You boys hungry?"

"Ain't et a thing since yesterday," Jesse admitted in a cheerful voice.

Katy, who was standing by Holt, said, "Well, you're lucky, is all I can say. We got a few biscuits and bacon left from breakfast. I'll make you some coffee."

"Obliged," Jesse said. "Who you boys plantin'?" he asked, looking curiously at the grave that Charlie One Eye was patting down with his shovel.

"Some dern outlaw. Called himself Texas Dan Simon. Never laid eyes on him before this mornin'. He rode in here to settle a quarrel with Billy Boy, there." Holt nodded toward Billy, who was still standing there, dumbstruck by the fact that he was face to face with one of his own dime-novel heroes.

"I'd say you must be pretty good with that sidearm of yourn," Jesse said to Billy. "Couple of boys that used to ride with me knew Simon. He had a right sizable reputation, you know."

Jesse's comment shot energy through Billy's sickened body. His legs suddenly felt stronger under him, and his face beamed as he blurted out, "Jesse James! Why, I reckon you're the most famous person west of the Mississippi!" As steadily as he could under the circumstances, he walked forward to shake Jesse's hand. He, too, offered up hospitality. "You and your brother, Frank, best get down and have some breakfast. Ain't a better cook to be found than Nikki Trapp!" he promised.

While the brothers ate, Billy was unusually quiet. He couldn't pull his eyes from the two outlaws, especially Jesse. In all his born days, he had never dreamed he would ever be in their actual presence. He had a ton of questions to ask them, but the combination of excitement and sickness left him only able to stare in amazement and listen as Jesse and Holt conversed.

Jesse finished the last of the biscuits and bacon and took a long drink of coffee. "You were right, Billy. These biscuits are as good as my ma makes. So." He looked at Holt. "You headin' toward Memphis, or what?"

"Not exactly. Thought we'd go over to Helena and catch a ferry 'cross the Mississip," Holt said.

"Well, if you'd been goin' to Memphis, Frank and I might have ridden along with you, at least to there."

"Memphis is little out of your territory, ain't it, Jess?" Holt asked.

Jesse blinked a time or two. "Now, that's debatable, but I do know what you mean. Memphis does lie in a different direction from Missouri," he said. "Unfortunately, though, too many folks with them little tin badges are lookin' for us there."

"Yeah, I heard about that ordeal up in Northfield, Minnesota," Holt said. "Hard to believe what happened to Cole and his brothers." He shook his head.

Jesse blinked more rapidly. "It weren't 'cause of me. I was against the whole idea from the git-go. But, you know, a man never could tell Cole anything."

Frank James tossed the remainder of his coffee into the dying fire and said to no one in particular, "I don't reckon Cole's the only one that won't listen to reason." He turned to Holt. "Helena. That's somewhat south of Memphis. You all wouldn't mind us riding along with you across the Mississippi, would you?"

Jesse looked off at their two horses. "Now, what you got in mind, brother?" he asked.

Frank shrugged. "Nothing. I just thought it would be nice to have some company. We could head north once we're over on the Mississippi side."

Jesse explained to Holt, "We was headin' up to Nashville, then on up to Kentuck." He thought of the bacon and biscuit sandwiches. "If me and Frank was to go along, I'd pay you folks for anything Frank and I et," he offered.

"Shucks, you don't have to pay us," Holt said. "If Nikki ain't got no objections, that is."

Nikki was folding some clothes that she had washed out in a nearby creek. She, too, was eyeing the James brothers curiously. Then she smiled. "You're welcome to ride," she said.

"Much obliged. You never did say where you all was headin'," Jesse pointed out to Holt.

Holt pulled out his tobacco and offered it around. "Goin' to Georgia."

"Georgia?" Jesse exclaimed. "What in the hell's in Georgia?"

"Billy Boy there and Betsy are gonna git married. What's the name of that town that Betsy's mama lives in?" Holt asked Billy.

Billy's face flushed red. He couldn't remember the name of the town, and it embarrassed him to seem so stupid in front of Jesse James. He coughed into his hand.

Betsy placed her hand on Billy's shoulder. "It's Ellijay," she said. "It's in Gilmer County in north Georgia."

"Well, I'll be! Goin' to Georgia to get married!" Jesse said. "That offer of a smoke still on?" He leaned forward to where he could talk to Holt confidentially and pretended to take the tobacco pouch. "Say," he whispered, "now, I don't wanta know, but by damn, I sure can't see you and Walter ridin' that far for a weddin'!" He laughed as he stood up, leaving Holt sitting there with the tobacco pouch in his hand.

Holt smiled at Jesse's observation. He stood up and stretched. Jesse was right. He and Walter wouldn't go halfway across the country for a wedding. But, friend or not, Jesse's business was robbing trains and banks, and to Holt's thinking, it could stay that way.

37

IT MIGHT HAVE BEEN THE FACT THAT THE MEN HAD STOOD up with Billy against Texas Dan that reassured him that they were, like Betsy said, still his friends. Or maybe it was because he was riding along with Jesse James, something Billy put a high value on. Whatever the reason, Billy's sickness disappeared. His wound started healing nicely, and he began to return to feeling normal again.

Billy's happiness at being in Jesse's company was not at all one-sided. Jesse took instantly to Billy, mainly due to the fact that Billy was plying him with questions as fast as Jesse could answer them, and his face held such a look of hero worship as Jesse had never seen. Jesse, of course, took an immediate liking to anyone who found him fascinating, and Billy was plainly in awe. He allowed Jesse no privacy, staying close beside him as they rode. Betsy seemed to understand, and rode along silently beside the pair.

They talked all the way to Helena, with Billy prompting a recount from Jesse of every instance of outlawing that he and Frank had been involved with. Jesse didn't mind a bit; in fact, it gave him a considerable lift in spirits to recall that he and his brother had been so successful at their trade. As he listened to Billy talk happily beside him, it occurred to Jesse that this was surely the most pleasant of times that he could recall in recent memory. He was thrilled by Billy's enthusiasm, but it went even deeper than that. He looked around at the other members of the group. They seemed to be a calm and happy sort, like their lives were in some sort of decent order. There was something about the bunch that made him feel melancholy. It would be nice, he decided, to live a simpler life. Jesse had been on the run for so long, he'd grown just plain tired—more mentally than physically. What would it be like to move along in life at a leisurely pace, without having to watch over his shoulder? He often wondered what life would have held for him if he had stayed back home, on the farm, and never gotten involved in outlawing. Life on a farm, he thought. It was surely something that could satisfy a man. Jesse had half a mind to go all the way to Georgia with Holt and his friends. But—he brought his mind back to the reality of things—that was impossible. Some of his impetuous impulses had gone by Frank unchallenged, but such a drastic notion was best left unsaid and undone.

Jesse was able to keep to his thoughts, even as Billy talked a blue streak beside him. It wasn't until they came upon the sign that Jesse was pulled out of his reverie. It was just an old piece of pine nailed to a fence post. It said:

PRIZE FIGHT—BIG GRUDGE MATCH
IRISHMAN CALVIN O'HERREN VS.
ENGLISHMAN GEORGE HOPE
SEE THE FIGHT THAT WAS OUTLAWED IN ENGLAND
AND WEST OF THE MISSISSIPPI IN AMERICA

Everyone except Chief gathered around to study the words that had been painted on the odd slab of wood. Even Charlie One Eye, who couldn't read a single word, stared at the sign like it had him spell-struck. He wanted in the worst way to ask Billy what in the world all those letters said, but he was too embarrassed. A feeling of relief passed over him when Jesse spoke up and gave him a hint as to what the sign said.

"Well, I'll be doggone!" Jesse said. "Ain't nothin' I like more than watchin' a boxin' match!"

Billy had heard of prizefighting, but he had never seen any such thing—that is, a fight by rules. He figured he had seen dozens, maybe even hundreds, of fistfights along the trails and ranches he had worked. They were as common as flies at a picnic. But those had been mostly between two cowboys, either half full of drink and fighting over some female, or trail-weary and snapping about anything. Cautiously, he said, "I'd sure like to see a good boxin' after myself."

Jesse smiled at him. "Don't give no date, but that's pretty fresh paint. If they ain't already had it, maybe we can go."

Billy felt overwhelmed that Jesse had spoken to him about such an important matter. He turned to Charlie One Eye, remembering what Betsy had said about including him. "What do you think, Charlie?"

"I don't know. I guess it'd be all right. I don't reckon I ever paid to see two men bustin' each other up before," Charlie One Eye said. He rubbed his hand over his head.

"What about you, Holt?" Jesse said.

"To tell you the truth, at the moment anything would beat this travelin'," Holt said.

When they had reached the edge of town, they met a man who told them all about the fight. It was to happen that very evening, on a piece of ground right on the banks of the Mississippi. For all the talk that the man did about the event, the town seemed like any other river town. Jesse queried the man.

"Where's all the folks at, if there's gonna be a big fight like this?"

"Some are comin' from the other side of the Mississip, I reckon. You know, they outlawed it over there. Then, there's quite a bit of interest among the folks here on this side."

Jesse wasn't satisfied at all with the answer. He'd been to several prize fights, and it was usually like a circus was coming to town. "Well, they better start showin' up, then, 'cause these fighters will want a big crowd."

"You're wrong there, mister," the man said. "They didn't come over here to fight for no crowds. You see, over in the old country, you know—cross the ocean? These two hates each other! Seems they tried to fight two times, and there was killin's and fights that broke out before their fight could even get under way. No, sir! They kinda slipped over here, you might say. Wanta fight, fair and square."

Jesse still felt he was right. The town looked to be no more populated than on any ordinary day, and this was supposedly a major prize fight. Jesse had heard of these two fighters, being a fan of pugilism. He had read everything he could get his hands on about the subject. There had been times when he had driven Cole Younger nearly crazy when he had ridden day and night—maybe three, four, or even five hundred miles—to see a fight.

As the evening approached and the fight time drew near, an amazing thing occurred. People started arriving from all directions. Several riverboats pulled in, and men with their pockets stuffed full of wagering money disembarked. Others came riding across the Mississippi in ferry after ferry. There were coaches and riders on horseback filling the streets and people streaming into the hotels and eateries.

Jesse's mouth watered at the sight of so many rich men, gathered together at one place. They carried fancy ladies on their arms, dressed in elaborate hats and lacy dresses. Jesse remembered seeing whores in New Orleans that dressed like that. Such women had been out of the question for the likes of him, even though he let very few things hold him intimidated.

Even more unbelievable to Jesse was the apparent absence of lawmen in the town. As far as Jesse was able to tell, the local sheriff and his two deputies were going to try to handle the situation by themselves. Of course, men as rich as these were of the docile variety.

Jesse, along with Holt and Billy, actually got a chance to talk to the Irishman, Calvin O'Herren. They were just walking down the street, looking the town over, when they nearly collided with the man himself. O'Herren stood five-feet-ten, and tipped the scales at the mercantile store at one hundred ninety-one. He was affable and full of Irish charm and wit, seemingly undaunted about his upcoming fight. He held court with anyone who would listen, telling limericks to anyone with a willing ear.

Holt and Billy took an instant liking to O'Herren. Billy was impressed with the fighter's celebrity status and the fact that O'Herren was paying him such considerable attention. For Holt's part, O'Herren was Irish, like himself. Jesse, on the other hand, smiled and was friendly enough, but the instant they left the pugilist, he commented, "I'll bet Mister George Hope will box that smile right off of O'Herren's face!"

Billy's face grew serious. "What makes you think that? I heard that there Hope feller weighed a shade over one eighty, and that O'Herren's a much stronger puncher."

"You mighta heard that," Jesse said, "but word has it that George Hope is a more refined feller with his fists. No, sir! For my money, I say he'll teach that O'Herren a good lesson tonight!"

Holt's Irish blood heated. He, like Jesse and Billy, had just gotten a glimpse of the taller, more slender Hope. From what he could tell, Hope was O'Herren's opposite. Not only in fighting, but in behavior as well. He felt suddenly angry at Jesse. On impulse, he stepped in front of Jesse and stopped.

"I got a hundred dollars that says O'Herren will wulp that Englishman tonight," he said.

Jesse blinked. He looked hard at Holt for a moment, then a smile started at the corner of his mouth and spread into a full grin. "You sure a hundred's all you wanta bet?" he asked.

"It is," Holt said.

Jesse pulled out a hundred dollars and handed it to Billy. "I say put your money where your mouth is, then." He looked at Billy and smiled. "Keep this for me, till after the fight."

Holt fished in his pocket until he came up with a hundred dollars, and handed it to Billy. The bet was a foolish one, he thought. After all, he'd never seen two men fight under rules before in his life. For all he knew, the Englishman just could be a lot tougher than Holt's fellow countryman.

They had just finished their wager when they spotted the others walking out of an eatery. Nikki looked around at the crowded street and exclaimed, "I never seen so many folks show up at once in my life!" she said. "We'd better git on down to the river and git us a good seat. I ain't never been to a fight for money before, and I sure don't wanta be so far away I can't tell what's going on."

Hearing a woman make such a comment struck Jesse as funny. He burst out laughing, while Nikki looked offended.

Just then, a boy of about seventeen walked up, staring at the group, and Jesse in particular. He was wearing an oversized shirt that had been patched so many times it was hard to tell the original color, and an old hat with a tattered brim. He circled a few times before he got the nerve to step up closer to Jesse, and said, "Pardon me, sir. Can I ask your name? You look awfully familiar."

Jesse took a hard look at the boy. "If it's any of your business, it's David Howard," he said.

"I'm sorry, Mister Howard," the boy stammered. He nervously scraped his toe in the dirt. "But you hold an amazing resemblance to Jesse James, the outlaw."

Jesse glanced around and over the boy's shoulder. The boy was clearly by himself. He was a local, too, from the looks of his clothes and bare feet. "Ain't never met the gentleman myself," he said.

The boy seemed embarrassed. He cleared his throat and said, in a voice that was a little stronger, "I did once, three and a half years ago. Over in Missouri. I was with my papa. Jesse gave me a nickel. I still got it." He reached into his pants and retrieved the nickel, holding it out for everyone to see. A proud expression covered his face.

"A nickel!" Holt said sarcastically. "Why, I'd always heard that Jesse James was a generous feller! That was mighty white of him, I'd say! Of course, I heard that Cole Younger handed out *dollars* to tadpoles like yourself," he added, stealing a glance at Jesse.

"Don't know about that. Never did meet any of the Youngers. Not that I know of," the boy said. He nodded and, with nothing more to say, turned to leave.

"Hey, boy. What's your name?" Jesse asked.

"Tory Barney."

Jesse flipped a ten-dollar gold piece. The boy reached out to grab it, but missed. The coin fell to his feet.

Everyone stared down at the money, including the boy, who was wide-eyed with surprise. "What's that for, mister?" young Tory Barney managed to say.

"It ain't for nothin'. Don't you know you ain't supposed to look a gift horse in the mouth? Now, git your money and git on out of here," Jesse said. He sounded cross, but there was the hint of a smile on his face as he watched the boy hurry to pick up the coin.

When Tory Barney had run off to show everybody his newfound wealth, Frank shook his head. "Hell, Jess. You might just as well have told the boy who you was."

Jesse was just about to tell his brother what he could do with his comments when a voice called out behind him.

"Jesse James."

"I told you, I'm David Howard," Jesse said. He turned around, expecting to see the eager face of the young boy come back to bother him some more, but instead he came face to face with a big man whose hand hung close to his Colt. "Who the hell are you?" he said, blinking rapidly.

The man was unsmiling. He wasted no words. "Name's Joe Harbin, and I intend on taking you and your brother, Frank, down to the jailhouse that's right down the street." He spoke simply and with no emotion, but stood there as if he expected Jesse to do exactly as he said.

Jesse's eyes blazed with fire. He pulled open his jacket to reveal four pistols affixed to his body. Frank quickly stepped in front of his brother. "No, Jess," he hissed. "This ain't the way to deal with this one. From what I've heard, he'll cut you in two before you can move."

Holt, who was watching Joe Harbin closely, said, "He's right, Jesse. I've seen his work."

Jesse's jaw worked back and forth. His breathing was coming in short, angry gasps. "Get out of my way, Frank."

"I ain't gonna do it." Frank shook his head. "This ain't the way."

The muscles around Joe Harbin's mouth tightened. He said, "Both of ya. Unbuckle your gunbelts, and make it quick." He slowly reached into his pocket and pulled out a poster. "Since that little ordeal in Minnesota, you boys have gotten right valuable. Picked up this poster a few days ago. Shows twenty-five thousand reward for Jesse James, and fifteen thousand for brother Frank. And it says right here in plain English, 'Dead or Alive.' So, you two boys make up your mind right now which way it'll be."

The members of the group were too surprised by the goings-on to react. Billy had suddenly felt his thirst for bravery falling away, as he and Charlie One Eye did their best to be as inconspicuous as possible. Nikki had pressed herself close against Walter, who didn't even seem to notice that she was clutching him by the arm. She tried to give a warning sign to her sister, but Katy was still standing next to Holt. She was staring at him in a peculiar way.

Wilford Jakes was almost frozen to his spot a couple of feet to the left and the rear of Harbin. He didn't want to make any sudden moves, so he started inching out of the way. He cleared his throat. "Mister James," he said. "For what it's worth, I ain't got nothin' agin' ya. But sure as the world is round, Joe Harbin is unbeatable in a gunfight."

Jesse's temper snapped at all the unwanted advice. He angrily pushed Frank aside. "Why, you arrogant sumbitch!" he said to Harbin. "I guess it'll just have to be 'dead,' then!"

Joe Harbin's hand was only a blur. His Colt was nearly out of its holster before Jesse's hand had even reacted. There, under the early evening sun in the Mississippi River town, time stood still, as all eyes waited for Joe Harbin's gun to explode.

Harbin's Colt cleared the holster, and was aimed dead center at Jesse's chest. Jesse's fingertips reached the handle of his own pistol. His brother, Frank, had just started for his gun.

Everyone in the group tensed, their hearts racing with fear and excitement. Katy felt Holt start to move beside her, but he pulled back. It all happened in a fraction of a second, but it seemed to Katy that every emotion she had ever known passed through her.

Harbin's finger tightened on the trigger, then stopped. His eyes widened, just before his body went stiff. He suddenly pitched face forward, landing so violently on the ground that his head bounced.

At first, no one said a word or moved a muscle. Jesse stood with his hand still poised, aiming his pistol where Harbin had been standing. Frank James wiped his forehead with his hand and holstered his gun, breathing heavily.

It was Wilford Jakes who finally stepped forward and bent over Harbin's still body. He felt the man's neck. Face ashen, he looked up at the others. "He's dead," he said.

Jesse blinked rapidly. "Dead?" he said. A look of shock came over him.

Holt stepped away from Katy and, almost reluctantly, knelt beside Wilford. Ever so gently, he turned Harbin over onto his back. The unseeing eyes were still open. Holt bent his head as a tear rolled down his cheek and fell onto the ground. Alarmed, Katy wanted to run to his side and see what was the matter, but something told her that she was not needed.

Drawn by the scene in the street, the curious townspeople were now starting to gather around the group. The crowd grew, and speculations about what had happened began to circulate. In the background, someone mumbled, "Is that Jesse James? I thought I heard his name."

Holt looked up at the people. His face had become red with anger. "Git the hell back!" he shouted. "All of ya! Somebody git a doctor!"

Katy knelt by his side. "It's too late, Holt. He's dead," she said softly.

Holt pulled away. He looked around him. "I said, somebody git a doctor! You!" he pointed at Wilford Jakes. "You're his friend! Go git a doctor!"

Wilford shook his head sadly. "Well, mister, I reckon it's too late for that. It's plain that he's gone," he reasoned. He took in a deep breath. "It was his heart, you know. He had an attack up in Crawford, Kansas, a little while back."

Suddenly, Holt grabbed Wilford by the shirt and shook him violently about. "I said git a doctor."

Billy, who was still wide-eyed over the fact that he'd seen two of his biggest heroes face each other off, looked around. He said to no one in particular, "What's wrong with Holt? That feller's right. He's as dead as any man I've ever seen."

It was then that Walter moved. He pulled free of Nikki and stepped forward. Silently, he rolled a fixin', lit up, and offered it to Holt. In a calm voice, he said, "We'll git a doctor. Charlie One Eye," he ordered, "you go and fetch a doctor."

Charlie One Eye gave Walter a disbelieving look, but Walter firmly motioned him on. Charlie One Eye shrugged and took off down the street, while everyone silently watched him go.

Holt bent back down over Harbin's body. Walter put his arm around Holt's shoulder. "Everything will be all right.

Charlie One Eye's gone for a doctor," he said.

Only then did Holt seem to relax. Walter glanced at the others, one by one, sensing a need for each of them to understand.

"This here feller," he began in a low voice, looking down at Harbin's body. "This here feller's real name is Joe Flynn. He was Holt's brother."

38

IT DIDN'T TAKE LONG FOR THE CURIOUS TO LOSE INTEREST in the man who lay dead in the street. After all, there was something more important on their minds. People died every day, but never before had anyone seen the likes of the big prize fight, between two men who had come all the way across the ocean. Soon, all but a couple of people had gone on their way, leaving Holt and his group to handle their own business.

For Jesse, tonight's big fight had lost its appeal. As the crowd had milled around them, he had heard more than just the one man murmur his name. It stood to reason that there was bound to be someone else who would want to seize the swollen reward that sat on the James Brothers' heads. Besides that, his near death at the hands of Joe Harbin had unnerved him, to the point where Frank was finally able to talk some sense into him. Within minutes, the brothers were atop their prize horses, bidding everyone a hushed and hurried good-bye. They caught a ferry to the Mississippi side, and when darkness fell, they headed north, riding hard for Tennessee.

Katy had tried to talk Holt into taking his brother to a funeral parlor right there in Helena, but Holt wouldn't hear of it. He wasn't about to spend any money letting a stranger handle his own flesh and blood. He'd have no part of that, he said. At first he had even announced that he wanted to take his brother back to Texas and bury him next to their mother, but when the initial shock wore off and he could see things more clearly, he realized the futility of the idea. He finally decided to bury his brother on the other side of the river, along the banks of the mighty Mississippi.

That night they, too, caught a ferry across, and made camp on the riverbank. As Katy feared, Holt spent a restless night, rising every so often to stand and look out over the moonlit water and smoke. She let him be, and spent a sleepless night herself, until she heard his deep breathing.

The next morning, when Holt awoke, he rose stiffly from his bedroll and stretched. Off to his left, Charlie One Eye was up, digging a grave next to a big, overhanging tree whose branches reached out over the river like a fancy Parisian umbrella.

Holt walked closer and watched the digging. "Much obliged to ya, Charlie," he said somberly.

Charlie One Eye nodded quietly. He wiped the sweat from his brow on his sleeve. "Sure am sorry about your brother," he said without looking at Holt.

Holt shook his head. "Don't be. I'm surprised he lasted this long. A man can only live the life of a gunny for so long. I guess Joe beat the odds longer than most."

Charlie One Eye thought about it a moment. "Yes, sir, I'd say he did." He nodded and went back to his digging.

Wilford joined the two at the gravesite, and soon Katy followed. Back at the wagon, which was a good twenty-five yards from the bank, some of the others were stirring. Walter was building a fire, while Nikki broke out cooking utensils and provisions. Chief had found a bush and was relieving himself. Under the wagon, Betsy and Billy were still asleep.

Wilford stared out across the water, at the Arkansas side, where the smoke from the dying campfires drifted upward, mixing in with the early morning fog. One of the last two riverboats was pulling out. Once again, the sleepy town looked for all the world to be facing just another day, as if nothing had ever happened. It occurred to him that one man's life didn't seem to amount to much in the total scheme of things. Not to the rest of the world, anyway.

Feeling more depressed than he could ever remember, he stepped close to Holt and handed him the envelope that Harbin had given him in Crawford. "Your brother gave me this," he said.

Holt stared down at the crumpled envelope. "What's this you say?" he asked, turning it over in his hand.

"Back in Crawford, Kansas," Wilford explained. "When Joe had his attack of the heart. He was recuperating at Mrs. Beavers's boardinghouse. He gave me this here envelope. Said it was in case anything ever happened to him. I hoped I was never gonna have to open it," he added, his voice faltering.

Holt tried to hand it back, but Wilford wouldn't take it.

"Go on," Holt insisted. "He gave it to you."

"If it's all the same to you, you're his brother, and I'd just as soon you had it," Wilford said.

Holt stared at Wilford, who stared right back. "Why, hell, then!" Holt said. He tore the envelope open.

Inside was a piece of paper. He pulled it out, unfolded it, and read:

Wilford,
I got sevn thousin dollars in San Antone bank. In Ft. Worth, I got nere four thousin. If I die, you tak this note to the banks in thes towns. You by the ranch for yersef. Wot mony is left over gos to my bruthr, Holt Flynn. You kin find him by axin in injin terytory.

Joe Harbin Flynn
1876

Holt held out the paper. "This just sounds like you got yourself a little money, Mister Jakes," he said.

Wilford took the paper and read, then shifted around uncertainly. "Don't know what I'd do with a ranch, all by myself. 'Sides, I reckon the money's rightfully yours," he said glumly.

"Why," Holt answered, "just 'cause he was my brother? No, you go and buy that ranch and hire you somebody to ramrod it. Get yourself a few beeves 'n let 'em run. You just find yourself a rockin' chair and put your feet up."

The logic was wasted on Wilford. He felt as low as he'd ever felt. He was out of a job and in a strange land. Harbin, who was bossy as they came and had near scared him to death on occasion, had been the closest thing to a friend he had ever known. Even the aroma of coffee brewing and fatback from Nikki's skillet filtering through the air failed to whet his enthusiasm.

Charlie One Eye finished his digging. He stepped out of the hole and looked for Holt's approval.

"Right nice grave, there, Charlie. I appreciate it," Holt said sincerely.

Charlie One Eye nodded. He put his hands on either side of his back and stretched.

"Come on, Charlie. We just as well go and have some breakfast," Holt said. "We'll bury him afterwards. You comin', Mister Jakes?"

It was then that Wilford finally let the fine aroma from Nikki's cooking efforts register from his nose to his brain. He spat into the Mississippi and eagerly followed Holt to the wagon.

Breakfast was pretty much a quiet affair, with everyone giving Holt their respectful silence. It was Holt who finally did the speaking. He stood up to get everyone's attention, and walked over to where Wilford was sitting.

"This here's Wilford Jakes, in case any one of ya don't know it yet," Holt said, gesturing toward Wilford. He frowned. "I guess all of ya must be wonderin' what's goin' on here. You see, my brother was a good man, once." He stopped and shrugged, staring out at the flowing waters of the Mississippi. "Hell, he might have *still* been a good man. Who's to say? Anyways, when he took to sellin' his gun, it hurt our mama real bad. I guess Joe didn't want to change his ways, so instead he changed his name."

Everyone stared at Holt wordlessly. It was hard for any of them to see just where Holt stood on the matter. He was clearly hurt, but it seemed to be a hurt that had been put away for years, and he had no further words of explanation to give. He pulled Katy to her feet. "I reckon I'll bury him now," he said.

It was done quickly. They gathered around the grave. Nikki read Scripture and said a prayer, then Holt filled the hole, shunning any offered help. That done, the group filed back to the wagon.

Holt lingered over the grave for a while with Katy standing silently beside him. When he returned to the others, he laid out Harbin's possessions. Besides the clothes on his back, Harbin had had one change in his bedroll. There was nearly four hundred dollars; his Winchester, Colt, and gunbelt; and a small knife and pocket watch, along with his horse and saddle. Holt picked up the money. "Here." He handed it to Wilford. "And don't say a dern word. You were his friend. Just take it."

Wilford stared at the money in disbelief. He swallowed hard at the lump that was forming in his throat. All his life, bad luck had been the only luck he'd ever felt. Now, for the second time, he was being handed a huge sum of money. He couldn't think what he had done to deserve such kindness from Joe Harbin, and now his brother, Holt. He reached up quickly and flicked away the tear that had formed in the corner of his eye. He tried to say thanks, but couldn't get the word out. Instead, he just nodded his head.

Holt turned to Charlie One Eye. "This here's a good saddle, and yourn is about gone. You take it."

He tossed the Winchester to Walter, who silently nodded his thanks.

"Billy Boy, I don't reckon I ever knew anyone that read any more about gunnies than you, and I hesitate to do this, but if you promise to take it as a keepsake and nothin' more, I want you to have Joe's Colt."

Billy's eyes widened. Even in the gravity of the moment, he couldn't hide his excitement. "My gosh! I thank ya, Holt. I'll keep this to my dyin' day!" he said.

"Let's hope that's a long time, Billy Boy, and if I ever hear of you wearin' that thing or usin' it, I'll come lookin' to take it back," Holt said sternly.

"No, sir! I swear I'll put it up and treasure it," Billy said. He held the gun and holster to his chest like he was carrying a newborn baby. He couldn't have dreamed anything better. He had actually ridden with Frank and Jesse James, and now he had in his possession one of the most famous Colts in the world. Even if they found a cave full of gold, it wouldn't match the way he felt at this moment.

Holt opened the pocket watch and closed it slowly, weighing it lightly in his hand. He put it in Katy's palm and closed her fingers over it.

"I can't take this, Holt," Katy protested. "Why, you need to keep something." She tried to put it in his hands. She couldn't hold back the tears that filled her eyes.

"I reckon with you keepin' it, it *will* be mine," Holt said softly. "I want you to take it." He stood there thoughtfully for a moment, while the others watched him somberly. "Guess I'll just keep this knife," he added, tucking it into his back pocket.

"I'll tell you what else I'll do," Holt went on. "I'll tie that ornery stallion I've been ridin' on the back of the wagon and take Joe's horse.

"Wilford." He gestured toward the others with a sweep of his hand, "I imagine the thought's crossed your mind about what this unlikely troupe is doin' out here in the middle of nowheres together. Fact is, we're goin' to Georgia. See that ole Injun over there? He says there's a cave full of gold, and he's gonna take us to it." Holt stopped and chuckled to himself. "By damn, when I left home to come on this trip, that's all I could think of. I believed in it!" He nodded, then shrugged. "Now, I don't know if there's any dern gold in Georgia or not, but if I don't do nothin' else, I intend on seein' this thing through. And, if you'd like to come along, as far as I'm concerned, you're welcome."

Wilford's eyes flashed with interest. "Gold?" His excitement turned to doubt as he looked at the Indian. "Well, gold or not, I guess I'd like to tag along. I ain't got nowhere else to go. Right now, that ranch ain't too appealin'." He thought about the four fine biscuits he'd just finished off for breakfast, and looked at Nikki. "Does she do all the cookin'?" he asked hopefully.

Nikki mouth twisted as she spoke up. "I sure do, and from the looks of that belly of yours, you haven't missed a meal in your life," she commented. "Supplies cost money, you know, so when we come to the next town, I expect you to dig down in that pocket and come up with some money for provisions. This ain't exactly a free excursion, you know." She caught Holt's hard glance, and quickly added a smile to her words.

Before they pulled out, Billy handed Holt two hundred dollars. "Here's your money from last night's bet," he said.

Holt gave him a puzzled look. "What bet?"

"The fight," Billy said.

Holt had forgotten all about the fight. He had spent the evening and all night remembering his childhood and his brother, Joe. Even the cheers from across the river had been blocked out of his mind.

"It's yours." Billy grinned. "The Irishman, O'Herren? knocked that Hope feller out in the forty-third round! I talked to some fellers last night who seen it."

Holt took the money. He thought about the bet that Jesse James had so eagerly wagered. He remembered how close his brother, Joe, had come to killing the Jameses, with only the hand of fate intervening. He smiled warmly at Billy.

Then, the smile turned to laughter.

"What's so funny?" Billy grinned back.

Holt held up the money. "I knew I was gonna win this bet."

"Why's that?" Billy asked, still grinning.

"Well hell, Billy Boy," Holt said, shoving the money into his pocket. "Let this be a lesson to ya. One good Irishman can lick any two Englishmen, any day of the week."

39

THEY TRAVELED ALL THE WAY THROUGH MISSISSIPPI pleasantly enough. There were no setbacks, except for the cooler weather that was setting in. The days began crisp and cool, settling into a perfect riding atmosphere by afternoon, but the nights were downright cold. The men were glad that Nikki had thought to pack several blankets in the wagon. Sleeping on cold hard ground was something they had become unaccustomed to.

In Alabama, they encountered cold rain—several days of it. Some of the areas flooded, and they were constantly on the watch for higher ground. The wagon repeatedly got stuck in the mud, and it could take an hour to get it unstuck. Finally, they sold the wagon to a farmer in Alabama, then packed what they could on the team of horses. Even though the farmer warned them that the horses would have a hard enough time making it through the rugged Georgia mountains, it was a difficult decision to make, especially for Wilford and Charlie One Eye, who had almost lived from one meal to the next. They could barely stand to watch Nikki leave behind so many of her cooking utensils. When the Dutch oven was added to the pile, Wilford's spirits sank considerably. This was a particularly devastating development. In all his life, he'd never tasted biscuits any finer than Nikki's.

They made it to the eastern side of the state, where the weather turned into a serious problem. There was no clear pattern to be seen. Cold rains would fall for great periods at a time, then freeze at night. It got so damp and cold, they couldn't sleep unless they were so tired they lost the energy to shiver. Then, the tables would turn for a week or two. Sunshine emerged, filling the afternoons with a humidity that made everything feel sticky.

The weather swings eventually had their effect. Billy, who was still a little weak from the infection, caught the first cold. Then Betsy got sick. Soon, everyone but the old Indian was coughing and sneezing through red runny noses. Sleep was impossible, and everyone grew tired and irritable. Holt pushed the group on, though, eager to move on to a more stable climate.

Walter was the hardest hit. He got so sick, Nikki was sure that he was going to die. Even though she was feeling poorly herself, she stayed right by his side and nursed him as patiently and lovingly as if he was her child.

Holt was finally able to buy several jars of homemade liquor and honey from a farmer whose house they passed by. That night, he heated up some water and dumped in a healthy dose of honey and a full jar of liquor, then passed the mixture around. It wasn't a cure, but at least they all seemed to feel a little better, and for the first time in days, most of them were able to get some sleep. Charlie One Eye remarked to Billy that they were surely the most pathetic lot he had ever seen. Billy just shrugged and blew his nose, glaring at Chief, who sat there without the slightest trace of a cold, old age and all.

The colds plagued them all through eastern Alabama. By the time they reached the Georgia border they were all starting to feel better. As they crossed into the state, their pace started picking up. They were getting closer to their quest, and their excitement was growing.

Walter had shaken his cold, too, but instead of returning

to his old crusty self, he had changed. All of Nikki's mothering had had an effect on him. He seemed to have given in to it, even to the point where he was now asking her to fetch him things, and to rub the soreness from his back whenever the day's riding was done. Then, at night, the two of them would curl up together to share their heat during the cold nights.

The sudden turnabout in Walter's demeanor wasn't lost on anyone, especially Holt and Katy. Holt was just plain flabbergasted that Walter had given in totally to such a woman. He had never seen Walter act so familiar with a female in front of others. It had never been his nature to be trustful of anyone, man or woman, and Nikki wasn't the normal kind of shy, submissive woman. Maybe that was what Walter needed—the dominant, motherly type. Holt couldn't figure it, but he didn't care, either. He wasn't sure if Walter was making a mistake or not, but he had to admit one thing. He had never seen Walter any more at peace with himself and others. Gone was the perpetual scowl and the sour disposition. Why, Walter acted almost pleasant! Holt had to hand it to Nikki for her patience.

As for Katy, she had known for a long time that Nikki loved Walter. A blind man could see that, she had told Holt. Still, she was surprised to see how Nikki would drop everything to wait on Walter, hand and foot. She would hurry to fetch anything Walter beckoned for. Why, Nikki had never done such a thing for anyone in the world—not even her first husband! It was almost like Katy was looking at a new person in her sister. Like Holt, however, Katy felt pleased to see Walter and Nikki getting on so well. Her sister had run a long and hard race to catch Walter, and to see him slowly starting to respond made her happy, even if it was a lopsided relationship of fetch-and-rub. Besides, if anyone could handle a situation, it was Nikki.

As the group moved farther into Georgia, they began to talk about the cave of gold again. The discussions were held in low voices, as if the slightest misspoken word might bring them bad luck. The cave was getting nearer by the day and, whether it was full of gold or not, it had made each of their lives a little bit richer.

A change began to come over old Chief. All of a sudden, he was sitting more erectly in the saddle. His eyes seemed to come alive, squinting in thought as he studied the horizon ahead. He would turn his head to linger on a stream or follow the flight of birds in the sky. There would be signs of recognition crossing his face as they neared his home of so many years before. The others noticed, and they watched old Chief curiously. Sometimes, they could hear him laughing gently to himself over some long-lost memory that had come back. Then he started to hum. There was no melody, just a low monotone that came from his throat. After a while, the humming took on a beat. It was the beat of his people, long ago when they had roamed freely in the thick Georgia countryside. He was nearing the land of his people, the Cherokee lands where they had lived and hunted and died for uncounted generations, until the time when the white men had driven them west, and out of their mountain home. As a young man, Chief had stored the sacred tribal melodies in his heart, and hidden them away for the day when he would return to his land.

Now, as he rode through the thick undergrowth, he smelled old familiar smells and remembered his youth. His heart raced inside his chest. He was happy again. The lines of time on his face had relaxed. He looked peaceful.

The countryside still held fresh scars that had been dug in by the great War Between the States. Only when he passed them by did Chief stop his humming and lose the gleam from his eye. It had been claimed, stolen, and ravaged by the white man's senseless battle, but this was still his Cherokee home.

As the group made a steady ascent up the Georgia mountains, they passed by the small homesites that had been dug into the sides. Chief studied the poverty of the mountain families. Children played in the tiny yards, shoeless, and with barely enough tattered clothing to ward off the cold. A few places had dogs, but the animals were so lean and hungry-looking they lacked the energy to do any more than sit and wag their tails. The houses were worn down and in need of repair. Many of the families had been left fatherless by the war. Or some men had come home without an arm or a leg. The sight was sad at best. The old Indian had mixed feelings about it. These were the greedy whites whose grandfathers had forced his people out of their land of plenty. And they had done nothing more with it than become destitute. It was hard for him to feel any pity in his heart.

Resentment stirred in him briefly, but it didn't last. They were getting closer to his home. In five or six days, they would reach the place of his birth. Childhood memories that had long been dimmed by the passing of time came back, crowding his thoughts and crawling all over him. He had come here to die, but strangely enough, he felt more alive than ever as his homeland welcomed him with its beauty.

After three days in the Georgia mountains, the group was starting to show signs of the hard travel. All of them were nursing cuts and scratches from the constant battling of tree limbs and the rough undergrowth. The horses were complaining, too, often refusing to go any farther until they had been rested for a spell. The rains were coming more frequently, but now they were laced with tiny droplets of ice, as the winter season approached.

At night, the group usually managed to find shelter under overhanging rocks or cliffs. It helped some, with blocking out the freezing rain, but still the travelers would wake up cold and wet from the day before. They would huddle close together around the evening campfire, but talk had died down. It was the end of the trip, and they were tired of trees and horses and sleeping huddled next to dying campfires, but still they kept on. It was the thought of gold that drove them.

One night, they happened upon a cave that opened out

upon a clear pool of water. It was too good to be true. Happily, they camped out for a two-day stay, drying themselves out and letting the animals get a good rest. Holt and Billy made several trips out on foot, and always came back with enough squirrel meat to feed them well. The woods, they said, were teeming with wild animals. Old Chief nodded wisely to himself when he heard Billy comment that the Georgia mountains weren't so bad, after all.

By the time they left the cave, the icy rains had stopped, and pleasant weather returned to the mountains. As the group pushed forward, Chief looked upward through the treetops at the skies. He knew exactly where they were, but he would say nothing to the others, yet. They were approaching a broad valley. When they crossed that valley and reached the next mountain, they would find the gold.

40

IT WAS AFTERNOON WHEN THEY RODE INTO THE SETTLEment of Spring Place, so named for the fine springs that sprouted out of the limestone rocks. They had found such a place and decided to make camp right there, washing the grime of travel from their bodies and drinking the cold water. They settled amid the hickory and white oak trees. There was a sodden carpet of fallen leaves underfoot from the heavy rains. It was a new and different world to the travelers, and the smell of a campfire in these woods was a quite unique and pleasant smell to experience.

They had pulled up some old fallen tree limbs to sit on, and collected enough dry sticks to get a good fire going. Holt had instructed everyone to look for dry hickory wood, if they could find any.

Soon they were seated around a healthy campfire. Nikki was about to break out her cooking utensils, when a large-boned woman of nearly six feet appeared. She walked up to the spring and stopped to look the group over. The woman was finely dressed, which came as a surprise after all of the poverty they had seen. With her was a small, freckle-faced boy.

No one spoke, so the big woman brushed back her gray-streaked hair with her fingers and said, "I declare! You folks look as if you've come a fur piece. Welcome to Spring Place!" She laughed. It came out naturally, as natural as the flowing water from the limestone rock. "Well, you folks just as well pack your belongin's back up, and come on to the big house!" She pointed. "It's up around the bend, there, behind those trees. I'll kill a couple of chickens. I been meanin' to get around to killin' 'em for a spell, anyhow! Got lots of cool, fresh buttermilk and good churned butter for your cornbread."

Without so much as a chance to even learn the woman's name, they found themselves hurriedly repacking. They were soon following after the woman, who walked ahead of them, tall and erect, as if it was natural for her to be in charge. They walked under the overhanging limbs of oak, chestnut, and poplar trees. Around the bend, they came to a big clearing. There was a well-tended yard that fronted a white, two-story house. A big porch wrapped itself around the front and side.

They walked through the yard. The woman turned to Holt, sensing that he was the group's leader. "You all can unsaddle your horses and turn them out inside that pasture." She nodded to a fenced area where there were several milk cows standing placidly around. "Name's Verna Kelly," she said to no one in particular. "And this here little varmint"—she rubbed the boy's head—"is my grandson, Paul."

Holt made a quick introduction of the group, to which Verna Kelly nodded pleasantly. She climbed the porch steps, then turned to the boy. "Go tell Asa to fetch me two hens," she ordered. "And you tell that Asa, don't be bringin' me no live ones. Best have their heads gone when I see 'em." She laughed that friendly laugh. "Asa's my nigra help," she explained. "He's all I got since the war. Claims he can't hear very well, but that's a lie. Tell you the truth, he hears what he wants to hear. Cantankerous old devil. Now, you all git on over there and unsaddle your horses. I'm gonna put some water on to boil."

She disappeared inside the house, leaving her guests to themselves. Like an obedient bunch, they walked their mounts to the corral and unsaddled them.

As they were turning the horses loose, Charlie One Eye said to Holt, "I don't like that woman." He frowned and stared back at the big house, biting his lip suspiciously.

Holt slapped the rump of the big gelding. "Why, hell, Charlie. You ain't knowed her long enough to form an opinion, I reckon. How'd she git under your saddle so quick, anyhow?"

Charlie One Eye took his hat off and wiped his head, then held his hand up to his face. He looked around to see where Nikki was. He said, "You know, that Nikki Trapp can be as bossy and talkative as any female I've ever seen, but that Kelly woman passes orders out to a man just like she was a trail boss or somethin'! Dern near bigger'n most men, at that!"

Holt smiled. "She does carry herself right well. I'll say that for her. But to tell you the truth, that fresh buttermilk and cornbread is about all I care to think about right now."

"Yeah, Charlie," Billy said, "don't be bringin' up any of your silly old fears. I ain't gonna miss out on that good fried chicken! Not fer nothin'! 'Sides that, we can handle ourselves just fine, can't we, Holt?" he added.

Charlie One Eye blinked angrily. "I ain't afraid of no female, I reckon!" he said.

It was good and dark by the time Verna Kelly called them to the table. There were so many of them, they had to eat in shifts. She fed the men first, even though she did comment that it was a custom that had no foundation, to her way of thinking. When the men were finished, she sat down to eat with the women. Katy and Betsy were silent through the meal, while Nikki and Verna Kelly talked like they'd known each other for years. It was plain that the two had a lot in common, both being assertive in nature and not without viewpoints.

When the last supper plate had been cleaned and put away, Verna Kelly lit a lamp, and the women joined the men out on the darkened porch. Katy sat down beside Holt on the top porch step, while Betsy plopped down on Billy's lap. Nikki sat on the porch floor at Walter's feet.

Verna Kelly settled back comfortably in her chair. "Where you folks come from anyway?" she asked conversationally.

"Out west," Holt offered.

"Out west, you say? Now, that could mean a lot of things to a lot of folks," Verna Kelly said. "Why, to me, out west could mean Alabama! But then, you folks don't look like Alabama stock to me."

"Well, some of us are from Kansas, some from Indian Territory, and some of us come from Arkansas," Holt said. He reached over and took Katy's hand.

"What about that old redskin?" Verna Kelly said. She pointed at Chief, who had positioned himself at one edge of the porch and was sitting cross-legged, and staring out into the night.

"That's a good question. Old Chief's originally from somewheres around here," Holt said, trying to see Verna Kelly's face in the dim glow of the lamp.

"Cherokee." Verna Kelly nodded. "Why, it's been near forty years since we seen the likes of his people. Has *he* got somethin' to do with you folks travelin' to this part of the world?"

Billy was sitting there studying the stars that lit the sky, holding Betsy's hand. At Verna Kelly's question, his face brightened, and he turned her way. Holt noticed, and spoke up quickly, in case Billy had any notions of mentioning the gold. They had talked about this, and Billy knew better, but sometimes Billy spoke before he thought. "You might say Chief's our guide," he said. "Betsy, there, the one with Billy Boy?" He nodded toward the pair. "That girl's mama lives east a ways, over that mountain. Place called Ellijay. Betsy and Billy is gonna get married there."

"I been to Ellijay," Verna said, "but that was a long time ago. Took the old Federal Road. Can't remember why I went, and for my money, I ain't goin' back. You just walk up one hill and down the next. These days, I leave mountain climbin' to the young ones." She chuckled.

"I'd think it would get lonely, all by yourself and in the middle of all these trees," Katy said.

"Can't say it don't, but a body gets used to it. 'Course, I got my grandson. God love him," Verna Kelly said. She turned back toward the old Indian. "Folks might not take too kindly at the sight of bad memories. You know, they ran his people outa here. Last ones left in '39. Sent 'em packin' west. They got a raw deal, for sure." She shook her head. "That big red brick house you all passed? That was built by one of 'em. James Vann was his name. From what I hear tell, he was half-breed. Daddy was Scottish, his mama Cherokee. Why, he had tradin' posts, blacksmith shops, and some say he owned four or five thousand acres o' land!" She leaned forward. "Would you believe he had pert near a hundred slaves? He must've been somethin'! Why, he even brought Christianity to this neck of the woods! Brought in some Moravian missionaries. One of his own people kilt him, though."

Chief looked up at her. His eyes twinkled in the lamp's glow.

"You remember, don't ya?" Verna Kelly said, nodding at him with a smile. She looked back at the others. "He had a son named Joe, who took over when his father died. Why, Joe was an even better businessman than his pap was. Folks around these parts called him 'Rich Joe.' Owned a couple of grist mills and had taverns 'n sawmills. Shucks! They say there wasn't much of anything in north Georgia that Rich Joe didn't have his hands on. Even had him two or three gold mines."

Billy went to coughing and moving around at the mention of gold. His excitement was showing. Holt noticed, and stood up, trying to act nonchalant. "Gold mines? Why, I declare! Never heard of no gold mines in Georgia," he said calmly.

"Well, there sure was. I hear stories that there's still gold hidden under some of these mountains," Verna Kelly said.

Holt tried to shift the conversation to another subject. "Whatever happened to this Rich Joe feller?" he asked, his voice full of interest.

"Probably the same as happened to that old Indian ridin' with you." Verna Kelly shrugged. "Got white man's justice dealt to him. Hired him a white man to oversee some of his businesses. Well, there was a law against such things. You know, whites couldn't work for Indians. Shoot! They just passed that law 'cause of Rich Joe. 'Course, Rich Joe didn't know 'bout the law . . . I declare! Overnight, he lost everything. They came in the dead of winter. Ran him and his family out into the cold."

She stood up suddenly and announced, "You womenfolk can sleep in the house. Men can have the barn if you don't mind the smell. We've had a damp year, and sometimes the stench gits so thick in there you can't hardly walk through it. 'Course, a lot of it has to do with the fact that Asa ain't cleaned the manure out in a month o' Sundays. But I got lots of nice warm blankets." She shook her finger. "Just make sure you men don't git to smokin' and burn my barn down," she warned.

Charlie One Eye mumbled under his breath, but Holt just smiled and said, "Yes, ma'am. We'll be right careful." He grinned at Charlie One Eye, who shook his head and blew out an exasperated breath at the woman's bossiness.

Verna Kelly lit some lamps and sent the men off to the barn. In the house, however, she stopped the women and motioned for them to sit down around the kitchen table. "You don't know how nice it is to have some women to talk to," she explained. "Around here—runnin' this place—all my dealin's are with men. And sometimes I get lonely for some women talk. Seems like all the women around here keep themselves busy with cookin' and makin' clothes and such, or else they're busy with the church. Methodists and Baptists, you know." She wrinkled her nose as she spoke.

Betsy frowned. "But you have a grandson. So you must have had a child," she said.

Verna Kelly nodded. "I have a son. He and my daughter-in-law are up north, 'cross the border in Tennessee. They found work up there and moved. I told 'em I'd keep their youngun until they could afford a house." She shook her head. "Right now, those two are livin' in a tent!" She stood up to fetch some cups from the cupboard, then poured four cups of tea. "Of course, my son could've stayed right around here and worked," she said pensively. "This place will be his someday, anyhow. But he says he don't like farmin'." She laughed. "So he got him a job cuttin' wood in a sawmill. Heaven knows we got plenty of sawmills right here in Georgia! But I guess he just wanted to get away. Why, when I married that boy's daddy, I felt lucky just to have enough land that we could grow our own eats on. Till the war, my husband owned and ran a grist mill, but do you think my boy—Verlin's his name—would work in a grist mill?" She sighed.

"What happened to Mr. Kelly?" Nikki asked.

"Same thing that happened to a lot of men around here," Verna Kelly said. "Boys, too, I'm ashamed to say. The blamed war. My husband was near forty, and he wouldn't have it until he ran out and joined up. Wasn't gone more than three months when I got the news. Oh, it was such a terrible war! I lost two brothers. My sister lost a son, and I had a brother lost two sons." Her face was strained as she talked, but there wasn't any emotion. She looked at the three women who stared hard at her. "I know what you're thinkin'. Where's my tears? Well, they've been put away for a long time," she said matter-of-factly.

The women sat there for a while in sympathetic silence, drinking their tea. Nikki appeared deep in thought. Then she spoke up softly, "It was a terrible war, indeed. And for what?"

"Well, the nigras will tell ya that they were freed by Mister Lincoln, and I can't argue that," Verna Kelly said. "A man should be free. But Lord, Lord! You look at the nigras today, and most of 'em are near starvin', the ones on their own are. We let all of ours go but Asa. He's got a little shed he stays in out back, and I pay him a little money. Well, every payday he goes right down to George Shaw's still. Stays drunk for two or three days. Got him an old nigra widow over there that cooks for the Shaws. I 'spect he lays up with her while he's drinkin'. Yep," she added, "Mister Lincoln's war may have freed 'em, but it sure left a lot of us with our hurts."

Verna looked at Betsy. "So you're goin' to Ellijay and git married? I must say, that feller's awful handsome. But don't let 'im git too much of a head of steam too early in life, or you'll spend all your time pickin' up after 'im and grievin' over 'im." She patted Betsy's hand. "You know, men are just boys that smell different. They don't really change that much. Oh, they slow down and git grumpier with age, but ninety-eight percent of 'em still don't think a woman was put here for anything other than waitin' on him and pullin' her bloomers down when he's a mind."

Betsy wasn't embarrassed, but she did blush red all the same when she glanced at Katy and Nikki. She wished they didn't know about Fort Smith, and the fact that she'd lived in a little room above Horst's saloon. "You don't worry about me, Mrs. Kelly. I've known a few like you're talkin' about. Billy's different. He's a little boy, all right, an innocent one," she said.

"Childish, if you ask me," Nikki commented.

"No call for that," Katy said. She smiled at her sister with everything but her eyes.

"I didn't mean nothin'," Nikki said apologetically. She smiled at Betsy, and for the first time it was genuine.

That night, when Betsy went to bed, her mind was far removed from any cave of gold. She, like the old Indian, was full of memories of a Georgia she had known as a child. She was excited about seeing her mama, and taking the man she was going to marry to meet her. The only dampening thought was the wish that her father was still alive and could meet Billy. She smiled, remembering the first time Billy had come stumbling into her room, all full of himself and nervous as a new father. She never would have thought that she would ever really fall in love with him. As she closed her eyes, she could see his face. She was, indeed, very much in love.

41

AT FIRST, HOLT THOUGHT HE WAS DREAMING. HE WAS, in fact, in the middle of a deep sleep when the gunshots rang out. Right away, his mind took the sudden noise and sent him visions of a terrible thunderstorm. Groggily, he rolled over and tried to block the dream out, but instead he saw a crowd of angry people growing under the black clouds. They were yelling and coming after him. He looked all around, but there was nowhere to run . . .

He came fully awake with a start and sat up, wiping his eyes. The thunder had stopped, but the shouting voices were still there, only getting louder. It was pitch dark.

At first, he couldn't remember where he was. Then the fresh smell of manure hit his nostrils and brought him to his senses. He was in Verna Kelly's barn.

He could hear light snoring in the darkness all around him. He strained to hear what the shouting voices were saying, but couldn't make any sense of it.

It was hard to get his bearings right away, so Holt sat there until he could remember which way was which. It reminded him of a time when he had gone swimming as a youngun. The pond had been deep where he and his friends were swinging from a rope into the water. Holt had rolled himself up into a little ball and hit the water headfirst. For a brief moment, under water, he had lost his bearings and didn't know which way was up. It had scared him out of his wits, and he'd shied away from swimming holes ever since. As he sat there in the darkness, he pushed away that old feeling and wondered instead what all the loud talking was about.

There was a flicker of light, and he turned to face the barn door. Through the cracks between the boards, patches of light shone through. Burning light. Quickly, he pulled on his boots and strapped on his Colt.

"Walter!" Holt called out low. "Walter? Wake up!"

It was Billy who answered. "Who's that talking? Holt?"

"What in tarnation's goin' on?" Walter's voice said sleepily.

Before Holt could answer them, one of the shouting voices called out. "You! In the barn! Come out here, before we come in for ya!"

By now, Charlie One Eye had also risen. "Who the hell's that out there?" he asked.

"I don't know," Holt said, "but grab your weapons and let's see." His voice was filled with trepidation, which did nothing to boost the other men's confidence any.

With the help of the flickering light, Holt was able to locate the cattle entrance at the back of the barn, where the cows were turned back out to pasture. In a loud whisper, he instructed Billy to take a look-see from there.

"Nothing," Billy said when he returned. "Whoever they are, they're all out front."

Holt nodded. "That's good. Walter, you, Charlie One Eye, and Wilford cover us with your rifles." He pointed to the door. "I reckon Billy and I had better go out and see what's goin' on."

Holt and Billy carefully opened the door and slowly stepped outside. What they saw nearly took their breath away.

About thirty feet from the barn door, there looked to be upward of twenty white-robed figures, standing in a semi-circle. They all wore white cloth that covered them from head to toe. Small round eyeholes had been cut in the masks, and the figures had to turn their whole heads to see around them. Some carried torches of fire that lit up the barnyard. All of them held weapons—mostly single-shot rifles, guns, clubs. Some even had hand axes and garden tools. It was the strangest sight Holt had ever seen. He could think of nothing other than to stand there and stare at these strange men who were all covered with what looked like bedsheets to him.

"If you fellers are lookin' to rob us, you've picked some mighty poor folks. We ain't got no money," he said finally, still trying to get a grip on the situation. He glanced over at Billy, whose eyes were as wide as they would open, and hoped he wouldn't decide to do anything sudden.

One of the white-sheeted figures stepped forward out of the semi-circle and waved his torch. "What's your business here?" he asked.

"Just travelin' through," Holt answered, his hand close to his Colt. "Billy here is gonna git married over in Ellijay," he added.

One of the men in the semi-circle spoke up. "He's just stallin' for time," he said impatiently.

The first one nodded. "The Indian," he said to Holt. "Bring him out here."

Holt frowned. "I don't reckon we're gonna bring anyone out," he answered calmly. "Not under these circumstances, at least."

"Well then, we're gonna have to come in and get 'im. So move aside if you know what's good for ya," the first man said gruffly.

"I wouldn't do that," Holt said in a stern voice. "You see, there's three repeatin' rifles right inside that barn there, pointed dead center. Now, any of you or your friends take another step closer . . . Why, between those repeatin' Winchesters and me and Billy, here—we'll drop half your asses where you stand."

Just then, Verna Kelly came out of the darkness and walked into the half circle of light. She was wearing a nightshirt. Her hair, which had been coiled into a neat bun that day, now lay long and flowing down her back. As she walked, it was caught up in the evening wind, almost transparent in the light of the flickering torches.

She marched up to the leader of the group. Her hands were held close to her sides, hidden in the folds of her nightgown. She looked the man over carefully, studying his shoes, then moving upward. Finally, she raised her right hand, and stuck a small pistol against the man's face. The eyes that peered through the small holes blinked in surprise.

"Git off my property, Silas Turner," Verna Kelly said, "or I'll put a hole right between your eyes. You can count on it."

"She's bluffin'!" a voice came from the crowd.

Verna Kelly held her look on the eyes through the holes. "I reckon you know better than that, don't ya, Silas?"

Someone else in the crowd hollered, "Take that dern pistol from her!"

She cocked the pistol, and the man called Silas Turner shouted, "Now just hold it a dang minute! Why, she's touched, I'll tell ya!"

"That's right, Silas, you ornery bastard," Verna said. "I *am* touched. Now, you all get off my property right now. The idea! Coming around here, tryin' to scare decent folks. They ain't done a thing to you! And as for that Indian in there! What are you afraid of? Is your conscience botherin' ya over what your daddies done to his people? These folks are goin' over the mountain to Ellijay. This young buck here wants to git married, and the girl's mama lives over there. Now, Silas, my patience is runnin' out. It's damp 'n cold out here. Am I gonna have to shoot you to get some sleep tonight?"

Silas Turner backed off, ever so gently, and rejoined the others. Some of them watched, while others formed a small circle and talked among themselves. Reluctantly, they soon started leaving her yard in pairs, disappearing into the night.

Before he left, Silas Turner paused and shook a finger at them. "I can't always protect ya, Verna. Some o' these men would just as soon burn you out as look at ya twice. Woman ain't got no business delving into men's affairs in the first place. A lot of these boys fought in the war, and they'll just not have the likes of you and your smart talk."

"Don't you talk to me about the war, Silas! I reckon my family left enough blood to cover the whole blamed county!" Verna said. She fired the pistol over Silas Turner's head.

Some of the white-robed men who had stayed back with Silas took off running at the sound of the shot. Verna Kelly laughed at the sight and turned to Holt and Billy. "Oh, they're not all bad," she said. "But I don't like nobody pokin' their nose into my affairs."

"Who were they?" Billy asked, his voice full of excitement.

"Just folks. Call themselves the Ku Klux Klan," Verna said. "You see, after the war, they got themselves together and said they wanted to keep peace. We might of needed 'em back then, I s'pose. A lotta women and children were left alone. But, for my money, they've served their purpose. We don't need 'em anymore."

"Why, I'll be danged!" Billy said. "Why do they cover themselves up like that?"

"Your guess is good as mine." Verna shrugged. "Maybe they don't want folks knowin' who they are, but everyone around here knows the Klan, and they know that Silas Turner is the head Klansman."

Charlie One Eye, Wilford, and Walter had stepped out of the barn. Walter was ready to go back to bed, and Wilford had a look of relief, but Charlie One Eye was as nervous and excited as Billy. Clutching his Winchester tightly, he kept his eye trained on the dark woods.

"I'm sure sorry about our lack of hospitality," Verna Kelly went on.

"Think nothin' of it," Holt said. "Back home, we don't have no Klan that I know of. We got a few cowmen associations, and they have some of the same ideas. But they don't wear no bedsheets. Not that I know of, anyway."

"All the same, I'm gonna fix you a good breakfast at daylight, and I'm sorry to say it, but you best be on your way," Verna Kelly said. "Git on over the mountain. I can't promise they won't be back, and next time, they might act first and talk later."

"We're much obliged to ya," Holt said, "but what about you? I ain't never run from a good fight in my life."

"Go on to bed." She smiled. "I'll be all right. Oh, the menfolk around here will stop speaking to me for a while, but that sure won't bother me!"

With that, Verna Kelly lifted the hem of her nightgown and padded barefoot through the wet grass back to the house.

The men watched her in silence, then Wilford said to Holt, "What time did she say breakfast was?"

42

VERNA KELLY ROUSTED THEM OUT OF THEIR BEDS BEFORE daylight was established in the thick Georgia mountains. It was mostly dark, with some blue light silhouetting the buildings and trees. There was a heavy mist covering everything. The weather was cold and crisp, and the men shivered as they made their way across the yard to the house. They could smell ham frying.

Talk was sparse around the breakfast table. Verna Kelly had the table set and ready with a plentiful breakfast. She urged them to sit right down. When they had finished, Wilford quickly did away with anything left that was edible. The women offered their help with cleaning up the dishes, but Verna Kelly declined. "No," she said somberly, "you best be on your way. Git on outa here before anybody knows ya even left. No use invitin' trouble," she added.

At the door, she handed them a gunny sack. Holt took the heavy bag. "What's this for?" he asked.

"Ain't that just like a man?" Verna Kelly smiled. She turned to Katy and touched her cheek. "It's a little somethin' for you to eat on your way to Ellijay," she said.

Holt held the bag and reached into his pocket. "Let me pay you for your hospitality," he said.

Verna Kelly shook her head. "Keep your money," she said. "I don't want you to be judgin' all us Spring Place folks by those Ku Klux Klan men that was here last night. Besides, I don't know when I've enjoyed anyone's company more." She smiled again at the women.

Holt tucked a bill into her hand. "Well, at least give this to your grandson. Tell him to buy himself somethin' at the store."

Before she could react, Holt pulled his hand back, leaving the money in her palm.

"Well, I'll do just that," she said. "Little Paul will think it's Christmastime."

When they were mounted and ready to leave, Verna Kelly said her good-byes and added, "I promise, I'm gonna talk to that Silas Turner. So, you folks be sure and stop back on your way from Ellijay." She waved until they were out of sight, one hand resting on her grandson's shoulder.

When they left Spring Place, Chief wordlessly took the lead. They traveled the Federal Road up the mountain. What had been a mist turned to light rain, and the cold hung in the air. No one seemed to notice. During the trip, there had been times when the gold had consumed their thoughts. Other times, they had hardly thought of it at all. Now, though, every member was in his own thoughts of what he would do with his share.

The rain fell steadily all morning, running down the mountainside and collecting in the low spots in the road. They had to stop often and let the horses rest. The cold wet air and steady climbing was hard on the animals' lungs. The trip had taken its toll on the horses. Not only was it hard to breathe, but the road was getting muddy, and their hooves were soon packed. They moved as if in slow motion. The travel was no lighter for the riders, either. They were all pretty wet, to the point where Betsy complained to Billy that her clothes felt like they weighed as much as she did.

In the afternoon, they came upon a thick wall made of rocks. It looked to be a fortress of some kind, built on top of the mountain. It stood nearly three feet high and ran for almost nine hundred feet. On either side of the wall, the earth dropped off sharply into cliffs.

They stopped there to rest a spell. Chief took a seat atop the wall and carefully studied the surroundings. He seemed to have a more youthful appearance all of a sudden. Holt watched him a moment, then joined him on the rock wall.

"Just what is it we're sittin' on, Chief?" he asked curiously, patting the large stones beneath them. "What in the world is a wall doin' on top of a mountain?"

The old Indian just smiled at the question. "Yes," he said, "it is old. My father's father spoke of the stone wall. It was old to him, also."

Holt pondered the mystery of the wall for a moment, but Chief didn't seem to have any answers as to where it came from and why. He wondered if the Indians had built it, or if any big battles had been fought from behind it. Whatever it was, the wall was too big to have just happened on its own.

Billy and Betsy walked up just then and joined them. "Are we gettin' close to the gold?" Billy asked.

"Yes, we are close," Chief said.

When it became apparent that Chief had nothing more to say on the subject, Billy shrugged and put his arm around Betsy, who was shivering. The rest of the group spread out blankets on the wet ground, while Holt and Katy set out to do some sight-seeing. It was too cold to just sit in one spot, he told her as they left the others.

Chief's elusive answer and the sight of the long rock wall held Holt's fascination. The base of the wall, he estimated, was at least ten feet wide. It was a curious sight, he told Katy, and there was bound to be some good story behind it.

Katy, who had been unusually quiet during their walk, finally pulled away from his side and sat down. "I'm tired," she said.

Holt grinned and sat down beside her. They listened to the rain pattering against the dead leaves at their feet for a while.

"This is pretty country," he said, noticing that the vapors that issued from his mouth were quickly swept away by the raindrops. He took a deep breath of the cold, wet air.

"It may be pretty, but I feel all closed in," Katy said. "Why, I'm used to bein' able to see for miles!" She looked up at the sky, which was barely visible through the treetops, and impatiently wiped the water from her eyes. "Wouldn't mind if the rain would let up for a day or two, either," she added.

"A body could do worse'n this," Holt countered. "Even in this cold and rain, there's a peacefulness here, unlike any place I've been before. Why, a man could build him a place and raise a whole passel of younguns. They could grow up huntin' the woods for squirrel and rabbit. And I'm sure there'd be plenty of berries to pick in the summertime. Yes," he said wistfully, "a man could sure do worse."

Katy took in a quick breath and squeezed his hand. "It's funny, but that's the first time I've ever heard you mention children," she said.

Holt glanced up at the dark sky, then turned to her. "Just 'cause you ain't heard me mention younguns before, it don't mean I don't think of such things," he said.

"Would you like to have kids?"

"I don't know how to answer that," Holt said slowly. "I'm not a spring chicken anymore. Why, I reckon all that cryin' in the night is better suited for young ears, more like Betsy and Billy's."

Katy's smile dropped from her face, and so did her spirits. Abruptly, she stood up and turned her face away from him to hide the hurt. "A child or two might do you some good, Holt Flynn," she said, barely able to control her voice. "It could give you some sort of purpose in life."

She started to walk back toward the group, when Holt grabbed her by the arm. He tried to pull her to face him, but she stubbornly held her ground and kept her face averted.

Holt frowned in confusion. "If you don't mind, just what did I say that upset you?" he asked.

Katy's body tensed when he reached for her again. "Just leave me alone. It's nothin'," she said, leaning away from him.

"Well, it's sure somethin', and I ain't lettin' you go until you tell me what it is." Holt tugged gently on her arm.

She turned on him. There was pain mixed with the anger in her eyes. She looked like she wanted to cry. "Let go of me! You're hurtin' my wrist," she said.

Holt lessened his grip a little. He didn't want to hurt her, but he didn't want to let her go, either. It was pretty simple to see what had set her off, but something inside him didn't want to reckon with it. He had thought about fatherhood, plenty of times, but that had been years ago, back when he was a young pup. He didn't know if he had that kind of energy left in him or not, in spite of the way Katy made him feel. He thought about his own father, who had been gone so much of Holt's life. Children needed their fathers as much as they needed their mothers, he reckoned. What if he did have children? Right now, he had his health. He felt good. But what about when the children got older? Would he feel good enough then to give them his full attention? His thoughts turned sadly to his brother, Joe. Just maybe, he thought, Joe wouldn't have lived by the blood of others, if only their father had been around. A mother could do only so much. It was the first time he had allowed himself to feel brotherly emotion since Joe had died on that Helena street. It almost choked him up, thinking about it.

He looked at Katy's angry face, and the pain in his stomach worsened. Her beauty was a marvel to him, and he couldn't help but admire the way she stood there, all womanly. He had to fight to keep from giving in to her persuasive ways all the time.

The two of them didn't speak for several seconds. Holt just stood there and held her by the arm and watched her as she looked downcast at the ground. Finally, he sighed and said, "I thought we was gonna go to San Francisco, then maybe catch one of those round-the-world boats. I'd like to go to where my grandpap was born, in Ireland," he said, hoping she would return to her old enthusiastic self. It was what they both had wanted, he had thought.

"Well, who's gonna stop you," Katy said, still mad. "Go where you want. I just thought there was more to life than all that."

"There is," Holt said. He was getting more confused by Katy's sudden change in demeanor. "Tell me what it is you're wantin' out of life. Maybe that's a more fair question," he offered.

"I don't want much," Katy said slowly, looking down at her hands. "I'd like to see those places, sure. But"—she looked up at him—"I want roots, dern it! Just like that Wilford feller was talkin' about! The ranch? Why, that would suit me! A ranch and a family might not of been pleasin' to him, but it sure would be pleasin' to me!"

"I guess I just don't understand you like I thought I did," Holt said. He let go of her arm and ran a hand over his brow. "Maybe we weren't meant to see the world together," he added, half to himself.

Katy set her jaw. "Maybe so." She turned on her heel and walked briskly back to where the others were sitting. Holt could tell by the stiffness in her shoulders that she was angry. But there wasn't anything he could think of to say.

He watched her all the way. Inside, he felt all confused. It upset him that she had gotten angry, all over some innocent statement. Still, another part of him wanted to run after her. Women had a way of making a man doubt himself, he decided. It was irritating the way they could get a fellow so twisted up in his thinking that right came out wrong, and wrong came out right.

It took a few more minutes before Holt decided that he had been right, after all. Katy had been wrong to get so mad. Women were emotional beings, and that made them unreasonable at times. As he saddled up, he tried to feel good about his conclusion. Still, as they headed eastward behind Chief, Holt felt an emptiness that hadn't been there before, when Katy had ridden at his side.

43

FOLLOWING BEHIND CHIEF, THE GROUP LEFT THE ROCK wall and headed east along Federal Road. Their pace was excruciatingly slow. The rain had finally stopped, but its presence was everywhere. The road was gummy with mud, and the horses had to lift their hooves high to keep from bogging down in it. There was a sweet, clean smell in the air. The winds were calm, and the quiet woods around them gave a serene effect.

Chief stopped often, pausing to study the surroundings and peer up at the dark gray sky. Holt noted that it was the most alert the Indian had ever acted, and it seemed to be wearing him out fast. Still, the old man was pushing himself hard.

Twice, he led them off the Federal Road to ride a ways into the woods. At these times, expectations among the group would rise high. No one talked, so that Chief could concentrate on searching for some familiar sign of where the cave might be. Eagerly, they watched him ride slowly through the trees, scanning the mountainside with his tired eyes. When at last he shook his head and turned back to the road, they felt disappointed, but only for a little while. There was still plenty of mountain to search.

Charlie One Eye was riding alongside Holt, since Katy

had put her horse in with Walter's and Nikki's. He felt as nervous as he could ever remember, and he wanted to talk about it. Maybe the others were just as nervous as he was, and surely if they talked, they could settle their worries some. Nobody seemed to want to make any effort, though. Charlie One Eye held his tongue as long as he could. After their second unsuccessful trip off Federal Road, he pulled closer to Holt and said in a low voice, "He—Chief, I mean—he sure acts like he might be lost."

Holt frowned and pondered the statement. He had been thinking mostly about Katy, but Charlie One Eye's thought had crossed his mind, too. Finally, he said, "Why, hell, Charlie! It's been near forty years for 'im. Why, I have trouble sometimes findin' my own ass in the mornin's. I suspect he'll git his bearin's in a little while."

"I sure hope so," Charlie One Eye said, still unsure.

Holt let the subject slip from his mind and glanced at Katy, who was riding silently beside Nikki. She didn't look any happier than he felt, but she never looked his way. Holt wished they hadn't fought.

They rode a little farther before Charlie One Eye spoke again. Just barely loud enough for Holt to hear, he said, "You know, Chief said he was comin' here to die."

Holt looked at him. "What exactly is on your mind?" he asked, wishing Charlie One Eye would resolve his worries in his own mind.

Charlie One Eye removed his hat, which was water-soaked and heavy, and rubbed his slick head. "Well, what's he gonna do in the meantime?" he said.

Holt studied the comment. "Your guess is as good as mine, I reckon," he said. "Hell, maybe he'll surprise everybody and take some of that gold and buy him a house, or somethin'."

Charlie One Eye fell silent to ponder such a thing, and Holt had to study the idea himself. It was plain that the old Indian was weak and tired, but still the fact remained that Holt couldn't remember hearing him complain even once during the entire long trip. He was old, but didn't seem to be ailing with anything. Why, for all they knew, Chief could have years of life left in him. The only problem might be those Ku Klux Klan fellers, he decided. They had made it clear that Chief wasn't welcome in his old homeland.

They rode all day, but their progress was slow. By the time the light began to fade, the group had gone only about four miles past the rock fortress. Distance didn't really matter to the group, being as nobody except Chief knew where the gold was, but time was on all of their minds. It was getting colder by the day, and the sooner they found the cave, the better. They were all worn out, cold, and tired. Tempers were getting shorter, but still no one said much to complain. Each held on to the hope that they would, very soon, reach the end of their long journey.

Charlie One Eye and Nikki were particularly concerned about catching cold again, as they had in Alabama. Walter still suffered from a hacking cough. They all bundled up as best as they could, but their clothes were wet, with no break in the weather to dry them out. The air in the mountains hung heavy and humid, even when the sun got its brief chance to shine.

That night, there was no cover for sleeping except for the trees overhead. After studying the situation for a moment, Holt directed the men to cut down several pine branches and lay them out. Next they spread the driest blankets over them, and used the wetter blankets for cover.

The group all slept together, side by side, on the bumpy mattress of branches. The women and old Chief were placed in the middle, with Holt and Wilford taking the spots on the outside. It was impossible to move, with the threat of sticky tree limbs poking them from every direction. Still, most of them managed to get a little sleep. The combined body heat helped some for those on the inside, but Holt and Wilford nearly froze, with little to help them escape the cold breeze that came in the night and swept across the mountainside.

To make matters worse, it started to rain again during the

night. By morning, the rain had turned to snow. The group huddled closer together, covering their heads in hopes that their breath would provide a little more warmth.

When Holt awoke at dawn, he uncovered his head and looked around them. There was a blanket of snow everywhere. The trees were all shrouded in white, hovering overhead like ghostly figures. He glanced at the figures beside him. There was no visible trace of a body anywhere; instead, it looked like a group of snow-covered logs, lying in a row. The way he was shivering, Holt felt sure that some of the others must have frozen to death. Pushing away the small feeling of panic that rose in his throat, he nudged them awake.

One by one, they arose and stretched their stiff muscles. Within an hour, everyone was up and complaining about the condition of things. There was no dry wood to be found for starting a fire. They broke out the ham and biscuit sandwiches that Verna Kelly had packed in the gunny sack and ate a cold and miserable breakfast. No one felt like talking. The bitter cold cut through their wet clothing and clung to them like second skin. Movement was the only thing that kept them from freezing, so they packed up quickly and put Chief back in the lead.

Once they were moving, their spirits seemed to pick up a little, as the idea of gold being within reach helped distract their thoughts. They kept a steady watch on Chief, hoping to be the first to see his eyes light up as he suddenly recognized the location of the cave. He was riding so purposefully, they were sure that he knew where he was going.

Holt had his high expectations, like the rest, but for the moment, his thoughts were consumed with Katy. It made him angry that she was having nothing to do with him. He had kept an eye on her all morning, but she hadn't so much as glanced his way. She seemed for all the world to be a total stranger. He felt annoyed, more than anything. It didn't make any sense to him at all. He took to muttering under his breath. Charlie One Eye kept trying to answer with an occasional "What?" but Holt would wordlessly glance at him and look away again. Charlie One Eye just scratched his head and wondered if the cold might be affecting Holt's thinking abilities.

They were about two and a half miles past the site of their overnight camp when Chief suddenly turned his mount to the east and left the Federal Road. He led them deep into the woods, then stopped to gaze upward. A smile played on his face as he watched the snow that had once again begun to fall, straight out of the sky. He moved his horse even farther into the woods, while the others followed, keeping a silence to help him concentrate.

They rode around through the heavily wooded area for over an hour, stopping once at the base of a great rock wall that rose straight out of the mountainside and into the sky for about forty feet. At the top were more trees. Chief dismounted and walked slowly back and forth in front of the wall. His old eyes seemed to be searching back through the years, remembering. The others sat on their mounts, waiting. Betsy clutched Billy's hand and squeezed it hard. Charlie One Eye had to hold back from asking Chief the question that burned in his mind: Was this the spot? Even Holt found himself holding his breath for a spell as he stared unblinking at the Indian.

Finally, Chief turned around and again mounted his horse. Slowly, he pulled on the reins and rode past the rock wall and around it. Disappointment again fell over the group. They followed the Indian around to the opposite side of the mountain, then traveled down one hill and up the next.

On the ground, the snow was steadily collecting. It was already a good three inches deep. The horses were cold, but they were still in good shape. Once, two young deer bolted out in front of them and bounded off again into the woods. Chief laughed softly at the sight, then his face turned serious again, a posture he had taken since they had left the slab wall. Fond remembrances were flitting in and out among his memories, but they could not be allowed to block his concentration on finding the cave. He must keep the word he had given to Billy and Charlie One Eye. Only then could he rest and wait for his final breath.

It was after noon when they rode down yet another hill and crossed through a small valley. The next hill looked oddly familiar, and, when they finally worked their way through the thick woods, they found themselves again facing the same slab wall, sitting there behind a thin row of trees.

Chief pulled up. He stared at the slab, which loomed stubbornly above them. His mouth hung open, and his eyes had lost the sparkle they had held for over a thousand miles.

Several hearts sunk. Charlie One Eye said, to no one in particular, "I believe he's lost." His voice was filled with dismay.

"I don't know about him, but I sure as hell am," Holt said dryly. He glanced at Katy.

Billy jumped down from his horse and ran over to Chief's side. "Tell us it ain't true," he said, his voice almost cracking. His eyes widened as he stared at Chief's fallen expression. "No, this can't be!" he pleaded.

Behind them all, at the rear of the group, Walter laughed. It wasn't the kind of laugh that goes with something funny. "Well, damn," he said. "That old buzzard don't know where any gold's at, any more'n I do." He, too, climbed down off his horse and tied it to the branch of a tree. "Shit."

Slowly, they all dismounted and stood there silently, looking at one another for a sign as to what to do next. Only Chief remained on his horse, staring at the slab wall. Once again, his shoulders were slumped wearily forward, and his face carried the deep lines of old age. He sat there until Holt insisted he dismount. He accepted help in climbing down from his saddle, but refused to join the others. Instead, he stood there, still watching the giant slab as if it would tell him what he most wanted to know. His mouth still hung open, and his eyes had filled with a sadness and disbelief in realizing that he had failed. He began to pace in front of the wall, back and forth, shuffling his old feet and hanging his head. As he paced, his steps became slower and slower.

Holt watched until he couldn't stand it any longer. He approached the old Indian and took him by the arm. "Billy," he called, "bring me his saddle."

Billy grabbed the saddle off Chief's horse and threw it down at the base of a big tree that stood so close to the wall it almost touched it. Gently, he and Holt eased Chief down to sitting position on the saddle, resting his back against the tree. Chief was still in the same state, staring down at his feet with a forlorn expression. His lips worked noiselessly, as if he was trying to remember some ancient incantation that would bring back his memory. It was such a sorry sight that Billy fell down on his knees in front of him and made a last desperate attempt.

"Just relax and think a moment, Chief," Billy said. "Maybe we're just in the wrong spot. There's bound to be lots more places around that look like this one. Maybe we just ain't found the right one yet. Why, after all, it's been pert near forty years!" he reasoned. "Maybe we just oughta do a little more lookin'." He leaned closer to Chief's face to listen for a response, but the Indian merely blinked his eyes a time or two and went back to staring at his feet. Billy started to say something more, but Holt stopped him.

"Leave 'im be for now," he said. "He needs to rest up some." Holt's voice was dry and unconvincing, but Billy nodded and moved away from Chief, anyway.

The snow had stopped falling, but there was no point in moving on when they had no direction to take, so they made camp right there. Charlie One Eye went off to search for some dry wood, and came back with just enough to make a small fire. They had to gather up some extra pieces of clothing to get it started, which pretty much took care of any dry pieces that were left. The fire did little to lift their spirits. It was puny at best, but they spread their blankets and crowded around it, anyway. The failed quest for the elusive gold haunted their thinking. They sat there, each as silent as the old Indian, and mulled over their disappointments. The woods around them lay white and still, without a sound to interrupt their ponderings.

Billy kept glancing at the old Indian. It wasn't his nature to give up on things so easily, and it clearly pained him that the group was sitting there, letting the good part of a day slip by. Charlie One Eye sat next to him, arms crossed, with his hands tucked under his armpits. Betsy was leaning close against Billy's other side, her hand resting on his knee in a comforting way.

Suddenly, there was a movement off to one side. A young doe had wandered close in. It caught their scent and started to run. At the same time, Billy, in his frustration, whipped out his Colt and fired a pair of quick shots.

The rest of the group jumped at the explosion. Holt said, "Hell, Billy Boy, if you're gonna take a little target practice, don't take it out on some helpless animal." His voice held a bitterness to it that made Billy frown.

Holt grabbed his Winchester and started off after the deer.

"Goin' huntin'?" Charlie One Eye called after him.

"Gonna try and find that doe. Billy's second shot hit it. I saw it jerk," Holt said.

"That dern Holt's got better eyesight than me." Charlie One Eye shook his head.

Billy's temper snapped. "What the hell!" he said. "Don't you think I could hit a movin' target?"

Charlie One Eye blinked at Billy, then looked somberly away, watching Holt disappear among the trees.

Betsy took Billy's hand. "There ain't no call for you to be talkin' to Charlie like that," she said. "He didn't mean nothin'."

"Maybe he did and maybe he didn't," Billy said stubbornly.

Holt could hear them talking, but their voices grew dim as he followed the deer's trail. He had been right. In the new snow, there was a bright red trail of blood. He followed it down a hill and into a brush thicket.

The deer was in the thicket, but the animal was so well-shaded it was impossible to get off a shot. Gently, he moved forward and prodded it back into the trees. He followed the doe for a ways, until it made the fatal mistake of glancing back at him. Holt squeezed off a shot. The Winchester exploded, and the doe jumped straight into the air, trotted about ten feet, then fell dead.

Holt stood his Winchester up against a tree and took out his knife. He made a deep, long cut, and steam rose up from the animal's body. He reached inside to pull out the entrails, and the warmth made him sigh. He'd forgotten how cold he was. This was the first time since they had left Verna Kelly's that his hands had felt warm. He let them linger for a moment, enjoying the small comfort that he could take from the animal before he finished gutting and cleaning it.

When he returned with the carcass, the group was still sitting there, as before. Holt commented that it reminded him of a wake, which caused Charlie One Eye to shudder at such talk.

Holt had hoped that having fresh meat for supper would spark a little spirit into the group, but only Charlie One Eye seemed to notice that he had killed the deer. He managed to catch Katy's eye and hold her glance for a moment, but then she turned away. Still, he felt a sensation go through him.

They managed to keep a fire going, and that evening they ate venison. They took the hot meal eagerly, and some even got to talking and complaining about the wasted trip they had taken. Others still held their silence.

Chief turned his head away from the plate that Nikki offered him. She gave Holt a worried look and shrugged. The Indian was still sitting on his saddle, leaning against the tree with his mouth open. He hadn't moved from the spot since Holt put him there. Knowing that it was a bothersome sight for the others to see, Holt tried to reassure them.

Maybe tomorrow, or the next day, he suggested. Maybe after the snow, things would look different to the old man. He could hear his own words coming out of his own mouth, but they sounded unconvincing, even to himself. Holt, too, was beginning to feel his dreams of wealth start to fade.

"Here." He stabbed a piece of venison with a stick and handed it to Charlie One Eye. "Give this to Chief. Maybe you can make 'im eat."

"Let 'im wait on hisself!" Walter's voice sounded loud in the quiet camp. "That ole buzzard's had somebody waitin' on 'im hand and foot since we left, and for what? So's we could all freeze to death in the middle o' nowhere!" He glared at the Indian, then at everybody else in the group.

Holt shook his head. "You know, for a while there, I thought there was some hope for you, Walter. But I guess I was wrong. Hell! I reckon Chief there, meant us no harm. Hell, any fool can see that! 'Sides, he might just git his bearin's back tomorrow," he said.

Walter snorted and gave another one of his humorless laughs. "I guess that makes you just about as naive as the rest," he said.

Holt was about to respond, when Charlie One Eye walked up to the fire, still holding the piece of venison on the stick. His face was almost as white as the snow. Holt frowned.

"Why, hell, Charlie! You look like you just seen a ghost," he said.

Charlie One Eye swallowed, causing his Adam's apple to roll up his skinny throat. His eye was wide open, jittery in his head. He looked first at Walter, then at Holt, and opened his mouth.

"Chief's dead," he said.

44

CHIEF HAD DIED IN EXACTLY THE SAME WAY HE HAD been sitting there on his saddle, resting against the tree that stood right up next to the rock slab. His eyes were closed, but his mouth was still open, as if he had planned to utter one last word before he passed. He had simply stopped breathing and died. It was almost like he had wanted to go with as little fuss as possible.

They all gathered around him and stared, while their last glimmer of hope drained away. If it was possible to be any more miserable than they had been before, then they surely were. Through all their grumbling and worrying, they had all held on to that human shred of hope that things would, somehow, work out. After all, Chief had lasted through the long trip better than most, and hadn't appeared to be sick at all, in spite of his age. Now, though, it was over.

Only Billy could speak the words that were on all of their minds. "Dead!" he said. "I can't believe it."

There was no answer in any of them. Nothing else needed to be said.

Their silence lasted through the evening. There was no place to go, and nothing to do when they got there, so they wordlessly regrouped around the fire and sat down together, each in his own thoughts. The ambitious plans that had dominated their thinking for so long, brought on by the promise of a life rich with gold, were crushed. The single death of one old Indian had brought them back to reality.

They might have sat that way deep into the night. No one seemed to have much of a care, one way or the other, what happened next. Getting rich had been so much a part of their futures, it was hard to remember what their lives had been before.

Holt sat there with the rest of them, feeling his regrets. It was a sad affair, indeed, giving up the big plans that he had foolishly let himself believe in. He looked around at the others and felt sorry for them, too. They all should have known better, he thought. Life just didn't hold such grandiose plans for the likes of them.

Somehow, though, he felt responsible for the group, and he sure couldn't sit there and let them freeze to death while they pined away about what would never happen. He was the first to speak up.

"I think we should bury 'im right at the foot of that tree, first thing in the mornin'," he said. He couldn't help taking a glance at the dark silhouette of Chief's body. They hadn't bothered to move him from his saddle, and he was still propped against the tree. They had waited too long to close his mouth, and the cold of death had frozen it open. Holt looked back at the solemn faces around him and added, "I reckon we all best sort our lives out. We gotta make some new plans."

No one answered for several minutes. Most of them took a quick look at Chief's body, as if to make sure that it really was over. They thought some more.

Finally, Billy sighed. "I guess Betsy 'n me are gonna go on across the mountain and see her ma. Then," he added nervously, "I guess we'll git married."

Betsy let out a shuddery breath and smiled broadly, clutching Billy by the arm and hugging him close. He gave her a sad smile in return. Holt had to feel sorry for Billy, who had twice as many regrets. Not only had he lost his dreams of life as a rich man, but he was also letting go of his lifelong ambition to be a gunny, for the love of a woman.

Walter spoke up next. He hadn't ever really supported the theory of gold in the first place, and if he did believe Chief's story, Holt knew Walter would never tell. With a smug grin, he said simply, "I'm goin' home."

"I'm goin' with Walter," Nikki said. "Reckon I'll open the store back up, if'n it's still standin'," she added. "Somebody's gotta git back there to take care o' them cowboys. Hard tellin' what they've been doin' to satisfy their thirst." She looked at Walter in such a way that said he didn't stand a chance against her wiles. It was, after all, a long trip back to the Territory.

"Wilford? Charlie?" Holt said. "Got any idees?"

Wilford shrugged. "Danged if I know. Maybe I'll mosey on down toward San Antone." He motioned toward Charlie One Eye. "We talked about goin' down there together, once. Ain't talked about it since."

Charlie One Eye didn't answer at all.

Holt turned to Katy. "What about you, Katy?" His voice softened when he said her name.

Katy's eyes met his, then looked quickly back down at her hands. "I guess I'll go back with Nikki and Walter," she said in a small voice.

"How 'bout yourself, Holt?" Charlie One Eye asked. "You headin' back home?"

"Why hell, Charlie. All this time, it looks like I've been travelin' in the wrong direction," Holt commented. "I think I might just slip on up toward Chattanooga and catch me a train. Might as well see San Francisco before I die. After this dern trip, I owe it to myself." He knew his words sounded harsh, but he said them anyway. He noticed a tear rolling down Katy's cheek, and his heart grew heavy in spite of himself.

They were all bone-weary, but there wasn't much sleeping done that night. They arose early the next morning and halfheartedly picked at a breakfast of venison and coffee. After he had eaten, Charlie One Eye got up and grabbed a shovel. He moved close to where Chief's body was propped, and started digging. It was a hefty chore. Not only was the ground cold and hard as rock, but having to dig with a dead body so close was giving Charlie One Eye the creeps. His eyes slid over to where Chief sat, frozen in death. The thought crossed his mind as to why he was digging the grave in the first place. No one had told him to, but then he'd always had an inner guilt that made him jump up and take on a job before anyone else.

He was working intently on his digging, while keeping a watchful eye on the body, when a voice spoke up from behind.

"Mornin'," Holt said.

Charlie One Eye jumped and let out a holler. He turned and saw that it was Holt. "You scared me!" he said. He felt embarrassed, but he was grateful for the company.

Holt pointed at the slight dent in the hard ground. "When you git tired, I'll take over," he offered.

Charlie One Eye poked at the ground with the tip of the shovel. "That might not take too long. This ground here at the base of this rock is awful hard," he commented.

Holt stood there and watched him dig for a while. Slowly, Charlie One Eye began to make some progress. After a bit, Holt went back to the others and sat down to drink a cup of the coffee. It tasted bitter, after sitting over the fire for too long. Holt drank it anyway, for lack of anything better to do. The rest of the group had repacked their belongings and were sitting around, waiting for the grave to be dug. Nikki had pulled out her Bible, and it lay waiting on a rock next to where she sat.

When Holt had finished his coffee, he turned back to see how the grave-digging was going. Charlie One Eye had worked up a sweat. He had wet spots under his arms and on his back. The hole was over a foot deep.

Holt stood up and said to no one in particular, "Guess I'll go and relieve Charlie One Eye of some of that diggin'."

No one paid any mind to his words except Katy. Once again, their eyes met briefly before she looked away. The effect was the same on Holt, causing him to feel all funny inside. He wanted to get mad, but he couldn't.

He was just turning away from Katy when a bloodcurdling scream came from the grave site. Holt jerked around just in time to see Charlie One Eye's head and shoulders disappearing into the earth at the base of the tree. A hand suddenly appeared, clutching desperately, and caught hold of the saddle that Chief was still sitting on. Just as quickly, the saddle, Old Chief and all, were sucked right into the ground behind Charlie One Eye. For an instant, Holt thought he was seeing things.

"Help me! Oh, my Lord! Help me!" Charlie One Eye's voice screamed from somewhere below. It sounded like he had fallen into a barrel.

Holt flung his coffee cup aside, ran to the tree, and stopped. In the place where Charlie One Eye had been digging, there now was a big black hole. Holt peered over the edge and squinted. From far down below, he could hear Charlie One Eye screaming in panic.

"Git him off of me! Oh, my Lord, git him off of me! Help!"

Holt could see nothing in the hole but blackness. From the sound of Charlie One Eye's voice, he judged him to be about fifteen to twenty feet below the ground. He sat back for a moment to study the situation.

By now, the others had grouped around and were staring in amazement at the strange black hole. No one was in a panic. From the sounds that were coming from deep inside, Charlie One Eye was still very much alive.

"Help me! Please! Oh, git this dead Indian offa me!" Charlie One Eye yelled again. His voice was starting to sound hysterical.

Holt wasn't sure how they were going to manage a rescue, but he tried to sound confident as he called down to comfort him. "Just try and relax, Charlie. Tell us what's around you. Feel around. Are you hurt?"

Charlie One Eye's terror was rising. "Oh, Lord!" he called. "Help me! Git him off! Chief's fell on top o' me and I can't move!"

Holt knew there was only one thing to do. "Grab me my rope, Billy Boy," he said. He took the rope and tied it around the tree. He pulled on it, checking its strength, then tied it around his waist. "I need some cloth and a big stick for a torch," he said, looking at Nikki.

"We done burned up everything that was dry last night," Nikki said, her face pale.

Katy stepped forward. "Give me your pocketknife," she said to Billy. She pulled open her coat and cut away her shirttails with the knife, then hurriedly wrapped the cloth around the end of a stick.

Holt was already starting to shimmy down the hole. "You all ease me down careful," he said. He took the rope in one hand, and accepted the torch from Katy. "Thanks," he said, looking her in the eyes. She nodded solemnly, but said nothing.

Down below, Charlie One Eye was still yelling as loud as ever. Slowly, Holt descended into the black hole. He had to push away the closed-in feeling as the dark earth surrounded him. The light from the small torch was dim, but right away he saw the underside of Chief's saddle. The Indian's legs were sticking straight up. Underneath, Charlie One Eye's panic-stricken face appeared. He was pinned underneath Chief and the saddle in a narrow opening, with no room to move.

Once Holt had found his footing, he moved as close as he could to where Charlie One Eye lay. Charlie One Eye had quieted down a little, but was still shaking. Holt looked the situation over. There was hardly any room with the rocks all around them.

"Try to relax, Charlie," Holt said softly. "This might take a spell, but everything's gonna be all right. You sure you ain't hurt none?"

"Not—that I know of." Charlie One Eye gasped. "I can't move, and Chief—oh!" he moaned. "I'm stuck in here like a fence post stuck in the ground."

From up above, Billy hollered down. "Is Charlie all right?" he asked, anxiety in his words.

"He's all right," Holt answered.

"Well, let's pull him up outa there," Billy said.

Holt strained his neck to see upward into the light. He could see the shapes of several faces peering down into the hole. He tried to change positions, but with both shoulders touching the sides of the crevice, he could barely turn around. Charlie One Eye said, more calmly, "Please, Holt! My heart's not gonna take this much longer."

Holt didn't answer. He was trying to figure out just what to do. There was no way to get Charlie One Eye and Chief out of that hole without first getting out himself. He said slowly and carefully, "Pardner, there just ain't no room here. I'm gonna have to have 'em toss down another rope and tie it around Chief. I'll have to get back out so's they can pull him up. Then I'll come back down and get you. It may take a little time, but we'll get you out. Do you understand?"

"Don't leave me," Charlie One Eye pleaded. "I can't stand it, being stuck down here with a dead man on top of me."

"I'm sorry, Charlie," Holt said truthfully. "I just don't see no other way. How's your arms? Can you move 'em?"

"I'm pinched in here somethin' awful," Charlie One Eye said in a panicky voice. He was getting hysterical again at the thought of Holt's leaving him alone with the body, even for a moment.

The torch was still burning fine, and Holt's eyes had adjusted, giving him a better view of the situation. He had been right in that the hole narrowed as it went downward.

"Can you feel somethin' solid under ya, Charlie?" he asked.

"What do ya mean?"

"Dern it, I mean are you on solid ground, or are you just caught in between the rock? Did the sides catch your fall?"

"No, I believe I've hit bottom," Charlie One Eye answered.

Holt nodded and called up. "You still with me, Billy Boy?"

"I am," Billy said anxiously. Holt could see the shape of his head as he leaned over the side.

"Well, tie me another rope around that tree and toss her down here."

He took the second rope and tied it around Chief and the saddle the best he could. With that done, he wiped the beads of sweat from his nose and took hold of the first rope. "Charlie," he said, "we're gonna have you outa here in just a minute. You hang on, you hear?"

Charlie One Eye merely moaned. As quickly as he could, Holt shimmied up the rope. Wilford and Billy helped him out of the hole. He shook his head at the group's questions and grabbed the other rope. "Give me a hand," he said. "Charlie's stuck down there, underneath Chief. We got to pull Chief out first, and then I'm going back after Charlie."

It took a real effort by the men, and longer than Holt had planned, to pull Chief out of the hole. By the time they maneuvered the body to the top, the rope had slipped, to where it was holding on to a stirrup and just one of Chief's legs.

They pulled the body out and laid it on the ground. Holt picked up his torch and held it up. "My light's all used up. I need some more cloth," he said.

"There's none left that's dry," Nikki said.

"Yes, there is," Katy said to her. "Git that dress outa your saddlebag."

Nikki's eyes narrowed into slits. "I don't have no dress in my saddlebag," she said.

Katy frowned a warning. "Don't you lie to me, Nikki! I seen it! You bought it in Little Rock! I ain't seen it since, but I know you didn't throw it away."

Nikki looked at them all pleadingly. "That dress cost me twelve dollars! I ain't about to burn it up!"

"The hell you ain't," Katy said. She took off for Nikki's horse.

Nikki started after her and yelled, "Don't you git into my saddlebag!"

The two sisters looked to be starting an all-out feud, when Walter stepped between them. "Give her the damn dress!" he snapped.

Nikki looked surprised at Walter, then glanced at the others. Red-faced, she turned away to hide her embarrassment.

Not long after, Holt reentered the hole, carrying a sizable torch. He found himself thinking about Katy's spunk in demanding that Nikki donate her new dress to help rescue Charlie One Eye. It was an admirable thing to do.

This time, he could see the situation much more clearly. Charlie One Eye was lying with his shoulders mashed together in the narrow crevice. Holt wondered how the fall had kept from killing him.

Charlie One Eye looked as glad to see him as Holt could ever remember a man being. He reached down and carefully eased Charlie One Eye up and into a sitting position. By now, Charlie One Eye had found some of his composure, but he was still shaky.

There was a crack in the earth behind where Charlie One Eye's head had been. Holt held the torch up to study it. The crack was a large one, big enough for a man to squeeze into. Deeper inside, he could see only blackness. "I wonder what's in there," he said, half to himself.

"I don't know, and I don't care," Charlie One Eye said. "Can we just git outa here now?" he pleaded.

"Just a minute, Charlie."

Holt stepped over him and eased through the crevice. As he neared the black part, the crevice started opening up. It was clear that there was a dark cavity in the earth, much larger than he had thought at first. He stepped in further. At the edge of the darkness, Holt held out the torch as far as his arm would reach.

It was a hole big enough to set a small house in. The darkness beyond the light of his torch told him that there was much more to the hole than he could see. But it wasn't the size of the hole that took his breath away.

The light of the torch bounced against the walls and ceiling. The rock walls were not even, but there amid the shadows, something shiny caught Holt's eye. He squinted to see better. Then he saw another shiny reflection. Then another.

His heart began to pump, hard against his chest. Behind him, Charlie One Eye hollered something, but Holt didn't hear the words. His eyes were as wide as a child's as he stared in disbelief.

He had to pause a moment to make sure he wasn't dreaming. Then he called out behind him.

"My Lord, Charlie! Come over here! We've just found Chief's cave!"

Charlie One Eye stopped his hollering and edged closer to peer into the hole. He stared for a full minute before he spoke in a hoarse whisper. "Well, I'll be derned! I knew that old Indian was right, all along!"

Holt stayed in the hole, while Charlie One Eye went up to tell the others. Holt could hear their excited voices, as they all insisted on seeing for themselves. One by one, they all went down into the narrow opening, with the men lowering the women, then sliding down the ropes on their own. Soon, they were all assembled inside the cave, staring at the cave of gold that they had dreamed about for so long. As quiet as they had all been in their sorrow over their failure to find the cave, the awe that they now felt as they gazed at the treasure around them held them even more thunderstruck. No words would come as a storm of emotions raged through each of them.

45

INSIDE THE CAVE WERE MANY SIGNS FROM CHIEF'S PAST. Well-used tools were found, as well as an old single-shot rifle, some clothing and a bone-handled knife. There were other relics, bowls and earthen jugs. They found an old rope ladder and several torches. But the most amazing find lay in one corner, just sitting there like a pile of coal. It was a stack of gold chunks, enough gold to fill a good-sized wagon.

"Would you look at that!" Holt exclaimed, waving his torch over the gold. "I reckon there's enough gold in that pile alone to make a thousand men rich!"

They were all staring at their surroundings, dumbstruck. Charlie One Eye rubbed the top of his head and said, "Why do you s'pose Chief would go off and leave a mess of gold like this? Why, he coulda been a rich man."

"Why, hell, Charlie! I reckon when they ran Chief and his people outa this part of the country, Chief just left things like they was." Holt shook his head in disbelief as he stared at the big pile of gold. "It's clear that he and whoever was with 'im was coming down here daily and chipping away. That must've been their storage pile. I reckon they used it as they needed it."

Billy suddenly let out a high scream that made them all

jump. "By damn! We're rich!" he shouted, and jumped into the air. His jubilation was catching, and everyone loosened up. Soon they were all hugging one another, laughing like children. Holt's mind left the gold long enough to pull Katy to him. She let him have the hug, but was stiff and patted his back, more like a friend than a lover. The gesture wasn't lost on Holt, even in the spirit of the moment. He released her quickly, and they both turned away without looking into each other's eyes.

The group spent the entire day packing gold into anything they could pack. They filled their saddlebags. Cooking utensils, clothing, blankets, and everything that had been on the packhorses was thrown away and replaced with sacks of gold. When they were finally loaded down to the last piece of gold that man or animal could carry, it was late afternoon.

Together, they decided to leave Chief down in the cave, atop his saddle. One by one, they each said good-bye to their quiet friend who had led them to wealth beyond their dreams. Nikki read from the Bible and said a short prayer, then they gently lowered him into the cave, and sealed it off with some big rocks and branches. There, Billy said, Chief could rest forever in his secret cave of gold.

A late afternoon sun had appeared and was shining brightly on the mountainside, melting off the snow. They all sat down to soak up the welcome warmth, drunk with happiness.

No one seemed in any hurry to leave. Instead, they talked again about their plans. Wilford announced as to how he and Charlie One Eye had decided to go on down to San Antone and buy that ranch. They would hire them a fancy cook and buy lots of fine beeves.

Billy and Betsy still planned on going over to get married at Betsy's ma's home. After a suitable time for Billy to get acquainted with his new mother-in-law, they would honeymoon in Europe, then maybe head for

San Antone themselves. Billy invited them all to the wedding.

Nikki held to her plans to return to her store. "But I got me a new partner," she said, squeezing Walter's hand. "Guess we'll put our money in the bank."

Walter managed a sheepish smile at her comment and said nothing.

"Well, hell," Holt said, squinting up at the sun. "You all's plans ain't much different from last night's, when we was all as poor as church mice. Now, there's some kind of lesson to be learned there," he commented.

"What about you, hon?" Nikki said to her sister. "You still comin' with me and Walter?"

Katy shrugged. "I don't know," she said, looking toward Holt. "San Francisco sure sounds good this time of year."

Nikki stood up. "Well, I'll tell ya one thing. I don't fancy sleepin' out here on the ground again! I say let's get movin' and find us a decent place to sleep. Ellijay shouldn't be much more'n a couple of miles from here. I hope they got a good hotel. We might even get acquainted with Betsy's ma." She gave Betsy a loving glance.

The group headed for their mounts and began to saddle up. "Guess you're still gonna make that round-the-world trip, huh, Holt?" Charlie One Eye said.

Holt looked at the slab wall and thought about the old Indian and the frustration that he had suffered when he thought he had failed them. He thought of the long journey, and of his brother, Joe. Remembered their lonesome childhood, and his days of robbing trains with Walter. He was amused at how Betsy had turned Billy's ambitions of being a gunny into a desire for domestication. Hell, he thought, for his money, he'd done been around the world.

They were all watching him, waiting. Holt looked at Katy, and her beauty swept over him. He pulled himself atop Joe's big gelding. "Why, hell, Charlie," he said. "All by yourselves, a couple fellers like you 'n Wilford may git in way over your heads in San Antone. I'm gonna buy me a big ranch, close as I can find to yours. Then, if she'll have me, I think I might marry me a pretty little Kansas girl and enjoy my golden years with a passel of younguns."